PRINCE OF THE SORROWS

ROWAN BLOOD VOLUME ONE

KELLEN GRAVES

For Mo
my one simple peace
who owns my heart,
my soul,
and my name

CONTENTS

Preface   vii
Pronounciation Guide   ix

Chapter 1   1
The Ring

Chapter 2   16
The Wish

Chapter 3   27
The Sprites

Chapter 4   42
The Prince

Chapter 5   52
The Geis

Chapter 6   79
The Wallpaper

Chapter 7   86
The Party

Chapter 8   101
The Deal

Chapter 9   108
The Library

Chapter 10   129
The Preoccupation

Chapter 11   140
The Fever

Chapter 12   156
The Medicine

Chapter 13   169
The Wolf

Chapter 14   181
The Apple

Chapter 15   194
The Queen

Chapter 16
The Silence   206

Chapter 17
The Raven   220

Chapter 18
The Lord   244

Chapter 19
The Circles   253

Chapter 20
The Night   264

Chapter 21
The Memories   280

Chapter 22
The Berries   290

Chapter 23
The Ridge   300

Chapter 24
The Undine   314

Chapter 25
The Spirit   324

Chapter 26
The Fruits   340

Epilogue   357

Acknowledgments   361
About the Author   363
Lord of Silver Ashes   365
Also by Kellen Graves   367

Author's Note

This novel is Fantasy-Romance for a New Adult audience, and contains tropes commonly found in that genre. Such tropes include but are not limited to:

CRUDE LANGUAGE

VIOLENCE AND DEATH

MENTAL AND PHYSICAL ABUSE/BULLYING

DESCRIPTIONS OF TORTURE

SCENES OF CONSENSUAL SEX

NONCONSENSUAL DRUGGING BY FANTASY MEANS

MILD THEMES OF SEXUAL HARASSMENT

THEMES OF INDENTURED SERVITUDE

THEMES OF FANTASY-BASED BIGOTRY

THEMES OF FANTASY-BASED GENOCIDE

Pronounciation Guide
(FICTIONAL & INSPIRED)

AILIR (FICTIONAL) *EYE-LEER*

ASCHE (FICTIONAL) *ASH*

AON-ADHARCACH (SCOTTISH-GAELIC) *OON ER-KACH*

BEANTIGHE (IRISH-GAELIC) *BAN-TEE*

BRÍGHDE (GAELIC) *BREE-JUH*

CONNACHT (IRISH-GAELIC) *CON-AH-KT*

CLYMEUS (FICTIONAL, GREEK INSPO) *CLAI-MAY-US*

CYLVAN (FICTIONAL) *SIL-VAN*

DERDRIU (IRISH-GAELIC) *DER-DRU*

EIAS (FICTIONAL) *EYE-USS*

ELLUIN (FICTIONAL) *ELL-OO-IN*

GEIS (IRISH-GAELIC) *GESH*

NAOILL (FICTIONAL) *NOW-ILL*

NAOISE (IRISH-GAELIC) *NEE-SHA*

NIAMH (IRISH-GAELIC) *NEEVE*

OISÍN (IRISH-GAELIC) *AUH-SHEEN*

SHAMHRADHÁIN (IRISH-GAELIC) *SHAM-RA-DIEN*

SÍDHE (IRISH-GAELIC) *SHEE*

TUATHA DÉ DANANN (IRISH-GAELIC) *TOO-HA DE DAN-AN*

Title Reference (FICTIONAL)

HE/SHE/THEY

LORD/LADY/GENTLE

KING/QUEEN/DANAE

PRINCE/PRINCESS/DAURAE

THE STARS ARE OUT, DEIRDRE, AND LET YOU
COME WITH ME QUICKLY, FOR IT IS THE
STARS WILL BE OUR LAMPS MANY NIGHTS
AND WE ABROAD IN ALBAN, AND TAKING
OUR JOURNEYS AMONG THE LITTLE ISLANDS
IN THE SEA.

THERE HAS NEVER BEEN THE LIKE OF THE JOY
WE'LL HAVE, DEIRDRE, YOU AND I, HAVING
OUR FILL OF LOVE AT THE EVENING AND
THE MORNING TILL THE SUN IS HIGH.

———

Deirdre of the Sorrows
JM Synge, 1910

1

THE RING

"*There are only two ways to compel a high fey; with their true name, or with wild fairy fruits.*"

Those were the last words Arrow said before disappearing into the forest, not even Saffron able to find them. Despite knowing the Agate Wood as well as he knew Beantighe Village, despite the woods being his safe place where nothing terrible ever happened. But perhaps the forest only extended that mercy to him. It devoured his friend in an instant.

But Arrow had only been gone for two days. There was still a perfectly good chance they were wandering without even noticing how much time had passed. Saffron had even shown them where to find fresh water or safe berries to eat, only later realizing perhaps they asked because they already knew they were going to wander off.

At least, if Arrow did find wild fairy fruits, they would know better than to eat them to live. Every human knew how to recognize the pink-powdered morsels, though most came artificially coated with magic dust to inebriate high fey enough to enjoy a party—or to reduce humans to simpering, giggling, submissive puddles on the floor, eager to do whatever was asked of them.

Saffron couldn't imagine what *wild* fairy fruits might do, especially if they could enchant even the unenchantable.

Why Arrow was searching for wild fairy fruits at all still made Saffron's head swirl. He hadn't actually gotten a chance to ask, and every moment Arrow remained gone made him kick himself for not being more demanding.

They would definitely be back before the sun went down. They had to. As Brìghde's stand-in that year, if Arrow didn't come back to sit on the stump and hear everyone's wishes, then... Saffron might have to accept the woods really had stolen his friend for good. He gulped. He tried not to think about it, instead focusing on what he would say as soon as Arrow's face appeared back in the village.

Let me guess—you didn't find your fairy fruits, did you? I told you there weren't any. I've never seen wild fairy fruits anywhere in the Agate Wood. You scared me half to death. I'm glad you're alright. Never do that again. Come on, you need to get ready for the ceremony...

Crunching through the undergrowth, he held his makeshift sketchbook under one arm while fiddling with a tin of charcoal sticks in the other. A teal blue pixie perched on his hand as he tromped, fascinated by the way he organized the drawing sticks in his box.

"What are you wishing for from Brìghde, Dewdrop?" he asked the sparkling thing, attempting to distract himself from the other pervasive thoughts. The answer was easy to guess as the pixie's eyes flashed to his pocket crinkling with honeycomb stolen from Cottage Wicklow's pantry. Perhaps Saffron should have asked a harder question, because the brevity of the exchange opened up more opportunity to dwell.

In previous years, Saffron had wished for simple pleasures not unlike that of the pixie who sat on his hand, or its colorful siblings who brought him flowers at night and always made nests in his hair beneath his veil while working. Wishes that were easy to manifest, so there would be no disappointment. *I want time to*

*make new charcoal sticks. I want to find more wildflowers or berries
to make paints with. I want to find something new in the woods to
draw.*

But for the first time in years, that Imbolc, Saffron had something he actually wanted. *Needed.* Another reason Saffron *needed*
Arrow to be back in time to hear it.

That year would be his last chance at a wish at all. His last
chance to beg Brìghde for mercy, to give him something that
might make the difference between life or death. A wish birthed
from pure adrenaline the previous Yule while visiting his patron-
fey in the Winter Court, when Luvon broke the news Saffron
prayed would never, ever come.

*"This coming Ostara, it's time I send you back through the veil
to the human world."*

To a world whose languages he didn't speak, whose maps he
didn't know, whose customs he couldn't navigate. A place he'd
only visited once before, where he was met with hostility by his
own birth parents who had traded him away.

I wish for an academic endorsement. He thought the words
intensely, as if to manifest loud enough for Brìghde to hear wherever she lived in the sky. Perhaps Arrow would hear it, too, and
finally turn around to trudge back to the village from wherever
they were. Saffron thought about it even harder: *I want an
endorsement to be tutored. I want to work at Luvon's winery permanently. I don't want to go back to the human world.*

Dewdrop gazed up at him, hands stained black with dust as
it rifled around in Saffron's charcoal tin still hanging open.
Saffron barely noticed the tiny handprints left on his thumb,
lost in a silent call for any god or goddess or otherwise to hear
him as he navigated the thick woodland path he'd memorized
long ago.

*I don't even care who endorses me, or what I eventually do at the
winery...* his thoughts trailed off. *Anything but the human world.*

Snapping the charcoal tin shut, he transplanted Dewdrop to a
shoulder, needing both hands to climb over a fallen tree. Three

more pixies found them along the way, Saffron recognizing them by their colors. *Flame, Moss, Goldie.*

"Have any of you seen Arrow nearby?" he asked, a pinch of desperation making his voice crack. But the pixies just fluttered like they always did, squeaking nonsensically, picking at the buttons of his doublet, pulling his hair, burrowing down inside his tunic in search of nipples to bite. He pulled Moss out unceremoniously, flicking them away where they tumbled before catching on their iridescent wings and squealing at him in annoyance. He apologized, but still swatted away their second attempt.

Stepping over exposed roots, touching trees in greeting as he wandered by, brushing through reaching foliage from the slope on his left, he shook hands with dewy maidenhair ferns and vines, snowberry plants. Even delicate flowers that, now that the True Season was returning to the Spring Court, would finally have enough warmth to grow into their natural sizes again.

Pausing at the creek where he always missed the crossover point, Saffron spotted the telltale cloud of more pixies enjoying the spray of water over a cluster of rocks. He hopped up onto the stones, as Dewdrop left to join the cloud, using the water to clean their wings like little birds. Others took Dewdrop's place on him, making more nests in Saffron's hair as he tried to focus on his footwork, not wanting to spend the rest of the journey with wet socks. They nipped at his earlobes and cheeks, squeaking demands, knowing he was the honeycomb-bringer, the human whose blood they could snack on beforehand as an additional treat.

Clambering up the slippery brae on the opposite side of the water, he yelped when his old boot lost traction. Slamming flat on his stomach made him groan miserably, creamy wool doublet instantly stained with mud and old grass. Behind him, two dozen shrieking cackles rang out over the sound of the creek, like wind chimes in a storm.

Finally reaching the top where sun filtered through the trees and undergrowth, at least four freeloaders still clung to his hair, ears, and newly dirty doublet. Pushing hair from his eyes, he accidentally tangled up two pixies between his fingers, apologizing sharply when they attacked his fingers in retribution. Down a narrow deer trail and through more green undergrowth as thick as the night was dark, he eventually found what he was looking for —within a clearing of long grasses and yarrow clusters, the familiar gnarl of an old willow tree stood out, hollowed-out trunk yawning like the mouth of an ancient dryad.

"Don't wake the others," Saffron quietly requested, his sparkly entourage squeaking and fluttering before quieting down. They might not understand his words, but they were familiar with his presence, having visited the hollow enough times to develop a pattern: if they behaved, he would give them the honey prize in his pocket. If they were nasty, he'd leave and wouldn't come back again for another month.

Focusing his breaths into silent sounds, Saffron stepped into the clearing. Parting the yarrow stems closest to the hollow, he smiled at the myriad of colorful pixies puddled on the other side. A few lifted their heads and fluttered their wings at the new peek of sunlight, before curling up again in annoyance. Dewdrop returned and tugged on Saffron's hair like the reins of a horse, and Saffron knelt down, knotting the tallest yarrow clusters out of the way to open up a window into the hollow. Pulling out the drawing charcoals and sketchbook tucked in his shoulder bag, his companions took seats on his shoulder, his arm, his hand, his head, to observe and offer critique.

Blowing a clump of light brown hair from his eyes, he flipped to a sketch page already dedicated to *"ranebow pixeys"*. Handwritten notes down the side described how pixies flocked around moving water, but only drank from cupped leaves and flowers; how one could tell when they were reveling by the flower petals and stolen downy-fur they wove into skirts, though otherwise fluttered naked; how they were inherent thieves, and the source of most campus rings and house pins going missing.

Lighting down a stick of charcoal, black pigment skimmed

over a line of printed text once belonging to a book on botany he'd snatched from a bench. As if the sound of compressed ash alerted them, more thumb-sized observers arrived, pulling faces at other iterations of their winged, shimmery, bug-eyed sketches.

Despite their combined sketches making up a stack of the sketchbook's pages, pixies were only the second most common mentions in his book, and every part of Saffron resented it. Of all the random creatures he'd observed, he'd bitterly dedicated the most paper to one type who didn't even roam wild in the woods: the high fey. With their pointed ears, tall frames, shining hair, smooth skin, and symmetrical features that could seemingly only emote disgust, resentment, annoyance, or arrogance. Saffron knew more than he cared about the high fey, including what they thought of humans like him, as well as how, on any night, he would much rather cross paths with a bloodsucking dearg-due than a high fey who would bleed him just for the fun of it.

He could practically hear Brìghde's voice in his head. *"And yet you wish to stay in Alfidel with them?"*

Yes! He thought, but it came with a grimace. Because there were at least *some* high fey who weren't as cruel as the students attending Morrígan Academy. Luvon's family had always been kind enough to him. Those who lived in the Winter Court where Luvon's winery was located always treated Saffron with at least a semblance of respect, even if they weren't particularly *friendly*. There were even some students on campus who ignored beantighes like Saffron rather than seeking them out just to play pranks or harass or bodily injure for laughs.

Listen, Brìghde: If I could just be academically endorsed, receive a formal education, and impress Luvon enough to be employed at his winery, I won't have to worry about high fey cruelty ever again, he insisted. Saffron could just live and work and die amongst the ice-painted fruit trees, the snowy mountains, the familiar faces of his patron family.

Goldie perched itself on the back of Saffron's hand as he quickly sketched, hoping to get enough detail down before the piles of color in the hollow deflated. Occasionally fluttering its wings, light yellow hands kept nudging the charcoal stick to mess him up, giggling in a frenzy every time he muttered for it to stop. When he accidentally sighed a little too loud in frustration, the breathing jewels in the tree came alive and filled the air with buzzing like a beehive.

They blanketed him with beating wings and tiny claws, nibbling at exposed skin, dozens more scrambling over one another to peer down at his sketch and offer opinions in more nonsensical, high-pitched noises. Burrowing into his hair, he barely nabbed a few before they slithered down his shirt.

Tucking his book away, he relented, removing the flattened parcel of stiff paper from his doublet pocket. Holding his breath as the cloud of squealing glitter nearly suffocated him in excitement, he unfurled the honeycomb before anything could crawl up his nose or into his ears.

The brief window of peace allowed Saffron to scour the hollow like a thieving fairy himself, burying his entire arm in as it slanted downward into a pit of treasures. Brushing past the flowers and colorful stones, his fingers curled around troves of stolen beantighe rings, crystal jewelry, Morrígan House pins, messenger-raven medallions, and, finally, the specific proof of thievery he was looking for—his friend Letty's golden hair clips.

"Found them, you little snipes!" he announced, a few pixies lifting honey-smeared faces in acknowledgement. Opening his shoulder bag and scooping every bronze ring in, he left the golden rings, house pins, and messenger tokens behind to feed his own high fey resentment. He then slid his friend's hair clips into his own messy bangs for safekeeping, at least three pairs of sticky pixie hands scrabbling at them while squeaking demands.

"No, no, no, you know the deal," he said like a scolding henmother. "I *might* convince Letty to let you keep her pins if you steal a *library ring* next time. Remember? Thin, gold, little lines on the inside. Don't give me those faces, you all know exactly what I'm talking about."

Accepting the licked-clean wax paper, Saffron folded and stuffed it away with the rest of the reclaimed property. More angry squeaks piped from the chorus of victims, and Saffron scolded every glittery thing that tried to burrow into his bag.

But as Saffron turned back toward the deer trail, a dark shadow stood directly in his path. His first thought was a black-bear—but it wore a bitter scowl and narrow eyes as if annoyed they hadn't gotten a lick of the honeycomb, too.

Stark against the bright sun, the stranger wore all black down to their heeled boots, with equally dark hair plaited into a snake-like braid over one shoulder. Their tunic was textured with embroidery and tiny gold beads, tailored pants snugly embracing long, lean legs. Saffron didn't mean to stare at the high waistband hugging their slender middle, eyes trailing up their chest and shoulders next. From their head curled a pair of horns shining like obsidian, carved with vines and leaves as works of art in themselves. Even the smaller details ensnared him, like their black nails filed into claws, the beauty mark beneath their right eye, the perfect shape of their mouth... Caught in the spell, Saffron stood momentarily captivated by the strange, surreal flawlessness of the person in front of him.

But the spell broke the moment Saffron's eyes returned to the point of their ears.

"How did you do that?" they asked, voice cold even in the morning sun, and Saffron finally noticed little spots on the fey's cheeks and ears resembling pixie bites. He would have laughed had it been anyone else; instead, he just rolled his tongue around in his bone-dry mouth.

"Do what?" he asked, trying to keep his voice flat.

"Escape with your eyes."

One corner of Saffron's mouth twitched upward, unable to help it. "They're, ah... more agreeable when you bring a trade."

The fey appeared wholly unappeased by that answer, and Saffron rolled his tongue around his mouth a little more. Finally, he relented, knowing he would age and die on that spot if he didn't. "Are you... missing something?"

The stranger's eyes flickered to Saffron's shoulder bag, irises like vivid amethyst coins. Saffron's hand twitched, realizing he'd frozen in the middle of tucking his sketchbook away.

"These pixies really only take campus rings from Morrígan Academy nearby," he went on, determining the person probably wasn't wild fey based on the lavish clothes they wore. Perhaps they were a student, but Saffron was sure he would have recognized them if they'd ever crossed paths on campus.

"Show me." The stranger's expression didn't change.

"Um... alright," Saffron sighed, pulling off his bag and kneeling down amongst the yarrow stems. Flattening a clump of grass into a cushion, he scooped out every bronze ring stowed away and dumped them into view. Swatting at any pixie who thought they could swoop in and steal them right back again, he barely glanced up to the intimidating stranger, inviting them to approach. They stomped forward, cursing under their breath and swatting at the tall plants as if insulted whenever their hands were brushed. Saffron just kept his eyes low, pulse quickening more and more as the distance between them closed.

The pixie hollow was close enough to the road that this fey could just be passing through, or maybe from Connacht, or even Hesper, he tried to reassure himself. Lost in the woods on a morning walk. Perhaps the trees really did devour anyone who wasn't Saffron—but that wasn't Saffron's problem, and he would sprint in the opposite direction the moment their exchange was through.

Saffron tried to make himself small, watching the fey's sharp nails scrounge through the pile of stolen rings like searching the bottom of a creek for diamonds. When they swore under their breath, Saffron secretly rolled his eyes as if to say *I told you so*—but then those startling amethyst eyes flickered back up to him.

"You said there were Morrígan rings here. But these are all beantighe rings, aren't they? So where are the others?"

Saffron grimaced. Perhaps this person was a student, after all, in which case he needed to be more aware of his throat. Still, he put on a practiced, polite beantighe smile, biting back any creeping natural disdain.

"Let me get them for you, my gentle."

Glad the pixies were still mostly sugar-drunk from the honey-comb, Saffron bitterly dug around in the hollow for the gold rings and house pins he'd left behind the first time. Returning to the scowling shadow in the grass, Saffron scooped the bronze rings back into his bag and dumped the gold ones in their place.

"Ah!" the fey exclaimed after another brief search, making Saffron jump as the scrounging hand finally hooked on something and flashed it away from the shiny puddle. Saffron sighed in relief and proceeded to gather the remaining gold rings, though he intended on just dumping them again as soon as the fey wasn't looking. But rising back to his feet, a sharp hand flashed out and grabbed him by the sleeve.

"Hold on," they said, and the air tightened further. "Are you a servant at Morrígan?"

Indigo eyes met Saffron's again, sending goosebumps down his arms. The fey smiled in a way meant to be charming, but Saffron knew better than to trust anyone so perfectly handsome.

"No," he answered, knowing a lie would be the safest option —but the fey's smile only widened slightly, rising to their feet alongside him. Standing at least a head taller than Saffron, not including their horns, Saffron had to lift his chin to meet their eyes. If they hadn't still clutched his sleeve, he might have finally turned and ran, but forced down that jackrabbit urge and braced for whatever would come next.

The fey held up the ring again. Golden and carved with swirling ferns, gaps between each tendril gave it a delicate, ethereal quality. On its face, a small, flat diamond was embedded, hardly bigger than a drop of rain.

"Don't you want to know what's so special about it?" they asked. Saffron frowned. He finally attempted to pull his arm free, but the stranger clung too tightly. Exhaling through his nose, he just tried to keep his voice calm.

"It's a very beautiful ring," Saffron answered with the same polite smile before offering another lie: "If you'll excuse me, my patron-fey is down by the river and probably wondering where I am—"

"It's more than just a ring," they insisted, tugging Saffron back when he tried to escape. "It's enchanted. Don't you want to know what makes it so special? Come on. Let me brag a little bit."

Saffron sighed, then smiled again in exasperation, turning fully to the fey stranger once more. They smiled another beautiful smile of their own, taking one of Saffron's hands without warning and tucking the ring on his finger.

"This ring belongs to a prince. Some say whoever wears one like it... gains the ability to compel any high fey."

Saffron's breath caught, gazing down at the pretty circlet sparkling in the sunlight. He didn't realize his mouth hung open in shock until the fey, still propping up Saffron's hand, surprised him again:

"At least, that's what I've heard. I've never been able to try it out for myself, since I don't have anyone I could trust not to use it against me cruelly. But seeing how you've earned the trust of these pixies... I wonder if you're someone I could trust to help me, too?"

"Wh—" Saffron jumped. "You—You want me to compel you?"

"That's right," they offered another handsome smile, and that time it made Saffron's heart race. "I would like to know if it works as intended, that's all. Before that, though—what's your name?"

Saffron gulped, touching the ring and turning it slightly to center the diamond on his finger. "My name is... um... *Dewdrop.*"

"*Dewdrop,*" they smiled, but looked like they were hiding an insult behind it. "It's nice to meet you, Dewdrop. My name is Sybil. When you enchant me, start with my name so the ring knows who you're influencing, alright?"

"What should I say?" Saffron asked, still unsure. A part of him swelled with curiosity, while another part of him wanted nothing more than to throw the ring back in the fey's face and run screaming in the opposite direction. But then he heard Arrow's voice again, talking about the wild fruits, about how there were so few ways to control a high fey. Could something as simple as a magic ring really be another option? And if Saffron found Arrow and told them about it, would they believe him and give up on finding the dangerous wild fruits altogether?

If Saffron... *showed* it to them, would they finally come home for good? Pressing his lips together, he adjusted the ring again. His jackrabbit urge returned to itch the back of his neck.

He could definitely outrun a stuffy high fey in heeled boots.

"Anything you like. I trust you enough," the fey in question kept smiling, taking a step back and extending their hands in invitation. "It doesn't have to be anything big. I'll be able to tell if it works."

"Um..." Saffron's brows furrowed, knowing he should pick an enchantment the fey wouldn't be able to fake.

Looking the stranger up and down again, Saffron's eyes lingered on the long, beautiful braid the color of raven feathers draping over one shoulder. Clearly well taken care of, grown out over decades, cherished enough that the owner meticulously checked it repeatedly for pieces of grass to pluck out.

Biting his lip, Saffron carefully removed the short foraging knife from his back pocket.

"Erm... *Sybil, I want you to cut off the very bottom of your braid.*"

Sybil stiffened. They stepped forward without a word, taking the knife and slicing the blade through their dark strands with a drawn-out sound like splitting fabric. Saffron just stared as they calmly handed the knife back, as well as the few inches of hair— before coming back to reality like a strike of lightning.

"You *bitch!*" they shrieked, lunging as Saffron stumbled out of reach, unable to help the shocked, sharp laugh that erupted from his mouth.

"It works!" he exclaimed, Sybil still cursing and clambering to tear him apart. He scrambled backward another few steps as claws nearly met his flesh, laughing again when the well-dressed fey gentle tangled up in the yarrow and fell face-first into the loamy earth.

"I'm really sorry, Sybil!" Saffron exclaimed, unable to bite back another grin. "I'm really sorry! Goodbye!"

Taking off in the other direction, Sybil shouted bloodthirsty threats of all kinds in chase, but Saffron knew how to leap through the yarrow field, knew how to fly through brambles and roots and long grass without getting tangled.

But the thrill didn't last long when Sybil suddenly, impossibly, lunged from behind a tree and clotheslined Saffron with an arm. Slammed back into the dirt, Saffron released another panicked laugh, before gasping and thrashing as Sybil pinned him.

"Get off of me—*Sybil!*"

The fey gentle scowled, returning stiffly to their feet. Saffron leapt up in turn, and considered turning and running again, but still couldn't wrap his head around how he'd been caught up to so quickly in the first place. All the while, Sybil fought against the enchantment, muscles straining, fingers flexing, a vein popping in their forehead.

Saffron nearly compelled them again, just for the fun of it— but the strained expression on Sybil's face made him pause, and a flicker of regret fluttered through him.

"Erm... sorry," he said. "I know being enchanted is... agonizing."

"The moment I'm free," Sybil hissed indignantly, "your tongue is mine, moon-ear."

"That's... rude," Saffron huffed. "You started this, dragon-head."

"D-dragon-head!" Sybil balked, and the enchantment wore

off again. They leapt with claws and teeth bared, but Saffron dodged out of the way.

"Sybil, *go back to the road!*" Saffron commanded, and Sybil straightened up. Turning stiffly, they stomped away through the grass, more curses and threats ringing out the whole time. The vitriol only increased when pixies found the shiny thread and beads on their tunic and picked at it.

Gazing down at the ring, Saffron wiggled his fingers, unable to swallow back insatiable giggles as he thought about it more. A ring that could compel high fey? He'd just seen it work with Sybil, but was it really so easy? They said it belonged to a prince—surely that meant it was something special? Saffron didn't even know any princes, in Alfidel or anywhere else—but coming from the royal family meant it had to be rare. Valuable. Important. And no one would ever think to check the hands of a lowly beantighe working at Morrígan Academy.

Sybil probably never intended on letting Saffron walk away from their interaction at all, maybe even prepared to kill him on the spot once the ring's ability was confirmed—and that summoned a nauseating mix of thrill and fear and excitement to swirl in his gut. Wait—should Saffron have compelled him to do something more permanent than just *go back to the road?*

He grimaced, but decided not to worry about it. Once Saffron stepped back into the trees, Sybil wouldn't know where to even start looking for him.

Taking the long way around the yarrow clearing, Saffron barely reached the edge of the brae down to the creek when a furious, shadowy mass erupted back into the field, barking commands and tearing at grassy clusters in search of the beantighe that'd tricked him. Saffron just smiled to himself, sliding down to the creek and hopping across. Gazing at the ring one more time, another thought occurred to him:

Not only could he potentially use it to convince Arrow to come back home, it might even help to grant his wishes, too. Any of them. All of them.

I want an academic endorsement.
I want a library ring.
I want to work permanently at Luvon's winery.

Pausing, one last indulgent thought whispered through the back of his mind. He pulled open his shoulder bag just slightly, where one other book sat nestled inside, spine worn away from months and months of daily appreciation. A book of old Alvish myths, dropped on campus a year earlier by someone named *Cylvan,* who had filled the margins with annotations that were thoughtful, sarcastic, romantic, poetic. The only book Saffron could never stomach the thought of burning, even though he would be punished if found with it.

I want... he thought timidly, but couldn't bring himself to even mentally vocalize something so irrational. He just bit his lip and appreciated the shining ring again, before closing his eyes and hurrying down the path, away from the hollering fey daemon at the top of the brae.

2

THE WISH

Saffron spent the next few hours searching for his forest-devoured friend while simultaneously avoiding any crossed paths with angry fey shadows, growing more and more frustrated every time his leads turned up cold. But he wasn't panicking, yet. Arrow had gone missing for longer times than that in the past.

Whenever he came dangerously close to pulling out his hair in agitation, he just frowned down at the magic gold ring again before huffing and continuing the search. But as the sun crept toward the horizon, he had to eventually accept defeat and just hope Arrow had made it back to Beantighe Village on their own to get ready for Brìghde's ceremony. To get ready to hear Saffron's wish, damnit.

Following another one of his memorized walking paths, Saffron wound through the trees toward the road. Stepping up onto the dirt flattened by centuries of horses and wagon carts, he barely made it another hundred feet before the pale, freckled face of Lettuce burst from the trees and scared the shit out of him.

"*You!* I've been looking everywhere for you, you—*Oh!* Oh, Ériu bless you, you found them!" She squealed, leaping and ripping the rescued clips from Saffron's hair.

Rubbing at his sore roots, Saffron's annoyance tempered into relief at the sight of his friend's smile, Letty nearly on the verge of tears as she tucked the clips into curly blonde strands. But even the relief didn't last long when something crunched behind them, and he recalled the big blackbird searching to gut him. Grabbing her arm, he towed her back to the main road to Beantighe Village.

"Any library ring this time?" she asked while dragged, a whirlwind of emotions flashing through Saffron at the question.

"No... not this time," he answered with a nervous laugh, pushing hair from his eyes. "Has Arrow made it back to the village?"

"Ohhh..." Letty trailed off. "Yeah, so... about tonight... Baba sent me to find you... Arrow's not back yet, and... they might have made you... their follow-up."

Saffron stopped short, staring at her.

"They what?"

Letty just kept smiling innocently, fluttering her pretty blonde eyelashes.

"But..." Saffron said weakly.

Brìghde stand-ins didn't get wishes of their own. And even with the stolen ring on his finger, he'd still hoped for a chance to join the candle line of others to beseech the goddess just once. Just once, before he wouldn't get another chance again.

He didn't know whether he wanted to cry or scream, so he focused on fuming as his steps turned into stomps, kicking at sticks and rocks as they made their way down the worn road. Pixies bounced up ahead and pointed out more things to attack as he went, giggling shrill laughs when he did as they told him.

"The one year I have a wish planned—*ugh!!*" he finally cried, and Letty offered an apologetic pat on the shoulder. "I even specifically picked the piece of grass I wanted to wish on! A long strand from next to the library..."

"I'll make your wish for you, if you want," Letty attempted to soothe him. "I was just going to ask for another box of chocolates on my changeling day. But I get them every year, so I guess I don't really have to keep wishing for them... Unless it's only because I make the wish that I get them in the first place... hm... damn... Maybe ask Hollow to give up his wish, instead. I think he's wishing for a scar on his face to make him more intimidating, or something."

"Oh—that's alright," Saffron grumbled, swatting at a branch with the audacity to hang low enough to brush his face, only for it to recoil and smack him. He ripped it down to thrash against the trail, pixies mimicking him, slapping each other with fern sprigs.

Traversing the sloping mountain path until it flattened out again, he shook out his sore leg muscles before stealing a sharp right down another narrow trail along the eastern edge of Beantighe Village. Letty kept in close, chatting about some recent gossip involving one of their roommates, left hand strumming the wrought-iron fence posts stretching down the length of the path. To their right, rowan trees stood like ancient sentries, protective berries burning red year-round because of their proximity to the iron of the fence. Surrounded on both sides by things the fey hated, there were few places Saffron felt safer than the iron-rowan corridor that circled the village.

Perhaps because they were so small, pixies were unaffected by both the trees and the iron, busy tying more knots in Saffron's hair as he and Letty entered through the creaking gate behind Cottage Wicklow. Crossing wobbly planks over the stream on the other side, Saffron's disappointment grew as he spotted the bonfire in the neighboring field prepared with spiced logs, yellow and green banners fluttering in the breeze, sun-wheels from earlier years dangling along the side of the gathering hall. Wanting to think about anything else, Saffron just commented on the saplings growing in the garden, knowing Letty had been on Wicklow's garden crew the Fall prior and it would make her happy.

Reaching the back of the old cottage, they climbed the stone steps, patted the churning water-wheel in greeting, and invited themselves into the sunroom. Saffron was hoping to slip by and up to Fern Room unnoticed, but should have known better than to think anyone could evade the owl-ears of henmother Baba Yaga working in the kitchen.

"Is that finally you, Arrow? Fetch your maidens, dear. It's time to get ready."

"It's me and Saffron, Baba!" Letty called out as Saffron groaned internally. "He said he'll be Bríghde this year!"

"Arrow isn't going to make it?" Baba's ancient face poked out from the kitchen, narrowing her eyes at the two human chicks in the wallpapered corridor. Her long silver hair was braided with yellow and green ribbons, coiled to form a crown on her head. Saffron just smiled awkwardly and shrugged. Baba clicked her tongue in disapproval and returned to kitchen prep, and Saffron sighed, sliding past Letty and hurrying down the hall.

Any pixies still clinging to him were immediately distracted by the flowers on the old wallpaper, then the hanging mobile made from collected river stones, then the sarcastic altar for Oberon set up by Cricket and their roommates by the door. Passing the sitting room illuminated by the stained-glass window on the far wall, Blade plunked at piano keys while Berry cleaned the glass, Hollow fighting off spiders in the rafters while Fleece attempted to hold the rickety ladder beneath his weight. Letty went to observe and offer suggestions as Saffron crossed the front vestibule into the kitchen, smelling like almond cakes with honey glaze, wild berry pies, dandelion wine, and watery coffee. It made Saffron's stomach growl, thinking he could snipe one of the small pies, but Baba Yaga's wooden spoon came down on his knuckles with a painful *thunk*.

"Pick your maidens and get to the barn, Saffron," she scolded. Saffron frowned and prepared to squabble back about the truth of Arrow's disappearance, but ultimately knew better than to argue with the old woman nicknamed after some wicked human witch.

"Letty, Hollow," he called into the sitting room, both of them glancing back. They looked immediately exasperated, realizing what he intended without having to ask. He sighed in agreement. "Come along, maidens. There are wishes to grant."

BRÌGHDE'S CEREMONIAL IMBOLC DRESS WAS WHITE, with embroidered leaves and yellow flowers along the boat-neck collar and down the long-sleeves, layered skirts of linen making it hang heavy. With only one ceremonial ensemble available for each holiday, Letty adjusted the laces for Saffron's waist as the garment had originally been prepared for Arrow's wider middle. Behind him, Hollow sat cross-legged on the sleeping mat that would be Saffron's bed that night, having found the driest place in the barn to lay it after it'd rained earlier in the week.

A mat, a candle, honeyed-milk, bread, and sweet cheese were set up like a mini altar for Saffron to imbibe in once the ceremony ended. In his hands, Saffron clutched his book of myths that would offer entertainment as he was expected to stay up for the rest of the night once the wishes were made. He'd tucked Sybil's golden ring in the gap of the spine for safekeeping, providing another reason Saffron would protect the text with his life.

Letty combed cinnamon-scented oils through his hair as late afternoon drifted lazily into early evening, and Saffron could hear the sounds of celebration beginning on the other side of the village. Between carrying chopped wood to the bonfire pit, placing more colorful ribbons around on the cottages and garden fences, and the occasional handful of humans stepping into the barn in search of bottles of alcohol missed in the original search, all of them greeted Brìghde's entourage with smug smiles like they didn't envy their night of abstainment. It made Saffron's stomach tangle up even more in disappointment. He'd been looking forward to the dancing, the drinking, throwing things in the fire, fucking the first person to ask, chasing off curious fey onlookers with screeching voices as if reduced to his most primal human state with everyone else.

Hollow claimed Letty's place in front of Saffron next, snapping open a wooden block of pressed pigments and dusting a dull gold over Saffron's eyes, then red on his cheeks and lips.

"What's on your mind?"

Saffron's frown intensified. Hollow could always read Saffron's mind, even when Saffron was doing the best job ever at keeping his emotions under control. Hollow, his best friend, roommate, and bedmate, who Saffron swapped off one of the shared Fern Room mattresses with morning and night when swapping shifts. He was tall and broad chested with brown hair always pulled back in a short ponytail, pretty brown eyes, tan skin, scarred hands, and missing part of his ear. Someone Saffron knew naked about as well as he knew himself. Damn it even more. He'd been looking forward to a fun, drunken, intimate night with him, too.

"I... don't have a day off tomorrow," he lied. "I wasn't expecting to be up all night as Brìghde. It's going to be a long day."

"Ah, you'll be fine," Hollow breathed, dusting more color across Saffron's cheeks. "I've kept you up all night plenty of times."

Saffron blushed, punching Hollow in the shoulder and making him laugh.

Nestling a crown of woven twigs, amethyst points, leaves, and rowan berries on Saffron's head last, Letty adjusted Saffron's hair until it was presentable, then summoned him to his feet. She handed him a fresh thrush of red rowan branches, and he pulled it into his chest. Exhaling through his nose, he closed his eyes for a moment, before following his green-dressed maidens out of the barn.

The sun barely slipped beneath the horizon in the distance, casting the world in a hazy purple that was the ideal time for spirits to wander. Leaving the barn, Hollow slipped away to let the pre-festivity humans know the ceremony was beginning, while Saffron followed Letty up the fence. Unlatching and stepping through one of the swinging gates, they paused on the other side and waited.

It wasn't Saffron's first time acting as Brìghde, but just like previous years when he wore her dress and clutched the thrush of rowan, watching a sea of humans with flickering candles appear between the other beantighe cottages, the storage houses, the stacks of chopped wood, the well, the tool sheds, all to stand along the safe side of the iron fence—it made the branches heavy. It made his breath tight.

Curling his bare toes into the grassy path, he inhaled another long breath as Hollow returned. In that moment of silence, Saffron begged Brìghde to come and dole out blessings—and began his journey around Beantighe Village.

Tips of the thrush grazed along the iron posts of the fence, reminding him of lute strings students played in music rooms. Right on the other side, more beantighes with candles stood watching him pass, occasionally offering him small smiles and nods of encouragement. Even if Saffron didn't get his wish, even if he never planned on being Brìghde at all—he would never not put his entire soul into the early spring ritual imploring the goddess for safety. Not when wild fey roamed on the other side of the rowan guard line. Not when other vicious high fey roamed on Morrígan Academy's campus where they all worked every day.

His feet creaked against the chill by the time they circled the entire village, Letty taking the lead again and walking him to the old rowan stump amongst the other trees. Saffron took his seat like a queen takes her throne, Letty helping to adjust the skirts of Brìghde's dress as Hollow kicked loose rocks and twigs out of the way of the path. Saffron let out another shaky breath, shivering in the chilly night air.

"Ten minutes," Hollow said, and Saffron nodded. Ten minutes alone to beseech Brìghde to remain a while longer, to bless the humans living on the other side of the fence with their personal desires. Their wishes.

Closing his eyes as Hollow and Letty left for the moment of

privacy, goosebumps freckled his arms and legs beneath the sheer sleeves and skirts. He pushed his own wishes away, manifesting all the things Beantighe Village needed most. *A new barn. A new cottage. New blankets and beds. A real healer. Medicine.*

One by one, red candles shivering with every step approached the stump. A wish, an offered strand of grass, a candle left on the ground in a flickering, crimson, crescent sea of flames so others could find where Brìghde sat, too. Wish, grass, candle, again and again until the moon was high and glowing wicks illuminated every inch of him.

I wish for health.

I wish for a new contract somewhere else.

I wish for more peaceful days.

I wish for bigger meals.

I wish for more days off.

I wish for a way out.

I wish for relief from my pain.

Saffron never said anything, just nodded and accepted the offered stems, weaving them one over another into a pinwheel that soon stretched across his lap.

I wish for safety.

I wish for happiness.

I wish for all high fey to die.

Saffron smirked. He tied that blade of grass with special intention into the others.

The moon was high by the time the line withered, replaced by a field of candles around the stump where he sat. Laughter and drunken music echoed from the glow of the bonfire in the distance, and Saffron felt another pinch of disappointment—until Hollow and Letty arrived last, and Saffron straightened to hear their wishes most of all.

"*I wish to become a knight*," Hollow said.

"*I wish for Saffron to find a library ring*," Letty said, before adding in a quick whisper: "*Also for chocolates on my changling day.*"

Saffron's heart twisted as he laughed, biting back the influx of emotion and knotting their grasses as the final pieces on the sun wheel.

"It's time to rest, Brìghde." Hollow offered a hand, and Saffron clutched it, holding up his skirts so they wouldn't catch in the flood of firelight. Letty took his place to watch over the flickering ocean in their absence.

Hollow's hand was warm, and it was only once they left the fiery embrace of the candles that Saffron realized how cold it really was. Guided back through the fence to the barn, Hollow kissed him teasingly before nudging him through the wide doors. Smiling as the groaning wood slammed shut with a clank of the latch, Saffron stood there a moment longer, watching Hollow's shadow through the old slats turn back to rejoin Letty and the candles by the stump.

Once alone, Saffron sighed again, pulling the crown of sticks from his head and shaking out his hair. Making his way to the makeshift bed, he hiked up his skirts and lowered himself down, pulling the train back over his legs like a blanket. Lighting his own candle, he drank the milk, ate the bread and cheese, and prepared for the night.

Letting out a sigh through his nose, he pulled his book from beneath the mat last, delicately removing the long strand of grass nestled safely inside. The blade he picked from the side of the library, hoping that by keeping it between the pages of his favorite stories, it might become imbued with a little more luck.

I want an academic endorsement, he thought, gently threading the grass between two fingers. *I want to work at Luvon's winery permanently. I don't care who endorses me, or what I eventually do at the winery. Anything, just so I don't end up in the human world.*

Coiling the grass around his finger, frustration and anxiety swelled up in his chest, behind his eyes. In that moment, his reality was heavy, crushing, suffocating. There were no whimsical wishes to cling to, no magic rings or planning ahead. Just him, alone, facing the reality that no matter what he did, it might still not be enough. It might never be enough. He might never have what it took to show Luvon his value as an employee instead of just a changeling-child. Luvon even thought he was showing Saffron compassion by sending him "home"—but Saffron just saw it as a death sentence.

He accidentally snapped the grass in his rush of emotion. Cursing weakly, his hands tightened into fists as his nerves twisted into more anxiety and made his heart race.

I don't want to end up in the human world. Anything but that.

He reached for his book. His most treasured possession, full of stories he'd read and reread a hundred times, words that drew him in deep enough that he could forget the world he actually belonged to. Annotated with Cylvan's beautiful handwriting, written with such personality that Saffron could almost pretend he was the intended recipient of the jokes, the comments, the explanations. As if Cylvan had included the notes just so someone like Saffron could better understand what was happening within the flowery language on the page. And the way they wrote about love, and trust, and comfort, and partnerships between the characters... Saffron wondered if Cylvan was really anything like the high fey he knew attending Morrígan.

Few things calmed his nerves like crossing his legs and hunching forward, opening the book, touching his fingers to the page to keep it from fluttering, feeling the worn texture of printed ink under his fingers.

Exhaling through his nose, he brushed his thumb along one of his favorite comments in his favorite myth. In the story of Derdriu and Naoise, where the author described Naoise with *hair black as crow feathers, skin pale as alpine mint, cheeks red as berries,* Cylvan had added a sarcastic response, saying:

DERDRIU HAS EXCELLENT TASTE IN LOVERS. BUT WHAT OF HIS LEGS?

Smiling to himself, Saffron closed his eyes. Cylvan existed as nothing more than a blur in his imagination, but Saffron could almost imagine their voice. Their hands. How they might have smiled while writing something so playful.

The golden ring slipped from the gap in the spine, clinking to the wooden floor and rolling to a halt amongst scattered hay. Saffron picked it up again, gazing at its shining surface in the light of his candle, more emotion swelling in the back of his throat.

He might still be able to use the ring to realize his more tangible needs, like getting access to the library. Finding someone to endorse him. Learning how to be more valuable to Luvon.

But it wouldn't be able to grant him that one wish he'd been too embarrassed to even consider in the woods.

"I wish... to one day discuss myths with Cylvan," he finally whispered into existence, tying the two strands of grass back into one.

3

THE SPRITES

"Morning, Brìghde," Hollow greeted sleepily as Saffron made his way into Fern Room the following morning, the other three night-shift roommates Feather, Splinter, and Quilt scattered in their own respective beds like warriors after battle. "Sleep well in the barn? Oh, I guess you didn't. Yet you have straw in your hair."

Saffron wrinkled his nose before turning it up completely. He undid the laces of Brìghde's dress, stripping it off and scattering more straw all over Hollow with a bark of laughter from his friend.

Pulling out the trundle drawer beneath where Hollow lay, Saffron removed his Morrígan servant uniform, tugging on the high-waisted gray slacks; the white, high-collar blouse with its v-shaped ruffle down the front and back, high button cuffs and puffy sleeves; black derby boots that were worn in perfectly to the shape of his feet. Opening the rattly wooden box in the drawer, next, he decorated nearly every one of his fingers with bronze access rings for Morrígan's campus, some settling all the way down at the base of his fingers, others shaped to nestle above his second knuckle to ensure he could wear as many as he needed at a time. It reminded him about the recovered rings in his shoulder bag, making a mental note to deliver them to Baba Yaga later that evening to be returned to their original owners. Last, he tucked his gold patron ring on his thumb, donning a sign of Luvon's family and ensuring Saffron couldn't be compelled by any fey word.

Finally, he pulled on the two pieces of fabric that made up his veil—a lace edged underpiece that pinned into his mousy brown hair and provided shape, then a top layer that hung like ghostly smoke over his face, fingertip length and just opaque enough to blur his features. With delicate eyelets sewn around the bottom seam, Saffron looped two through the matching line of buttons down his shoulders and arms to keep the flowing fabric out of his way for the time being. He tucked his book into the back of his waistband last, deciding it would be a nice comfort in case he found any moments of free time between chores.

"Good luck with that hangover, good ser knight Hollow of Wicklow," Saffron teased, making Hollow laugh drowsily again. A chorus of weary *"have a nice day, Brìghde"*'s emerged from the other sleeping bodies, Saffron just rolling his eyes with a smile and slipping into the hallway outside.

Fellow day-shift residents of Maple, Clover, Dandelion, Pebble, and Grass Rooms passed by him in the hallway, all yawning and donning matching white veils to cover the exhaustion and brewing hangovers as they descended to the bottom floor. Saffron joined at the back of the line, finding Letty in the kitchen, drinking from the tap and still in her green maiden dress. Through the front door, Saffron's other roommates, Berry and Fleece, raced up the stairs to get changed.

"Staying home today?" Saffron asked as Letty lifted her exhausted eyes to meet his. She smelled of candle smoke and had loose leaves in her hair, making him wonder if anything wild had happened at the stump after they relegated him to the barn.

"I let Hollow head to the bonfire around two," she grumbled. "He was supposed to come back at four, but he didn't. That ass."

"He's upstairs right now. You should go pour water on him."

"Ooooh," Letty growled, vengeance glowing in her eyes. Saffron offered her an encouraging pat on the shoulder, before following the parade of white-clad ghosts back into the morning air. Pressing a goodbye kiss to Baba Yaga's cheek, she lingered as she normally did by the exit and fussed over her passing chicks' veils and wrinkled shirts, long white hair messy and still plaited with ribbons. He wondered if she'd taken her chance to get drunk with the other henmothers like every other year, but the fact none of them were found naked and dancing in the woods praising some human god made him doubt it. Perhaps those ceremonies were only reserved for Samhain.

Leaving Beantighe Village for the dirt road through Agate Wood, Saffron kept to the tail end of the ghostly parade, suddenly self-conscious about the Brìghde makeup he'd forgotten to wipe away. Weaving in and out through the trees, passing lush grottos, the wildflower meadow, a few streams with planks of wood acting as bridges, they arrived at Agate Bridge at the very end, Saffron's campus access ring tingling slightly and allowing him to cross the campus barrier like normal. It was that light sensation that compelled him—and every other beantighe who walked with him —to pull down his veil and hide his face, making him just another ghost. Another nameless spirit mopping the floors and sweeping the walkways, one to be ignored and disregarded. Ideally, anyway.

The buildings of Morrígan were older than every beantighe combined, constructed with dark stone and metal in ways that were both smooth and sharp at once. Delicate, colorful-glass windows sat within dark metal frames, like ice held in old tree branches. The exterior stone was dark and discolored from centuries of rain and wind, porous and prone to mold and moss clinging to the exteriors. Perhaps that was the real reason beantighes rarely received more than one collective day off for holidays—if the buildings went without upkeep much longer, they would surely crumble to ruin overnight.

Pathways between buildings were paved with centuries-long polished stones worn flat, green hedges and rose bushes filling in gaps between the paths and walls, decorating the center square where the fountain gurgled clear water. While the towers, buttresses, stained-glass windows, marble floors, vaulted ceilings, and looming gargoyles of Morrígan's campus used to fill him with wonder, the sights had since muddied into more reason to resent the fey who attended the school. Scrubbing mold out of cracks in the floor tiles, chasing rats from closets, climbing ladders to polish the tall windows and dark bronze chandeliers, scaling tiled rooftops and slippery metal gutters in the rain, none of it was so stunning beneath calloused hands and broken bones.

The building for morning assignments was set behind the dining hall, beantighes clustering in the walled-off courtyard decorated with crawling vines and blind arcading, crumbling around the top edge and stained dark with centuries of weather beating down on it. Through the double-doors into the office where the line spilled out, the smells of breakfast floated through and made every collective, starving human standing around groan in envy, taking guesses about what the fey residents could have been eating that morning—toast with sweet berry jams and pine nut compote... honeyed ham, sugar bacon... rainbow skinned potatoes sliced and draped with sprigs of rosemary... wine-soaked cakes with cream centers... eggs whipped into clouds and adorned with a drizzle of salted syrup... fresh coffee brewed from roasted beans and hazelnuts with sweet cream to cut the bitterness...

In the village, they rarely had more to look forward to than mashed beans with an egg from the shared chicken coop, fresh or steamed vegetables from individual gardens, an occasional rabbit if Blade or someone else managed to get a trap to work, a slice of bread or pancakes if old flour was gifted from the Morrígan kitchens. For the luckiest cottage, it would be their week with the shared milk cow, before she waddled off to provide cream and butter and something to drink to the next cottage down the hill. Or, for those beantighes who came from wealthy patron-houses, they could indulge in leftovers from the kitchens after student meals—though even those trays were hardly more than morsels or scraps.

In the assignment office, on the furthest wall from the entrance, cubby holes labeled with names waited with gaping mouths and gifts inside. Saffron made his way through the crowd for the familiar place designated to him, reading *Saffron dé Patron dé Mag Shambradháin* just like every other morning. But upon sticking his hand in, he was surprised when no assignment ring waited to be grabbed. Even dragging his hand over every inch of the cubby in confusion, there was nothing tucked in the back, and he wondered if his contract had ended overnight and no one told him.

"I heard you sat in for Brìghde during Imbolc last night, Saffron. Does that mean you didn't get your last wish?" Merith, assignment director and elevated beantighe, human like the rest of them but with a venomous superiority complex, approached him from behind.

She had her gold-embroidered veil pushed out of her face, copper-brown hair twisted into a low knot at the nape of her neck. She tucked a piece of hair behind her ear to show off her gold unrestricted ring and anti-aging ring. Saffron's eyes lingered on them a moment too long. That was his second mistake. The first was humoring her in the first place.

She smiled in a way he hated, and he already knew what she was going to say.

"Lord Kaelar is still interested, if you'll just swallow your pride," she told him like it was anything new, or particularly generous. "He's even upping his offer. Now, if you agree to his patronage, he promises to be the only brother you have to spend nights with."

There were only a few elevated beantighes on campus, and Saffron had made the mistake months earlier of asking *Merith* if she had any advice for getting an academic endorsement. Merith, raised by a high-noble family, endorsed and taught to read and write from an early age, promoted to assignment director at

Morrígan without ever having to raise a finger to work first. Merith, who, on the same day Saffron asked for advice, went straight to the youngest son of her patron family, a student on campus with an equally bitter superiority complex and something to prove. Thus began Lord Kaelar's obsession with Saffron's patronage up for claim.

All things considered, becoming a silken-beantighe, a courtesan for a fey lord, especially one from a wealthy noble family, wasn't the *worst* Saffron could do—but he would keep that option far in his back pocket for when he lost all other hope. He couldn't stand Lord Kaelar, a part of Saffron constantly debating whether he would be better off drowning in Lake Elatha on campus.

"Lord Kaelar certainly knows how to entice me," Saffron answered with a sarcastic smile, hoping that was the end of it so he could ask about his assignment for the day. "I don't have anything in my cubby. Is there some kind of mistake?"

"No mistake," Merith smiled, plucking a silver ring from a matching loop on her belt. Handing it over, Saffron's heart thudded when he saw the unicorn engraving on the front.

"This—"

"There are new students moving into Danann House tonight, and Elluin insists on throwing a welcome party. Apparently Caetho walked in this morning to find an infestation of fairy bugs. You're the local bug lover, so..."

"Wait, but—" Saffron stammered, but Merith was already grabbing and steering him through the door. He didn't have a chance to ask for any more information before she flipped her veil and turned back inside, just watching her go before slowly adding the silver ring amongst his bronze collection. Bronze represented places he was allowed to access indiscriminately, mostly supply closets, main buildings like lecture halls and the Administration Building, the gardens, Agate Bridge, the stables, the sports fields; but silver meant the ring was expected back when his shift ended. That normally wasn't anything to be worried about, except

—*Danann House*, Saffron couldn't recall if he'd ever actually been inside that old dormitory in particular, seeing as it was so rarely inhabited. Most beantighes thought it was abandoned. Haunted. Left to be reclaimed by the woods, as if something terrible had happened inside and no one wanted to step foot through the door again.

Closing his eyes, he just let out a breath and trudged his way up the path. Technically, Merith said the dorm was infested with *fairy bugs*, not ghosts, so perhaps he wouldn't be so in over his head. Although *fairy bugs* could really mean anything to those who didn't know any better, and his mind went wild with possibilities. Damn, should he have brought his sketchbook? What if it was something new? Something he'd never seen before?

Following one of the side-paths between buildings, he kept close to the exteriors and stopped only once on the way to his assignment—outside the Grand Library. Standing on his toes and peeking inside, he sighed longingly at the way the sun cast glorious beams of light through the tall windows, illuminated the spines of books, shone like portals of gold on the floors.

It was empty so early in the morning, as to be expected as most students were still away for the holiday, which gave it the air of a tomb. A place where no life walked, but still radiated warmth. He used to mentally beg every morning for a library assignment, even just to scrub the floor, before learning it was the one building normal beantighes like him weren't allowed. Those privileges were reserved for others on track to become elevated like Merith—which Saffron thought was a crime in and of itself. Did they think because he never *formally* learned how to read, he wouldn't know how to take care of the books? Wouldn't be mindful of his hands? The volume of his voice? Even though, technically, his same hands had burned a handful of books from the same library... but not because he wanted to. Because otherwise Elluin might just chop his hands off if she learned he was snagging books from benches and reading them in secret in the barn.

Sighing again, he returned flat to his feet and trundled off toward Danann House, keeping his eyes down just in case someone else dropped a library ring while he was away and Brìghde wanted to give him one nice thing that morning.

Set away from the rest of campus, while Morrígan's other dormitories had courtyards and gardens of their own, none compared to the swath of land claimed by Danann House. Gardens in the front overflowed with neatly trimmed grass, bushels of curling ferns, fish ponds that croaked with frosty toads despite magic to keep the water thawed, marble statues of nude forms caught up in wind and draped in flowers, similarly carved fountains spewing water from mouths and pitchers while dancing with wings like butterflies.

The menagerie continued around both sides of the house to the back, which was its own gallery of marble statues, florals, hedges, and fruit bushes, with a terraced patio and sweeping apple orchard, punctuated with a man-made pond at the far end that was nearly large enough to be a lake of its own. Pure luxury for the particularly affluent students who lived there year-round—no wonder it sat vacant for so long. And Morrígan Academy only admitted high fey of nobility, so the thought of there possibly being families even *more* wealthy, *more* affluent, *more* self-important than the ones that already terrorized him and other beantighes daily... Saffron's resentment reached a new peak.

He'd been in the other three dormitories plenty of times, and always thought them to be luxurious on their own. House Pallas for those studying military history, world history, and diplomatic politics; House Erce for studying government, economics, social philosophy, public works, and ensuring the wellbeing of all high fey; and House Nemain, for the arts, literature, philosophy, sociology, anthropology. Pallas was for future knights, Erce for future government officials, Nemain for oracles and philosophers— which apparently reserved Danann House for nobility who only wished to impress the right people and attend lavish parties while rubbing elbows with royalty for the rest of their lives. Saffron already hated the two students who would be moving in. He wondered if there was some sort of curse in the form of toads he could catch and release in their beds.

Waiting at the gate for Caetho to come and give him more instruction, Saffron watched other beantighes who'd arrived slightly earlier already at work trimming hedges, fluffing ferns, carrying armfuls of potted plants, baskets of old apples, and what looked like entire uprooted juvenile trees around the yard. Others touched up the white gazebo and swinging daybeds closer to the house, offering him polite waves when they noticed him looking.

The facade of Danann House was of worn gray stone like the rest of Morrígan's campus, another reminder of its age. Three stories high with a fourth attic area at the very top, tall latticed windows stood stark against the rough facade, vines crawling up the sides of the chateau and bursting with early spring flowers in yellow and white. It had to be the size of three beantighe cottages combined, and Saffron briefly wondered how hard it would be to reside in one of the rooms without ever being found.

"You! Saffron, thank the gods," Caetho exclaimed from the doorway. Failing to respond even a polite *hello*, she was already flattening him: "We had a thousand irises delivered last night, and someone left a back window open. There are little fairy insects *everywhere*, so *please*, we need them all gone by this evening."

Grabbed and dragged toward the door, Saffron tripped over his words while trying to ask what she meant—but Caetho pulled him through the front entrance, and he understood instantly.

An ocean of indigo-blue irises in golden vases decorated the floors and every other flat surface, overtaking his senses with their sweet-smelling blooms—but behind that loveliness, there was chaos. Sparkling blurs flitted in every direction, occasionally giggling as they *thwumped* drunkenly into windows, knocked down wall hangings, wrote rude words in tree sap and pollen across the mirror over the fireplace. They tugged curtains from their loops, random shoes and jewels from light fixtures scattering across the polished floors and couch cushions. A bottle of rich perfume laid half-spilled on a rug in the study, a diamond-encrusted pocket watch with a golden chain and at least thirty wine corks scattered around it like spent arrowheads.

"Oh... my god," he whispered. "What am I... How am I... This is too much, Caetho, I can't—"

"Come on, buck up, we all have to carry our weight. Here, I got you this." She tucked a glass jar and cloth topper into his hands. He stared at them blankly. "Get to work. If there's a single pixie left in this house when the kings and prince arrive for dinner tonight, it'll be all of our heads."

"The—the kings! The *prince!*" Saffron choked, mind racing back to Sybil in the woods. They said—stolen from a prince—the ring tucked in Saffron's book, tucked in his waistband—

Caetho just smiled tightly at him.

"But why are the kings—for Imbolc—And the prince?" He went on nonsensically as Caetho attempted to wave him off to get to work. "Is he—the new student? The—the prince...?"

Saffron had to run. He had to dump his book. The ring. He needed to be far away before anyone could find him with a magic *fey-compelling* ring stolen from a thief who stole it from a prince—

"I don't have time for jokes, Saffron," she continued through her tightening smile. "Get to work, or we're all dead."

She walked away, leaving Saffron in shock in the entryway, staring down at the empty jar in his hand. A pair of squealing creatures suddenly knocked a ceramic bust of the late King Elanyl from its pedestal at the bottom of the stairs, the fey majesty's nose skittering across the floor and bumping into Saffron's shoes. He lifted his eyes back to them, fighting to swallow the lump in his throat. He focused on one single distracting detail.

They were just flower sprites. Nasty, crude, feral cousins to the cute creatures Saffron befriended in the woods—but they were only sprites.

Watching the three responsible for King Elanyl's beheading, they just fluttered their wings, called him a *ninny cocksucker*, and zoomed off again. He gulped. If he just... kept his veil on. Focused on his work. If he just didn't speak or bring attention to himself, perhaps he could finish the day and narrowly escape with his life before anyone showed up for any party at all. And he would remain anonymous. A ghost. Just another veiled beantighe.

WHILE FLOWER SPRITES WEREN'T ANY MORE OR LESS *intelligent* than rainbow pixies, they were a damn lot more chaotic —but in other ways, also more predictable.

Morning hours melted into midday as Saffron gathered as many he could by hand first, carefully peeling a thousand iris petals apart to scoop up anything snoozing drunk inside. A part of him wished again that he had his sketchbook whenever one looked sort of cute—until its snoozing eyes bulged open and it went straight for his mouth to steal his teeth.

When the easiest prey was all gathered, Saffron resorted next to his own tricks for those that remained hiding or clustered in horrifying spider-sacks near the ceiling. He didn't know much about them as a whole since they were generally less genial than their pixie cousins, but there was at least one thing: they loved crows and all parts of them. Their eyes, their beaks, their feet, their tongues. Stealing their feathers, the sprites would strip the dark, iridescent barbs to weave into clothing, and there was nothing quite like watching a cloud of them drag a whole bird from the sky to pluck a dozen of its feathers, and then its eyes for fun. Sybil was lucky they didn't cross sprites in the woods, instead —the little buzzards would have gone straight for their amethyst eyes first.

Gathering black feathers from the private raven paddock in the backyard—hoping the sprites wouldn't notice the difference —he left the dark bait around the house, trapping more sprites one by one in his jar. Meanwhile, around him, Danann House was being overrun with even more flowers as the hours ticked by; some matched the irises cluttering the walkways, others coming in gigantic bouquets of roses and tulips and dangling wisteria, others wrapped in paper like twigs bundled for kindling. Flowers from fey courtiers wishing the new residents luck in the school year, wishing them a safe transition, wishing them a home filled with peace and love and overseen by Danu. With them, boxes upon boxes of candies and cakes, new cloaks, boots, silk scarves, hair pins, makeup, jewelry. At one point, a new horse was delivered with a wreath of pine berries around its neck, and Saffron couldn't help but secretly laugh as Caetho stared and had to figure out where to put it. Unfortunately for Saffron, the responsibility of clearing out an additional pen in the back stables fell on him between rounds of sprite-wrangling, scraping gunk from the walls and sweeping dirt and straw from the floor as the horses already housed there watched in curiosity.

He was in the middle of a brief lunch break with other beantighes in the front garden when yet another overflowing bouquet arrived, Caetho calling out to him to carry it in as he was closest to the door. Groaning, he shoved the rest of the dry sandwich into his mouth and accepted the ridiculous, overflowing bouquet into his arms.

Following the dark banister and carpeted stairs all the way to the Aon-adharcach Suite on the third floor, he sensed the moment he passed through an unexpected internal barrier at the top, the rest of the house falling away beneath that last step. Silence greeted him, stark enough that it made goosebumps prickle the back of his neck.

Deciding it made sense for there to be some sort of sound-softening magic for the comfort of the *highly-affluent, sensitive, easily-ruffled* residents of such an affluent house, Saffron pulled a face of disdain and made his way down the long passageway. Early afternoon sun came in warm yellow beams through the corridor window, curtains pulled open wide as if attempting to summon as much light in as possible. More curtains hung from the high ceilings to break up the length, which explained why even Saffron's footsteps on the carpet runners came as muted as the air he inhaled. Approaching the single doorway at the end, it sat propped wide open, and he invited himself inside with a brief, habitual bow.

Searching every flat surface for a place not already cluttered with other extravagant deliveries, he couldn't help but pause and appreciate the luxurious interior despite himself. Black paper with muted bronze flourishes covered the walls above dark wood wainscoting, floorboards glossy and protected by a thick area rug stitched around the edges with white mushrooms and leaves. Overhead, a bronze coffered ceiling printed with more floral motifs reflected daylight streaming through tall repeating windows opposite the door. Claiming a majority of the wall, a few of the windows opened up onto a balcony overlooking the side garden, latches molded like swirling leaves from metal that matched the ceiling.

Over the mantle of a fireplace as wide as Saffron was tall, a mirror reflected the crystal chandelier hanging from the ceiling that cast little colorful spots on the dark walls and sheer black canopy of the massive bed. It was—excessive, in a way that almost made Saffron burst out laughing. He couldn't help but approach the bed to run his hand over the matching black sheets, wondering what sort of shadow creature could enjoy the dark so much. It made him think about Sybil again, grimacing, glad to know there was no chance *that* shadow creature would be coming anywhere near the suite's lavish interior.

He regarded the entire corner of the room packed with waiting luggage next, seeing how some poor beantighe had been tasked with hanging tunics, slacks, leggings, doublets, blazers, and other articles of clothing in the wardrobe, or folding them into the dresser drawers next to it. Saffron paused with curiosity when something caught his eye from the dresser in particular, approaching a well-worn violin sitting on top. Plucking one of the strings, it made an enchanting sound, reminding him of Cottage Dublin's henmother, Hector, and the fiddle he played after too many drinks.

Searching for the instrument's missing bow, he was in the

process of collecting it from the floor when he spotted a paper card that must have fallen from one of the bouquets, as well. Grabbing both, he placed the bow next to its instrument before searching for which bouquet the card belonged to—but stopped short when he read a familiar name within the swirling words.

A humble gift for dear Prince Cylvan. Congratulations on acceptance to Morrigan Academy. Here's to new beginnings.

"P—" Saffron choked, eyes going wide as his world suddenly clicked brighter, louder. "P-P-P-Prince—*Prince* Cylvan?" he finally squeaked. "*Prince? Prince* Cylvan?"

He wasn't sure he kept breathing—or even remained upright. Everything spun, but he didn't know from which way, or how to escape it. The same words just kept repeating in the back of his mind, reading the note over and over and over again. But—it was right there, in front of him.

"Cylvan is the *prince?*"

Oh—Saffron wanted nothing more than to drop everything, strip down naked, and sprint full-tilt into the woods, never to be seen or heard from again. Suddenly his silly wish in the barn felt *loud*, like a landslide.

Prince Cylvan! PRINCE Cylvan! How could a stupid beantighe like him ever even look a *prince* in the eyes? Let alone— expect to impress him with his childish appreciation of myths?

Myths from his stolen book that also hid his stolen magic ring that Saffron stole from another high fey in the woods?

Saffron slammed the card on the dresser and ran. Down the stairs, his hand on the banister was the only thing keeping him en route and not slamming through a wall. At the bottom, he sprang straight through the exit—only to be greeted with another cruel, ludicrous development on the other side.

Was Brìghde punishing him? Had he asked for too much? Had he cursed himself by making a wish despite not being allowed one? Was she purposefully going to ruin his life because he couldn't keep his one indulgent desire to himself?

"L-Luvon!" he exclaimed, voice cracking as he attempted to sound excited through the pure hot anxiety.

Luvon grinned at the sound of Saffron's voice, shallow laugh lines creasing the corners of his cloudy eyes. His tinted glasses allowed him to perceive aural colors and shapes, and Saffron tried to make himself as yellow as possible despite the deadly pounding of his heart. As yellow as the gold shimmer on Luvon's dark cheeks and eyelids. As yellow as the flowers crawling up Danann House.

"Are you here to wait on the evening, Saffron? I was hoping to stop by the village later, but you seem to have come to me instead," Luvon said cheerfully, standing alongside one of a handful of carriages that had arrived while Saffron's world split apart in the Aon-adharcach suite. Putting out an arm for a hug, Saffron slumped defeatedly into Luvon's rich purple jacket, smelling his patron-fey's familiar perfume combined with wintry mountain air. If anything—it did help to slightly temper his urge to sprint into the woods. Slightly. Only slightly. He might still lightly jog into it if the chance came.

He only needed to remain a ghost. Unknown, unnoticed—and perhaps he could still finish the night and narrowly escape with his life.

4

THE PRINCE

There were dozens of wines the mag Shamhradháin Winery was famous for, and that night, Luvon provided one of his most expensive and most sought-after—a special sparkling apple that, when paired with fresh slices of frost-fruit, changed flavor profiles entirely. It was the same kind he always gifted Saffron on his changeling day, so it held a special place in Saffron's heart—but it also meant Saffron was left in the kitchen slicing up special wintry apples, pears, plums, and various berries in preparation, dropping one of each into a myriad of crystal dessert cups. His back hurt halfway through, but at least regularly gathering sprites from his traps helped get blood back in his legs.

Around him, beantighes continued bustling with decorations and snapped commands at one another, lighting a fire in the parlor and crowding the kitchen with dinner preparation. The sun reached early evening, and the temperatures outside crept lower with the fading light. More flowers accentuated the entry-way, the front hallways, the sitting room and parlor, creating a walkway out the back doors to the tables where pristine wine glasses and other dinnerware sat waiting to be eaten off of. Green and silver of Alfidel's capital city, Avren, hung in pine garlands pinned with little bells over the fireplace and between windows, curtains pulled open wide to allow for views of the thoroughly organized gardens and inevitable Imbolc moon once the sun eventually set.

As shadows lengthened around him, his natural light shifted into orange and then pink. Soon, Saffron couldn't swallow back the return of his apprehension. He just kept tapping the book hidden in his waistband, using it to remain tied in reality.

He considered his options.

Leave the moment courtiers arrived. Stay completely out of the way. Watch from afar. Make himself small. Run into the woods forever. Only come back out again to say goodbye to Luvon around midnight.

Or... the more the day crept on, the more he realized... perhaps he didn't need to be so terrified. Perhaps—*perhaps* Brighde wasn't trying to *curse* him, but... to thrust exactly what he wanted into his hands.

What if...?

I'm so sorry to bother you, your highness...

I ran into this miserable asshole in the woods yesterday, who claimed they stole this ring from you. They were so ugly and rude. I tricked them so easily. Not like you at all with your beautiful golden hair, tan skin, brown eyes, broad chest, strong hands, thoughtfulness and intelligence...

Oh! Are you the same Cylvan who once owned this book? Your name is so unique, surely there can only be one of you? I, too, love to read about myths... Oh, how did I learn how to read? Well, I taught myself, actually... Does that impress you? Oh, you'd like me to join you at your chateau by the sea, where we can eat cakes and drink mimosas and talk for hours and hours and hours?

"Pffft," he sighed, but a rogue smile cracked the corner of his mouth. Was that really so impossible?

Yes. But...

Still, he fantasized about all the ways he could tell Cylvan about the book. About how much it meant to him. How Saffron was infatuated with his humor, thoughtfulness, intelligence, romanticism. Maybe Cylvan really would be impressed. Maybe he would see Saffron's potential, and... offer an academic endorsement on the spot. Maybe he would write a recommendation for someone in King Ailir's court to patronize him, if he couldn't do it himself. Maybe he would suggest to Luvon to keep Saffron around like Saffron ultimately wished, and Luvon would agree because he couldn't possibly send someone so cunning and smart into the human world. In fact, maybe Cylvan would want to keep Saffron for himself, to appreciate for long hours and hold even longer discussions with, until eventually they grew so close to one another, knowing each other's deepest thoughts and wishes, that they would be inseparable in every way...

He held his face as it went hot, embarrassed by his own thoughts and letting out a small sound that was both a giggle and a pressure-release. It was easy to pretend while he stood uninterrupted over his chore, but the words just kept repeating in his head. *Why not?*

"The courtiers will be here any minute now!" Caetho announced frantically from the parlor, heads turning before pulling down veils to disappear into the woodwork. Saffron took that as his cue to do one final check of his sprite traps, wiping his hands on his apron and slipping from the kitchen.

He barely made it into the front corridor when the front door opened and an elegantly dressed Headmistress Elluin, her assistant Silver, and a few luxuriously dressed students entered. Saffron just stepped out of the way and adjusted his veil, Caetho greeting the first arrivals and bowing. She snapped her fingers, calling out for wine and finger foods to be served, Saffron lingering out of the way before initiating his last check with haste.

Whenever more noble high fey arrived, he just silently stepped off to the side to allow them through. Again and again, small groups approached the doors of Danann House, dressed in lovely flowing gowns, suits, jackets, hats, smelling of perfumes and fresh flowers pinned to their collars, wishing one another *"blessed*

Imbolc" and shaking hands. They sparkled with crystal beading and dusted makeup, grabbing offered wine from trays, stuffing their faces with appetizers before even sitting down. Bodies packed the house in less than an hour, voices practically shouting over one another in order to enjoy conversation.

Saffron just focused on his work, on the last remaining sprites, swallowing back the anticipation, the anxiety, the embarrassment as more and more fantasies plagued him. Fantasies like—Cylvan approaching from behind, commenting with concern about Saffron's dry, calloused hands. Offering a velvety cream to soothe them before asking what made them so worn in the first place. Saffron would tell him about his art, and Cylvan would ask to see it, before lauding Saffron with praises and asking if Saffron would be willing to draw him, too...

Fully ensnared by the delusion, he didn't notice when Lord Kaelar found him even with his veil on. Snapping out of it, Saffron hated how it felt to emerge from such warm, romantic scenarios to find Kaelar crouching on the balls of his feet and meeting Saffron's eyes.

"What are you working on, Saffron?" he asked as Saffron tucked another flower-drunk sprite into the jar. "Ah—Morrígan has a pest problem, do they? And here I thought you beantighes were the only blight on campus."

Kaelar's hand tucked under Saffron's veil to push it up, and Saffron politely knocked it away again. Insisting he needed to stay focused, Kaelar disregarded the request like he always did.

"Did Merith tell you my new offer?" he went on, attempting to push Saffron's veil up a second time. Saffron huffed in restrained annoyance, side-stepping and digging around in another bundle of flowers as Kaelar continued. "I saw Luvon was here—we could talk to him, together. I could have you at my family's estate by morning. I could come visit you every weekend, or perhaps I'd ask you to be assigned to keep me company in Pallas House—"

"No thank you, Lord Kaelar," Saffron finally answered,

glancing at him for the first time. Even dressed like nobility, with a jacket of deep gold, rapier on his belt, makeup over his gray eyes, shoulder-length blonde hair pulled back into a half-up braided style, Saffron's stomach turned at the sight of him. Every beantighe knew who Lord Kaelar was and how he normally acted, and a shiny facade didn't hide the insufferable refuse beneath. "Please go enjoy the party. I have not made any decisions yet."

"You know I could just go speak to Luvon myself, right?" Kaelar continued with an arrogant smile, and Saffron had to bite back his frown.

"I appreciate your patience," Saffron told him otherwise. "And your willingness to let me decide for myself."

"I know Luvon sends his beantighes back to the human world when they get too old and useless. Aren't you worried?"

"Please, go back to the party—" But Saffron stopped short when the sound of horses in the courtyard made him lift his head. He clearly wasn't the only one to notice as every guest crowding the sitting room leapt to their feet and rushed the door, knocking over decorations including the flower vases. Scattered blooms were flattened beneath heeled feet as Saffron just watched in horror, praying there weren't any sleeping sprites in them he might have missed.

Overhearing the words whispered excitedly amongst fey courtiers next, his heart froze for a different reason.

"Is that Prince Cylvan at the back?"

"How ironic for him to arrive at night, don't you think?"

"Shush—don't speak so loudly. Do you want to curse us all?"

Saffron craned his neck to peer through a nearby window, spotting the gold-embellished carriage drawn by six black horses displaying the royal family's emblem, a barn owl encircled by fern stems and thorns. Behind the carriage, a dozen riders followed, one of them draped in a thick cloak and hood of emerald green velvet.

Even with his face shadowed, Saffron didn't have to see to know. By the decorated reins of the horse, the luster of their saddle, the color and design of their drapery—that was Prince Cylvan. It had to be. And he was right out on the drive.

Saffron's hand crept to the book tucked in his waistband, knowing instantly, it was foolish to ever think he would be able to just stand to the side. Watch from afar. Pretend he didn't exist. Not with Cylvan, not with the person who taught him how to love myths, whose silly annotations helped his reading improve, how everything about his book brought Saffron so much comfort and grounding and joy, even in his darkest nights. Even if it would end in disaster—the potential for even one of his fantasies to become real was worth the risk. Even just to thank the prince for his passive, beloved presence in Saffron's life. Saffron might even return the stolen magic ring, if it meant Cylvan would smile at him in gratitude for a brief moment.

His heart raced faster—but before he could do anything else, his wrist was suddenly grabbed, and he snapped back to reality. Kaelar was still kneeling next to him, a wicked smile on his face.

"*Oh,* I see where your intentions lie. You might be pretty for a beantighe, Saffron, but Prince Cylvan's tastes are particular. You know, though—I'm actually already acquainted with him. Why don't I, in my chivalry, introduce you?"

"What—!" Saffron gasped, but was already being dragged to his feet. Wrenching his arm back, he dug his heels until his boots squeaked against the polished wood. "Lord Kaelar, no! Stop it!"

"What for? Not many beantighes—will ever get the opportunity—for a face-to-face introduction like this," he grunted as Saffron resisted, clawing at his hand. "Go on, take this off, too. Your face is the only thing Cylvan might give any shit about, anyway."

Kaelar snatched Saffron's veil, tossing it to the floor before dragging him through the exit. Saffron clamped his mouth shut at the sight of Kings Ailir and Tross stepping from their carriage, Ailir with his hair and beard like spun gold, shimmering paints gilding the dark skin of Tross' shaved head like a crown. Approaching the walkway hand in hand, applause and words of adoration plumed from the guests lined up to the door as Kaelar tugged Saffron off to the side.

"Kaelar—stop it! Let go of me!" Saffron hissed, still attempting to tug himself free.

That wasn't how he wanted to meet Cylvan—he didn't want Kaelar anywhere near him, knowing he would definitely say something crude, or cruel, or otherwise horrible—not when Saffron had spent the last day, the entire last year, fantasizing about his first meeting being simple, maybe even romantic—

Kaelar waited for the kings to pass before grinning in a way that made Saffron's heart stop.

"As you wish," he granted, and released his grip.

Saffron crashed to the gravel driveway. It scraped his hands, the book skittering out of his waistband and across the drive. Wincing, he caught his breath before rushing back to his feet— but in the process of righting himself, froze at the sight of two dark boots standing in front of him. No, not just standing—waiting. Waiting to pass by, to enter through the front door. Saffron had tripped—right in Prince Cylvan's way.

Gulping, Saffron's eyes lifted slowly, following the line of the prince's long legs, his hips, his waist, his shoulders, the pale column of his throat—until finally, Saffron laid eyes on black hair, amethyst eyes, and curling obsidian horns.

Him. Sybil, who Saffron left shrieking threats in the woods. Who Saffron had stolen the magic ring from. A magic ring— likely belonging to Sybil, himself, never stolen from any prince at all.

"*You,*" the prince hissed, impaling Saffron like ice.

Kaelar rushed from the crowd, insisting something about his *stupid beantighe.* He grabbed Saffron by the hair to drag him out of the prince's way, but Saffron barely felt it, even as tears filled his eyes and his scalp erupted into flames. Attempting to reclaim his balance, he just scraped his palms against the gravel again, unable to think straight, hearing the hushed whispers of disgust amongst the courtiers, their disapproving eyes trailing over him. But the worst moment of all was when Sybil—Cylvan—knelt and picked up the discarded book. He examined it briefly, frowned, cast Saffron on his knees one last fleeting glance—and walked into Danann House.

Saffron finally snapped, throwing his hands up to tear free from Kaelar's grip. Kaelar just laughed, joining the others inside and leaving Saffron alone in the front yard.

Saffron's fists closed around handfuls of gravel as his whole body shook, gasping and clenching his muscles to keep the misery at bay. No, no, *no*—that wasn't how any of it was supposed to happen.

Cylvan, who wrote such beautiful things—had looked down on Saffron with such pure resentment, turning his blood to ice and ash until he didn't feel like a person at all. Only a swirling pool of dust, smoke, debris.

His Cylvan—was the same wild, angry shadow in the woods that spewed threats after flashing shiny rings used to compel high fey, luring Saffron into trying it on. And Saffron *had* compelled him, before taking that ring altogether. No wonder Cylvan hated him.

Saffron had done this to himself.

"Saffron! Hey, Saffron!" Saffron jumped at the last voice he expected to hear—Arrow's.

Glancing over his shoulder in disbelief, he saw his long-lost friend regurgitated by the woods, standing on the other side of the garden fence as if they were coming out just to say hello. Except, they looked flushed with exertion, as if they'd run all the way from Beantighe Village just to greet him.

"Hey, Saff!" Arrow continued, and their voice cracked. "Would you—would you be willing to help me with something? It's about those fairy fruits I mentioned the other day—remember? Listen, I think I found them! But I can't get to them—I need your help, please, Saffron!"

After leaving Saffron to take their place as Brìghde. Leaving Saffron to sit all night in the cold barn and revoking his last chance at a wish. Forcing Saffron to stir the goddesses' ire, her curse, to ruin the one good thing he had. Arrow—still had the nerve to come emerging from the woodwork, still prattling about wild fairy fruits. When Saffron's entire world had just been rent apart, every piece of him stripped away with one look from the person who had, until that night, been his only joy in life.

Saffron hunched over his legs. He tried to ignore them, but Arrow was persistent. They just kept asking, again, and again, and again—

"No!" Saffron finally screamed, tearing to his feet. "Enough about the fucking fruits, Arrow, god! Can't you see—! Can't you see what you've fucking done! Isn't it enough! Please, I can't...! I can't do this right now, please...!"

Arrow flinched. The air between them shifted, Saffron breathing heavily as he did everything he could to hold back tears burning behind his eyes. Finally, Arrow just smiled awkwardly and nodded.

"Oh—sorry, I didn't mean to be such a nag. I'm sorry you're having a bad night, too, but... hey, I'm sure there'll be lots of wine left over. Save some for me, huh?" They rambled uncomfortably, rubbing the back of their neck. Before Saffron could say anything else, they turned and hurried off again, straight back into the trees. Saffron called out, flooding with annoyance, but it snuffed again as quickly as it came.

Saffron pressed his face into his hands. He just tried to breathe. Inside the house, applause broke out, and then cheers.

There was nothing else he could do. Cylvan wasn't who Saffron thought. Cylvan took his book back, and his magic ring was tucked in the spine. There was nothing left for Saffron at all, except perhaps consequences for compelling the Prince of Alfidel to slice off his own hair and then leaving him to wander in the woods. At least—whatever Sybil, Cylvan, had in store for him would be better than the veil. Better than the human world.

Saffron returned to the house with his eyes turned low. He picked up his discarded veil. Grabbed the jar of sprites by the window, releasing them through the front door. He'd nearly closed it when a noise pealed from the woods on the other side of the fence, like a fox kit shrieking for its mother. A barn owl's shrill cry as it swooped for a mouse. He pulled the door shut before any vicious thing could leap through and take him, next, though hesitated before letting the latch click.

5

THE GEIS

Courtiers hurried onto the back terrace once dinner was announced, where namecards painstakingly hand-written by Caetho lined the tables like a long snake winding down into the gardens toward the apple orchard. Beneath black trellises decorated with dangling wisteria, the crowd of high fey were illuminated by thousands of novel glass orbs woven between the slats, and Saffron didn't envy whoever had to go through and place individual candles inside each bubble.

The way noble fey courtiers celebrated Imbolc was a far cry from beantighe traditions, Saffron doubting the night would end in naked dancing and a bonfire, bigger humans threatening to throw the newest contract workers into the flames. Surely none of the fey feasting on the snake's back would have anything to wish for, either—no patched roofs, or blankets, or new pairs of shoes because their only non-uniform pair had finally worn through. It made Saffron sick, watery acid scraping at the inside of his empty stomach, having been given only the sandwich at lunch to tide him over for the day. He couldn't even snack on the leftover fruits for Luvon's wine.

One beantighe tradition remained, however—downing

mouthfuls of whiskey in the kitchen whenever someone came in and complained about something a high fey had said or done while being served appetizers and bowls of fruit for the wine. It quickly became a game, beantighe humans practically begging some fey to say something nasty so they could go inside and request another shot from a frazzled Caetho who took her own sips directly from the bottle. She was kind enough to offer Saffron his own multiple gulps when he finally emerged to pull on another apron and join the others, face puffy and red as he'd spent the ten minutes prior sobbing in the bathroom. He just thanked her and downed the offering without breaking concentration. It probably wouldn't be the last time that night, so long as the alcohol lasted.

It helped to warm his body against the chilly bite of early spring air, as well as soak his nerves so that he could think straight again. Perhaps once Saffron told Prince Cylvan about the hidden location of the magic ring, he would let Saffron go. They could forget all about it, and about each other.

If not, Saffron would beg for death and be gladly done with it. All of it. Simple enough. Straight alcohol had such a compassionate way of making everything so easy.

With his veil on, there was a chance he might not be confronted by the prince at all. He was sure Cylvan wouldn't want to disrupt his own party to accost a beantighe like him, anyway. He would surely be too busy with his own courtiers asking if he liked all of their gifts, wishing him luck in his classes, jerking him off for being the most beautiful creature to ever walk on hind legs and spew venom. *Ugh.*

Saffron searched for Luvon along the tables, his patron-fey having requested him by name, stomach falling out of his ass when he finally spotted him at the head of the snake. Furthest from the house, nestled amongst the hedges, the sculptures, and the rose bushes, Luvon sat with the two kings within the foliage like creatures of myth. But with them—Prince Cylvan, Head-mistress Elluin, Silver, Lord Kaelar, and two other high fey students joined them on either side, meaning Saffron not only had to weave between hedges and over guests to reach them, but he would be vulnerable to Prince Cylvan's icy gaze all night, after all. He secretly cursed Luvon, and then Brìghde, and then Arrow all over again. At least, maybe, Cylvan wouldn't accost a beantighe like him *in front of Luvon and the kings*.

Gathering nine crystal bowls piled elegantly with his cut fruits, Saffron weaved past other beantighe servers, high fey guests, rose clusters, and marble statues, straight for where Luvon sat with the members of royalty and one shadowy venom-spitter. He nearly lost all of it in one go when an additional body suddenly shoved past him, claiming the open seat next to Cylvan with a huff and a fluff of his hair. Cylvan just frowned at him, lazily turning a knife on the table with his finger on the tip, the newcomer grabbing it and throwing him a look.

"Glad you could join us, Lord Taran," Luvon greeted politely, and Saffron wondered what color the new fey lord's aura was. He was breathing heavy like he'd sprinted across campus, running late for the soirée where he, apparently, had a seat reserved next to the guest of honor. On a second glance, Saffron realized he recognized Lord Taran's shoulder-length hair, copper skin, and golden-green eyes as a student he'd passed on campus probably a thousand times. Was he the second new resident of Danann House? Did his family find an opal vein in the Fall Court, or something?

Setting crystal cups in front of every guest, being especially careful to hold his breath behind Cylvan who hadn't recognized him yet, he motioned that he would fetch another for Taran—but Taran took one look at the offering and stole the cup from in front of Cylvan, instead. Saffron made a face under his veil, before biting his lip as Taran muttered:

"There are apples mixed in."

"Thank you, Taran, I could see that," came Cylvan's icy retort. "I was only considering how fun it would be to put myself out of my misery."

Saffron nearly turned and half-sprinted back to the house

with his initial task done, but Luvon was smiling calmly at him, like he always did after they'd been apart for a long time. Saffron tried to smile back. Maybe, if he just remained safely behind Cylvan, like in the blindspot of a bloodsucking dearg-due, he could actually relax. Have a fine-passing evening on the fringes. Even with the dearg-due threat within reach, his patron-fey's comforting smile was enough to help Saffron feel a little bit more at ease, at least. If Cylvan suddenly sprang, Saffron wondered if Luvon would hesitate before whipping the blade from his seeing-cane and skewering the prince in front of everyone. Saffron would offer to drag Cylvan's body away so it wouldn't ruin the night. King Ailir would say something like, "*thank you for finally taking care of my rude son, he was starting to really get on my nerves, that's actually why I sent him all the way to Morrígan so I wouldn't have to listen to his bitching any longer—have you met my next born, Silvan? He sometimes uses his older brother's name in books because he's embarrassed to enjoy such romantic stories...*"

How interesting, the way devotion turned to hot resentment after two shots of whiskey.

"Are these Morrígan apples, headmistress?" Taran's voice broke Saffron's fantasy. The fey lord plucked an apple chunk from the bowl while, next to him, Cylvan just sighed and rested his chin in a hand. Saffron couldn't help but bitterly appraise every inch of the prince he now hated, including every stupid detail about his outfit. Maybe pixies would come and pick it apart, too.

His black hair had a natural, shiny wave to it, cascading over his shoulders and down his back. Curled bangs separated to show the paleness of his forehead and the purple of his irises, eyelids painted with shimmering gold eyeliner and dark red shadow. His lips were tinted dark, turned down in a permanent scowl as he repealed his attention from Taran and took an angry sip of water, leaving a smudge behind on the rim. He donned a stiff tunic with a high collar lined with raven feathers, golden embroidery shaping his broad shoulders and spilling in beaded threads down his chest and back beneath his hair. The dangling strings chimed lightly and sparkled with every movement, and Saffron, admittedly, found himself momentarily hypnotized, before wondering how hard it would be to tangle the prince's hair in them and ruin his night even more.

"Actually," Luvon spoke before Elluin could, and Saffron noticed the headmistress' face scrunch up slightly in annoyance. "These are honeyed frostapples from my winery, your grace. We grow all of the fruits that pair with my wines to ensure quality."

"Surely these apples did not travel all the way from the Winter Court," Elluin responded with a faux smile, new tension fluttering to life like a spring flower. Or like she had a knife in her belt and wanted a reason to draw it.

"Amber Valley is named after the cold apple cider it produces, Elluin," Luvon responded with ease, as if he'd been mentally preparing for that exact conversation. "We know how to ship our goods around the world without losing any of their quality."

"Is it true you were the first to cultivate frostfruits, Master Luvon?" One of the fey Saffron didn't know spoke up, and Saffron peeked at their name card, reading *Gentle Eias*. Thinking about it, he peeked at the other fey next to them, reading *Lord Magnin*.

"Yes, dear Eias," Luvon smiled, dabbing his mouth with a napkin. "My apples are also cold-pressed, which gives them their extra sharp flavor. Not to mention hand-picked one by one."

"You do not have to exaggerate for the kings," Elluin's voice remained teasing, but the hostility remained. Saffron was in the middle of refilling Luvon's glass of water when Luvon's arm suddenly wrapped around him, tugging him back with a tiny yelp of surprise.

"This beantighe here is one of my own patron-children, headmistress. He will tell you, himself. Go on then, Saffron."

Saffron's heart raced, mentally reminding himself how Cylvan didn't know his real name, probably wouldn't recognize him just by his voice. So long as he kept his answer short and polite, kept his veil over his face, he would probably be fine. Cylvan wasn't paying attention, anyway, twirling another knife beneath a finger and watching the house as if eager for the main course to finally arrive.

"I—it's true, ma'am," Saffron said with perfect pitch. "As a child, I even picked and planted several of Master Luvon's fruit trees, myself."

There. Done. No concern at all—

"Luvon—ask your child to lift their veil, would you?" Cylvan's voice came at the tail end of Saffron's words, all heads turning to him. "I prefer to see the faces of the people speaking to me, if you are comfortable."

The stone walkway vanished beneath Saffron's feet. His soul nearly expired when the prince's cold indigo eyes locked with his, gaze sharper than the knife on the table and cutting straight through Saffron's veil. The prince then leaned forward slightly in his chair, wearing an expression of wild, smiling anticipation. His eyes remained locked on Saffron as the request hung in the air, and Saffron suddenly worried there would be claw marks down his cheeks if he pulled the white chiffon away.

"Ah, of course. Go on," Luvon encouraged, nudging Saffron around the waist again. "Prince Cylvan is right. I apologize for the thoughtlessness."

Saffron's mouth dangled open in another long moment of hesitation. He briefly wondered how hard it would be to vault over the hedges at his back and disappear into the orchard. Or would Cylvan just chase after him? Every possible scenario played out in his mind, jumping when Cylvan shook his head the tiniest amount, as if recognizing the jackrabbit urge clearly in Saffron's eyes.

He accepted his fate with a silent, haggard breath. Carefully sliding his fingers under the veil to undo the placement pins in his hair, he looped an eyelet through one of the buttons on the back of his collar. Keeping his eyes low and holding his breath, he tried to move elegantly as he pulled it off over his face, his hair, allowing the airy fabric to drape behind his shoulders like a cape of smoke.

"You've always had quite pretty patron-children, Luvon," King Tross commented with a smile. "Such pretty green eyes on this one."

Saffron flushed in response. Of all the guests, King Tross was easily the most beautifully dressed, but not by ornate patterns or gold accessories or jingling baubles. He had a specific air of grace that made him more breathtaking than even Cylvan, whose own pretty face remained twisted in its unique mix of fury and exhilaration. Saffron nodded slightly in thanks, Luvon laughing and jostling Saffron by the waist again.

"I pick them like I pick fruits for my wine, your majesty. I always said the sweetest, loveliest things come from the Winter Court. Just look at yourself!"

Tross feigned flattery in a way that confirmed the long-standing friendship between himself and Luvon. Saffron would have found it charming if he wasn't on the receiving end of the dearg-due's sharp teeth.

"I will admit, Saffron has always been my favorite," Luvon went on, rubbing his hand up and down Saffron's back. "Though he's also my last, at least for now. Humans just aren't invoking fey deals like they used to, and the run-in Saffron and I had with his human parents has made me reconsider my changeling-swapping days."

"They're going through an industrial revolution on that side of the veil," Eias spoke up, adjusting a pair of round glasses. "Because of it, they're losing interest in magic and the occult that leads them to making deals. My parents are actually going mad over some human invention called a *lightbulb* at the moment. Made of glass, apparently it shatters whenever you try to pass it through the veil, but it's a new way of lighting a room..."

"What happened with his human parents?" Tross asked conspiratorially, leaning forward in his seat. Saffron wished he'd asked Eias to describe the *lightbulb* more, having no interest in being reminded of the terrible memory on Luvon's tongue.

"Ah, well, I return all of my changeling children after 20 fey years, since that's the amount of luck I give their parents in return," Luvon answered. "I like to take them through the veil and introduce them to their birth family around year 19, to offer them a chance to learn their heritage but also to offer the family a chance to welcome their child back into the fold…"

Tross's eyes were wide, practically licking his lips as if it were the juiciest drama he'd heard all night. None of the other fey except Eias and Magnin seemed particularly interested, though Cylvan continued staring silent daggers into Saffron as if wishing he'd die on the spot. Saffron did his best to ignore him, but accidentally made eye contact at one point, where he stubbornly made a face that commanded *stop it.* Cylvan narrowed his eyes in threat.

"You should have seen Mister Maddox when we arrived on his doorstep, going red in the face and erupting into a rage. Barely invited us in, probably only because he's still frightened of me. Going on about how I'd promised 20 years, getting even angrier when I reminded him how time moves differently in Alfidel, how I explicitly told him his child would be a fully grown adult in only five of his own. Absolutely *furious*, enough to pull one of those little handguns and start waving it around. I should have melted his bones right then."

Saffron jumped when Luvon raised a fatherly hand to tuck some hair from his eyes, making him go red in embarrassment. It summoned him back from the safe place he mentally floated around in as Luvon spoke, hating the reminder of his first and only trek into the human world and how it molded his entire perspective the moment his birth-father threatened to blow his brains out if he ever saw Saffron's face again.

"Do you enjoy working for Luvon, child?" King Tross asked Saffron directly. Saffron nodded, a nervous pinch in his chest.

"Y-yes, your majesty," he answered quickly. "I adore Master Luvon. He's always been very kind to me."

"Can't you keep him, Luvon?" King Tross asked, and it made Saffron's heart dance even more. He didn't mean to, but a hopeful smile crossed his lips, gazing down at Luvon.

"I've thought about it," Luvon admitted, "but it's my own code of ethics as a changeling-patron to return all of my children, eventually. I already have a few offers from associates on the other side as well, which are highly promising. One is looking for a young husband to keep her company, another needs a new head of household..."

Saffron's growing hope withered in an instant. Those words were news to him, and he suddenly knew how it felt for a knife to slice through his back. Had Cylvan leapt from the table and attacked him, after all?

And if Luvon was already making preparations, did that mean, even with an endorsement to stay in Alfidel...?

It was suddenly hard to breathe, Saffron attempting to clear his throat. He clutched his hands over his stomach so no one would see them trembling.

"Have you considered offering him to another patron-fey?" Kaelar asked next with a coy smile, sitting forward with fingers interlaced under his chin. "I'm actually in the market for a new bedchamber-beantighe, Luvon."

Luvon's fingers pressed into Saffron's side as Saffron stiffened more.

"Unfortunately, I'm steadfast in my morals, Lord Kaelar. I send all my beantighes back once their time is up. I've even kept Saffron a few years longer than others before him, since I cherished him so much—"

"And when will he go?" Cylvan interrupted next, lifting the wineglass to his mouth. Saffron just glanced at him and then away again—but before Luvon could answer, a sudden, electrifying jolt thundered in Saffron's chest, and he lunged to smash the flute out of Cylvan's hand. It drenched Taran sitting next to him, Taran leaping to his feet with a snarl—but Saffron's wide eyes just stared at the prince.

"A-apples..." he choked, though the thought was still forming. A vague memory from Cylvan's annotations. A tongue-in-cheek note left in the margins of Connla and his fairy maiden's apple.

THEN AM I CURSED TO DIE ALONE, IF EVEN MAGIC APPLES MAKE MY THROAT SEIZE?

"Saffron!" Luvon hissed as the world rushed back, grabbing Saffron by the waistband and wrenching him back. "What's gotten into you!"

"It's apple wine!" Saffron exclaimed frantically. "The—the wine is made with apples! I only just realized, and the prince is allergic..."

Cylvan looked genuinely surprised, King Tross lifting a theatrical hand over his mouth as King Ailir, who'd been engaged in conversation at the next table, boomed with laughter and leapt to his feet. Grabbing Saffron's hand to shake it wildly, Saffron's face went hotter and redder than the roses on the bush behind him, bowing repeatedly in apology, then doing the same for Lord Taran. Stripping off his apron as an offering, Taran snatched it with a look of disgust, wiping wine from his face and chest and storming off.

"We've always joked about Danann House's apple orchard!" Ailir laughed as he collapsed heavily back into his chair. "Planted by that old fool Elanyl—Danu made sure we knew how she felt about it when she made my first-born allergic. Elluin, are you sure my son won't get into any trouble while he's here?"

Ailir just kept laughing, but Saffron's eyes locked with Elluin's. They didn't blink. The headmistress didn't even breathe, just glaring at him as if she thought he might burst into flames if she manifested it hard enough. Combined with Cylvan's continued knife-twisting, Saffron was cornered. How had he managed to eviscerate even more of his already thin thread of life?

Did everyone laughing at the table know Elluin was going to gut him as soon as they left, and Cylvan would probably agree to hold Saffron's arms out of the way? Would Taran offer to pull his insides out one by one, last?

Saffron took a timid step back, apologizing again and bowing low from his hips. Grabbing his serving tray, he barely resisted the urge to sprint all the way back to the house, Elluin's gaze following still and striking matches to light him on fire.

He kept himself calm—until at the edge of his escape, he overheard Cylvan excuse himself as well. Commenting on how he wished to check on Taran. To warm up in the parlor. To take a break from the festivities.

Saffron walked faster. Weaving in and out of other beantighes serving fruit and drinks, he just kept swallowing his heart back down his throat.

When Cylvan remained some distance behind him as he reached the terrace, Saffron's survival instincts kicked in hotter. Slamming the tray on the prep table in the kitchen, he hurried through the swinging doors, past the laundry room, the servant washroom. He was just reaching for the door into the main corridor—when Cylvan exploded in behind him, and Saffron became a jackrabbit.

Bursting into the main hallway, he sprinted straight for the front door, but had to reel backward so he didn't slam into a group of courtiers right on the other side. Panicking, he raced up the stairs instead, barely flinging himself beneath the architrave up to the second floor as a giant raven streaked after him. Cylvan's enthusiastic pursuit made the banister rattle, tearing up the stairs two at a time, eyes wide with an eager, bloodthirsty smile that made Saffron shriek.

Scrambling faster, he barely avoided a set of reaching claws as he flung himself toward the third floor. Cylvan lost his footing and slammed against the opposing wall with a grunt and a curse, but Saffron just kept running. He didn't know where he would go once he ran out of stairs, what he would do once Cylvan inevitably cornered him—but if he could just find a place to hide—

Crashing into the Aon-adharcach suite, Saffron attempted to whirl and slam the door behind him—but Cylvan burst through, knocking Saffron to the floor.

The prince slammed the door. Still grinning ear-to-ear, orange fire from the hearth illuminated him like a wild animal, breathing heavily and dotted with sweat on his perfect forehead. Saffron could only clamber backward and put his hands out in defense, all while attempting to get back to his feet.

"Alright! Okay!" he attempted in a shrill voice, struggling for words as the vengeful fey stalked toward him. "I'm sorry!"

"Sorry for *what*, Dewdrop-Saffron? Be specific," Cylvan hissed wickedly. Saffron bumped his back against the wall, squeaking when Cylvan immediately clutched the front of his shirt and wrenched him to his feet. Slammed back, Saffron grabbed at Cylvan's wrists, attempting to smile, to be polite as ever, but Cylvan's handsome, perfect face twisted into something more and more unreadable the longer he resisted spilling Saffron's blood.

"Well—!" Saffron's voice cracked when the innocence didn't work. "For stealing your magic ring, I guess!"

"You know a wild animal could have eaten me? When you cursed me to wander aimlessly in the woods, totally lost and out of control of my own body?" Cylvan shoved Saffron against the wall again, knocking the air from him. "What would you have done then, idiot, with royal blood on your hands?"

"Oh, stop it! My command wore off after just a few minutes! I saw you back in the—*urk*—clearing!" Saffron grunted when Cylvan shoved him against the wall again. "Maybe next time be more careful about who you trust in the woods!"

Saffron clamped his mouth shut, kicking himself for choosing the moment he stared down ravenous death to be sarcastic. He tried to give the prince another pretty smile, returning to innocence, but Cylvan's expression didn't change.

"Where's my ring?"

"What?" Saffron said, crying out when Cylvan suddenly pinned him entirely, hands groping every inch of his body in search. Saffron attempted to shove him away, face going hot, too many overwhelming emotions coursing through him to think straight. But when Cylvan didn't find anything, his frustration reached its peak, hand lashing out and forcing itself between Saffron's teeth. Saffron bit down in surprise, making Cylvan growl—but he only pushed his sharp nails in deeper.

"If you won't give me my ring—then you'll give me the tongue you owe me!"

Pinning Saffron back with his forearm, Saffron attempted to jerk his face away, pressing his hands into Cylvan's chest again, but the prince was too strong.

"I don't owe you—my tongue!" Saffron garbled against the fingers. "Stop it!"

His head clocked against the wall with another thrust of Cylvan's body, slumping slightly as claws buried further in his mouth. Saffron clamped down hard again, Cylvan hissing and ripping his hand back out, only to hook a thumb inside Saffron's cheek and pull.

"Your thupid ring ith probably in the same plathe it was when I firtht found it—the pixthie hollow!" Saffron lied, suddenly determined to never give this dearg-due daemon anything he wanted.

"*Pixies!*" Cylvan hissed, pulling harder on Saffron's cheek. "You think you can blame—*urk*—*pixies* when I know you took it for yourself, you godsdamned púca rat!"

"*Púca!*" Saffron growled. "I didn't thteal anything! You gavthe'it to me!"

"It doesn't matter—according to the law of names, this tongue is mine!"

"The law of—fucking *namthes*—what'th that thuppothed to mean!" Saffron finally jostled free of the invading thumb, thrashing his head back and forth as the digit attempted to find purchase again. "All of this, even after I saved your stupid life! I should have let you drink that fucking wine!"

"They would have just accused you of poisoning me." Cylvan's eyes sparkled with a venomous thrill. "But poisoning me would be *nothing* compared to using my name to compel me. Taking your tongue is merciful compared to what I could really get away with, púca—"

"Wait—!" Saffron asserted, hitting Cylvan in the chest. "What did you just say? Did you just—'*using your name to compel you*'? Are you telling me—"

Saffron hit him in the stomach that time, Cylvan grabbing his wrists and thrusting them against the wall. Saffron just breathed angrily through his nose, heart racing.

"Is Sybil your true name?" he insisted. Cylvan eyed him darkly, which was confirmation enough. Saffron attempted to yank his arms free, but the prince held him tight. "So is the ring magic or not? If I was just using your true name to compel you—!"

"The ring—"

"And did you tell me just to trick me into using it?" Saffron went on, voice rising. "Did you do it—knowing you would take my tongue after? Or try and kill me? You told it to me before I could even agree to anything—You told me without even warning me first! You didn't give me any chance at all! I would have said *no* if I'd known, damnit!"

He finally shoved Cylvan away, the prince taking half a step back, though the glare never left his expression. Saffron just shook his head, before pressing a hand to his face. He'd always known high fey to be cruel—but Cylvan was worse. Cylvan, his dear Cylvan... was so much worse than Saffron could have ever imagined.

"Goddamnit," he groaned miserably. "None of this was how I wanted any of this to happen..."

The words formed a lump in his throat as he still couldn't pull his hand from his face. He didn't want to see, didn't want to face the prince he'd once fantasized about so much. The prince Saffron once imagined might be kind, and gentle, and thoughtful, and passionate. Who Saffron had come to love in his own way. Who, instead of snapping at him on the front drive, might have knelt down and offered to help Saffron back to his feet. The prince—who truly only existed in the margins of Saffron's favorite myths.

"You poor thing. Boo hoo. *Waah,*" Cylvan mocked, and Saffron finally pulled his hand away to glare back at him. Cylvan's handsome mouth curled into another smile, suddenly grabbing Saffron by his blouse and dragging him to the couches by the fire. On the ottoman in front of the hearth, tossed like an unwanted gift amongst the ocean of others—Saffron's book.

Saffron instinctively jumped for it, but Cylvan shoved him into the couch before he could get far. Bouncing against the cushions, Saffron sat back up as soon as he could, watching the prince wave the book around with another cruel smile.

"Is this what you mean by *not the way you wanted this to happen?* Do you feel some sort of perverted kinship because you stole something belonging to me?" he asked, Saffron's eyes never leaving the precious text in his hand, like a mother bird watching a magpie eye her hatchlings. "You know, stealing from a prince usually ends with all your fingers being bent back until they snap —and this is the *second* thing you've taken from me. What good will you be as a maid *or* Kaelar's whore with no tongue and no hands?"

"Give it back!" Saffron finally snapped. Leaping to his feet, he crashed into Cylvan's chest to reach for it, but Cylvan held it too far away. "Please, you can have my tongue! Just—! Just, please, just let me keep my book!"

"*My* book," Cylvan hissed. "And I think I've shown you enough mercy, beantighe. My patience is wearing thin. I'm taking this back, and I'll do whatever I want with it."

Cylvan tossed the myths into the hungry flames behind him.

Saffron screamed and lunged to rescue them, but Cylvan's arm hooked around his waist and wrenched him back.

"*Why!*" Saffron begged as tears filled his eyes. "Why would you do that! I've done nothing to you! I haven't done anything!"

He slammed his fists against Cylvan's chest, again and again, growing more and more incensed as the prince just *laughed* like Saffron was the most pathetic thing he'd ever seen. He pushed Saffron down onto the couch again, creating a cage with his body and trapping him against the cushions.

"You weren't supposed to be like this!" Saffron cried again, hitting his chest more, then attempting to kick him in the stomach. "You weren't supposed—! *To be...! Ugh!!*"

"What am I?" Cylvan urged, grabbing Saffron's wrists again so he could no longer thrash. Saffron just met his eyes, breaths shaking, prepared to light the prince up with everything he felt— but that cruel gaze made his hatred deflate back into misery. He just closed his eyes, body going heavy as he sniffed.

"Connor," he murmured. It came with bitter humiliation, wishing he had anything else more cutting, more insulting, but his will to fight back slipped away as the sound of his crackling book faded.

"Who?"

Saffron averted his eyes, pressing his lips together. "C-Connor," he mumbled again. "Connor mac Nessa..."

Cylvan considered that for a second, before bursting out laughing. More embarrassed tears dripped from Saffron's eyes. Attempting to pull his arms free, Cylvan maintained his hold, hanging over Saffron like a miserable curse.

"The one who stalked Derdriu? Who wanted to kill Naoise?" Cylvan asked in amused disbelief.

"... Yes..." Saffron sniffed.

"Does that make *you* Derdriu? Someone as sad and pitiful as you? You must think quite highly of yourself."

Saffron shook his head, but couldn't speak. He knew if he

tried, he would only embarrass himself more—and he was beginning to realize, there was no point after all.

Still shaking with laughter, Cylvan finally let go and sat back on the ottoman. Saffron pulled his arms into his body, rubbing where the prince had clutched his wrists.

"You need to read more than stupid myths," Cylvan scolded him, and Saffron's face went hot again. "Perhaps burning that book was the kindest thing I could have done. There is no Naoise to come and rescue you, beantighe. Not from me, from Luvon, from Kaelar, or any other human who puts their hands on you through the veil. Accept that now, or you're going to be a lot more miserable soon enough, my dear Derdriu of the Sorrows."

Saffron sniffed again. He thought about how the prince's precious ring was in the book he'd just burned.

"Good luck ever getting your ring back from the pixies," he grumbled. "There's nothing they hate more than bitter old crones like you."

Cylvan's amused expression flattened, lips pursing. Saffron buckled when the prince lunged and grabbed him by the arms again, hissing threats worse than merely taking his tongue. Saffron swore back at him, kicking him in the stomach and landing a center purchase that made the prince wheeze like a horse.

Cursing more when Cylvan hooked the curve of his thumb under Saffron's knee and shoved his leg away, his body collapsed on top of Saffron to pin him into the cushions and claw at his mouth—but someone suddenly called Cylvan's name from the hallway, and the prince stiffened. Saffron sucked in a breath and attempted to cry for help, but Cylvan slammed a hand against Saffron's mouth.

"Be quiet!" he hissed, Saffron biting at his hand. "*Ack—* damnit, púca! Shut the fuck up! Be silent—*and I might let you keep your tongue!*"

Saffron glared at him—but clamped his mouth shut, against his better judgment.

When the door clicked, Cylvan heaved Saffron into his arms,

vaulting over the back of the couch and into the wardrobe against the wall. The cabinet swung closed within an inch as the bedroom door opened, Saffron pulled chest-to-chest against Cylvan as the prince's hand remained smashed against his mouth. Pinned hard enough to hear how fast Cylvan's heart pounded, Saffron instinctively held his breath.

Lord Taran stepped inside, but didn't remove his grip on the lever knob. He paused, looking around, before calling out Cylvan's name again. Cylvan stiffened, fingers flexing against Saffron's mouth, silently begging him to ignore that little voice telling him how easy it would be to kick the wardrobe wide open and announce themselves—but the way Cylvan's heart pounded harder, faster, the moment Taran glanced in their direction, made Saffron hesitate again. Without thinking, he slid a hand up to touch the side of Cylvan's neck, as if the sound of his pulse would draw Taran's attention on its own. Cylvan just stiffened more—before letting out a slow breath.

Even when Taran left with a slam of the door, Cylvan still didn't release Saffron right away. When he did finally remove his hand, it trembled slightly, and then he spoke into the darkness.

"Thank you," he said flatly. "There's a... particular conversation I'm trying to avoid with him."

"... Did you not mind when I poured the wine on him, then?" Saffron muttered sarcastically. Cylvan chuckled in response, and the sound made Saffron's heart skip.

Pulling back a few inches, firelight glowed through the open crack in the wardrobe, a line of orange drawn down Cylvan's face, neck, chest, reflecting off his shiny horns and making one purple iris look crimson. Saffron might have lost himself in the sight, had Cylvan not finally closed his eyes and nudged Saffron back into the open room.

He should have sprinted for the door. Should have attempted to flee all over again—but Saffron just flexed his fingers in apprehension. Something unseen clung to his shoes through the floor, rooting him in place. Something about Cylvan's laugh, Cylvan's heartbeat, the warmth of his neck when Saffron touched it... made Saffron hunch his shoulders. He braced himself, and then turned around right as Cylvan stepped from the wardrobe, himself.

"Can we just... talk?" Saffron asked breathlessly, tightening the muscles in his legs in case he had to sprint away, after all. But despite the skeptical look Cylvan gave him, the prince neither refused nor lunged. Saffron sucked in a deep breath and held it until he could pretend the fire in his chest was confidence returning. His next words rode the wave of his exhale, though came out a little more shrill than he'd hoped.

"I don't intend you any harm, your highness," he said first. "With your true name or otherwise. In fact—after tonight, I would very much like to never see one another, ever again."

"Morrígan's campus isn't that big," came Cylvan's unappeased response. Saffron sucked in another breath and summoned that fiery false confidence back.

"You won't even know who I am under my veil."

"I suspected you as soon as you brought the fruit at dinner, even with your veil on. Turns out I was right."

"Oh... How?"

"You have nice legs," Cylvan answered, eyes flickering downward as he said it, as if to remind himself. "For a beantighe."

Saffron's face went hotter.

"Well... then..." he rasped. "Is there any other way... for us to keep the peace, my lord?"

Cylvan crossed his arms, leaning back against the wardrobe and looking Saffron up and down again. Saffron averted his eyes, subconsciously smoothing down his messy hair and wrinkled blouse. Finally, Cylvan sighed, rubbing one of his temples.

"Unfortunately, I just can't let you run around knowing my true name," he said pointedly, but his tone had settled into something that just sounded *tired*. "So you understand why I need to take your tongue. For my own protection."

"Can't you just trust me?" Saffron mumbled. "I won't use it

against you. Like I said, I didn't even *want* it, I have no need for it..."

"And I have no reason to trust you. So unless you have another idea, I have no choice but to take your ability to speak."

"What about threadweavers? They could pluck it from my head."

"*Threadweavers?*" Cylvan muttered. "They would *also* see that I gave it to you in a moment of my own damn hubris. That information would be *worse* for my reputation if it ever got out."

"Well..." Saffron huffed. "Luvon... intends on sending me through the veil soon, anyway. It won't be a problem for you then, will it?"

"Hm. When does he plan to do that, exactly?"

"Ostara, I think." *Unless I can convince him otherwise.*

"Which Ostara? Yours or ours?"

Saffron didn't like the way Cylvan said *"yours,"* as if Saffron claimed any part of the Ostara on the human side of the veil. Though human Ostara came sooner than fey Ostara did, and he suddenly had another reason to be grateful for Luvon choosing the latter.

"Ostara on this side."

"That is still months away. What until then?"

Saffron furrowed his brows in growing frustration. Fidgeting with the patron ring on his finger, his mind was blank, but Cylvan just kept standing there in expectant silence.

"Why did you have to tell me in the first place? Were you just looking for a tongue to steal? Out of boredom?"

Cylvan didn't move to answer, and Saffron crossed his arms to silently mimic him. Finally, Cylvan squeezed his eyes shut and pinched his nose.

"I was... indeed, trying to trick you. But not because I wanted your tongue. I have no use for human tongues, except when protecting secrets."

Saffron still didn't speak, patiently waiting. Cylvan frowned. He huffed. He flexed his folded arms before giving in again.

"You will *really* force me to rip out your tongue if I tell you. Is that what you want?"

"You're going to tear it out either way. Tell me."

Cylvan sighed again, closing his eyes before gazing down at the hand resting on his upper bicep. He considered his options for a moment longer, before finally giving in to the death-glare Saffron tried to melt him with.

"I was under the impression... that ring was charmed like your patron rings, but the opposite. So that whoever wore it could not compel me, even with my true name."

Saffron's folded arms loosened, and they fell to his sides as curiosity sparkled in his veins.

"Oh," he said in consideration, voice light with intrigue. "So you were using me as a test? To see if it worked?"

Cylvan nodded stiffly, jaw tight. He looked almost embarrassed when considering the giant mess his ego caused, and Saffron found it strangely humanizing. It made his posture, his expression, relax somewhat.

"Why do you need a magic ring like that? Am I not the first random person you've shared your true name with?"

Cylvan scoffed, shaking his head.

"It's none of your business *why* I needed it—I only told you to sate your own curiosity. Now, come come. That squishy tongue is all mine."

Cylvan wiggled his fingers in threat, but Saffron obviously didn't approach. He just bit on the tongue Cylvan wanted so badly, before gazing down at his feet. Maybe he should have run out of the room, after all.

"What if I could just... figure out another way to forget your name?" he went on, even though Cylvan rolled his eyes and leaned back against the wardrobe again. Saffron puffed himself up and kept going despite the disinterest. "For example, there are plenty of herbs we use in Beantighe Village to make memories blurry. Perhaps there's something stronger I could find—"

"*Herbs?*" Cylvan muttered, and Saffron scowled at him.

"Or—I don't know! Perhaps some sort of fey magic? I'm sure there are plenty of things you all have done to protect yourselves against true names in the past... certainly someone came up with some sort of defensive spell along the way... I don't know, do you really expect someone like me to have a solution for your own *hubris* or whatever you want to call it?"

"What exactly do you think *hubris* is?"

"I don't know! Perhaps the thing that makes you so disagreeable!"

Cylvan laughed, which came as a surprise. Saffron fiddled with his patron ring again, lifting his eyes to the prince, and then averting them again, peeking at the wardrobe, the fire, and then— the walls of books on either side of the mantle. It made his uncertainty fizzle, lips parting as a thought formed.

"Perhaps I could..." he breathed. His eyes returned to Cylvan, specifically to his hands, though they were empty of his own campus rings. Saffron pressed his lips together. Cylvan's eyes traveled to where Saffron's had hovered on the bookshelf, before flickering back with a new curiosity.

"If... you were to let me into the library at night, perhaps I could... find another way to forget your name, or find a spell you could use to make your ring work, while also... allowing me to keep my tongue. And then you can also keep an eye on me, to make sure I don't do anything against you..."

"You want me to let you into the library?" Cylvan clarified. "What, every night?"

"Y-yes..." Saffron said with a nervous smile. It wasn't a full-fledged library access ring, exactly, but it would do for the time being. Perhaps after proving himself, he could even earn a ring of his own in order to come and go as he pleased. In the meantime, relying on Cylvan seemed doable enough. "Um, besides... you're the one who said I needed to read more books than just myths, right?"

"Don't be coy with me."

Saffron just kept the nervous smile, scratching at the back of his head. "Um, well, also... if I can't find anything to help you before Ostara, I will be long gone into the human world and you won't have to worry about me. Or, if Lord Kaelar somehow convinces Luvon to transfer patronage... then you have my expressed permission to actually cut out my tongue. Maybe without it, I won't have to bother with Lord Kaelar at all, which I'm also fond of..."

Something about that made Cylvan smile, though it was sarcastic.

"You have my interest," he finally said, pulling a handful of hair over one shoulder and combing fingers through it. "But all you really want in exchange is just me letting you into the library? Don't you have any imagination at all? Go on—make it worth your own while, so I know you'll be determined to work hard and show up. If you could have anything at all, what would it be?"

"Well..." Saffron whispered before fully considering it.

Cylvan's handsome, encouraging smile made it hard to think. But even in Saffron's flustered brain fog, one vivid desire came to mind. The same one that would always come to mind whenever asked if there was anything in the world Saffron wanted.

"I want... an academic endorsement," he finally whispered. "I want someone... to patronize me, or convince Luvon to continue patronizing me, and endorse me while I go to school, where I can earn an elevated status. I don't actually want to go back to the human world... or be Lord Kaelar's silken-beantighe."

"Ooooh." The corners of Cylvan's mouth lifted into a different smile, and Saffron's heart pounded. He suddenly felt nervous again, like he was indeed getting caught up in a deal with a fey thing his human ancestors always meant to warn him about.

"Do you... agree to those terms?" Saffron went on apprehensively. "I'll find a spell for you by Ostara, and you'll—"

"I'll offer you an academic endorsement," Cylvan finished. Hearing the words out loud summoned a desperate, relieved smile from Saffron, about to rain gratefulness all over the prince—but Cylvan stepped forward, taking Saffron's chin and pressing their mouths together. It made Saffron's chest tighten, holding his breath and closing his eyes as he was overcome with the sensation of drinking fairy wine.

"I accept this geis." Cylvan pulled back an inch with a teasing smile.

"A-a geis?" Saffron asked in uncertainty. Cylvan's fingers remained curled under his chin, a thumb brushing his bottom lip.

"That's right. Just like Derdriu and Naoise."

Saffron's face went hot. He nodded, offering: "Then, I... also accept this geis."

Unable to resist the temptation, he leaned forward again slightly, but Cylvan was already pulling back.

"I have two conditions," he said, and Saffron groaned internally.

"You waited until I agreed first on purpose, didn't you?"

Cylvan's smirk was answer enough. Saffron just frowned at him.

"First... you're going to go into the woods and retrieve my ring from the pixies."

"Oh," Saffron perked back up, before smiling awkwardly. "Umm... yeah. It's not actually... in the woods. It was in the book you burned, so I imagine it's nice and warm in the fire..."

"... *Second*," Cylvan hissed with a furious smile. He stepped in close again, reminding Saffron how it felt to be a rabbit beneath a fox. "If, while I am so graciously and empathetically trusting you with my true name, I get even a *sniff* that you've let the syllables *Sy-bil* leave your mouth... I will lock every single beantighe human in their iron cage around Beantighe Village, and burn it down, cooking them alive. And then I'll tear a hole in the veil, myself, and shove you through without hesitation."

Saffron stared at him, unmoving, as his heart had stopped. Cylvan's smile pulled back into something handsome again, offering Saffron another delicate kiss.

"I look forward to our deal, beantighe. Now dig my ring out of the godsdamn fireplace."

Saffron remembered how to blink, and then how to breathe, jolting back to life with a high-pitched noise and hurrying to the fire. Digging around in the remains of his book with a metal poker—and biting back more tears as he did—he managed to uncover the golden ring. Cylvan watched from the couch, pouring himself a glass of red wine.

"Keep it for now. It's useless, anyway," he muttered as Saffron offered the tarnished circlet, swallowing back a mouthful of his drink. "Now go away."

"O-oh—alright!" Saffron exclaimed, making Cylvan jump at the volume and scowl at him.

The moment Saffron was back in the corridor and the bedroom door slammed shut behind him, he could only stare straight ahead as the reality came down around him like a theater curtain.

His stomach suddenly swelled with butterflies, and he almost squealed as they attempted to flood out of his mouth. Oh—perhaps not everything was lost, after all. Perhaps Saffron wouldn't have to go to the human world. Perhaps he wouldn't have to ever resort to Kaelar's offer. Perhaps—he could still, one day, stay with Luvon after going to school, earning an elevation, and becoming exactly what Luvon needed to keep around.

Hurrying down the stairs, overwhelmed with pure elation, he only stopped at the sight of courtiers still clustered outside the open front door and gossiping about something. When one of them perked up and called out to him, waving him over, Saffron practically floated out to ask what they needed. Another drink? A snack? Would they like to know exactly how compassionate and merciful the great high prince of Alfidel was?

"There's a horrid sound coming from the woods, there," the old fey man said, looking quite offended. "Like an animal dying. Go take care of it before it ruins the entire mood."

"Sure," Saffron answered with an amiable smile. After announcing how happy he was to help, next, he stepped past the gaggling group of fey and made his way to the fence. Finding the gate out of the yard and into the reach of the trees, he forced himself to take a breath and focus past the elation in his bones, quieting his heartbeat to better listen. There was nothing at first, no *horrid sound of a dying animal*, but he was happy to stand there in silence and pretend if it meant he could enjoy the afterglow of his good mood for a moment longer. Just a moment longer—

"*Saffron?*"

Saffron jumped, eyes snapping more to his left as he heard his name called. Glancing back over his shoulder, the group of high fey still watched him curiously, clearly not the source of the noise. Some had hands to their mouths in dramatic awe, others looking annoyed that there was any sort of disruption to the party at all. Saffron gulped, turning back toward the trees.

"Hello?" he responded, wondering if it was some sort of wild fey attempting to lure him. So long as he didn't follow it deeper into the woods, he should be fine—but something about the way it said his name remained carved in the back of his mind, ringing like a death toll. As if—he recognized it.

Risking a few steps into the trees, he called out again for whatever had called to him first. When nothing responded, he nearly gave up when a groan suddenly rattled from behind a fallen tree, making him stumble backward. Freezing again, Saffron held his breath, before risking a few hesitant steps forward, just far enough to lean over the log where it stemmed from.

Like a struck match, Saffron could suddenly, practically taste blood in the atmosphere, enough to shift the temperature of the air. He nearly stumbled backward once more upon realizing it really was some poor animal attacked and left for dead—but then the voice returned, and every muscle in his body calcified.

"*Saffron... please,*" it gurgled, and Saffron realized—he actually knew that voice.

Lurching forward, Saffron leapt over the downed tree, nearly toppling backward again with a scream when he found the source.

Arrow. On their back, chest and stomach torn open, struggling to breathe as blood filled their mouth.

"Arrow! Oh my god!" Saffron shrieked, plummeting to his knees and gathering his friend in his arms. Arrow just groaned, eyelids fluttering as they struggled to stay awake. Hot blood soaked Saffron in an instant, Arrow's chest and throat mangled with raking teeth and claw marks, blood spilling and pooling beneath them.

"Arrow! Arrow, hey!" Saffron gasped, attempting to get their attention, but Arrow's eyes just rolled back toward the sky. "*Help! Somebody—!*"

Arrow's trembling hand lifted, touching Saffron's face and summoning his attention back. Saffron leaned in close as Arrow's voice was hardly more than a whisper, but still begged to be heard.

"The wolf... Saffron, the wolf... fruits for..." Arrow hiccupped, whole body shaking. Saffron kept repeating their name, shrieking for someone to come and help, *please, someone come help—!...* But the fey courtiers wouldn't cross the fence. They just watched from the safety of the garden, whispering to one another.

When other white-clad beantighes finally rushed through and met him, Saffron was already bent over, sobbing into his dead friend's chest.

6

THE WALLPAPER

They wrenched Saffron from Arrow's body first. A hand clamped over his mouth, his patron ring snatched and allowing him to be compelled.

"Be silent. Be silent!"

They dragged him from the Danann House yard, gardens, courtyard. Down the path toward campus, the sun was still an hour from cresting over the horizon, but close enough to bring up the color of the overcast sky. He thrashed the entire time, Arrow's blood smearing everywhere he touched his hands. All over him—Arrow's blood covered every inch of him like bleeding sap from a tree, and everytime he tried to wipe it away it only grew thicker. Stickier. Until he thought he might drown in it.

Taken to the Administration Building, they tossed him into Elluin's office with another compelling command: *"Don't move."*

He recognized the voice that time as Lord Kaelar's. The rush of fury nearly allowed him to overwhelm the enchantment and lunge to attack through the doorway, but Kaelar just snapped the command again and Saffron fell on his face to the floor.

Kaelar—did Kaelar kill Arrow? Kaelar, who wore that stupid rapier on his belt, even when in his school uniform? The wannabe knight, Prince Cylvan's alleged friend, the one who insisted on harassing Saffron to the brink of his sanity? Would he do something so horrific as a prank? Kill one of Saffron's friends, leave them there for Saffron to find and never forget?

Headmistress Elluin arrived eventually, by then the sun peeking across campus through the spindle-latticed windows behind her desk. On her heels, Lord Taran joined her, and Saffron bit his tongue as they entered together and locked the door behind them. They both still wore their party clothes—Elluin in her slacks that sparkled with crystals and blouse with billowing sleeves; Taran in his red velvet doublet and silk shirt underneath. Both still pristine, as if they could turn right back and continue the party. Neither of them with even a drop of uninvited blood on them.

Meanwhile, Saffron just kept dripping on the headmistress' rug.

By then, Kaelar's paralyzing enchantment had worn off, but Saffron remained silently on his knees in the middle of the office. It wasn't an unfamiliar place for him to be—Saffron had spent plenty of time in that cramped, lifeless, miserable little room every time he did something wrong and needed his hands lashed, his pinky finger broken, his hair cut off, a nick in his ear, a hot needle pressed under his nails. But historically, it had been Elluin's assistant, Silver, doling out the consequences. Saffron had never seen a student like Taran offered the pleasure.

"I do not think I've ever met anyone so determined to ruin a good night in any way possible," Elluin's voice came, and Saffron sank into more anger at how those words diminished the actual terrible thing that had happened. As if Arrow's death was a spot on her perfect ledger as party host, and not a mutilation on her campus. He clenched his fists on his thighs, squeezing his friend's wet blood between his fingers until it made his stomach turn. Cylvan's fern ring was still on his finger, though stained red and unrecognizable—and Saffron wished it had been magic, after all. There were a thousand things he would like to say to Elluin with a ring that could compel her to obey.

Taran stood behind the oak desk, fiddling with a long silver instrument, like a sharp knitting needle. Illuminated in the soft morning light, rain speckled the diamond-paneled glass at his back as Elluin approached with an excited smile.

"Remove your blouse, Saffron," she ordered without warning, and Saffron's hands moved without permission. Undoing the line of buttons down the front of his shirt, tugging the thread looping around the buttons of his sleeve cuffs, removing his arms from the sleeves—that was when he truly witnessed the extent of Arrow's blood spilled on him, and it nearly made him sick. But he just grit his teeth, bit his tongue, closed his eyes, and folded the garment over his lap as Elluin's next command came.

"Turn and face the wall."

He rotated on his knees to turn his back to the headmistress and Lord Taran. Goosebumps freckled his skin from the chill on his naked torso, mentally preparing himself for whatever punishment would come. Elluin was always careful not to scar the face, though relied on other physical consequences without hesitation. She thought it was merciful of her, but Saffron knew the morality stemmed from a high fey's instinct to commodify utility. Saffron was less likely to be offered new patronage, new working contracts somewhere else, if he didn't have enough positive traits to make him valuable. And since he wasn't particularly strong, or charming, or smart, or detail-oriented, or crafty, his average looks became the thing that gave him worth—and Elluin would never insult Luvon by leaving scars where they could be seen.

Saffron's hands, arms, and legs were riddled with little white lines where even the healer's magic couldn't remove them entirely. And despite the headmistress' mercy, he'd still received scars on his face just from the day-to-day work—on the side of his neck where he'd tripped while scraping residue from a window with a flat blade; on his cheek where a rosebush had whipped him while trimming hedges; the nick on his top lip from a student prank; the one in the outer corner of his eye after falling from a ladder;

the scar curling up the side of his jaw from... oh, he couldn't actually remember that one.

Glancing over his shoulder, Saffron watched Elluin appreciate Taran's offered needlelike wand in one hand, while Taran placed a pad of parchment and matching silver quill in front of her.

"Hold on," Taran muttered, retrieving the wand again and approaching Saffron on the floor. Taking Saffron's palm, he jabbed it with the sharp end of the instrument to draw blood, and Saffron jerked his hand away in confusion. But Taran seemed only interested in the tip of silver that had gotten a taste, tossing Saffron's patron ring to the floor before returning to the desk. Saffron scrambled for his ring, hurriedly sliding it on over the blood drying on his thumb.

"Mix this into the ink, first. Right. Now dip the quill, and—ah. Perfect, headmistress. You're a natural."

Saffron continued watching behind him as the pointed rod suddenly wobbled, floating in front of Elluin, who grinned even wider. She wiggled the nib of her quill, the rod following suit and only making her smile more.

"Queen Proserpina was a visionary," she whispered, and more goosebumps flushed Saffron's arms at the name. "I always knew it. I am honored to use one of her tools, Lord Delbaith. Ah, now let us begin. Saffron—press your hands flat on the wall. Don't dare make a sound."

Saffron hesitated, but bit his lip and obeyed, even without being compelled. Flattening his palms into the office's faded floral wallpaper, his fingers trembled in anticipation. Red fingerprints stained wherever his skin brushed, spots blurring as his fingers twitched. Just like he did at dinner when Luvon recounted their experience in the human world, Saffron compelled himself to float away from his body. Float away to a safe, light, warm place far away from the rain and Elluin's faded floral wallpaper.

"Are you familiar with Queen Proserpina's *Ten Hindrances to Human Perpetuity*, beantighe?" Elluin went on. Saffron just closed his eyes and shook his head; though knew if it came from the late Veiled Queen of Night, it was certainly something cruel. He encouraged his mind to drift even further into the distance.

"You see, beantighe, Queen Proserpina believed the reason humans age so quickly, and so poorly..." Saffron jumped when an ice-cold nib tickled his back. Looking over his shoulder again, the sharp wand drew light circles around on his bare skin. "... is because they are born burdened with shortcomings that exhaust them into an early grave. Shortcomings that, if overcome... would allow them to live as long and as freely as high fey do. Some even say that by overcoming all ten, a human can ascend into high feyhood entirely. Now—from last night alone, it's clear you're *heavily* burdened with a myriad of said shortcomings, beantighe, and I want to help you overcome them so that you, too, might live a more fulfilled life. Lord Taran, if you please. What of Proserpina's ten do you think Saffron is most burdened by?"

"Selfishness," Taran answered immediately, before adding: "Arrogance."

"Very rational, my lord. I choose *impertinence*. Seeing as Saffron suffered all three, each with harm done to our guests' enjoyment of the night... I would like to hold him accountable for all. Any disagreements?"

"None," Taran answered forcefully. "Please, only allow me to administer my own."

"Of course," Elluin purred. "Well then, I will go first."

Saffron perceived the tiny sound of a quill's nib stroking on parchment—and the sharp instrument buried itself into his back, making him scream.

Every stroke of Elluin's pen, mimicked by the knife, carved deep into Saffron's skin until blood dripped down his spine. His whole body locked up, buckling forward and tearing his fingernails into the wallpaper simply for something to hold on to. Taran snapped at him to *stay silent,* and Saffron bit down on his tongue in an attempt, but the horrific pain of silver tearing into his back nearly gave Cylvan what he wanted as Saffron edged closer to biting his tongue off in the effort.

I-M-P-E-R-T-I-N-E-N-C-E.

Sweat drenched him as she finished, whole body trembling as he struggled to breathe, tasting bile in the back of his throat. Coughing miserably, pink spit dripped from his mouth as his teeth had cut into his tongue, more red prints smeared and stamped across the wall from his hands.

Bodies shifted behind him, but Saffron's head was too heavy to lift and look. And then the torturous sensation started all over again, right below Elluin's line of letters. He tried to direct himself far away again, tried to cast his mind out entirely so that the pain would pass faster—

But cracking open his blurry eyes, gazing wearily across the smear of red on the wallpaper, Saffron was reminded—none of the blood on his hands was his own. Despite the amount that spilled down his back, his spine, soaking into the back of his pants and dripping to the floor... none of what he painted across the wall came from the silver instrument.

He pulled himself back. Back into his body, as if the needle really did stitch his soul in place with every movement.

As if to pay for how he'd turned his back on Arrow—shouted at them, ignored them, told them to *leave him alone, hadn't they done enough*—perhaps experiencing the same agony of being cut open would mean Saffron never forgot what he'd done when his friend needed him most.

S-E-L-F-I-S-H-N-E-S-S.

A-R-

Taran started the third line of letters, but a loud knock suddenly came at the office door. Elluin muttered something, pushing hair from her eyes and stalking past Saffron to answer it, though Saffron barely noticed.

"The kings are ready for breakfast." Saffron's pounding heart muffled Kaelar's voice. "They're on their way. Said they want to go somewhere in Connacht, and want you to join them."

Elluin sighed, a mixture of annoyance and disappointment. She turned back to Taran, who sighed as well, and Saffron felt the chilling sensation of the silver needle leave him, floating back to its master at the desk.

"Take him somewhere to get cleaned up," Elluin said, and it took a moment for Saffron to realize she was talking about him. "Don't let the kings' travel party see him."

"Yes, ma'am." Kaelar's voice smiled, and Saffron couldn't do more than agonizingly slide his arms through his blouse's sleeves before being roughly grabbed and yanked to his feet. The fabric of his shirt suckered itself to his dripping, bloody back, like a wet bandage instantly stained crimson.

Sunlight pierced through cracks in the cloud cover as Saffron stumbled along behind Kaelar's commanding grip on his elbow. The air was, somehow, cold and hot at the same time. Thorny vines snarled his thoughts and kept him from gathering his composure.

He never knew words could pierce him physically, emotionally, mentally. Impertinent. Selfish. Arrogant. Words he barely understood, words used against him for—

For screaming when he found his friend slaughtered in the woods, after Saffron had done nothing to help them.

Those sounds of fox kits, barn owls—had they actually been Arrow dying within reach?

Hot tears pricked the backs of his eyes, mixing into the muddy colors already flowing in his vision from the pain, the exhaustion. He didn't know where Kaelar was taking him, and a part of him didn't care, just wishing he could lie down and close his eyes.

"Take some time to wash up," Kaelar's mocking voice emerged through the fog—and then the earth vanished beneath Saffron's feet, crashing into the icy grasp of Lake Elatha. Water as sharp as the silver that maimed him rushed down his throat, filling his lungs with thorns.

7

THE PARTY

"Seems you haven't changed at all."

Dark teal skin shimmered with scales, eyes yellow like gold coins, hair long and silvery like seaweed and starlight. Webbed fingers with claws drew lines up and down Saffron's bare chest. Rasping with breath, his lungs bubbled and sagged with uninvited lake water. Frozen solid, all the way to the bone. Weeds and creeping roots infiltrated the gaping words in his back, and he suddenly knew how it felt to be buried. To return to the earth as food for the plants.

"I didn't do this," another voice came.

"Perhaps, but those who kiss your feet did."

Webbed fingers trailed the center of his sternum, touching his neck, drawing a line down the square of his jaw.

"What will you do to make it right?"

"Will you forgive me, then?"

"I will forgive you when you have earned it, Night Prince."

SAFFRON WOKE WITH A JOLT, SOAKING WET, CLUTCHING something soft into his chest. He first thought he was still soaked with lake water—before realizing it was his own sweat. Hair clung to his face, shivering and gasping as someone rubbed scratchy paste over his back. Pulling the pillow closer into his body, he bit down on the fabric as the poultice made the fresh wounds sting, gasping when a voice questioned him by name.

"Are you awake?"

He only nodded weakly, collapsing back into the pillow. The voice belonged to Silk, Beantighe Village's informal healer. Without a human healer to rely on for years, the responsibility had fallen on her with little choice, but her herb and medicinal work was as good as it could be for someone otherwise untrained. Saffron had scrounged in the woods for roots and leaves and other plants at her request many times, wondering if the catwort she spread across him was something he'd once gathered with his own hands.

Trying to take stock of his body, his surroundings, a part of him was sure that silver instrument had pierced all the way through his back, his spine, his ribs, into his chest—and the painful burning of every inhale was him trying to respirate his own blood.

He was back in Fern Room, in his bed, soaking the sheets and blankets with his own sweat and what looked like more old blood. His palms were scraped, one of his cheeks speckled with dirt as if he'd crawled on his hands and knees all the way from campus. But the more he searched his memory, the more he realized he couldn't remember returning to Beantighe Village at all. There were hardly even flashes to offer hints, except for that hazy dream of voices and shimmering teal hands and seaweed-starlight and golden eyes...

"What happened?" he asked, voice barely more than a rasp.

"That was going to be *my* question," Silk answered, and Saffron grimaced. "Night-shifts on their way back from campus found you dumped just outside the front gate this morning. No one knows how long you were there."

Saffron groaned, pressing his face into the pillow again. It was quiet while Silk continued to dab at his back, and Saffron's face slowly peeked back out from the pillow. He swallowed back the uncertainty before asking:

"Did someone take care of Arrow?"

Silk's fingers slowed, but never fully stopped.

"Yes," she whispered. "Others got Arrow away before Elluin could stop them. They were buried this morning in Verdant Cemetery, next to their sister, like they always wanted."

Saffron bit back tears, nodding and pressing his face back into the cushion. Good, good—that was *good*, wasn't it?

"Did they..." he breathed. "Did they find the thing that did it?"

Another moment of silence. Saffron vaguely recalled sobbing about the wolf while clinging to Arrow's body as other beantighes rushed to help, but not much more before he was pulled away.

"I don't know," Silk said quietly. "The henmothers say it was probably just an accident... but that we should keep our eyes out."

Saffron wanted to argue, wanted to tell her "*I think Arrow knew it was coming*"—but Baba Yaga joined them first, claiming the stool from Silk and pushing fingers through Saffron's hair.

Offered a cup of hot tea, Saffron propped himself on his elbows and sipped, rubbing his thumb over the circle of random hatchmarks painted around the edge of the matching saucer. One of Baba's special cups, one she claimed to be instilled with her own special magic. No matter the injury, the illness, the woe, she had a cup and saucer for anything any beantighe needed—and just like promised, his own misery numbed as the tea filled his empty stomach.

The more he drank, the more Baba's folk magic spread through his body and quieted the racing thoughts, the pounding heartbeat in his back. A tiny flicker of logic in the back of his mind knew it was due less to actual magic and more to the hot whiskey Baba included in all of her medicinal teas, but there was less whimsy in that reality, so he ignored it.

As his nerves slowly melted like wax to a magic flame, his

henmother sat close and hummed while stitching together a cloth bundle. Apparently Ribbon from Cottage Monaghan offered to let Saffron have his old chest binder to keep bandages in place if Baba sewed him a new one, and Saffron sat mesmerized by the way the old woman's hands stitched with such control, threading needles and fastening the fabric as if her fingers that normally trembled with age felt no twitch at all.

"Is it strange to sew binders after years of sewing breasts?" Saffron mumbled with a flush of inebriation, and Baba laughed. It had been a long time since she laced herself into her hand-sewn brassiere, shaped with handfuls of rice that eased her nerves when her silhouette didn't reflect how it should be. Perhaps it grew too heavy with her age, or got in the way while she did chores throughout the day, though she made sure to always sling it on again when dancing naked in the woods.

Silk returned eventually to peel bruised medicinal leaves from Saffron's back, reapplying more with fresh water from the creek. When Saffron felt well enough to sit up, Baba wound him securely in bandages before pulling the binder on, all while Saffron bit back tears and groaned miserably. He asked for another magic cup with *extra* whiskey, but the woman just clicked her tongue in refusal.

Successfully wrapped like a corn husk, Baba and Silk left Saffron after telling him to get some rest. And he tried—but then spotted the burnt, bloody fern ring on his finger, and his heart throbbed.

He pushed hair from his eyes and held it there—but the reminder cracked the dam holding back everything else. His eyes burned, his lips trembled as he fought to keep his composure—before shuddering, pressing his face in his hands as he couldn't stop seeing it, hearing Arrow's voice, both when they called out to him in the front yard to when they lay dying in his arms. How Saffron couldn't do anything at all, except call for help and beg them to stay awake. Saffron had been there when Arrow's breaths slowed to a stop, when their expression went limp, when their eyes stopped moving. He'd seen it, up close, drenched in their blood—

Pixies papped hands on the nearby window like children demanding to be let inside. They found a crack in the frame and squeezed through, fluttering to the bed where Saffron sobbed. Something pricked at his finger, and Saffron pulled his hands away just as a pair of shimmery creatures attacked the gold ring. It summoned a miserable laugh to rattle out of him, swatting them away. They just chirped and squeaked threats in response, nibbling on his hand to show they meant it, offering him a picked flower in exchange.

For a split second he considered making the trade, before pulling his hands under his chest to hide the ring entirely, forcing the fairy creatures to find something else to entertain themselves. They crawled on the walls, pulled at wallpaper hangnails, pushed each other off the wooden bedpost.

He forced the misery down, down, down, far enough that it couldn't reach him—though perhaps it didn't matter. Every time his back throbbed, he just heard Arrow's blood-choked voice calling out his name.

AFTER AN ENTIRE YEAR OF NEVER HEARING MENTION OF the name *Cylvan*, for it to suddenly be on every fey student's tongue was jarring. Saffron couldn't escape it no matter where he went, particularly with the student body returning from Imbolc holidays and flooding Morrígan's walkways, buildings, and campus square.

They mostly discussed how beautiful he was. How they hoped there would be parties in Danann House now that there were people living back in that dormitory; how good he and Lord Taran looked together; how they hoped Cylvan would notice them; how they did their makeup specifically to stand out and catch the prince's eye.

None of them mentioned Arrow. None gossiped about the

beantighe who died outside of Danann House only two nights prior. Saffron didn't know if that was a blessing or something to make his insides coil in anger.

That morning, Saffron just wanted to stay out of the way. Wanted to hide the discomfort of his aching back beneath the bandages. He knew from experience the moment a student recognized injury on a beantighe, it would be like pixies on honeycomb —and even with Baba's magic tea and Silk's poultices to ease as much of the pain as they could, Saffron did not want to know how it felt for fingernails to drag down his wounds.

While the stark white of his veil made him stand out visually amongst the ocean of maroon blazers, matching slacks and skirts, jackets, embossed shoulder bags, dress shoes, and the occasional peacoat for warmth, at the same time, it also helped him to better hide. He could blend with the walkway, blend into interior walls, disappear as nothing more than seafoam on the edge of a cresting dark red wave of bodies. It made Saffron wonder if the prince really would be able to recognize him by the shape of his legs like he'd implied in his suite, especially when, if it wasn't for his horns, Saffron surely wouldn't be able to pick Cylvan out from the crowd, himself.

Tasked with mopping marble floors of the Pallas lecture building, he swirled the head of braided fabrics up and down the corridors between classes, stepping aside as lectures ended and students passed by. But when he finally made the mistake of wincing after leaning against the wall, his fate was sealed in an instant. He soon lost track of how many hands punched him in the back; how many fingernails scraped down his spine; how many heckles and insults were thrown as he just hunched over his work and focused on anything else. Every time, he just braced himself, biting back tears and curses before laughing lightly, as if he was in on the joke. *Yes, thank you my lord, thank you my gentle, my lady, yes, very funny. I enjoy your attention so much. You are so kind to find me amusing. I hope we cross paths again soon. Thank you.*

The harassment reached a fever pitch when he silently entered one of the study halls to swap candles in window sconces with Fleece. Plucking half-withered sticks and trading them for new ones while Fleece balanced the ladder from below, he focused on how nice it would be to finally get new candles in Cottage Wicklow as the others were becoming skeletal. He focused on ensuring all of their replacements were perfectly upright, like femur bones in candelabras. He specifically ignored the whispers from the tables below, how at least one hand seemed to motion to him as if they knew exactly who he was and what hid beneath his blouse.

A sudden eruption of laughter made him jump, turning and flushing with goosebumps when he recognized Prince Cylvan stifling laughter with a band of five or six others a few tables down. Quickly averting his eyes, Saffron took it as further proof Cylvan was full of shit and definitely didn't recognize him with his veil on. Still, at the sight of him, Saffron couldn't help but peek at the fern ring on his finger, dusted with dirt so it wouldn't stand out from the other bronze accessories.

"Is it true beantighes are afraid of heights?" Someone asked from nearby, but Saffron ignored them as Fleece turned and offered the joking fey a polite smile. Saffron's eyes just flickered back to the far table, glad Cylvan still hadn't noticed him despite the callout. That was—until someone suddenly leapt from their seat, shoving Fleece out of the way and grabbing the rungs of the ladder, twisting it and summoning Saffron straight to the floor.

Slamming on his back, Saffron barely swallowed his gut-wrenching scream, buckling inward and curling his body tightly to suppress the simultaneous vomit that raced up the back of his throat. It left him gasping and shuddering, hands pressed into his mouth as sobs threatened to tumble out. Did it—rupture his back wide open? Did his spine snap in half? His pounding heart gaped through the wounds, as if a hole had torn through and the organ tumbled out onto the floor.

Fleece took on the role of laughing politely with the others, thanking them for the entertainment, knowing better than to address Saffron writhing on the floor right away. Saffron knew he couldn't lie on the floor much longer, either, not wanting to show how badly it hurt, not wanting the one who knocked him down to think he had actually been injured. That would be insulting. High fey were only playful, they were not vicious or cruel. Of course. *Of course. Of course.* It would be rude for Saffron to imply otherwise.

"Excuse me."

Saffron lifted his head, seeing Cylvan suddenly standing there through blurry eyes. He was speaking to Fleece, who bowed their head and stepped quickly out of the way. The prince then passed by without a second glance, leaving the room with his entourage. The study hall fell silent.

Saffron watched him go as Fleece knelt down and asked breathlessly if he was alright. Saffron nodded, strangely reassured the excitement would die down with no royalty to impress. Though—it left him wondering if Cylvan had recognized him, after all.

That evening when his shift ended, Saffron excitedly waited off to the side of the library for the prince to come and allow him inside. Bouncing on the balls of his feet, about to tear out of his skin in anticipation, throwing looks through the windows whenever he needed something to quell the overwhelming excitement —but when Cylvan never came, Saffron had to swallow back the disappointment that was too large to stomach, and amble silently back to the road.

Perhaps Cylvan had only forgotten. Perhaps he was busy with his grand appearance at Morrígan, and Saffron shouldn't worry about it too much. Shouldn't take it personally.

But the more the days dragged on, Saffron waiting by himself as the sun set only to tromp off in annoyance when the prince didn't appear again, soon the quiet force of patience mutated into annoyance, and then edged on fury. Every time he overheard someone mentioning the prince and his beauty, how his placement tests already put him at the top of the class, how he'd joined the hurling team as a primary forward, how Cylvan spoke a hundred-thousand languages, how he could bend over backward and kiss his own ass, how he'd been born directly of the goddess Danu and a horse, how his royal shits were flecked with gold—Saffron realized he was sick of hearing about perfect Prince Cylvan, period.

It didn't help that, while his back slowly healed at first, the wounds soon showed signs of festering. Inflamed, stark red like roses, leaking mysterious liquid that Saffron pretended not to notice and Silk grimaced at every time she pulled his binder and bandages off to wipe down and apply more herbs and healing pastes.

It didn't help that, on top of the injuries on his back, there was something else rankling the inside of his lungs. Like water from the lake still lingered, growing heavier as it spawned creeping moss and clay and formed its own thorny mire in the places he used to breathe. And even despite the irritating cough that trickled in, he couldn't seem to do anything to ease the lingering heaviness.

His frustrations only grew as Cylvan could never be found alone, witholding any chance Saffron had to approach and make requests—or demands. The prince was always with Taran and Kaelar and Magnin and Eias, as well as a rotating roster of others that came and went like the changing seasons. Saffron seemingly couldn't do anything at all, and the edging fury grew hotter as days kept passing.

Until the night came that, upon reaching Agate Bridge as the day-shift ended, Saffron overheard a handful of students giggling about *getting Cylvan into bed* as they hurried for the path that branched toward Danann House. It piqued Saffron's curiosity, slipping away from the white sea of beantighe veils to follow the students in silence.

Lamps guided him down the edge of campus in the growing dark, like wisps captured in glass cages. All the while, more students hurried out from behind other buildings to join those already on their way, none paying him any mind as if he really were invisible. He didn't mind it that night, just like every other night—there was only one fey whose attention he wanted, and, ironically, Saffron really thought catching Cylvan in the middle of a party might be the most natural way to do it. He could pass as a servant assigned to the fete, offer the prince more wine, whisper a threat during the exchange. Catch Cylvan smoking out back and motion for him to come and face the consequences—but then wondered if the prince would actually obey a request like that.

The closer he got, the more he realized maybe he shouldn't have bothered so much with evicting the pixies before the kings' dinner, considering how most of the bottom-floor windows of Danann House were pushed open, terrace doors around the back and side hanging wide both to let fresh air inside and to offer more places for guests to wander and puke after they drank too much. Saffron wouldn't be surprised if he received another frantic Danann House assignment in the morning, demanding he take care of a second infestation.

Nearly every window glowed with light, shadows bustling around between panes of glass. There was even cheerful, whimsical music coming from somewhere inside, a violin, a harpsichord, wailing notes throughout the parlor and across the gardens and courtyard where already-drunk fey attendees laughed and roughhoused while stumbling over one another. If they were all so inebriated, it might be easier than Saffron thought to slip in and back out again with only one fey noticing him.

Reaching the gate around the front yard, students sat amongst the once perfectly preened greenery, smashing down grass and ferns, sitting in the apple trees and knocking down fruit. Saffron mentally noted how he didn't spot any other beantighes serving drinks or cleaning up amidst the chaos—but tried not to think about it, just double-checking the proper draping of his veil and forging ahead through the front door.

Saffron didn't make it far before stumbling backward as three brawling students tore at one another while hissing threats and slamming into walls. He hurried by when the path cleared again, wanting to be nothing more than a mouse. A mote. A ghost. He just needed one moment with the prince, and then he could go back home where his bed was waiting for him.

Careful never to look too eager, or like he was looking for anything at all, Saffron pretended to be very focused on a wine puddle on the floor, a stain on the staircase carpet, adjusting a tilted painting as he wandered down the front corridor, peeking into the study, up the stairs, into the kitchen. He was sure he never saw the same fey student pass by twice, many still wearing their school uniforms while others had changed into casual clothes, some so revealing that he was even more grateful for his veil when he couldn't help but stare.

Peeking into the main parlor, his survival instincts shrieked at so many high fey in one place. Strewn over couches and in one another's arms, between each other's legs, more wine spilled across the floors and cushions as hands clutching glasses whipped and waved in conversation. Through the open terrace doors, even more milled about the gardens, plucking mint leaves to chew on as distant sounds of passionate moaning came from at least every direction. In the center of the indoor festivities, platters of suspicious-looking chocolates in shades of brown and pink joined trays of fruits, both natural and with artificial pink fairy dust coating them. The sight made him almost turn and flee in an instant, but his nails gripped the edge of the wall to ground himself.

"What made you come to Morrígan, my prince?"

Saffron's eyes flickered to the circle of buttonback couches and armchairs around the fireplace, easily crowded with the most people in the room. In the center, a dark-haired daemon reclined in an armchair with his chin in one hand, his opposite spinning a glass of wine. Three fey draped themselves over him as if rendered too weak to remain upright by Cylvan's beauty, smiling and flirting and simpering in a way that made Saffron pull a face.

There was one detail that tempered the disgust, however, and that was Cylvan looking bored out of his fucking mind.

"What classes are you taking, your highness?"

"Can I get you more wine, Prince Cylvan?"

"Has anyone told you your eyes are like flowers, my lord?"

Even with that look of pinched annoyance, Cylvan was handsome as ever amongst the groveling. He wore a sheer black blouse that showed off his skin underneath, Saffron's eyes lingering briefly on his collarbones, his chest, the slight musculature of his stomach, as well as gold shimmers in what Saffron realized were jewelry pierced through his nipples. The prince's hair draped long and loose around him, wavy and shiny in the light of the fireplace, the candles in the sconces, the overhead chandelier. Shimmery lavender eyeshadow sparkled over his dark lashes whenever he moved and blinked, the shade of it making his indigo irises stand out even more.

Saffron especially noticed their color when Cylvan's eyes lifted and met his across the room, embarrassment escalating a hundred-fold as they then glided down to observe Saffron's legs, mouth curling into a knowing smile.

Saffron gulped, but ignored the implication and did what he'd set out to do. He lifted a hand and timidly motioned for Cylvan to *please come here.*

He should not have been even a little bit surprised when Cylvan curled his own finger for Saffron to approach *him,* instead. Feeling bolder than he should have, Saffron attempted one more time to request the prince obey his own beckoning, but Cylvan just repeated his motions with a little more emphasis and a sarcastic smile.

Sighing, Saffron accepted his fate, and stepped into the snake pit.

At least five people bumped into him, two stepping on his feet, a dozen more in every direction giving him a double-take. More and more, Saffron's nerves amplified the closer he approached, especially when those seated around Cylvan all tore their eyes from him like insects on tree sap to look at Saffron, instead. When he reached the edge of the simpering cluster, Saffron just smiled politely through his veil, nodding a few times in apology as he shuffled his way through.

The moment he stepped within reach, Cylvan shoved his closest admirer away, grabbing Saffron's hand and yanking him down. Saffron bit back a noise of surprise, slamming to his knees between Cylvan's legs. His face went hot again, leaning away when Cylvan leaned in close with a smile. He tugged playfully on Saffron's veil, messing up Saffron's hair underneath.

"I was praying for something to come and break up this boring fete," he purred. "Looks like I've been blessed with an adorable little púca fairy."

Saffron shook his head slightly, before glancing to his right, his left, seeing all the eyes bulging and digging into him as if touching the prince would get him killed on the way back home.

"I just..." Saffron suddenly couldn't remember what he wanted to say, holding his breath when Cylvan's hand touched his chin beneath the chiffon and coaxed his eyes forward again.

"Look at me when you speak," he breathed.

"S-sorry..." Saffron's entire soul left in an exhale, wondering if Cylvan had just cast a spell on him. He realized he had his hands on Cylvan's thighs for balance, quickly pulling them away as his face went even hotter. He spoke in a whisper just loud enough for Cylvan's pointed ears. "I just—I just wanted to ask... ask if you'll..."

But it was impossible to focus on his words every time someone behind him moved. Breathed. He just kept glancing over his shoulder, expecting someone to grab his veil, break his arm, slam one of the fruit knives into his shoulder. And every time he did, he accidentally leaned slightly more into the curve of Cylvan's body, as if a part of him really thought that was the safest place to hide.

"Ah..." Cylvan smiled, and Saffron glanced back at him again nervously. "You wish to ask about the library, don't you?"

Saffron nodded, and then jumped when someone muttered something from the neighboring couch. Cylvan's warm hand slid under Saffron's arm and down his back in response, pulling him in slightly more. It made Saffron wince, biting back a sound of pain and turning quickly back to Cylvan again, only then realizing how close they'd gotten.

"I've been too busy to meet this week," Cylvan whispered, his eyes hovering over Saffron's shoulder as if to keep watch for him. "But... how about we make another deal?"

Saffron grimaced. "I know better than to make any more deals with you, your highness."

Cylvan smiled darkly, like he took it as a compliment.

"Just one. Just for tonight. At least hear me out."

Saffron sighed, peeking over his shoulder at the others surrounding them again. Despite knowing he and Cylvan spoke quietly enough that they wouldn't be overheard, he still worried a word or two would pass through the intimate barrier. Cylvan's calm voice brought him back.

"You stay right where you are for the rest of the evening, and do whatever I say," he offered, "and I promise to meet you at the library tomorrow night after curfew."

Emotionally, that was the easiest *"yes"* Saffron would ever give —but the reply hung in his mouth for a moment longer. He regarded Cylvan's demeanor one more time, searching for true intentions behind his words. Obviously, with the addition of *"do whatever I say,"* Saffron should have assumed there was already something on his mind... but even gazing up at his intimidating face, surrounded by three dozen high fey watching with bitter resentment, and trays of pink-dusted fairy fruits spread out at his back—Saffron still felt pure elation at the thought of finally getting his chance to step foot in the library.

"Alright," he whispered with a nod. "But, ah... only if I get to leave my veil on."

"Of course," Cylvan smiled, petting a hand down the back of

Saffron's head, smoothing the airy fabric. "They would gut you in the woods after this, otherwise."

Saffron peeked one more time over his shoulder, and could hardly stomach the looks of envy emanating from the prince's admirers. But before Saffron could say or do anything else, Cylvan slid a glass of wine beneath the edge of his veil and encouraged him to drink.

8

THE DEAL

The glass of wine in Cylvan's grasp never fully ran dry, even between him and Saffron sharing it. There was always a bejeweled hand appearing to refill it, or to offer their own, all while drizzling the dark prince in endless compliments and groveling as if Cylvan was one penstroke away from declaring war on their family names.

To Saffron's relief, he easily disappeared back into the woodwork once the excitement died down and Cylvan returned to looking bored as the other fey made conversation. Saffron might have believed even he forgot about the beantighe kneeling between his legs, had his fingers not sat trailing below Saffron's ear through the veil, drawing endless circles, like a man subconsciously twirling the fur of a cat on their lap. Saffron actually enjoyed the thought, to be a cat over a beantighe.

"Choose a piece of fruit and feed it to me."

"Tell me again how handsome you think I am."

"Pick one of those pink chocolates you think I'd like."

"Will you tuck my blouse back into my waist?"

"My ring is crooked, why don't you straighten it?"

"Reach around my neck and untangle the hair from the back of my collar, will you?"

The orders came sporadically, and Saffron obeyed each one, though never fully relaxed every time the prince shifted and he anticipated another on his tongue.

Though once he felt safe again, there came a point where Saffron didn't mind each request for fruit or chocolate or some other snack from the trays, because it meant he could turn and gaze around the rest of the room, in secret. For the first time in his life, with only the task of shoving strawberries into Cylvan's handsome mouth, and he was able to actually observe high fey outside of campus activities like he did sleeping puddles of pixies. His previous pages of notes had all been scribbled with animosity, rather than birthed from actual observation—and to actually, safely indulge for just a moment, he found himself unusually fascinated.

Some had facial piercings like Cylvan had in his nipples. Some had natural hair colors like humans did, while others flipped strands in varying shades that Saffron had only ever seen in wildflower meadows. They had the same variations in skin tone and body type as humans as well, even the length and points of their ears varying between one another. In fact, apart from their ears, high fey shared enough physical traits with humans that it made Saffron *uncomfortable*. They admittedly lacked the scarring, the wrinkles, the sun damage, the acne, the crooked teeth... but their eyes, noses, mouths, while all diverse from one another, could pass them as any beautiful human if their ears were round instead of sharp. Perhaps they did have an additional air of ethereality, or their overall beauty was more heightened... but by whose standards? Saffron could count the number of humans just in Beantighe Village he found more attractive than any of the fey in the room, save perhaps only Prince Cylvan.

"What are you thinking about so seriously?" Cylvan must have heard his name in Saffron's thoughts, whispering into Saffron's ear. Saffron jumped, not realizing how long he'd sat there and observed the room in silence, still holding the prince's intended strawberry.

"Oh... nothing," Saffron muttered, pressing the ripe fruit between Cylvan's lips and rolling his eyes when a flirty tongue curled over his fingers. "Only that... you high fey aren't actually as magnificent as I always thought, now that I am sitting in a room with you."

"Is that so?" Cylvan appeared intrigued. "Even me, púca?"

Saffron sighed, offering a polite smile.

"Of course not, your highness. You are the most magnificent creature I've ever laid eyes on."

Cylvan smirked. "Tell me more about how ugly everyone else is."

Saffron nearly did, before laughing softly and shaking his head. "On second thought, perhaps I shouldn't. I've already been threatened with gutting once this evening."

"I would never let anyone gut you," Cylvan promised, but Saffron waited for the punchline. "Not with wine this expensive in your stomach."

Chuckling under his breath again, Saffron rolled his eyes and picked another strawberry from the trays to press into Cylvan's mouth. Cylvan accepted it, that time curling his soft lips over Saffron's fingers and making Saffron's breath catch.

There was one observed pattern of behavior Saffron was very much *not* surprised by, and that was a high fey's propensity for pure, stupid levels of inebriation that would have killed a human much sooner. Saffron wasn't exactly sure where the wine was coming from, or when the whiskey and rum were introduced into the mix, but soon even Prince Cylvan struggled to remember his words and laughed every time he stammered. When one guest accidentally drenched Saffron with a glass of wine, the prince was even drunk enough to lunge and shove the fey away with a near snarl. He might have ripped them clean open if Saffron hadn't gently prodded Cylvan back and assured him everything was fine. By his bright eyes, though, Saffron knew Cylvan was looking for any reason to start a brawl at all; it didn't actually have anything to do with how Saffron was now soaking wet and tinged pink.

There was only one person Saffron noticed who didn't imbibe with every reach of their soul, and that was Lord Taran. Taran, who mostly lingered on the fringes, making conversation with anyone and everyone, but who Saffron noticed never actually took a sip of wine from his glass. He would lift it to his lips and pretend, but the level of the red drink inside never lessened.

Saffron didn't think much of it at first, deciding Taran must not like the taste of that flavor specifically, or perhaps he just wasn't in the mood to embarrass himself like all of his peers—until a different pattern emerged that made Saffron's nerves itch with anxiety. Every time someone refilled Cylvan's cup, it was only after Taran pointed it out. A whisper, a finger indicating the prince's near-empty glass, a nod. And the admirer would grab the nearest bottle and approach, introduce themself, and offer Cylvan a top off of his glass. Again and again and again, never allowing Cylvan a break, never even allowing Cylvan a glass of water—though Saffron tried—and slowly the prince grew more and more intoxicated until he couldn't stop laughing under his breath, teasing Saffron's veil, threatening to pull it up and show everyone his face. Saffron just swatted his hand away, averting his eyes, growing more and more uncomfortable the longer the night went on.

He was eventually distracted watching a group of fey laugh over a stolen beantighe veil when his own veil shifted again. Sighing, he turned back to Cylvan to ask him to knock it off, but the prince just pressed something into his mouth, and Saffron bit down without thinking. A sweet strawberry coated his tongue, and he smiled at Cylvan in polite exasperation—before the fruit was pulled away, and Saffron saw pink dust coating its flesh.

Icy fear slammed into him. He grabbed Cylvan's hand, staring at the fruit, and then staring up at him. Behind him, a few amused laughs came from those seated around on the couches.

"Why..." he begged, before instinct flooded and took over. He jolted to his feet—but Cylvan flashed out a hand and grabbed his arm, pulling him back down onto his lap and pushing up the rest of his veil. It made Saffron's injured back scream, attempting to hide his face from the others, but it was too late. Cylvan just shoved his arm away and forced the rest of the pink berry into his mouth as he laughed.

Spitting, clenching his teeth, smashing his lips together, the effects of the first full bite were already making his skin tingle, his heart flutter, his nerves melt. In not much more time, he would laugh, too. He would spread across Cylvan's lap, smile at him, touch his face, beg to be kissed and compelled.

Thrashing, Saffron ripped himself free and raced for the nearest open door. Someone howled excitedly behind him, and a dozen feet leapt from couches to take chase.

Saffron didn't bother searching for a gate, leaping over the fence as soon as he reached it. His boot caught in one of the prongs, and he hit the earth with a miserable grunt, scrambling back to his feet as the chasing animals only tore closer. Flinging himself into the trees, darkness drenched him in an instant, but he forced himself deeper, deeper into the woods until even he didn't know where he was, or if anyone else could ever find him.

The fairy fruit's effects were already in full force by the time he could no longer walk straight, stumbling over his own feet and giggling. He pushed hair from his eyes as sweat beaded on his forehead, laughing more every time he scraped his hands on a tree or tumbled into painful thorny brambles, every time he tripped into the stream and came out soaking wet.

It made him hot in every way, until the base of his stomach sparkled like champagne and his cheeks flushed in embarrassment because he just kept thinking about Cylvan's tongue, his lips, touching and kissing and curling around Saffron's fingers every time he fed him a strawberry. How he licked his lips every time he took a sip of wine, how those same lips parted slightly in concentration while tucking the same glass against Saffron's mouth. How his fingers held the stem, how the tendons in the backs of his hands shifted with every movement. The feeling of a hand petting the back of Saffron's head. Coaxing Saffron's own hands back onto two thighs for balance. How Saffron could see the movement of Cylvan's stomach muscles every time he even just breathed—

Any remaining sober part of him tried to force the thoughts away before they could evolve into anything more, before they could become fantasies or memories he would think were real in the morning. He forced himself to recall Cylvan's face as soon as Saffron realized the fruit he'd taken a bite of—that dark amusement, as Cylvan knew exactly what he'd done. Cylvan knew *exactly* what he'd done and still pulled Saffron down to feed him more. If Saffron hadn't been able to get away in time, what else might have happened? Would Cylvan have watched as the others tore Saffron apart? Would he have helped?

Saffron grabbed the nearest tree and shoved fingers down his throat, puking up as much as he could. Wine and fruit and chocolate, hoping at least some of it was the fairy powder he'd ingested. But even when there was nothing left in his stomach, his blood still pounded with magic inebriation, and all he could do was groan. He thought about Arrow, about their search for *wild* fairy fruits, and Saffron felt even more anxious nausea climb up his throat. If just powdered fruits did this to a human, what in Ériu's name would wild fruits do?

He stumbled more. He tried to follow the moon through the trees—before realizing it wasn't the moon at all, and he'd been imagining the glow the entire time. He followed the stream instead, ignoring the insidious night-wisps that called out to him, knowing they would likely send him over a cliff or into a sinkhole instead of anywhere useful.

When the exhaustion hit, but the drug's effects continued stronger than ever, Saffron woke up on his side, never realizing he'd fallen at all. Hanging over him, a dark shadow that would have made him scream had he been more in control of his body. Instead, he just laughed, something about the old crone's face filling him with wonder.

"Baba?" he giggled. He swore she smiled, leaning down and

pressing something between his lips. He should have reacted, fought, thrashed—but he saw the round curve of her ears, and his wobbly self-preservation determined her a human friend before his conscious mind ever did.

A bitter, crunchy coffee bean reinvigorating his senses. It didn't so much purge the unwanted magic from his blood as it just helped him think more clearly, a few more being popped into his mouth. Eventually, his thoughts opened up enough to gaze at the trees overhead and string complete sentences together again.

"Cloth," the old woman said without warning, voice like branches raking on the side of Cottage Wicklow. It startled him, jolting upright—but the woman was gone as quickly as she came, leaving only one thing behind: a beantighe veil with Arrow's name stitched along the edge.

9

THE LIBRARY

Saffron eventually stumbled back to Beantighe Village and collapsed facedown in bed with a groan, still clutching Arrow's veil in his hand. His legs ached from wandering so far into the woods, his feet hurt from doing it all in his uniform derby boots; he could feel his heartbeat in his back again, the herbs having done some work to numb the pain but ultimately didn't stand a chance against the exertion, the whipping tree branches, all the times he fell. At some point in the night, whether at the party, while fleeing, or somewhere amongst the trees, he'd lost his own veil, too, making him grateful to be clutching Arrow's—even though it was still a blur how he'd ended up with it at all. There was an old crone, or something—but how had she gotten it? Maybe she just found it randomly in the woods; maybe she was a wild thing drawn by the smell of Arrow's blood...

He was too exhausted to question.

Morning came far too quickly, Saffron sure he'd barely closed his eyes before Hollow was there, nudging him back awake. Like a corpse, he felt extra heavy with water in his chest and feverish as his back boiled, but he just weakly nodded at his friend, pushed himself up, and got dressed with the others. He might have had a conversation with Letty—or was it Berry?—but he couldn't recall the details. Did he give Baba Yaga a goodbye kiss on the cheek like he always did? When did he leave the house? How did he walk all the way to campus without recalling even a moment of it?

Arrow was always losing their veil, and the one Saffron claimed for himself was still stiff with newness, smelling of starch and soap as if Arrow had barely broken it in. After arriving on campus, Saffron took an extra moment away from chores in favor of a side trip to the lake, crunching down one side of the bank out of sight of student eyes to drench the chiffon in water.

Washing away the stiffness and massaging the layers into lovely, delicate, flowing waves he preferred, he sighed the whole time. It made him think of the time Arrow's veil was sucked up in a wind because their hair was too short to pin it; or the time it caught on a branch while hunting tobacco and marijuana in the woods together, tearing far enough down the middle that not even Baba could rescue it. It made him laugh under his breath, whispering thanks to his friend for letting him hold on to that one.

He was just breaking up the starch from the second layer when others joined him, turning to find Letty and Berry making their way carefully between the trees and the weeds. Letty crouched on the balls of her feet to watch as Berry offered to hang the first piece of fabric from a nearby branch to dry.

"Are you doing alright?" she eventually asked, voice quiet. "You've been acting strange lately."

"Strange?" Saffron feigned confusion, but Letty just frowned at him. He should have known that wouldn't work, letting out a huff. He scrubbed wet sand into the chiffon as he considered what, exactly, he could possibly say. Finally, he closed his eyes and let out a quick breath.

"I... made a deal with a high fey," he whispered. His friend smacked him, then shrieked and apologized, grabbing his face to rub his cheek. Saffron choked on a laugh, unable to blame her.

"A deal for what?" she asked weakly, still embarrassed by the instinctual response. "Are you in trouble?"

"I'm not in trouble. At least, I don't think I am." He grimaced. "But with it, I'm supposed to be able to go into the library, Letty, as soon as they let me in. Maybe even tonight."

Letty's groping hands softened, and then a hesitant smile crossed her mouth.

"You must be... really desperate."

Saffron realized he still hadn't told Letty about Luvon's intentions for Ostara. In fact, he hadn't told anyone at all, not even Baba Yaga. He turned his eyes back down again, wringing the veil in his hands.

"Yeah," he whispered. "But not desperate enough to be a fool. I promise."

"Which fey?" Berry asked from behind them. Saffron narrowed his eyes, and Berry narrowed them right back.

"Just some dark lord."

Letty rolled her eyes. "Come on, Saff."

"Swear you won't tell anyone?"

"Of course."

"I don't make promises like that," Berry said on the contrary.

"Hm," Saffron sniffed. "Then I guess that's my secret to keep."

"Damnit Berry!" Letty hissed, splashing water on him as he complained. Saffron just laughed, wringing out the rest of the fabric and hanging it to dry with its companion in the tree.

WITH IT BEING THE END OF THE WEEK, THERE WERE NO classes on campus, and therefore no students to roam between lecture halls. They mostly stuck to their dormitories, the dining hall, the roads out of Morrígan into nearby towns, the athletics fields. Some rowed out onto the lake to smoke, others taking hikes through the woods along safely-designated paths that never strayed too far from civilization. But of all the people Saffron expected to see showing off a new outfit, running laps around the field, or otherwise making a mess for some weekend entertainment, Cylvan was nowhere to be found. Saffron even began to wonder if the prince was dead. Too hungover to move. Did he even remember making their deal the night before, or had Saffron negated it when he ran for his life? Like a claw dragging down the back of his mind, the closer the sun crept to the horizon, the more Saffron was subjected to the nauseating thought of facing more disappointment once it got dark.

If Prince Cylvan actually came, he would finally step into the Grand Library. Walk the shiny floors. Touch the books. See what exactly was painted on the murals overhead. He would finally have the one thing he wanted more than new drawing charcoals, or watercolors, or apple wine on his changeling day. The thing that could allow him to earn an honest, legitimate, bonafide academic endorsement on his own merit, without the use of true names or magic rings.

If Prince Cylvan actually came.

"*Ugh,*" he grumbled for the hundredth time, hanging back in the trees as other day-shift beantighes trudged off into the setting sun for Agate Bridge. Once they were gone, he helped himself to a candle lantern in the supply closet, spending the last bit of sunlight unearthing treasures from a nearby stream until he was sure curfew had come and gone. Students would be fully back in their dorms. There wouldn't be anyone else out wandering to bother him.

Except one. He hoped.

Exhumed quartz points clinked in his hand as he pulled on his veil and hurried back into the open. Stealing between the buildings, past flower bushes and trimmed hedges, dark walkways, wisps captured in lamps, he walked intentionally so his shoes wouldn't make any sound on the stone. The movements, the intentional silence was no different than all the other times he approached in secret, but that night was different. There was real promise he clung to.

God—Saffron really hoped Cylvan would be there.

Rounding the stairs leading up to the library doors, his racing heart made its way into his throat—but there was still no one waiting outside.

He thought he might cry. He stopped at the bottom steps, breathing hard through his nose as emotion swelled behind his face and threatened to creep over his eyes. Really? Truly? Had he signed his life, his only opportunity for survival and happiness, away to someone so inconsiderate? How could someone with such a honeyed voice, a sharp tongue, a charming laugh be so cruel?

He nearly turned to leave—but a click from the doors made him whirl around, eyes going wide and mouth dropping open when Cylvan appeared in the entryway, looking annoyed.

"Come on, idiot," he said, and Saffron wasted no time racing up to meet him.

Practically hopping up and down as he reached the entrance, Cylvan just rolled his eyes and stepped off to the side. But before Saffron bolted in—he paused.

Beneath his feet, he finally saw the dark wood floors he'd only ever regarded on his toes through windows.

The air inside was warm, despite there being no fireplace burning. It smelled of light incense made from sandalwood, and what Saffron knew was the soft scent of old pages. A scent he only ever held in his stolen books for a day before the fresh air of Beantighe Village washed it away.

These would be books he didn't have to burn. Books he could read more than once until he actually understood them, instead of having to store them in the barn and dispose of them quickly to avoid being found. Books he could take his time with. Books he could learn more than just new words and spelling from. Books—that could change his entire life. Finally. With just one step through the door.

His breath shuddered. It all suddenly felt very heavy—and Saffron wasn't very strong. Even at his fastest, it could take him weeks to read something cover to cover. And even then, he rarely understood more than a few parts. What if he couldn't do it?

What if he couldn't read as well as he thought? What if he was too slow?

What if Cylvan—laughed at him?

"What's wrong now?" the prince asked sharply. Saffron's eyes snapped back up to him, mouth still hanging open in uncertainty. He pressed his lips together. He didn't know how to say it. *What if it's not like I thought? What if I can't do it?*

Instead, he held out his hand, washed clean of mud though there was still some clay under his nails. Cylvan frowned, but extended an open palm, gifted with the small cluster of quartz points. Cylvan made an initial face of disgust, before it melted into restrained curiosity, eyes lifting back to Saffron in question.

"I got these... for you," Saffron said, but didn't look at him, just gazing apprehensively into the dim library ahead.

He took his first step inside.

The lantern was hardly bright enough to illuminate the front vestibule, but Saffron stared in awe as Cylvan closed the door behind them, still frowning at the dirty crystals given in offering.

Saffron wondered how it was possible for something of stone and wood to caress delicate windows of glass without crushing them, immediately taken by the colorful inlays between dark metal traceries, lancet windows lining the clerestory above. Below, framed paintings hung from the wood wainscoting, and his breath caught, making the back of his throat itch. But coughing made him self-conscious, trying to suppress it, the sound of his struggling lungs echoing off the ceiling and polished floors.

When was the last time the walls saw a human face? Would they be offended that he walked beneath them? Would they finally give way beneath the weight of the stone roof, and crush him as punishment for thinking he had any right to breathe in the air of the books?

Cylvan started to say something with a step forward—but Saffron's hand flashed out, taking a handful of his blazer. The prince narrowed his eyes like he wished to incinerate Saffron in that moment, but Saffron barely noticed, still too busy staring at the sweeping landscape mural on the ceiling. The adornments in the tall corners, the wainscoting, the paintings, the stained glass windows, how there were mushrooms carved into the floor.

"P-Prince Cylvan..." he whispered, finally finding the strength to speak. Tears of elation burned in the backs of his eyes. "I'm... I'm sorry, I... can't explain, but do you think... you could wait here a moment? Just for a moment. Just..."

"Seriously?" Cylvan hissed, rattling his handful of quartz. "You unload muddy garbage on me, then you expect me to...?" But he trailed off as Saffron's desperation grew, until he finally sighed. Then he nodded, motioning for Saffron to go on ahead. Saffron smiled brightly, Cylvan making another face of exasperation and waving more emphatically for him to *get going*.

It took Saffron another moment of gathering his nerves to take a step further. But his lantern cast shadowy leaves on the floor ahead of him, and he could almost trick himself into believing it was no more than another walk in the Agate Wood.

With another step, Prince Cylvan fell away entirely. And then all of Morrígan, all of Alfidel, all of the fey world; even all of Saffron's anxiety sloughed from his muscles, his heaviest parts torn away at the doors, like a rain-soaked coat left on a rack. The lightness allowed his heart to race for a new reason. A bird held and protected for years in his chest until the moment he could finally release it. Rattling the inside of his ribs excitedly and making every inch of him tingle. Making him cough, making him softly suffocate in the most satisfying way.

The vestibule split into a bottom floor that continued straight ahead, or two wings of wooden stairs like arms open for an embrace. Saffron timidly made his way up the steps and into the long central nave of the second floor, mouth dropping again at the sheer size, the height, the decor embellishing every inch of dark paneled walls where shelves weren't stacked with books.

Wood columns carved with magpies and ravens climbed before flourishing into fan vaults on the ceiling. Winged trouping fairies reveled with instruments in a line along the baseboards, trailed by mischievous sprites exactly like the ones Saffron plucked from irises in Danann House. Three-moon motifs crowned rounded tympanums over archways, curtains pulled open in sections down the length to break up the dizzying expanse. Even the stairs up to the balcony level were carved and painted with pixies and leprechauns, merrows slithering up columns between shelves, unicorns laying in fields of wildflowers. Narrow ladders perched within every book-walled aisle donned creeping vines along each rung, the balustrades along the edge of the balcony carved like gaping rose hedges. Down the center, long study tables stretched not unlike the snake's back at the kings' dinner, separated into the three sections of the nave. More chairs than Saffron could count lined the sides like headstones, and Saffron couldn't help his fingers tracing over them.

But nothing compared to the murals overhead. Stunning depictions of beautiful fey, unique compositions on the three main ceilings, painted within the spaces between blooming vaults of the support beams. And the thing that made the bird in Saffron's chest trill the loudest—was his ability to recognize every one of them.

In the first chamber, an elegant, dark-skinned, pointed-ear fey in a flowing dress stood on her toes to kiss her pale companion perched on a steed, the rider's red hair tied in a braid over one shoulder. Over their heads, three magpies flew by; at their feet, two of the horse's hooves crossed out of a circle of mushrooms, legs charred and turning to bone.

"Oisín and Niamh," he whispered with a tiny smile.

Following the well-worn river of wood into the next section, Saffron couldn't resist the urge to tuck cushioned chairs neatly back into place as he passed. Candelabras broke up the length of the tables, repeating every few chairs down the line, interspersed with white wax pillars of varying heights. Like abandoned finger bones beckoning Saffron further.

In the second mural, four swans were painted starkly against a torrential, white-capped ocean, rain and lightning crashing amongst dark clouds behind them.

"The Children of Lir!" Saffron acknowledged under his breath, with a giggle and an excited hop on his toes.

His fingers trailed along everything within reach as he passed. The books, the tables, the chairs, the carvings on the walls. He might have even scooped up the tiny mice that occasionally scurried under his feet, but couldn't be sure they weren't púca fairies in disguise, wanting to bite his nails off.

He just wanted to remember everything. Every single detail, to think about while he fell asleep or to draw in his sketchbook the first moment he got. One day, whether when his geis with Cylvan ended, or he was shoved through the veil, or Cylvan grew tired of Saffron's games first—Saffron would want to remember exactly what it all looked like. How it felt.

"Oh..." he couldn't help the fluttering in his chest beneath the final mural. A crimson-haired maiden wrapped up in a wind, clutching the bleeding body of her dark-haired lover. Pulling them in close, tears streaming down her eyes as scenes of the woods, the ocean, meadows, stone quarries made up the landscape behind them.

"Naoise and Derdriu," he whispered reverently. The recognition made more emotion well up in his eyes, blissful as if he'd passed every test that would allow him to stay. *Oisín in the Land of Youth, The Children of Lir, Derdriu of the Sorrows.* Saffron knew all of them—and felt like maybe he wasn't so out of place, after all.

Taking a few steps back, he placed his lantern on the table before taking a seat, himself, fully appreciating the lovers overhead. Naoise, who died at the hands of jealous King Connor mac Nessa, trying to protect the person he cared for most. Derdriu, who then chose to die instead of being loved by anyone else.

As someone who had only ever known romance by the pages of those myths, Saffron wondered if it was actually possible for someone to love another person so deeply. Painfully, excruciatingly. Enough that they would rather die than be without them.

"Are you done having your moment?"

Saffron's foot caught in a chair and sent it crashing to the floor, scrambling in surprise. Stumbling upright again, Prince Cylvan just observed him with restrained laughter, making Saffron's face go hot.

"What, did you forget about me?" the prince smirked, and Saffron balled up his hands.

"N-no! Of course not! I'm sorry, I only—"

"Don't apologize, púca. I'm only teasing," Cylvan sighed, lifting his shoulder bag onto the table. "I actually quite enjoyed watching you appraise this old building like you've never seen a ceiling before. Is this really your first time inside? I asked the caretaker when they assigned my campus rings, and they said this is the only building normal beantighes aren't allowed to clean."

"Um... yes," Saffron flushed. "I've only ever seen it through the windows, so..."

Illuminated by the soft glow of the lantern, the way Cylvan's eyes lingered on him didn't help to put Saffron at any more ease.

"Why are you still wearing your veil?" The prince said next. "It's just us. You can take it down."

"Oh—sure!" Saffron jumped, grabbing the white chiffon and tugging it off.

His hair must have come out a mess by how Cylvan bit back more amusement, but the prince said nothing else, claiming the first seat within reach and pulling texts and bound parchment from his bag. Saffron watched in silence, intrigued by the way Cylvan's hands moved while opening the pages of his book, removing his raven-feather quill from its golden case, uncorking the writing ink and setting it on a little plate to keep from dripping on the table. Then he pulled a match from a long box, striking it to light the candles on the table. Saffron never knew stationary could be so... elegant.

"If you're waiting for a command..." Cylvan muttered, blowing out the match. "*Get to work.*"

"O-oh! Right," Saffron squeaked, turning quickly and hurrying off without thinking where he was going. He just claimed the first aisle of books behind him, a thousand titles and authors staring him down in an instant. A hundred witnesses to the moment he remembered—he had no idea what he was doing.

Not just that he didn't know where to start, either—Saffron didn't know *anything*. And since he'd finally had his moment to stand beneath the murals, to release that little bird in his chest and let it sing, Cylvan had come along with a crossbow to shoot it back down so they'd have something to eat for dinner.

Saffron didn't know how to find a *spell*. Would he even recognize one if he saw it?

Did fey even use "spells" like the ones Baba Yaga painted on teacup saucers? He'd never even seen a student drawing magic circles or anything like that—so how did they do magic at all?

It had been easy to pretend in the wake of his excitement, all the way up until that very moment, armed with a crossbow and told the little bird had to prove itself useful.

Licking his lips, he steeled his nerves. Hopping on the balls of his feet to summon some courage, he nervously hooked a finger over the spine of one text and tugged it down.

"You might need this."

Saffron slammed the book to the floor. Cylvan just stared at him as Saffron gulped and stammered.

"Oh, I... I thought the book said that."

The horned daemon's grip on the lantern wavered, and then trembled, laughter rising out of him like it was the funniest thing he'd ever seen. Saffron just snatched the light in embarrassment, grabbing the book from the floor and shoving it back in place. He tried to look more confident as he skimmed the other titles next to it, but Cylvan clearly wasn't convinced by the way he hovered.

"Can I help you with anything else, my lord?" Saffron asked in a tone that said *you're very distracting to my important work.*

"Why are you beginning your search in *mathematics?*"

Saffron stared blankly at the shelf. He opened his mouth to lie, before closing it again and pulling his searching hand away.

"Well..." was all he managed, and another laugh escaped the prince.

"I've certainly gotten myself into something here, haven't I?" he muttered, before motioning for Saffron to follow. Saffron did so silently, stepping back into the main nave, a lump forming in his throat when he realized Cylvan was leading him toward the exit.

"Um—!" Saffron started, hurrying to match Cylvan's pace. "Please—I'm sorry! I've just never been in a library like this before. I promise I just need some time to learn the layout, I can still—!"

"What?" Cylvan asked with a frown. "Relax, I'm just taking you to the register tome."

Saffron floated behind Cylvan's line of sight again in embarrassment, following him all the way to the end of the central corridor. Against the balustrade railing overlooking the vestibule, a massive text sat on a pedestal, already opened to a page. Inside, columns upon columns of classifications, numbers, and other symbols that made Saffron's head spin with just a momentary glance.

"The library is separated into sections based on subject matter. Then there are then subsections, and then sub-topics," Cylvan explained, putting a hand on the open pages and glancing back at Saffron. Saffron's heart fluttered, realizing Cylvan was... offering advice. Something about it made the indigo gaze even more intimidating, and Saffron could hardly bear to meet it for longer than a few seconds. "Each section has its own book like this with every volume listed, and where to find it. Understand?"

"Um... yes," Saffron whispered, wincing when Cylvan huffed in doubt and hooked an arm around his waist to drag him closer. Clutching his hands over his chest, he worried a single touch to the book would reveal him as an uninvited guest. He just unconsciously leaned more into Cylvan, as if he could disappear into the prince's body and the book would be none the wiser.

But upon actually standing close enough that they touched, with Cylvan's instructing voice calm and gentle, his clothes smelling like sweet perfume, long hair tickling the side of Saffron's neck... Could Cylvan hear how loudly Saffron's heart pounded for a different reason?

"Now—this is your task, so I won't tell you what to do, but... if *I* were you, gods forbid, I would begin my search... hmm..." he considered it, trailing a finger down the tabs like golden teeth sticking out of the side. "Perhaps in the Opulentology section?"

Saffron wanted to ask *"the what?"* but Cylvan was already hooking a finger under the appropriate tab and heaving a thousand pages over to reveal his desired section. Dragging a finger down the first of four columns per page, Saffron caught sight of a few different sub-sections: *History of...; Philosophy of...; Literary Reference; Religious Applications...*

"Erm—how much do you actually know about Opulence, beantighe? Perhaps that is where we'll start." Cylvan glanced down at Saffron, who gazed back with what he knew was the look of a frightened deer staring down a bear.

"... You're kidding."

"I'm—!" Saffron yelped when Cylvan's nails burrowed into his side.

"You offered your abilities as if you knew exactly what you were doing," the prince said with an exasperated smile. "And now I find out—*not only* have you never been in the library before, you also don't know what Opulence is, let alone how it encompasses true name magic... Oh, Danu drag me screaming to the mounds—"

"I know I can do it!"—He didn't. But Cylvan didn't need to know that—"I only need somewhere to start! So just tell me where I can find this section you're thinking about, and I'll figure it out..."

Cylvan smirked. "No, I don't think I will. Here—you see

these numbers and symbols next to the subsections? Those tell you where to find the books you're looking for. I want to see you find it yourself, to ease my uncertainty."

Saffron wanted to complain more, but just puffed up his chest.

"F-fine," he said with faux confidence, returning to the book to locate the *History of Opulence* line in the column, notating the ᚦ *HIS;01* at the end. Grabbing the quill next to the book, he dipped it in the inkpot and jotted the notation down on his palm. Cylvan muttered, "*There's paper for—Oh. Alright,*" as Saffron turned and walked away stubbornly.

Cylvan followed close behind, whispering teasing discouragements as Saffron just ignored him. He then felt extremely smart when he noticed symbols carved over each aisle of books, pulling a face at Cylvan when they accidentally met eyes. Around the room, he observed every archway, admittedly growing more and more frustrated the more they just kept *going*.

Finally, he located the ᚦ section on the upper floor in Derdriu's section of the nave. With an accidental sound of relief, he searched the shelves for *HIS* next, and then *01*, smacking his hand on the located prey and eviscerating Cylvan with a smug smile.

"Ah, yes, good job, beantighe. You managed the most basic of library navigation after I literally gave you all the instructions you needed," Cylvan said with a sarcastic smile. "Now. That entire shelf is Opulent History, so... better start reading. Ostara only creeps closer."

Saffron's stomach fell into his ass as he craned his neck just to see all the way to the top.

"Oh, god," he muttered. Cylvan chuckled in satisfaction before heading back to the stairs, making Saffron jump and call out again. Hurrying to where Cylvan paused, Saffron looked at him with fresh uncertainty.

"Wh-what are you going to work on? Should we make a plan, or...?"

"Me?" Cylvan smiled. "I'm doing my philosophy homework."

Saffron waited for the punchline, but Cylvan just raised his eyebrows.

"... You're not going to help me?" he finally whimpered.

"No," Cylvan responded flirtatiously, twirling a piece of hair around his finger. "Like I said, this is *your* task, beantighe. But I look forward to being *very* impressed when you figure it out all on your own. So don't let me down."

Saffron watched him go, forcing himself to breathe as anxiety clutched him again. He flexed his hands. He took another deep breath.

Seeking out the sub-section register at the end of the aisle, Saffron pushed it open with a grimace, scanning line after line as the beginnings of rain tapped against the window in front of him.

SITTING CROSS-LEGGED ON THE POLISHED WOOD FLOOR, it wasn't long before Saffron surrounded himself with more than a dozen books, one particularly giant text spread open on his lap as he sat hunched and reading. Though unlike when he used to read myths in the same posture, that time it only made his back hurt.

It was harder than expected to only pick a few off the shelves —a *few* for him clocking in at almost twenty—as every single title sounded interesting. *Origins of Opulence; Is Opulence of the Blood or the Soul?; How Opulence Changes the Anatomy of the Mind in Both Practitioners and Intendees; Can Opulence Be Learned From Nothing?; Wild Fey Opulence: How Does it Differ From That of the High?;* the titles captured every single loose thread of his curiosity, slowly unraveling like a wool sweater every time he climbed up and down the leaf-carved ladder.

Careful not to cough anywhere near the pages, Saffron didn't realize how much time had passed until Cylvan suddenly appeared in the aisle again, kneeling down and catching Saffron off guard.

"Have you figured out what it means to be opulent yet, beantighe?" he asked, grabbing one of Saffron's discarded books and aimlessly flipping it open. Saffron straightened up, clearing his throat, coughing, then nodding—before sinking into a frustrated scowl.

"It's... more than just a fey's ability to do magic. And has something to do with the soul," he whispered. "Right?"

"Hmmmmm." Cylvan smiled slyly. "That's a good primary-school answer, I suppose. Out of all these books, that's all you've gleaned so far?"

Saffron frowned, glancing back down at his lap.

"None of the authors actually *define* opulence clearly, as if they assume whoever is reading already knows, which is... presumptive of them..." He sighed in defeat. Cylvan flipped through another few pages of the book in his hand, not looking up when he asked:

"Did you learn anything else?"

He asked it in a way that could be either sarcastic or genuine. And while the thought of Cylvan being capable of sincerity, especially with someone like Saffron, made Saffron doubt everything else he knew—he decided to pretend, since he actually did learn a few interesting things of note.

"Well..." he stretched out his legs. "Did you know the terms 'seelie' and 'unseelie' originated amongst humans? Back when the veil was still open. And that they actually refer to how friendly different types of fey are to humans? I had no idea, especially since I've heard so many high fey use the terms to insult one another... I also think it's interesting how, in modern usage, 'seelie' seems to be the negative one in your circles, when all it means is you're friendly to humans..."

"Calling a high fey 'seelie' is a quick way to insult their entire family line," Cylvan told him. "I would be careful if I were you."

"Oh—I would never," Saffron promised. "I have better instincts than that... especially after recently making a deal with an actual unseelie lord, who is intent on teaching me my place."

The unseelie lord smirked. "You mean between his legs?"

Saffron went red, smiled, and then quickly looked away again before Cylvan could see. Luckily, Cylvan just tossed his book back to the pile and went on.

"How many of these did you actually get through?"

"Um... just this one," Saffron admitted, curling his fingers over the pages. "The writing is more complicated than reading myths, obviously... and I have to re-read some of the sentences a few times..."

"You know true name magic is one of the oldest, most complicated, most nuanced spells in all opulent systems?" Cylvan interrupted, as if it was something he'd been dying to tease Saffron with all night. Saffron just scrubbed his nail up and down the corner of the pages in his lap.

"Yes. Which is why you employed a human to help you," he responded sarcastically, unable to help the pout that pursed his lips. "You know I'm starting at a disadvantage, even if I know how to read."

"Barely."

"Well, I'm sure *you* could read from the day you popped out of Oberon's ass, and yet... heh. Um, what I mean... is..."

He internally kicked himself, pressing his lips into an apologetic smile. Cylvan smiled back, though his was a unique combination of surprise and insult.

"That's not a kind way to speak to the unseelie lord you've promised your tongue to."

Saffron bit back another sarcastic smile.

"You're right, your highness, unseelie Prince Cylvan. I swear to never insult you again."

"Good. Back in your place where you belong."

Cylvan papped Saffron on the knee, then smacked him with a flip of hair while standing. "Come on, it's midnight. I need to get some sleep."

"Oh! Can't you—can't you leave me here?" Saffron scrambled

to his feet, clutching the enormous book. "I promise I won't get into any trouble!"

"Considering the number of holes in the promises you've already made me, I doubt that."

Cylvan clearly hoped for Saffron to argue more, like it was his favorite game, but Saffron just grimaced.

"Alright. That's... fair. Only small holes, though, really... Well —can I take some books home with me, then? Isn't that a normal thing to do? I promise I won't burn these ones—" he tripped over his half-circle wall of texts, glancing back as he'd launched one into the nearby shelf.

"Burn... *these ones?*" Cylvan muttered, but paused when Saffron met him at the end of the aisle with a look of sincerity. Cylvan just pursed his lips, before nudging Saffron away and shaking his head.

"Not tonight, beantighe. Earn some of my genuine trust first. There are actual reasons I'm not helping you in your search, and borrowing texts like the ones you want would go against those reasons."

"Oh..." Saffron trailed off, but barely felt the sting of the dismissal, replaced by curiosity. "What reasons?"

"None of your concern," Cylvan answered, flipping hair into Saffron's face again before making his way down the stairs. Saffron huffed, hurrying back to his squirrel's nest and gathering all his things to return them where they belonged.

Racing down the stairs to meet Cylvan at the bottom, he tripped on the very last step and crashed into the prince's arms. Cylvan just pushed him right-side up again, telling him to *"take it easy,"* but the bird in Saffron's chest was going wild.

"Will you come again tomorrow?" he asked, trying to keep up as Cylvan made a direct line for the exit. "I feel like I've already learned so much! Like the proper way to spell unseelie, or how to find the books I want! You know I didn't realize there were so many things people have written about? And this is only one library! And—you know, even after only one night, I'm confident

I can find the spell you need. So can we meet again tomorrow night? Oh, *please*, Prince—!"

"Terrier."

"... What?"

"Ah, yes, I'm sure of it. Fox terrier, specifically."

"I—I don't know what that means."

Cylvan opened the door for himself to leave, allowing it to smack Saffron in the face. Before Saffron could complain, Cylvan just turned to him with his eyebrows raised.

"Fox terriers love jobs, don't you? That's why you became a beantighe."

"... What??"

"How about this—from this point forward, if I am not waiting for you here when the sun sets, spend your evening snooping around listening for what the other students are saying about me. You seem like you'd be very good at that."

He turned and continued walking, Saffron standing confused at the bottom of the library steps before hurrying to follow.

"I'm not sure I understand—"

"I was perfectly clear."

"... So we're *not* meeting tomorrow night?"

Cylvan exhaled sharply. "I don't *know*. Don't you have, like— hobbies? Little human parties you can attend? Dinner to eat? More rocks to dig up? Fish to catch with your hands? Anything else to keep you busy on the days I don't have the strength for you?"

Saffron smiled awkwardly, trying to remain polite as Cylvan seemed to just keep quickening his pace. "I'm just... excited to help you find your spell. And, I think, if I could spend all night, every night in the library, I would gladly give up everything else—"

"Well—I *wouldn't*."

"Oh—I mean, of course, I just—"

"*Cylvan?*"

A voice interrupted, making Saffron jump. He hurried to pull his veil over his face just as Lord Taran emerged from the shadows of the neighboring lecture hall. He gave Saffron a distrustful look before turning his attention to Cylvan, whose shoulders slumped as he rolled his eyes. Despite standing at equal heights, the way Taran spoke could have fooled Saffron into thinking he was twice as large.

"I have been looking everywhere for you," he growled, grabbing Cylvan's arm. "Where the fuck have you been?"

"Studying," Cylvan answered easily. "How was the fete?"

"Obviously I didn't stay long when you never showed up. Why didn't you tell me you weren't coming?"

"I didn't realize you were my chaperone for the night."

Taran's jaw clenched like he wanted to spew acid instead of words, turning sharply to Saffron next and shouting for him to *fuck off*. Saffron jumped again, offering a quick bow and having to physically resist sprinting away. Just before he was far enough to escape eavesdropping, he heard the final words Taran said:

"Don't you dare ever speak to me like that again."

Its vitriol compelled Saffron to throw one last glance over his shoulder, watching as Cylvan pulled his arm free of Taran's grip. He thought back to that tense moment in Cylvan's suite, in the wardrobe, where they intentionally hid from the fey lord. How Cylvan's pulse raced like he faced down a wild animal rather than his friend.

Friend? Dorm-mate? Lover?

Shaking his head, deciding it was not only *not his business* but that he also *didn't particularly care*, Saffron hurried to Agate Bridge, moving swiftly through the dark woods back to Beantighe Village. He arrived around one in the morning, doing his damndest to stay silent while creeping through the front door and up the stairs, trained with exactly where to step so nothing squeaked beneath his weight. But upon slipping into Fern Room, he immediately knew something was off. Letty wasn't snoring.

A match struck. Letty sat straight up in bed, curly blonde hair pulled back into a bonnet.

"Do you mind explaining where you've been all night? *Again?*"

He glanced around the room, finding Fleece and Berry tangled up in one another on Fleece's bed. Fleece was also wide awake, wearing a conspiratorial smile as they curled pieces of Berry's hair around a finger.

"Yeah, Saffron. Go on. We want names," Fleece reiterated.

"I wasn't sleeping with anyone," Saffron insisted with an embarrassed smile, glancing at Letty before tugging off his veil and stripping down to his braies. Pulling on his sleep shirt from the trundle, he collapsed into bed, breathing in the smell of Hollow on the pillow and observing the pixie offerings on the nightstand. Letty and Fleece, meanwhile, didn't look convinced. Berry just stirred in his sleep, muttering something about lake monsters stealing his lunch.

"I mean it!" Saffron said, sitting up and blowing out Letty's accusatory match. "It's nothing. Just go to sleep."

But as his friends settled into their pillows, Saffron's mind wouldn't stop racing. Finally, he cleared his throat, and Fleece sat up expectantly.

"Do any of you, um... know what a *fox terrier* is?"

10

THE PREOCCUPATION

Another day, another disappointing evening.

And another. And another. Saffron needed to learn not to get his hopes up so much every afternoon, but like clockwork, as soon as his shadow started stretching long, he couldn't help but wiggle his fingers in anticipation. Smile. Forget to breathe.

Or maybe that was the persistent sludge in his chest. Every night as he went to bed following another Cylvan no-show, sipping Silk's teas to keep the coughing at bay, he told himself he would wake up in the morning refreshed and better than ever.

Instead, he seemed to only grow worse. It became harder to open his eyes. Harder to stand the weight of his own limbs. Just sitting up left him trembling and breathless, hunching over his knees and fighting to get a hold of himself. More than once, Letty attempted to coax him back into bed, but every time, Saffron could only think of one thing—what if that was the night Cylvan finally waited for him outside the library? The simple hope pushed him to his feet, forced his spinning head to slow. He clambered down the stairs where Baba made him drink medicinal teas from her magic cups, which helped to clear him out at least until he got to campus. At least once he was on his feet and working, it was easier to remain upright. It was getting to his feet that remained the biggest hurdle.

Three days without a step into the library felt like years, stretched long like hot candy, cooled and on the verge of breaking with even a breath of added weight. Watching Prince Cylvan from afar in the meantime was both relieving and perpetually infuriating—a reassurance that he was still on campus; a reassurance that he was purposefully choosing parties and social events over Saffron's fate.

Though since their first session, Cylvan no longer disregarded him entirely when they crossed paths. Saffron was even occasionally sought out on purpose, as more than once, while hunched over a flower bed digging up weeds and resisting the urge to cough, a finger tapped him on the shoulder. And each time he turned to find Cylvan, who asked for directions to the botany clearing in the woods, or where to make dorm-repair requests, or who to talk to about a snag in his uniform. Every time, Saffron rolled his eyes, straightened up, wiped sweat from his forehead, caught his breath, and provided his most polite and thorough response. Cylvan never said thank you, only nodded and walked away.

Meanwhile, whenever he witnessed the continued push and pull between Prince Cylvan and Lord Taran, his curiosity always got the better of him. How Cylvan always provided Taran his most charming, sparkling smile, before turning away and letting it drop when he thought no one could see. How Taran never seemed to smile with Cylvan at all, and always spoke to him in close, as if every conversation had to be in secret. How whenever another student approached them, they always greeted Taran first, pausing before acknowledging the literal prince right next to him.

Saffron stewed over the dynamic aimlessly and endlessly, made easy by the mindless chores he was given day after day. Scraping scum from the ponds in the Elathan Gardens, sweeping lecture halls, helping Cauldra package foodstuffs to be taken to Beantighe Village, cleaning the hooves of student horses in the stables.

He started to stop by the library in the mornings again, standing on his toes and peeking inside wistfully. Appreciating the sight in the daytime, whispering that he hoped to visit that night if the unseelie lord would let him. While stepping inside at all had been like something from a dream, Saffron still craved a moment within the walls when sun spilled through the windows, when there were other students amongst the shelves grabbing books for classes, just... the feeling of being there because he was meant to be, rather than as a secret.

At the rate Cylvan intended on helping him, though, Saffron was beginning to feel like he might not even get much time as a secret, either.

On the fourth morning, when assigned to collect raven feathers for Morrígan's only human staffer, Professor Adelard, Saffron decided to use it to his advantage. If Cylvan was going to drip-feed his access to the library, then Saffron would just have to seek more information elsewhere. And Adelard was a walking library, especially once Saffron got him talking.

As a professor of anthropology and biology, Adelard had helped to identify and properly label more than half the things in Saffron's sketchbook, and always seemed eager to hear about his adventures and the wild fey behaviors he observed. Even after years, Saffron still had to read many of his descriptions out loud as the educated man couldn't always make sense of his attempted spellings, but Adelard never mocked or laughed. He never offered to correct Saffron's spelling, either, to avoid the appearance of *teaching a beantighe*—but the fact he listened at all was enough to make Saffron feel... important, in the saddest of ways.

Gathering feathers from the raven paddock alongside Lake Elatha, Saffron scowled at the cerulean water and blooming lily-pads, wondering if they were what made his chest so tight—and a forgotten memory suddenly poked to the surface, like a frog emerging from a frozen pond in spring.

"I will forgive you when you have earned it, Night Prince."

Frowning more, he kicked a stone into the water with a humble *thwunk*. Even just standing on the edge reminded him of Elluin's punishment, the words on his back, Kaelar telling him to *wash up* before throwing him in. He'd assumed that strange conversation on the banks had only been a dream, or perhaps overheard from students passing by...

Shaking his head, he just adjusted his veil, counted the feathers in his hand, and determined them to be enough to buy a session with the human professor.

In the Nemain Lecture Building, Saffron waited outside the anthropology hall where he could hear Professor Adelard's voice muffled through the doors. Keeping his eyes down, he rolled back and forth on his heels as the occasional student passed by, just trying to blend in to the stone walls and marble floor. When the class finally let out, he was almost crushed beneath the wooden door that sprung open and belched out maroon-clad students, pressing himself flatter until the tide ebbed and he could peek inside. At the base of the tall room, he spotted the short, black-haired, bespectacled human trying to gather far too many things at the front podium.

As a human student in Alfidel before the veil closed, Adelard had been fortunate enough to step into professorhood right before Queen Proserpina entered her reign and made it impossible for humans to ascend past elevated beantighehood. Even the high fey students treated him like anyone else, despite his round ears and obvious ring of perpetuity that kept him an energetic mid-thirty year old, human age-wise. He never gave Saffron a straight answer when asked how old he *really* was.

"Professor?" Saffron invited himself inside. Adelard recognized his voice and greeted him by name, grinning and clapping his hands together when Saffron waved his bundle of feathers. Thanking him and taking the offering, Adelard turned right around and asked if Saffron had a moment to help carry some things back to his office. Saffron had been anticipating it.

Balancing an armful of tall scrolls printed with anatomy drawings, a stack of heavy books, a jar of something that looked like it belonged inside a body, and a stack of lecture notes, Saffron kept close to the chatty professor as they crossed back to the Administration Building. Stepping into his office, Saffron tripped over the upturned rug on the floor, but managed to slam all of Adelard's things on his already-cluttered desk without any casualties.

Adelard's office never changed, always cluttered to the brim with knick-knacks, books, skeletons—and every time Saffron had a chance to step inside, he found something new to grab his interest and make him spin with silent questions. Biting them back was even more difficult that morning, wanting to exclaim everything he'd seen and learned in his first library session, but— even in private, Saffron knew to always be aware of lines and boundaries and places they shouldn't cross. Despite being a legitimate professor, an expert in his field, Adelard's humanity also meant his position perpetually balanced on Elluin's mood, who might gladly use any reason she could find to accuse him of stepping out of bounds. It was one of many reasons Adelard wasn't an option in endorsing Saffron, either—an unspoken frustration that ate Saffron alive every time they crossed paths.

Sitting in one of the creaky chairs with legs pulled up into his chest, Saffron's eyes skimmed the books stacked on top of each other at the edge of the checkered floor, Adelard apologizing for the mess as he fixed his rug then swiftly poured Saffron a cup of day-old tea to drink. Saffron barely took two sips before Adelard asked all about the sprite infestation in Danann House on Imbolc, catching Saffron off guard. Apparently they'd tried to rope Adelard into purging them, first, but obviously Adelard had more important things to do, so he recommended Saffron for the job, instead. Saffron didn't know whether to thank or curse him.

Describing how he'd used raven feathers to lure them out, searched through individual irises to remove their drunken bodies, and used a glass jar and cloth topper to keep them, Adelard scribbled madly on a piece of parchment the whole time.

It always made Saffron smile, the pure giddiness radiating off the human professor warming him to the bones.

"I actually had a question about that..." Saffron went on. "Do wild fey like pixies and sprites have *true names?*"

"T-true names, child? Where did you hear about those?" Adelard asked after dribbling his tea in surprise. Saffron's thoughts scrambled. Was that something he wasn't supposed to know?

"Oh, um... I heard some students joking about them."

Whether Adelard believed him or not didn't matter, because the professor accepted that lie with ease. As if all he really wanted was something to use, himself, if their conversations ever came into question. Wiping the front of his tartan suit, he cleared his throat.

"I do not believe wild fey have true names, no—that is a high fey tradition, as far as I know."

"Do all high fey have two names, then? Are they born with them? Or are they given?" Saffron went on, keeping his voice casual and sipping at his own cold tea. With Adelard's first show of surprise, Saffron knew he was already walking close to the line where the professor would cross, bumble, get flustered, and then nudge Saffron out in embarrassment.

"Both are given, just like our names are given to us," Adelard nodded, but clearly picked his words.

"Why don't humans get true names?"

"Because we are already compellable enough, don't you think?" the professor's nerves clicked.

"Well—why would the high fey give themselves true names, if it just makes them compellable, too? If they didn't use true names, would they be non-compellable? Seems silly to me..."

"Oh, dear," Adelard fumbled his tea again, and Saffron knew they were reaching critical mass. "Who's to say true names aren't a protection rather than a vulnerability, hm? Perhaps narrowing a person's vulnerability to a single word protects them from a more general compellability, and then by hiding that vulnerability they become... well... ah, would you look at the time, Saffron, I wouldn't want to keep you from your other chores!"

Saffron sighed, but placed his drink on the professor's desk so it wouldn't spill as Adelard engaged in his standard *time to go before I say anything else!* dance of self-preservation. That was fine, Saffron had learned how to anticipate and work with it—and Adelard had given him plenty to consider, even if it didn't offer any more clues about his geis with Cylvan, specifically.

PERHAPS PUT IN THE MOOD BY HIS CONVERSATION WITH the professor, Saffron sparked a heated debate with Letty that afternoon about whether wall paint could *go bad*, Letty assuring him the entire way to the Pallas Lecture Hall that the paint they had was *fine*, it was going to be a perfect match, she would bet her dessert on it—only for Saffron to burst out laughing when her swatch was yellow compared to what they needed. She just muttered curses under her breath, stirring the thick pigmented slop with vigor while insisting it was only because the powder had separated from the oils, when a familiar finger tapped Saffron on the shoulder.

Closing his eyes, he exhaled through his nose in exasperation, before turning and getting to his feet. Letty followed, offering the prince a polite bow as well, but Cylvan only acknowledged Saffron.

"Can I pretend to yell at you?" he asked, and Saffron made a face of *"excuse me?"*. Cylvan sighed in frustration. "Quickly. Please. I need to be fully preoccupied."

"I'd really rather—"

"What the *fuck* is wrong with you, you godsdamn round-eared moron? Do you really believe a mere apology can make up for splattering paint on my shoes? What are you, incompetent? I should have your hands stapled to your ass, you know that?"

Saffron watched him boredly. He let Cylvan go on and on with whatever he felt he needed to, on the verge of interrupting to tell him about the school counselor if he really needed to blow off steam—but then he spotted Taran suddenly enter at the other end of the corridor and look up and down in search. He had the same look on his face that he did the first time in the suite—one of someone on the hunt. Saffron stiffened, eyes quickly flashing back to Cylvan, who continued to ramble. He thought again about Cylvan's racing heart as they hid in the wardrobe. How Taran had grabbed him so roughly outside the library.

Snatching his brush, Saffron actually splattered the tiniest amount of white paint across the toes of Cylvan's shoes. The prince erupted into nearly a shriek as his anger detonated into something far more believable.

"Threaten to take me to Elluin. Come on, drag me away," Saffron muttered beneath Cylvan's insults. Cylvan's words fumbled before burying a claw in Saffron's arm and announcing his intention to do just that. Saffron just offered Letty an apologetic smile, stumbling as Cylvan dragged him opposite Taran's direction.

Cylvan didn't thank him that time, either, standing behind the lecture hall as Saffron wiped the paint from his shoes.

"As if it never happened," Saffron told him, getting back to his feet before adding: "There's a cluster of study rooms without windows in the Erce Lecture Hall. They make excellent hiding places."

"I'll remember that," Cylvan said. Saffron took it as the closest thing he might get to a real *thank you*, and sighed.

"Is there anything else I can help you with, my lord? Otherwise—"

"Actually—" but the door behind them clicked, and Saffron yelped when Cylvan dragged him into the bushes. A hand clamped against his mouth, and he rolled his eyes as Taran stuck his head through, gave a brief glance up and down the walkway, and pulled the door shut again.

"Why do *I* have to get pulled down into the mud as well?" he asked. "I'm literally wearing white."

"I thought beantighes loved mud. You gave me a handful of muddy treasures just the other day."

Saffron sighed again and pushed himself to his feet, coughing into his elbow before offering Cylvan a hand up as well. The prince was heavy despite his lithe form, Saffron not bracing well enough and plummeting back into Cylvan's chest with one tug.

His face went hotter than Baba's medicinal drinks, attempting to stand again, but Cylvan grabbed his wrist and yanked him back as a few more students passed. Hanging over him, waist caught between Cylvan's bent knees, hardly a few inches from his handsome face as they waited for the walkway to clear, Saffron found it hard to breathe for an entirely different reason. Namely—Cylvan smelled of fresh pine and gardenia, making Saffron's insides feel sunshiny.

He turned his gaze down, to the right, then up, trying not to meet Cylvan's eyes, but knowing the prince kept his own gaze on Saffron the whole time.

"What's wrong?" Cylvan finally teased. "I thought you liked being—"

"Between your legs?" Saffron muttered, seeing it coming from a mile away. "It's... your perfume. It's making my eyes burn. Why are you wearing so much?"

"*Hm.* Perhaps I wear *so much* to block out you stinking beantighes. *You* smell like..." Cylvan leaned in, pressing his nose into Saffron's veil beneath his ear as if he really wanted Saffron's heart to stop. "Creek water and shit. Are you sure it's only mud?"

Saffron couldn't resist a smirk when the walkway cleared and he could finally shove Cylvan away. Rising to his feet, Saffron adjusted his veil as Cylvan emerged behind him. He proceeded to brush grass and hedge leaves from the prince's uniform without thinking, before pulling his hands away and apologizing.

"Will you... be at the library tonight, your highness?" he

prompted next, watching as Cylvan pulled a twig from the flap of his shoulder bag and flicked it away.

"Perhaps. I have another party invitation, but to be honest, I'm tired of them. Unless you agree to come and entertain me again, of course."

"No, thanks."

Cylvan smiled in a way that gave Saffron goosebumps, habitually smoothing wrinkles out of his blouse. He swallowed back another round of coughing before shaking his head.

"Well—I guess I should get back to Letty so we can finish repainting the wall... Um, the next time you want to run from Lord Taran, you don't have to scream insults at me, either, you could always just... I don't know. Would you like a secret phrase?"

"Sounds fun. Why not, *'I need you to get Taran off my ass'*?"

"Huh. Admittedly, I expected more from someone at the top of his class. Goodbye."

Saffron left Cylvan chuckling on the walkway, touching the place below his ear where the prince had nestled his nose. *You smell like the creek.*

It made Saffron laugh as he rounded the corner of the building, walking straight into someone waiting for him. Saffron went stiff at the sight of Lord Kaelar, hands tucked in his pockets and wearing a curious smile.

"Since when were you so friendly with the prince of darkness?"

He barely caught a breath before Kaelar twisted him into a headlock, and everything that followed happened in a rush. Claims of a ghost in the woods resembling Arrow, and how Saffron was the only one who could appease them; his veil being torn away, wadded up, and shoved in his mouth; the belt from Kaelar's peacoat cinching Saffron's wrists together before he was dragged off campus and tied to a tree out of sight.

. . .

It was already long dark before someone found him, slumped against the tree and shivering, drool dripping from his mouth still cramped open with the chiffon. By the time they cut Saffron down and slung him over Hollow's shoulders to be carried back to Beantighe Village, Saffron's wrists were bruised, his fingers stiff from the cold, his mind spinning as even his insides trembled. All he could think was—would Cylvan be angry that Saffron made him wait?

11

THE FEVER

It was a different teacup spell Baba Yaga gave when the curse was a fever. When he was drowning in his own lungs, when he couldn't feel his hands from the cold, when his whole body suddenly weighed six times as much and he couldn't balance on his feet. The next morning when he tried, he buckled to the floor like a sack of flour, and Letty bodily forced him back into bed. Hollow took her place when she had to leave for assignments, pinning Saffron against the blankets as Saffron thrashed, dripping with sweat, shivering, fading in and out of consciousness, mumbling nonsense, coughing, choking, suffocating.

No one seemed to know if the fever was from the infection on his back or the sludge in his lungs. Baba just paced the room, bringing him more teas, asking Silk what she thought, before kicking everyone out, removing Saffron's patron ring, and pushing up his nightshirt to smear thick paste in a circle around his chest. He just stared up at the ceiling with a drunken smile, watching as the orange house cat floated between rafters and chased dust motes. No one else ever saw the cat float around like Saffron did, fat stomach dangling like a plum on a tree as if the levitation only worked on its front legs.

He giggled and squirmed when Baba applied something

particularly icy down the center of his ribs. He wanted to tell her he was fine, he just needed to sleep, he'd wake up again totally refreshed like always... but then recalled his promise to meet Cylvan at the library that night.

He couldn't quite recall why he was back in bed in the middle of the day in the first place. Or how he got there. Or why the sun was so low and sun singers were chirping. Or how his conversation with the prince even ended. Or where Cylvan went after that. In fact, all of his memories globbed around like thick cabbage soup without a spoon.

All he knew was—he needed to get going, or he would be late.

Despite Baba watching over him for what felt like hours, how he fell asleep a few times, had at least two meals, and then slept some more, he still managed to leave Cottage Wicklow with enough time to spare. It was even easier to escape when Baba hurried away to discuss something with the other henmothers about *cloth* or *the wolf* or *the woods*, though the rest of the words were quickly swallowed by Saffron's mental soup.

The sun was on the edge of setting when he hurried from Beantighe Village, pushing himself to chase the remaining light. Crunching through undergrowth and using trees as support whenever he got too dizzy, the fresh air offered him just enough clarity to avoid the road. For some reason, he was sure if anyone saw him out and about, they would force him back into bed.

He wasn't that sick. He would never be too sick to miss a night in the library, anyway. Not when his chances were so rare.

Approaching campus from the side of the trees, the sun barely passed the horizon, stars peeking through velvety clouds that made the air smell like rain. Saffron grinned with hands outstretched to catch the first icy drops, before wobbling when the ground tilted slightly beneath him.

When Cylvan wasn't waiting for him outside, Saffron thought nothing of it. The prince said he'd come, and Saffron trusted him. Wait—did he? Since when?

"Since always," he argued stubbornly, taking a seat outside the doors and crossing his legs. The cool air felt good on his skin—until sweat soaked through his doublet, and he pushed it off. But that turned the rainy breeze into needles, so he pulled it back on. Then he dripped even more with a rush of heat, groaning and pulling it off again with chattering teeth. All of the movement made his back ache, trying to remember if Baba reapplied his bandages after wiping him down earlier.

What was taking Cylvan so long?

Saffron coughed into his elbow, pink-tinged spit trailing when he pulled away.

Had the prince chosen to attend his party after all?

Just as Saffron weakly pushed himself to his feet to go searching, a horned shadow appeared at the bottom of the library steps. He looked breathless, cheeks flushed, hair askew, as if caught up in a whirlwind right before turning the corner. His eyebrows raised upon spotting Saffron, Saffron just looking back at him in question.

"Where were you last night?" Cylvan finally asked, climbing the stairs as his expression shifted into ice. "I waited for you!"

Saffron blinked a few times when Cylvan was suddenly close, jabbing a pointy nail into his chest. Saffron licked his lips, taking Cylvan's hand and holding it, not sure what else to do.

"Was I not here?" he questioned with a frown, swimming in his cabbage-soup brain and pressing Cylvan's fingers against his forehead as the chill of them was heavenly. "Wait... oh, maybe I was... tied to a tree. Or was I painting your shoes? Hollow carried me... It's... all sort of a blur..."

"... *What?*" Cylvan asked in exasperation, yanking his hand away. But before Saffron could try and clarify, someone called out Cylvan's name from around the corner, and the prince snapped up to stare across the lantern-lit walkway.

Saffron frowned more, instantly troubled by the look of apprehension on Cylvan's face. He felt a sudden rush of protectiveness, grabbing Cylvan's hand again. His boiling brain summoned words to his mouth:

"Do you need me to... beat Taran's ass? No, I mean—get him off my ass. Your ass. Your highness."

Cylvan turned back to Saffron slowly, and Saffron realized, perhaps he wasn't as alright as he originally thought. Cylvan just opened his mouth to say something, before closing it again. Without another word, he grabbed Saffron by the arm and shoved him through the doors.

THAT NIGHT, CYLVAN DIDN'T LIGHT ANY CANDLES. HE glanced toward the doors repeatedly, especially when there were noises on the other side. Saffron knew they were only students exploring past curfew, or night-shift beantighes getting work done as normal, but Cylvan went still every time. He barely said anything at all, except to hiss when Saffron spoke too loudly, or accidentally dropped a book, or coughed a little too much.

Saffron wanted to ask what was wrong, despite knowing it definitely had something to do with Lord Taran. But unlike their first night in the library, Cylvan seemed to want nothing to do with Saffron at all, like he was annoyed Saffron was even there. As if something in the prince's flawless facade had cracked, and Saffron could see the little porcelain chips left behind on the floor, at the study table, on his shoulder. But instead of picking them up and offering them back, Saffron just disappeared into his little corner on the balcony and hunched over his books.

Except the books suddenly weren't books, they were portals of rushing water. Sweeping the text away, soaking the paper through until the words all blurred together and Saffron couldn't read them at all. One by one, he tried to find a single volume that hadn't been drenched, worried there was a leak in the ceiling where rain poured through—but when he shouted down at Cylvan in concern, the prince just slammed a hand against the table and commanded him to be quiet.

He hadn't taken them outside to wash in the creek, did he? As much as he loved washing books in the creek, he couldn't quite remember. Was he in the rainy section? He tried to find where the dry books were, weaving in and out and around all the aisles. He wanted to search the floor below, too, but couldn't remember how to get down.

Soon the water soaked into his clothes, blouse clinging to him like paper on a wet rock. His hair dripped no matter how many times he slicked it back. He couldn't stop shivering, wrapping arms around himself and quietly begging the library's chilly breeze to leave him alone. Where was the warm spot he'd sat in the first time? Why couldn't he find it again?

In his frantic search for a warm place to sit, he found a single-person study table at one end of the shelves, tucked between the window and the aisle. So well hidden that Saffron nearly tripped over it. Dragging his fingers up and down the surface, he considered hiking his own waterlogged books over to get them off the floor and let them air out... but then thought of the frightened raven on the floor below, afraid of the doors and voices on the other side. Maybe if... the raven couldn't see the doors... or hear the voices... he might cheer up. And then maybe he would help Saffron find somewhere to sit, where the books stayed still and didn't go blurry whenever he tried to read them.

With thoughts churning slow like milk to butter, Saffron searched for the stairs until he found them, then approached the big, grouchy raven at the lower table.

Cylvan held himself tightly, bent over a piece of parchment with two textbooks open, though his quill never moved. It just hovered over the paper, a few drops of ink indicative of his long pause.

Tapped on the shoulder, Cylvan whirled so fast he nearly ripped the chair into pieces, making Saffron squeak and jump backward.

"What the fuck do you want, beantighe!" he shouted—but once the shock wore off, Saffron just smiled. Cylvan was so handsome, even when he was angry. Such a pretty bird.

He reached out, clasping one of the prince's talons. Cylvan

snatched it away with another hiss, but Saffron shook his head with a pout and took it again, before patting him on the shoulder.

"It's alright," he said. "Come here. Come with me. Come on~ I'm just a leanan sídhe here to seduce you, and I say come upstairs with me, please."

"What the fuck?" Cylvan grumbled, but Saffron just tugged on his hand again. Finally, Cylvan threw his head back with a groan and got out of his chair with a kick.

"Why are you so sweaty?" he asked next, but Saffron was busy searching for the stairs again, pulling Cylvan up them while clutching his hand the entire time. He lost his footing at the top, crumpling to the floor with a yelp before hopping up again, still never letting go.

It took a few rounds between the shelves until Saffron found the little desk again. Stopping next to it, he appreciated the sight, before turning and smiling at Cylvan. The prince just made another face of annoyance, and Saffron saw complaints forming on his perfect mouth.

"It's safe," he insisted, pushing more sweaty hair from his eyes before pointing. "Do your homework here, bird."

"Bird?" Cylvan muttered, before turning his nose up at the desk. "I'm not going to be relegated to—"

But Saffron yanked him forward, shoving him into the seat with a clatter and a net of hair. Cylvan glared at him, attempting to jump right back up again—but Saffron planted his hands on Cylvan's shoulders. He squeezed them a little on accident, making a small sound of interest.

"Oh... strong bird," he whispered, world spinning more as he flushed over his already-raging fever. Pulling his hands away, he put them up again.

"Safe here," he promised. "Taran won't be able to find you. I'll watch you. And if he comes inside—I'll jump on him. From the balcony. He won't see me. Um—like a ceffyl-dŵr."

"... I thought you were a leanan sídhe."

Saffron smiled coyly, putting a hand on his hip and leaning against the shelf.

"Are you impressed?"

"... With what, beantighe?"

"How much I know."

"... About?"

Saffron opened his mouth, closed it, rolled his eyes with a sarcastic smile, then looked at Cylvan more pointedly. Admittedly —he'd forgotten what they were talking about, hoping maybe Cylvan had, too. Cylvan just pulled another face of confusion, before tapping his fingers on the desk.

"I don't quite know what's happening, and that's all very fine and good—but I don't have any of my *things* here, so I can't *study* here," he smiled just as sarcastically, tapping his finger on the desk again. "Do you understand? Or am I to just sit in silence while you sweat all over the floor?"

Saffron put his hands up again. He pulled a random book from the closest shelf and gently tucked it into Cylvan's hands.

"Read this. I'll get your things."

"Use the stairs, púca!" Cylvan called out when Saffron briefly considered the balcony as a way down, making him jump and hurry away.

It took three trips, a storm of coughing, two bruised knees, a long minute of forgetting where he was, getting startled more than once by Derdriu on the ceiling, and a bloody nose to carry all of Cylvan's stationary, books, shoulder bag, coat, and parchment to his desk, not including the number of times Saffron lost him in a panic and had to cry out for directions. Cylvan watched him the entire time, asking if Saffron tripped again when he saw the smeared blood on Saffron's lip. Saffron just shook his head, handing Cylvan his parchment with a few red thumbprints on the front.

Cylvan handed the random book back.

"Did you read?" Saffron smiled.

"Oh, yes. The entire thing."

"The... entire thing? Really?" he asked, immediately discouraged. "You're... so fast."

"Yes, and you're terribly *slow* and *noisy* like a toad." Cylvan's polite smile went tight. "And now that you've carted all my shit up here, I'm going to ask you to take it all back."

"N-no!" Saffron insisted, slamming the book back on the desk. "I..."

He trailed off, tongue turning to cotton in his mouth.

"I can keep you safe up here!" he finally exclaimed, and Cylvan glared at him. "Just! Just stay here and stop being so mean, you stubborn bird!"

"Stop calling me a bird!" Cylvan shouted, but Saffron snatched the feather quill and tucked it into the prince's hair, running away when Cylvan snarled at him.

Despite all the stubbornness and complaining, the prince did remain in the little desk at the end of the aisle. He uncorked his ink and started writing, flipping through his textbook and mumbling under his breath as the nib scribbled across parchment pages. It allowed Saffron to relax, too, though it didn't help to quell the hot fog cooking his insides like bread.

His return to the shelves still didn't result in anything legible, either. No text stood clear on the pages long enough for him to follow, words washing away in that feverish water that infiltrated his lungs more and more and made it more difficult to breathe as the hours ticked by.

Every time he had to cough, he hurried as far as he could from where the prince sat, crouching on the balls of his feet and pulling his arm into his mouth to silence it. Sometimes he coughed so hard he slumped onto his knees, gasping wet breaths that left the whole world spinning, sweat dripping into his eyes and making them burn, mixing with strained tears as he suffocated.

Once, Cylvan even called out to him in the middle of a fit. Saffron croaked back an apology, trying to hold his breath as more body-jolting coughs attempted to escape—but they eventually erupted hard enough that red spit smeared across the back of his hand, and he could only frown down at it in spinning frustration.

In brief moments where his lungs settled, he floated behind the ornery bird just to peek at what he was writing, every time losing himself in the familiar letters he'd once fallen in love with. He didn't realize how much he missed appreciating Cylvan's handwriting, and had to resist reaching out to touch it on the page as he passed by. But as Cylvan glanced over his shoulder and asked what he wanted on yet another less-than-subtle appraisal, Saffron grew a little bolder.

"Um..." he whispered, holding his hands behind his back and leaning over the prince's shoulder. "How do you spell... *quartz?*"

Cylvan sat back in his chair. "Q—"

"No!" Saffron huffed, pointing. "Will you write it for me?"

Cylvan rolled his eyes, but sat forward again.

QUARTZ.

"Ohhh..." Saffron tried to sound aloof while his heart exploded in appreciation. "What about... um, what about *agate?*"

AGATE.

"B-Beantighe Village?"

BEANTIGHE VILLAGE.

Saffron smacked him on the arm. "Don't tease me!"

"What?" Cylvan asked in annoyance. "That's how it's spelled!"

"*Ban-tee*, Prince Cylvan! I thought you were supposed to be smart!"

"It's old Alvish!" Cylvan insisted, but then cracked a smile, like Saffron's incredulity finally pricked deep enough between his porcelain cracks to tickle.

"... Cottage Wicklow?"

COTTAGE WICKLOW.

"mag Shamhradháin?"

Even Cylvan paused on that request, before complimenting himself under his breath when he recalled the spelling and wrote it out. Saffron smiled more, grabbing Cylvan's shoulders and bouncing slightly. He was in the middle of requesting "Luvon" when Cylvan unexpectedly went off-script, writing something of his own:

BEANTIGHE SAFFRON MAKES A LOT OF IMPERTINENT DEMANDS.

Saffron's heart raced at the sight of his name—but the joy was quickly smothered by the word *impertinent,* making his breaths shudder as he was rushed back to that morning on his knees in Elluin's office. He tried not to sink too deeply into the memory, treading water of the reawakened agony, fingers trembling as his back throbbed hotter.

"Wh-what does that word mean?" he asked quietly. "'Impertinent'?"

"Bold. Annoying. Disrespectful," Cylvan answered easily, writing the word again, larger with more flourishes.

Saffron slowly pulled his hands away, wringing them together. He saw Elluin's wallpaper smeared with Arrow's blood. He heard Elluin's excitement as Taran prepared the needle. He rubbed his thumb over the spot on his palm where he'd been poked for the silver to taste and learn him. He felt the first drag through his skin—

"Do you... really think so?" Saffron asked weakly. Cylvan turned with a sarcastic smile—but it faded when he met Saffron's eyes. His throat shifted as he swallowed back whatever he meant to say, looking back down at the paper.

"Erm... no, not really, I suppose," he muttered, tearing the parchment away and turning it facedown on the desk. He sat motionless for another moment, before dipping the nib and adjusting how he sat.

"What else?"

Saffron bit his lip. He leaned in again, carefully returning his hands to Cylvan's shoulders. Cylvan shifted, but didn't pull away, just hovering his pen over the blank page.

"Will you... write my name again?" Saffron asked in a tiny voice.

"Hmmm," Cylvan twirled the feather.

PÚCA.

"You mean like that?"

"N-no!" Saffron giggled, though it took him a moment of swimming through the fog to figure out whether that was true or not. He squeezed Cylvan's shoulders in disapproval. "My real name!"

"Ah, right, of course," Cylvan re-dipped his pen.

BEANTIGHE PÚCA.

"No! You stupid prince!" Saffron complained, shaking him. Cylvan apologized again, *swearing* he would get it right the third time. Finally, Saffron watched with a dancing heart as his name fluttered across the page.

SAFFRON DÉ PATRON DÉ MAG SHAMHRADHÁIN.

"Oh..." he breathed. He hopped on his toes slightly, giggling more. "You... make it look so beautiful."

"What else?"

"... What about *your* name?" Saffron requested, leaning in even closer as Cylvan obeyed.

DARK UNSEELIE PRINCE CYLVAN DÉ DAY KING AILIR AND HARMONIOUS KING TROSS AND PROGENITOR MOTHER NAOILL DÉ FIANNA DÉ TUATHA DÉ DANANN.

"Oh..." Saffron whispered. *"... Really?"*

Cylvan chuckled lightly.

"Of course not," he sighed, crossing out the unnecessary bits. "I was only teasing you again."

PRINCE CYLVAN DÉ TUATHA DÉ DANANN.

"Will you... take away those other parts, too?"

CYLVAN.

"Ah... that's how you wrote it in your book," Saffron whispered, not meaning for the words to come out so wistfully. "It's... strange to see it again. But it makes me happy..."

He smiled at the letters for a long time, allowing the horrible sights of Elluin's office to drown beneath the soft, lovely memories of his favorite stories... Cylvan's notes... spending long nights in the barn with only a candle... reading them again and again until he was sure he understood them... dreaming about the kind of person Cylvan must have been to love the same things he did...

"... What else, Saffron?" Cylvan coaxed under his breath, and Saffron emerged from his cloud.

"What about—" but a tickle caught the back of his throat, and he pulled back quickly, attempting to gulp it back. When it was stronger than he could fight, he shook his head in apology, turning to hurry away—but Cylvan put a hand out to stop him.

Before Saffron could explain, the fit claimed him, and he bent his knees to cough and hack into his elbow. It seemed to never end, hardly able to wheeze an inch of breath between the crushing pressure, cracking open his eyes once air finally whispered back into him. Gazing down at his sleeve, more red flecks of blood scattered like stars, surrounded by dark spots where new sweat had soaked into the fibers.

"S-sorry," Saffron croaked, pressing a hand to his head as the floor tilted under him. He knew it would pass, it always did, he just had to wait... but with Cylvan there watching him, his bones solidified in humiliation, and he struggled to lift his head. Suddenly he hated himself for ruining the light moment, knowing Cylvan would curse at him again, tell him to be quiet. Why couldn't he just have one moment of peace?

"I'll... let you get back to studying." He offered the prince a weak smile. Cylvan balked, grabbing Saffron before he wobbled straight back to the floor.

"Actually, Saffron, you know what?" he said. "I... hate being all by myself. What if someone comes and finds me while you're away? Why don't you stay and keep me safe, just in case?"

"O-oh, alright," Saffron's weak smile twitched higher. "Of course, your highness. I'll only step away when I have to—"

"No, no," Cylvan insisted, shepherding Saffron to the floor next to his desk. He quickly skimmed the shelf at his back, pulling a book and tucking it into Saffron's hands. "Here. *Opulence Amongst Wild Fey and Fairies;* that shouldn't be too hard to read."

"Um, alright..." Saffron smiled more in uncertainty. Cylvan paused for another moment, before getting back to his feet and returning to his things. Saffron watched him settle in, then addressed the book in his lap.

"Oh, thank god," he breathed, cracking it open to find the words on the page blurring slightly, but not washing away completely.

PRINCE CYLVAN WHISPERED TO HIMSELF WHILE HE wrote. The nib scratched as he argued under his breath, whether with himself or the author of whatever he studied, and Saffron closed his eyes and listened every time. Did he do that while leaving notes in the book of myths, too?

"It's cold in here tonight, don't you think?"

Saffron nodded. It wasn't long before he had his arms wrapped around himself, shivering like pixie wings, enough that his whole body was sore from clenching. Even when Cylvan draped his peacoat over his shoulders, Saffron couldn't draw it in close enough. He couldn't stop sweating. He couldn't stop coughing. Soon, even the words on his one dry book turned wet, printed letters drifting away as his eyes blurred with fever and dripping sweat.

"Why don't I take you to the healer, púca?"

Saffron clenched his teeth, shaking his head.

"Why not?"

"I-it won't m-matter," Saffron stammered, furrowing his brows. "I—I haven't saved up two days of meals, yet, mhh—m-maybe I'll start tomorrow, though..."

He hunched in closer to his knees, pressing a cough into his thigh.

"What does that mean?"

Saffron shook his head again, wiping sweat from his forehead, though it mostly just smeared as his sleeve was already soaked through.

"The—the campus healer won't see b-beantighes until they give up two—two days of meals, first. As payment."

Clack. Cylvan set his quill down, but Saffron insisted.

"If we go now—it would only w-waste your time. Besides— we don't know—where Lord Taran is, right? We should— shouldn't risk it, I don't think."

He managed to smile back at the prince, who watched him silently. Another stitch clutched his throat, and he coughed into his arm again, heaving with sticky breaths and slamming his feet in frustration.

"I'll wash your jacket for you," his voice crackled. "Sorry, I'm sorry..."

Pink spit dripped from his mouth as he tried to blink the spinning blur from his eyes, tried to clear his throat, tried to swallow back the tight dryness making it impossible to breathe.

"You're... not well, Saffron. You could have stayed home; I would have understood..."

Saffron managed a shaky smile and a laugh.

"This was... only my second time inside," he rasped. "Who— who knows when my next chance would be... I knew I couldn't risk it..."

His smile twitched in distress, pressing his hand to his head as it became difficult to find his mouth at all.

"I suppose, at least, at this rate... you won't have to w-worry about my tongue much longer, your highness, hah... and... you can keep... going t-to your... parties..."

Like creatures from a lightning strike, any remaining words fled as fire sparked between his eyes, devouring every inch of his mind in a second.

He slumped. Everything flickered away, like a candle snuffed in darkness.

When it wavered back, Cylvan's feet appeared, dropping to one knee.

Saffron's ears popped, and the world sank under water. Ebbing and cresting over him, allowing brief moments to lap and cross—only to sink away again just as lazily.

Hands took his face. Patting his cheeks and whispering his name.

They wiped sweaty hair from his forehead.

They lifted him from the floor. He dangled like a doll, the weight of his head and limbs straining the tenuous scabs connecting the words on his back.

From beneath the ebb, Saffron made out the watercolor shapes of—someone familiar. Someone he knew without knowing, someone he would recognize without ever having to see their face. Someone who—used to be there when he fell asleep at night.

"Cylvan..." he breathed with an uneven smile.

"... What do you need, Saffron?"

But Saffron just closed his eyes again, smile lingering as every part of his body found a different piece of gravity to cling to. A different tide of sand pulling him this way and that, slowly tearing him apart, drawn and quartered by his own fever.

"Brìghde... must finally be granting my wish," he said over the scraping of his bones. "Which one was your favorite, Cylvan...?"

"My favorite what, púca?"

"I always liked... Derdriu, or Niamh," Saffron answered, but wasn't sure how. He didn't know how he spoke without a tongue in his mouth. Still, Cylvan somehow heard it, because he eventually reponded:

"But Oisín and Niamh's story was so sad... don't you think?"

Saffron giggled, though it was stolen by the wind as the floor vanished beneath him. His arms dangled, chilled all the way to the tips of his fingers, as if dragging through creek water in winter. He tried to splash, but realized, perhaps it was all of him beneath the water. Needles poked every inch of his skin to prove it—except his chest, hot and biting enough to melt any tips that pricked.

"Though now I think... I like Eithlyn..." he went on, sinking forward into something soft. It smelled like... gardenia, and pine. "Who dreamed of Ciann before ever even meeting them..."

He'd lost his eyes entirely in the waves, somewhere, only starry skies up above as he drifted. He wondered if Luvon could see the stars, too. Were they just bright flickers of aura?

"Do you remember... how Ciann was a Tuatha dé Danann?" Cylvan asked, and Saffron laughed under his breath.

"Were they a prince, too? Ah..." he teased with a sigh. Something cupped the back of his head, holding him. He tried to find his eyes again, but there were only stars. Only stars, and warm breath, and gardenia and pine, and needles, and water, and wind. So much wind.

"I think I know how she felt..." he whispered at last. "I dreamed about you for a long time, too..."

The hand on the back of his head stiffened—before gently petting him.

"I'm sorry for disappointing you."

Saffron smiled. He giggled, nestling his face closer into the warmth.

"No," he whispered. "You can't disappoint me—not when you made me so happy..."

The hand flexed again, and pulled Saffron even closer. Every part of him protected. Hidden from the needles that dug.

"That's..." the voice returned, but the words snagged on the breeze. Saffron lost them between his fingers, sinking further into the wind, the ice, the dark water—until even the stars couldn't shine through.

12

THE MEDICINE

he wolf. The wolf.

Teeth buried into Saffron's back, piercing all the way through his flesh until bones crunched like ice beneath winter boots. Filling his lungs with blood until he exhaled like rain, coughing red fluid until each gasp was nothing more than a gargle. Harder, harder, the jaws clamped down, hot breath pluming from the beast's wrinkled nose, growling every time Saffron dared to even twitch.

Left in the woods, on the cold, muddy forest floor, begging anyone to come close enough for him to call out. To wheeze out a request for help—only to be abandoned in the dark until his eyes froze solid.

SAFFRON WOKE SLOWLY. ONE BY ONE, HIS SENSES plucked through the darkness, allowing him to perceive the crackling of fire, the smell of burning wood and breakfast foods, soft fur tickling the lower half of his face. When his eyes finally parted open, he had to blink a few times before his vision cleared enough to see, head pounding and drenched in sweat. His breaths came ragged as ever, eyes swollen and heavy and stinging as he glanced around.

Reclining on a thick-cushioned couch, Saffron's feet lay angled toward a fireplace easily as high as he was tall, and as wide as the couch where he lay. It was familiar—in fact, the entire room was familiar, and he might have known who it belonged to right away if his mind was anything more than dirty pond water and a thick haze. Still, he searched through the muck, like hunting for toads in forest ponds. Eventually, he grabbed something. A wriggling memory, slimy and slithering and hard to keep a hold of.

The library. Sinking into water. Stars. Pine trees and flowers.

Dredging deeper, he grasped other muddy moments like the roots of an oak tree: the sound of a violin; water dribbling down his chin, a mouth pressing into his lips and forcing him to drink; a hand touching his forehead and pushing damp hair from his face; a voice whispering, *"why aren't you waking up?"*

A rush of coughing claimed him, twisting his body into the crook of the cushions to muffle the sound. And while they came hard and gasping as ever, something about the coughs themselves was... different. Lighter, sharper. As if his lungs weighed less than before he fell asleep.

He was still fighting to catch his breath when the sound of a door opening caught his attention. Peeking out from under the blanket, he painfully glanced at the bedroom door, but it remained closed. He craned his neck in the opposite direction, slumping back into the cushions when he set eyes on the prince emerging from a steamy bathroom, hair hanging damp over his shoulders and wearing a flowery, black silk robe. He didn't mean to glare, though Cylvan appeared amused when he saw it.

Cylvan approached with his flushed skin, exposed chest, naked legs, wet hair dangling past his navel. Reaching the couch, he pressed the back of his hand to Saffron's cheek before pulling away again, like he wasn't sure he was supposed to do that.

"Erm... how are you feeling?" he asked. "You've been asleep a little more than two days—"

Saffron lurched upward, but Cylvan grabbed him before he hit the ceiling.

"Two whole days!" he shrieked before Cylvan could say anything else. His voice was raspy and desperate, the sudden gasp of air making him cough again.

"Shhh," Cylvan breathed, taking a seat on the edge of the couch and causing Saffron's hips to sink toward his weight. He pushed hair out of Saffron's wild eyes that time, before his fingers twitched away like he wasn't expecting the human's forehead to still be so sweaty.

"I put in a specific request for you to be assigned to Danann House every day, and reported you in attendance for all of them... Said we had another sprite infestation." He smiled unevenly. "Ah —and some giant brute and a little blonde accosted me on campus on the first day, saying you were a friend of theirs. Called me a... oh, what was it... a *prince of darkness*, or something..."

"Dark lord," Saffron whispered.

"Ah—yes. That's it." The dark lord smiled. "I take it you know them?"

Saffron grimaced, but he nodded. Of course; Hollow and Letty.

"I told them where you were and why. I even let them in, and they changed your clothes and applied some medicine on your back. Erm—why didn't you ever say anything about those wounds? I don't think I've ever seen anything so infected. No wonder you were so messed up..." he trailed off when Saffron just watched him, as thoroughly soaked with confusion as he was sweat.

Perhaps Cylvan thought that explained everything, but it only brought up more questions. *How did he get back to Cylvan's room at all? Had Cylvan really brought him, himself? Why not just let him cook alive like a hard-boiled egg?*

"Because... I felt obligated to give you a soft place to sleep. At least once, before you died."

Saffron stared at him a moment longer, before flushing in

embarrassment when he realized he said that last thought out loud. He bit down on his tongue to keep anything else from slipping out, deciding he must still be feverish enough to not have all his bearings gathered.

"That is all... very kind of you," he said with an awkward smile. "I hope I did not inconvenience you too much, your highness. Um... if you'll excuse me, I'll give you your couch back..."

Throwing the fur blanket aside, he attempted to bend his legs around where Cylvan sat, though ended up just tangling his feet in the prince's robe.

"I—I would also like to apologize for my behavior last night— it was wholly embarrassing... and inappropriate... and—!"

"Hey! Relax, púca," Cylvan grabbed Saffron's ankles before they could heel him in the gut, and Saffron fell back into the pillows with a *fwump* of air. It was only then he realized—he was wearing a nightshirt that definitely wasn't his, the bottom hem bundled up over his short braies and revealing the bare skin of his legs all the way up to his hips. He almost passed out from overheating again.

"I... should have helped you sooner," Cylvan said, averting his eyes but not yet releasing Saffron's ankles. Still, Saffron's panic tempered slightly. "Those scars on your back... who did that to you? Was it the night of Imbolc? And who threw you in the lake afterward? Is that why you're coughing?"

"How did you know they threw me in the lake?" Saffron asked, and Cylvan offered him an exasperated look. Something clicked, and Saffron's face went hot again. "Y-you! Were you the one who found me? And took me back to Beantighe Village?"

Cylvan nodded, but his jaw clenched.

"I assumed the blood on your clothes was from your friend who died... if I'd know it was your own, I would have done more."

Saffron looked at him skeptically, wanting to mutter "*no you wouldn't have*," but saw what he thought was actual *remorse* behind Cylvan's eyes.

"Well... thank you for taking me home, either way," Saffron

offered meekly, finally tugging his legs back and tucking a piece of stiff hair behind his ear. He didn't want to mention anything else about what happened to his back, worried those names might come back to bite him—but Cylvan kept watching him expectantly.

"I don't remember who threw me in the lake," Saffron finally said.

"You're a liar."

"Um... prove it," he countered, but the intimidation fell flat. Still, Cylvan sighed, rubbing his temples before meeting Saffron's eyes again.

"*Fine*. But at least let me do something about the other night."

Saffron raised his eyebrows in question. Wasn't carrying him all the way back to Danann House and hiding him like a pet rabbit enough?

"I... knew you were unwell, from the moment I saw you outside the library. I should have turned you right back around to go home, but..." Cylvan frowned, picking at something on his robe. "I was angry that you'd blown me off the night before. I was angry after my argument with Taran. And a part of me... liked seeing that you'd come despite being so sick, like I was all you could think about even on your deathbed. But it was selfish of me, obviously. It was also cruel of me to be so harsh with you all night, even when you were trying to help... and I'm sorry."

Saffron watched with his head tilted in curiosity, a part of him certain he was still asleep. Cylvan was... apologizing to him. First, there was a flicker of remorse in his eyes, and then he was *apologizing*. Oh—Saffron had definitely died the night before. He was definitely still asleep. Still dreaming.

"And," Cylvan continued, taking Saffron's hands. "Saffron, I... want you to use my name on me. Anything you want. In exchange."

Saffron recoiled slightly, before smiling in more confusion.

"Erm... that's not necessary," he said. "We don't have to..."

But Cylvan squeezed Saffron's hands tighter, and Saffron's words died.

"Please. For my own conscience."

"Um... No, I don't want to do that." he insisted. "I can see how sorry you are. You even took care of me while I was sick, so I believe you when you say—"

"But—"

"I don't want to compel you!" Saffron exclaimed, before smiling apologetically as it came out shriller than intended. "Your highness, please, don't make me do that. I don't want to. Being compelled is agonizing—and thinking about *doing* the compelling again makes my skin crawl. A part of me even regrets compelling you the first time we met. Even if you deserved it."

Cylvan was clearly torn by that confession, shifting where he sat.

"Then... do you forgive me?"

Saffron looked at him again. He attempted to clear his swollen throat, instincts commanding him to navigate the conversation carefully, delicately, with the same detail-orientation as pulling flower sprites from iris blooms. Cylvan's sincere gaze didn't help to keep Saffron's thoughts straight, though, suddenly worried he was going to make the prince cry. Was Prince Cylvan really capable of *so very many emotions* that weren't annoyance or boredom or bitterness?

"You're... incredibly gracious, your highness. Perhaps the most generous student on this entire campus. I'm eternally grateful—"

"Stop," Cylvan interrupted. "That's not what I asked."

Saffron took a deep breath before putting on his most falsely polite smile ever. Taking his hands from his lap, he folded them over Cylvan's gently.

"I forgive you."

"... Oh, you really lie every chance you get, don't you?"

Saffron's practiced expression dropped into exasperation.

"I'm not lying. I forgive you."

"I don't think you do."

Saffron huffed again. "Alright, well—! I *am* grateful for your care while I was sick, and I can see how repentant you are. I do believe you genuinely feel bad, so thank you for your apology."

"Then you do forgive me."

"... Yes. I forgive you."

"Stop saying it like that! Say it properly!"

"I am saying it properly!" Saffron didn't mean to laugh, coughing again as Cylvan held his hands in a death grip. "I mean —I don't really know *what* to say, since I'm... I'm not all that surprised, I guess... I mean, I'm not really bothered... I don't know..."

He smiled weakly, unsure if it was possible to explain without being totally insulting. *I'm used to high fey being selfish and inconsiderate, but I'm not used to them apologizing for it afterward, so I don't actually know how to navigate this conversation...*

"It was my own fault for going to the library when I was sick, anyway, so really you didn't do much..." Saffron tried again, but trailed off as Cylvan just shook his head. He wore the face of someone who'd just been told *"no"* for the first time in their life.

"Well—I would still like to make it up to you. Would you like new shoes? Some perfume?" he sniffed Saffron's wrist before frowning. He pinched Saffron's finger, instead. "I can get you diamonds; do beantighes like diamonds? Anything at all, just ask and it's yours."

"I—I don't know what I would even do with diamonds," Saffron said in uncertainty. "And I would only get mud all over new clothes."

"... I suppose you would wash the perfume away in the creek, too, wouldn't you?"

"Probably," Saffron smiled again. He rubbed the backs of Cylvan's hands, unsure what else to say. "Erm... how about, instead of any of that, why don't you just... agree to turn me back home the next time I have a fever?"

"... Alright. Agreed. Now you forgive me."

"I—I suppose so..."

"Ugh!" Cylvan collapsed dramatically across Saffron's legs, and Saffron laughed more before coughing into his arm. "I can't live like this! A prince cannot live with debts unpaid!"

"Even beantighe debts?"

"Yes!" he jolted back up, taking Saffron's hands again. Saffron attempted to bite back another surprised giggle, but it spilled out. *"Especially* when the beantighe in question knows my true name."

"I've also heard you say the words *'I'm sorry,'* which was a little out of character."

"You know too much. You've become too dangerous. I will have you stripped of your beantighe title and sent into exile at once—no, that's probably exactly what you want, isn't it? I'll have to think of something else..." Cylvan finally cracked a smile, too, and Saffron's last remaining anxiety ebbed away. He chuckled a little more, coughed again, and Cylvan squeezed his hands.

"I have something coming by raven for your cough," he said, catching Saffron by surprise. "Let me go see if it's arrived yet. Ah —you're also welcome to my bath if you'd like to wash up. I had your clothes and veil cleaned as well, they're folded on the bathroom counter. You're also welcome to any of my nightshirts, if you'd like to relax a bit longer."

"O-oh," Saffron blinked, not expecting so many offers in one breath. "Are you sure you weren't reserving those favors only for when I, erm, forgave you? I wouldn't want you to give away all of your bargaining chips..."

Cylvan smirked. It made Saffron smile again, strangely enamored with the idea that Cylvan found him at least *a little bit* amusing in ways that weren't painful or embarrassing or bodily dangerous. The prince even touched Saffron's forehead again, but seemed to still not quite know what to expect from it as he just made a face and got to his feet.

"Wait!" Saffron sat up when Cylvan headed for the exit in only his robe, one of the shoulders slipping down and showing off his chest. Saffron looked away immediately, struggling to remember what he'd wanted to say.

"Um—ah—what about—" he gulped. "Aren't you worried about Lord Taran? Does he... does he know I'm here?"

Cylvan smiled darkly, like the name was enough to ignite fiery disdain in his gut. "Taran hasn't been back to Danann House since our argument; he's staying in his old room in Erce House. I think I scared him off, hopefully for good."

A stab of intimidation made Saffron shiver, and Cylvan barked an arrogant laugh before pulling open his robe to prove his point, leaving the room with fabric fluttering behind him. Saffron was definitely just dreaming.

Considering whether bathing in Cylvan's room was really the safest of bets to make, Saffron's fingers tangled immediately in his hair and he knew he didn't have much choice. His whole body was sticky and crunchy with sweat, even more dripping down his face and back as he moved around. And—he would have to give Cylvan opportunities to earn trust if Saffron really intended to ever give him the forgiveness he craved. Forgiveness for behaviors Saffron expected of most high fey—but perhaps the catch was that Cylvan didn't *want* that behavior to be expected of *him*... and the thought made Saffron bark his own laugh.

The tiled walls of the bathroom were still slick with steam from Cylvan's time inside, humid air smelling of a hundred unique perfumes, shampoos, soaps, lotions. But it was hard to observe the full extent of the lavishness beneath the clutter. The spilled potions across the marble vanity countertop, splatters on the long mirror over the sink, a war zone of horsehair makeup brushes and pigments and lip colors, decanter corks of mystery liquids in colorful jars along the windowsill over the corner bathtub. Laundry draped the cushioned chaise next to the tub, along with at least three used towels, something that looked like a long party dress, and a single abandoned shoe.

Still covered by Cylvan's blanket, Saffron approached the tub framed by rainy windows. Drawing the tap with a loud *clank* and a rush of spluttering water, he knocked something over into the basin, muttering under his breath. Checking the label on the side, he shrugged and proceeded to dump the rest in. Instantly, the room smelled like mint and grass, a flurry of bubbles swelling up on the swirling water.

Digging around in the pile of discarded clothes on the chaise, Saffron removed a white linen undershirt, sizing it up before hanging it over the side of the tub. Peeling the sweaty nightshirt off over his head next, he found the binder laced underneath, embarrassed when he thought about Hollow or Letty tying him into it while he was nothing more than a corpse. Pulling the laces from the side, loose herbs scattered around his feet.

"Oops," he whispered, scooping the flattened leaves and tossing them into the bath, thinking whatever oils they had left wouldn't hurt to steep like tea. Or would it be more like a stew? Did that make him a potato? Or a carrot?

Tugging the undershirt on last for an ounce of modesty, he carefully lifted a foot over the edge of the tub, tucking the bottom of the shirt down as it barely reached mid-thigh while dangling loose. He sighed when the water was hot and inviting, nothing like the barely lukewarm temperatures they managed in Beantighe Village, or the icy bite of the creek when bathwater wasn't available. Not only that, it was strangely velvety with the minty mystery concoction, draping over the rest of Saffron's body like a luxurious blanket as he settled down into it.

"Oh, *damn you,*" he whispered to no one, sinking far enough that the bubbles decorated his chin.

A knock came at the door moments later, as if Cylvan had been summoned. Saffron sat up just enough to glance over his shoulder, watching a horned head poke in and smirk at the sweaty beantighe melting in his ridiculous bath.

"Doing alright? How do you feel now?" Cylvan asked, inviting himself fully inside. He'd changed into slender-fitting pants beneath a baggy maroon tunic, hair pulled back into a low ponytail. In one hand he carried a plate burdened with toast and fruit, two flutes of what Saffron assumed were mimosas balanced in the other.

"Like... a potato," Saffron responded without thinking, blaming it on his fever. The heat of the bath. How Cylvan's legs looked in his pants.

"... Oh, you mean in a pot?" Cylvan caught on to the nonsense, taking a place on the cluttered chaise and balancing his dish on the edge of the tub. "But why would you be a potato, when you're already a spice?"

Saffron raised his eyebrows in question, and Cylvan raised his right back.

"Erm... because *saffron*."

"... Oh! My name!" Saffron exclaimed, making Cylvan shake his head before smiling. Leaning over the open bath, he knowingly grabbed and dumped his own concoction of potions into the water, making it swirl with pastel shades like meadow flowers. Saffron couldn't help but trail fingers through the colors until they swirled.

"I'll fetch some cabbage and leeks and, before you know it, we'll have a whole tub of colcannon for lunch..." Cylvan went on, saying it under his breath like he wasn't sure it was as funny as he thought. But Saffron laughed, and Cylvan smiled in relief before shaking his head again.

Pulling a wrapped package from his pocket, he tore it open, removing a glass vial of blue liquid. He poured it like syrup across a piece of toast already spread with butter and jam, before holding it up to Saffron.

"Medicine, for your cough," he explained. "It's supposed to take on the flavor of whatever it touches, so don't let the color intimidate you."

"M-medicine?" Saffron asked in surprise, a part of him thinking Cylvan had been exaggerating earlier. "But—the healer doesn't have human medicine on hand, it'll only make me sicker..."

"I ordered it from a healer in Connacht; they have a specialist shop there," Cylvan promised, urging the toast closer to Saffron's mouth—but Saffron's whole body had gone stiff. His heart pounded, just staring at the bread, the apricot jam, the blue syrup. His eyes flickered to the additional fruits on the plate, next, thinking about the party when Cylvan forced him to eat fairy fruit.

"I'm..." he said nervously. "I'm actually... feeling better already, I don't think I need... Maybe some rest was good enough, I don't know if I have to..."

"Púca," Cylvan insisted, but Saffron still pressed his lips together.

"Is it... is it really medicine, your highness?" he asked, feeling embarrassed. Cylvan was quiet before setting the toast back on the plate. He tucked a finger under Saffron's chin, silently requesting Saffron's eyes to meet his.

"It's proper medicine," he promised. "I'm not trying to trick you, Saffron."

Saffron still wasn't sure whether that was the truth, but bit his lip and nodded. He couldn't see any other way out of the situation, anyway, so perhaps it would be easier to obey and find out how genuine Cylvan could really be.

Cylvan returned the toast to his lips, and Saffron risked a bite. To his surprise, and mild relief, he tasted only seed-packed wheat bread with apricot jam and butter, just like he was told. There was no tingling of fairy fruit, no strange aftertaste, nothing that made him feel fooled.

"Oh..." he perked up, balancing the toast on his fingers and stealing another mouthful.

"How does it taste?" Cylvan asked.

"Like you said."

"Good." Cylvan smiled. "You know... I just wrote down all your symptoms, and they sent me a potion without much trouble. Truly, if what you said about seeing the healer is that complicated... I'll have to have a word with Elluin."

Cylvan was quick on the draw as soon as Saffron finished his first piece of bread, offering the second one already prepared with butter and the fruit spread. He nearly lost his fingers as Saffron snatched it.

"Good... good," Cylvan repeated, pushing up Saffron's hair to feel his temperature again.

For a moment, it was easy for Saffron to lose himself in the prince's handsome face. The way his features were so elegant when they looked at him... like *that*. With an ounce of tenderness and concern, his eyes muted slightly in the overcast light, dark eyebrows furrowed in concentration. While Prince Cylvan had always been beautiful, when his expression was relaxed... it was enough to make Saffron's heart race in the same wanting way it did when he read romantic stories. As if, when the prince was calm, and sincere, and focused on him, Saffron could actually see a shadow of the Cylvan he'd come to love written in the margins of that book.

The thought made his face go hot, turning down his eyes as Cylvan let out a frustrated breath and asked if the medicine wasn't working. Saffron just buried more toast in his mouth as the embarrassment was overwhelming.

13

THE WOLF

"Does no one come and clean here?" Saffron asked from the bathroom doorway, dressed in his newly-washed doublet and dabbing at wet hair with one of the prince's ridiculously plush towels. Cylvan narrowed his eyes from the bed, a book open on his lap and papers spread in an arc around him. Saffron just motioned to the disaster that was the bathroom counter.

"Beantighes come every few days," Cylvan answered. "But I don't allow them in my room. My bathroom always looks like that. I prefer it."

"You *prefer* it?" Saffron smiled in disbelief. "This—this *disaster?*"

"It's not a *disaster,*" Cylvan grumbled. "I know where everything is. And I'm very particular about my things and exactly where they all go. And I *will* know if you touched anything at all, and I *will* take a finger for each infringement."

"Oooooh," Saffron feigned intimidation. "Are you attached to the mystery stains on the counter, too?"

"Yes, yes, yes, alright, no more criticisms from the bath-beantighe, please." The prince flourished his quill declaratively. "Are you leaving now?"

The bratty behavior made Saffron smile. Still, he nodded, folding up the towel and tossing it into the laundry basket. Cylvan cleared a path through his homework to step from the bed and join Saffron at the door, but neither seemed ready to say goodbye first. Saffron was too busy gazing at the carvings in Cylvan's horns while Cylvan lifted a hand to touch Saffron's forehead again.

"Will..." Saffron trailed off. "Will you be at the library tonight, your highness?"

Cylvan smiled—and then frowned. Saffron's heart sank a little, but he kept the smile on his face.

"That's alri—"

But Cylvan suddenly removed something from his finger, taking Saffron's hand and pushing a thin golden ring onto one of his own, right above the delicate fern ring.

"This... is my library ring," he whispered. "You can use it to visit whenever you like, so long as you promise not to get yourself spotted. I, um... I trust you, Saffron."

Saffron's mouth hung open slightly in disbelief, skin buzzing with uncertainty, wondering once again if he was dreaming. But then pure elation struck him, and he hopped up and down, a noise of excitement squeaking out of him.

"Oh—! Prince Cylvan! *Thank you!*" He threw Cylvan in a tight hug, before scrambling away just as quickly and apologizing with a frantic bow. Cylvan just smiled in uncertainty, before opening the door to let Saffron out.

"Perhaps I'll stumble into you one of these nights," he said. "Imagine my surprise when I learn a beantighe can read."

"I can write some, too, you know," Saffron added, laughing when Cylvan pretended to be shocked. Saffron just bowed one more time and hurried from the room, practically skipping down the stairs and out the door.

A light drizzle fell that morning, the sun attempting to push through thinner parts of the clouds overhead. The gardens of Danann House sparkled with rain, dangling leaves dancing with every additional *pap pap* from the sky. Like a chorus of everything Saffron loved most; the sounds, the smell, the gray light, all of it emphasized the pure, medicated elation in his chest as he gazed down at the newest ring on his finger. He stumbled into a rose-bush, tripped over a root, walked straight into the metal gate with a *thud* and *clank* and swore softly in embarrassment, all the while with his eyes locked on the circlet of gold. He couldn't actually bring himself to look away, fearing it might disappear as soon as he did.

There was perhaps only one thought that ebbed in stronger than his glee over the ring—and that was the memory of Cylvan's face while Saffron sat in the bath. His soft voice, the gentle movements of his hands. His apologies, how his amethyst eyes, for the first time, didn't bore holes into Saffron as they looked over every inch of him. Instead—it was like they searched for gaps carved from Saffron's skin, with every intention of filling them in, patting them flat, so nothing could grow or fester there ever again.

It was hard to believe. The High Crown Prince of Alfidel, who would eventually become king, who would pass laws and have his hands kissed and live for centuries and go down in history in name and legacy... had spread apricot jam on toast for Saffron to eat with medicine.

Saffron flushed. And then giggled again, though it was a little shrill.

Rounding the corner toward Agate Bridge, Saffron's pace slowed the moment he spotted a crowd gathered. Beantighes huddled on and around the stone path stretching over the creek, leaning to get a better look, grabbing each other so they wouldn't fall into the water, gossiping and whispering excitedly to one another. Gulping, Saffron picked up the pace again, wondering if there was a fight going on.

But upon reaching them, he stopped short at the sight of a bloodstained body being pulled from the mud. They draped weakly in the healer's arms as Cassila, the beantighe liaison, followed close behind. Without a veil to cover her pale face, while

Saffron didn't know the victim's name, he recognized her from Cottage Dublin.

Stepping out of the way, a red-stained hand suddenly flashed out to grab his veil, and he was wrenched into the girl's face as the healer yelped in surprise.

"Saffron—Arrow—the wolf," she guttered. *"That lord—he—for the fruits—the prince—"*

Cassila jerked Saffron away, the girl's arm drooping back to her side as her gray eyes reflected the sky, and Saffron watched them cloud over as if rain would spill from their color, too.

The name *Cloth* whispered between beantighes behind him, and he thought of it while gazing down at her handprint staining Arrow's old veil.

Arrow. The wolf. The lord. The fruits.

The prince. Saffron stared at the red stain as rain speckled it, making the fresh blood run pink.

WICKLOW BEANTIGHES SHUFFLED THROUGH THE FRONT door of their cottage, just like those of Monaghan, Galway, Dublin, and Carlow cottages did around the rest of Beantighe Village. Both day-shift and night-shift workers crammed into the parlor room, whispering amongst one another, holding hands, a few crying softly and wiping eyes on their sleeves. It wasn't often the entire cottage was together in one place, which only made Saffron's nerves spike more. Would someone be able to read his thoughts from the proximity? Smell Cylvan's fancy soap and shampoo from his bath? Would they be able to tell his clothes had been properly cleaned in student basins, not scrubbed over a metal plate in the creek?

Would they know what Cloth whispered to him in her last moment? Before her eyes became the sky and she was carried away?

Another thought gripped him—if he'd left the library on his

own that night, would the wolf have found him, instead? He clutched Arrow's veil until his knuckles turned white.

It had been easy to forget there was danger at all. Easy to trick himself into accepting Arrow's death as a wild animal attack and nothing more. But now—

Saffron had to consider the other possibility. Every beantighe working Morrígan would have to consider—there was something out there hunting them on purpose.

Silk sat holding hands with Blade on the old couch; Fleece and Berry were in the middle of a hushed, intense conversation across the room as rain pattered the window behind them. Letty eventually shuffled in and found Hollow and Saffron, giving Saffron a tight hug and commenting how glad she was that he was safe.

Standing against the back wall decorated with peeling wallpaper, Saffron couldn't stop counting the surrounding faces, notating their shift and assigned room. Some sat on the staircase as the parlor filled to the brim. Others argued about lighting a fire because of the rainy chill through the windows, as even more argued against it because they would all be sweating in another few minutes. Saffron just kept counting, again and again and again, wondering if there was anyone else missing from any of the other cottages.

It was on his fifth round of mental attendance that he heard Pepper ask a question of Hollow that made his blood run cold.

"Cloth was a foundling too, wasn't she?"

Saffron turned his eyes slightly to Hollow, who was in the middle of stiffly pulling his hair into a short ponytail. He nodded.

"That makes two," Hollow muttered. "I don't think that's enough for a pattern, at least. Just a coincidence… definitely."

Saffron knew Arrow was a foundling, a human beantighe without a formal fey-patron. He didn't know Cloth was, too— but so was Hollow next to him. Instinctively, he reached out to take Hollow's hand, holding it protectively. Hollow squeezed him back, as if to reassure Saffron he was still right there.

When Baba Yaga finally entered the cottage, the conversation died down. The Wicklow henmother shuffled to the fireplace where everyone could see her, wearing her moth-eaten moon and star shawl that dangled with tassels and twinkling silver charms. The look on her face when she turned and gazed across the plethora of humans she vowed to keep safe made Saffron's heart break, as if she immediately counted all of their faces room-by-room like he had. It took a moment before she bowed her head to speak.

"Everyone listen to me, please," she announced, voice deep with solemnity. She tucked one of her silver braids over a shoulder, adjusting the cuffs of her sleeves. "The other henmothers and I have just finished speaking with Cassila and Elluin about Cloth's death this morning. I would like to reiterate what they've said on the matter."

"You mean what they told you to say?" Blade asked, and Baba gave her a dry smirk. She straightened up and put on her best Elluin-voice, heavy with faux-pompousness. A moment of light-heartedness within the mire of uncertainty.

"We are aware of the rumors being spread amongst you. At this time, we have no reason to believe there is a wolf hunting humans around campus..."

A wave of murmurs washed over the Wicklow audience. Candle mentioned the claw marks on Cloth's body, and nausea twisted in Saffron's stomach.

"For now, we will continue our schedules as normal, with no new curfews..." Baba Yaga went on, voice catching as if distressed to speak them. She closed her eyes and gathered herself again, letting out a controlled breath. "Until we know if this is truly an animal, or merely two unfortunate accidents... the other henmothers and I only ask that you all watch out for one another, and report to us if you see anything strange."

"And what if someone else gets slaughtered?" Thread exclaimed from the staircase, leaning over the railing so Baba could see them. A chorus of scattered agreements followed, even Saffron nodding slightly.

"Unfortunately, even in these cases, Morrígan has always held to the law of threes," Baba explained, steepling fingers over her stomach and gazing down at them as if those were words she was particularly unhappy to repeat. "Once is an accident, twice a coincidence, three times an intention—"

"So someone else has to die before Elluin gives a shit?" Hollow spoke that time. Baba looked at him with a pained expression, as if begging them all to remember she wasn't the one who made any of the decisions. She was only the messenger, no matter how bitter the words were to repeat.

"There will be no changes to morning and evening assignments, or any change to normal village routines. Further, Elluin let me know that if they find anyone putting up unnecessary traps, organizing hunts, or otherwise, they will be..." she cleared her throat. "They will be punished for stirring undue fear. The headmistress does not want any students thinking there is reason to worry for their safety—"

"Fuck the students!" Basket's shrill voice responded, even more dissent growing around the room.

"What about us!"

"Fuck Elluin if she thinks we'll just wait to die!"

"Elluin would rather we all die than let her school look bad!"

"Cloth said something to Saffron while she was carried away!"

The room went silent, even Baba Yaga going stiff as she gazed at where the voice came from. Wax seemed to regret the callout right away, especially once their neighbor elbowed her in the side to stand up and keep going. She got to her feet, clearing her throat and wringing her hands together. "I'm—I'm sorry, it's just... I saw Cloth grab him and say something. And—he's the one who found Arrow, too. Arrow told you it was a wolf, didn't they, Saffron? What did Cloth say?"

Saffron squeezed Hollow's hand hard enough that his knuckles cracked. He cleared his throat, though his voice still came out in a rasp.

"She mentioned the wolf as well."

"Did anyone see Cloth last night? Before she died?" someone else asked, and voices bounced around the room too quickly for Saffron to follow.

"Yeah, who was the last person to see her?"

"Last I saw her was a few days ago."

"Me too. She was looking for..."

Silence fell again, and Saffron realized with a strike of fear that faces were slowly turning to look... at him.

"Wh-what?" Saffron asked. "She was looking for me?"

Leaf stood from their place tucked slightly into the kitchen, face wet with tears. They quickly wiped them away, keeping their eyes on the floor as if also regretting drawing attention to themself. "She said... you know about the woods and how to navigate them."

"Didn't Arrow go into the woods with Saff a few days before they died, too?" someone else continued, and Saffron's blood ran cold.

"Wasn't Saffron really sick the other day? When he ran off? When did Cloth disappear? Maybe they went into the woods together?"

"He hasn't been around the village at all lately."

"He showed up this morning, right in time for Cloth to be carried away—"

"Hey, cut it out!" Hollow boomed, making everyone flinch. "Don't act like you all haven't asked Saffron where to find marijuana and other shit in the woods. Don't start spreading stupid rumors that could get someone else killed for Elluin's own ego."

Saffron looked at him with gratitude, Baba Yaga clearing her throat to reclaim everyone's attention.

"Listen to Hollow, everyone, please," she beseeched her beantighe chicks. "Remember who stands to benefit from our harm, fey or not. We cannot sow contention amongst ourselves— that will only allow Elluin the opportunity to blame the wrong person and further the reason to mistrust us. Alright? Now— since you're all here, why don't we take this opportunity to catch up on the chores you all skipped on Imbolc... don't whine to me, it was your own faults for getting too drunk to move, come on, get to work. Stop crowding my parlor..."

DESPITE ELLUIN'S WARNING TO NOT GO HUNTING, SET traps, or do anything else out of the ordinary, a handful of beantighes from each cottage met at the gate a few hours later. From the combined counts, there were five people unaccounted for from the village. Two had been missing for a considerable amount of time, even before the wolf ever became a concern; one ran into the woods after eating some strange berries, though it wasn't confirmed whether or not they were fairy dusted; one had simply not come back from assignments one night; and the fifth had, worryingly, gone missing around the same time Cloth had, and was even a close friend of hers —Sunbeam.

The news was particularly shocking for Berry, who had apparently been courting the girl from Dublin Cottage, and he showed his fear in every movement.

Partnered with Saffron while searching the nearby woods, every time they came across a strange mound of soil, or a dead animal, or rot-mushrooms that reeked of decay, Saffron had to explain every time that the signs didn't belong to fresh human remains.

"Those are just roots under the soil."

"That's only a deer carcass."

"Those mushrooms smell terrible, don't you think?"

Every time Berry snatched Saffron's hand drawn map from his grip to frantically search the area, Saffron had to tell him that all the places he wanted to search next were hours away by foot. There just wasn't time.

All the while, Saffron's own mind spun with the last words Cloth said to him. The wolf. The lord. The fruits. The prince. Like being handed puzzle pieces, but no reference for the final image, no confirmation that those were all the parts he needed to figure it out.

There was one thing he did know for certain, though—by her own words, Cloth's death had to do with the same wild fairy fruits Arrow was obsessed with finding, too. And, if the current pattern was any indication of intent—whatever it was was targeting foundlings. Which meant, not only was Hollow potentially in danger—but somehow, the wolf could tell beantighes from fey students, and knew how to pick out those who didn't have patron-families to complain to Elluin when their changeling-human was killed without explanation.

The lord. The prince.

Returning to Beantighe Village before noon, the other teams had apparently found one long-decayed skeleton, though there was no way to determine who it belonged to or if it was even human. That left just as many technically unaccounted for as they started with.

Saffron's mind thundered with more thoughts than the sky as rain picked up and drowned out the village, relegating all the humans into the cottages whether they liked it or not. Most in Wicklow crowded in the upstairs bedrooms or the attic where they smoked like they thought Baba couldn't smell it, Blade practicing her piano while Silk looked over Saffron's infected back and commented on its improvement. Saffron shrugged and told her he must have gotten lucky.

When there were no more obvious chores to complete, he went to Baba asking for anything at all to keep his mind off the wolf-prince-fruit shaped storm in his head. Eventually she gave in, sitting him at a little table in her bedroom off the kitchen with a piece of paper and every magic cup she owned, asking him to rub down the red paint on the saucers and refresh the designs. He attempted to get more information out of her in the process, but Baba just smiled and told him it was only an old folk myth from the human world.

Baba Yaga never spoke much of where she came from or who

she was before becoming Cottage Wicklow's henmother; Saffron knew she could read and write, knew she was in Alfidel before the veils were closed, knew her ring of perpetuity to slow aging had been taken away before being given back again, which was how she reached old age at all. Her actual human name was Nora, and her formal beantighe name was Hearth—and she was never quite clear where she got the nickname Baba Yaga. Every now and then her human chicks could pluck another detail out of her, usually when she was drunk and being overly affectionate, but even totally inebriated, she tended to remain a lockbox of secrets.

Wiping down the cups, Saffron studied the hand-drawn circles and their accentuating lines around the rims, like cracked rings in an old tree. Beneath each circle, of which there were nine, he read the labels one by one: *sleep, wake, pain, fever, fright, illness, antidote, strength, truth*. Painting one circle onto each of the nine corresponding saucers, he was careful to make every stroke absolutely perfect, wanting to ensure that, even if it was only hopeful folk magic, the intention would be there to protect anyone who ever sipped from the rims. And then, before Baba returned to appraise his efforts—he copied the folk circles into his sketchbook. Perhaps there was something in the library to explain them, if Baba insisted on keeping her secrets.

ALL OF THE VILLAGE'S TENUOUS CALM CAME TO AN END as soon as the sun went down, Leaf and Berry racing inside with wide eyes to exclaim—there was something pacing on the other side of the rowan trees.

Rushing out the back door, Saffron was one of the first to find a place on the stone steps, a group of other Wicklow residents joining him, others pushing open windows in the attic and bedrooms to all stop and listen. Overhead, thunder rumbled and wind scattered through windchimes like screeching pixies. Saffron just held his breath and tried to listen as the thunder rolled away.

Before any other sounds came—there was a smell. One of rot, wet fur, blood, breath.

And then, through the trees—crunching. The slow, repetitive *crunch, crunch, crunch* of heavy feet making their way through the undergrowth. In the last light of the sun, Saffron managed a glimpse of it—blacker than the night sky, hunched with wiry fur, standing larger than a horse or a bear. Unlike anything he'd ever seen.

It was the wolf.

14

THE APPLE

Crimson-stained cotton. Carrying Hollow's sagging body, a few inches taller and wider than Saffron even when Saffron stood up straight. Heavy. Crushing. Staining his doublet as they dragged themselves through the woods, the path never changing.

A tiny, flickering light beckoned to Saffron far out of his reach, Saffron just focusing on its little glow, knowing, surely, it would lead them out of the darkness.

"We have to hurry," Hollow whispered. "They only give us an inch. An hour."

"What?" Saffron asked weakly, and Hollow lifted a finger to point. Saffron focused on the light up ahead, realizing it belonged to one of the inch-tall funeral candles used for human burials, burning away faster than Saffron could chase it.

"N-no," Saffron begged. No, no, no—he had to get Hollow to safety.

"Saffron," Hollow's voice changed, and Saffron nearly lost his footing, weighed down suddenly by someone colder, long black hair swinging with every dragging, weakened step. "You have to forgive me."

Saffron groaned beneath the prince's weight. "I will, Cylvan. I'll forgive you."

Only an hour. Only an hour to find the other side. Beantighes were hardly given any time at all to search for the afterlife. What would happen if Saffron didn't make it in time? What if Saffron couldn't carry Cylvan into the light?

A flock of crows suddenly swept from the sky. Saffron stumbled back, ducking, pulling Cylvan in close so the birds wouldn't scratch his face, pull out his hair. When the shadowy mass dissipated again, Saffron cracked open his eyes—but the path was blocked. In its center, a massive, snarling wolf, the color of the night sky. Blood dripped from its mouth, ears bent back, snout wrinkled and baring its red teeth.

He could only stare at the blood dripping from its mouth. Like bright berries warning Saffron to keep away, or else he would be drenched in his own rowan-red crimson just like the others.

It continued raining the following day, Saffron joined by a gaggle of fellow hooded beantighes as they made their way in tense silence toward campus. Any time a noise came from the trees, or someone spoke a little too loudly, or moved too quickly, a dozen heads turned in alarm. Saffron, himself, could remain calm, but the composure was only visible on the outside. In his gut, his heart, he was still reeling from his dream, replaying the sight of the wolf over and over again. Reliving how heavy Cylvan's body was, slumping from his shoulder, too weak to walk on his own.

You have to forgive me.

Damnit. The words made him shudder, trying to force them away.

Reaching campus, he claimed his assignment ring to clean out the raven paddocks and went to work. Sweeping out old straw and replacing it with new handfuls; sweeping stolen trinkets from each cubby as the ravens were no different from pixies when it came to thieving shiny objects; plucking the occasional dangling feather from any bird he pet on the head and scratched under the beak; replacing their trough of honey and seeds; organizing the messenger token and counting how many were missing. It was mindless, but that was exactly what he needed to pass the daylight hours.

Finishing up right as evening came, Saffron double-checked his waistband for his sketchbook and mentally prepared himself for the wet waiting period outside the library before curfew came and went. He was barely settling down in a hidden spot of muck right off the walkway when he spotted Professor Adelard hurrying from the Administration Building, looking giddy, poor Letty on his heels and burdened with a stiff leather satchel, an easel and canvas, and what Saffron realized was a chunk of raw meat wrapped in wax paper by the way it dripped a red trail behind them. He considered letting them go on their way, but leapt out and grabbed the slipping canvas seconds before Letty dropped it. She thanked him with a tired expression, Saffron just smirking before offering Adelard a greeting.

"Saffron, good, good! I meant to call for you, but Lettuce was sweeping the hallway outside my office. She was polite enough to assist me tonight."

"Assist you with what?" Saffron couldn't resist, gazing down at the canvas, the meat, the painting tools again and feeling a little envious that they weren't his.

"I've heard recently—oh, Saffron, you're going to *die*—there are *undines in Lake Elatha!*"

"U-undines!" Saffron exclaimed, and Letty made a face when she realized she was outnumbered by fairy-obsessed weirdos. "Are you going to lure her out? I'll come with you! Oh, I even have my sketchbook! How lucky!"

Adelard practically squealed in matched excitement, beckoning the humans to quicken their pace before it got too dark.

Hurrying down the length of the dock, Adelard dumped his

things. Unable to get a handle on his excitement, he shook out his hands and attempted to give logical instructions. "Come, come, come! Come on, hurry! Lettuce, dear, do you still have that lamb flank? Ah, yes! Go on, unwrap it and toss it in! Let's see if these ladies like blood!"

Saffron offered to take the canvas supplies while Letty scrambled with the chunk of meat. At the end of the dock, she did as she was told, both hers and Saffron's stomachs growling as the perfectly good slab of potential food hit the water and wobbled down into the darkness. Behind them, Adelard pulled book after book from a shoulder bag, before setting up his art easel and tugging the canvas from Saffron's hands.

"I didn't know you painted, professor," Saffron commented, still staring dejectedly down into the murky water.

"I don't, dear child—but the undine doesn't have to know that. They're attracted to artists and poets, you know. Oh—you said you have your sketchbook! Go on, pull it out! Get into position! Letty, do you know how to sing? Or could you recite some poetry?"

"Some what?" Letty asked as Saffron crossed his legs on the edge of the dock. Pulling out his sketchbook, he flipped through the pages until he found a blank one, snapping open his tin of charcoals and beginning to idly sketch the lakeside. He wrote *"Undeen"* at the top of the page for good measure, before doubting his spelling.

"Oh—*I see something!*" Letty suddenly exclaimed, grabbing Saffron's arm and pointing into the water with her opposite hand. "There! There, Saffron, did you see it! A shadow, way down there, like a giant snake!"

Saffron squinted, but saw nothing. Letty remained crouched and peering into the water next to him—screaming when bright yellow eyes suddenly peeked through the surface directly beneath her. It startled Saffron and Adelard, too, the professor tumbling backward and nearly taking Saffron down with him.

The undine's eyes were the color of gold coins, skin shimmering with dark teal scales that moved like wind on a grassy field, or raven feathers in the sun. She regarded Letty with piqued curiosity, before her eyes traveled to Saffron, where she smiled in a knowing way.

Saffron almost spoke, trailing off when a vague memory along the lake surfaced in the back of his mind. Behind him, Adelard leapt back to his feet, nearly shoving Saffron into the water with how fast he rushed to get another look.

"Feeling better?" the undine directed at Saffron, voice gargling as if her throat was full of water. Saffron gulped, the sound of it confirming what he thought. Cylvan might have carried him from the lake after Elluin's punishment and returned him to Beantighe Village... but it must have been this undine who pulled him to the banks in the first place. He nodded timidly, almost thanking her before Adelard interrupted.

"Hello! I was hoping to have a discussion with you!" he announced, on his hands and knees and adjusting his glasses. But the undine didn't look at him, moving her eyes back to Letty. Saffron nudged his friend, who jumped and glanced back at him.

"Um... what's your name?" Letty asked in uncertainty.

"My name is Nimue," the undine replied, smiling with her sharp, yellow teeth. "What is your name, pretty flower?"

Letty blushed, pressing her hands to her cheeks. Next to them, Adelard excitedly took notes, muttering, *"the lady of the lake; must know the myths of Arthur; perhaps from the human world?"*

"My name is Lettuce... but everyone calls me Letty."

"Letty," Nimue mused. "You have hair like the sun, Letty."

Letty's nervous hands tangled in her wild blonde curls, as if she'd never thought about it before.

"Your hair is like the moon," she whispered in reply, and Nimue grinned wider.

"I will answer anything you ask, so long as Letty is the one who poses it," the undine told them matter-of-factly, Letty's face going even redder. Saffron bit back a laugh as Adelard immediately pounced, rushing Letty with a thousand different questions to ask in a very specific order.

"Careful, beantighe, the professor might kick you in as bait."

Cylvan's voice was cool and teasing in the evening air, Saffron and the others turning in surprise. He immediately leapt to his feet, sketchbook tumbling from his lap and accidentally kicking his tin of charcoals into the water. He cried out in tandem with his heart breaking, Letty politely asking if the undine would swim down and grab it. Nimue obliged.

"Are we making friends with the local fauna tonight?" the prince asked, approaching to gaze over the edge of the dock right as Nimue reappeared and offered Saffron his tin, though the drawing utensils had turned to mush. Still, Saffron sadly thanked her, pouring the black sludge back into the water.

"Prince Cylvan," Adelard prompted. "Is this the undine you told me about? She said her name is Nimue."

"Oh, yes. That's her alri—" a beam of water sniped Cylvan in the face, like an arrow from a bow. He stumbled back with a bark, Saffron's mouth hanging open as Nimue hissed venomously from the water.

"Sídhe scum!" she snarled. "How dare you speak of me to anyone, poxbottle! Do not dare claim to know me!"

Saffron put out his hands as Cylvan nearly leapt in to brawl with the undine, though his assault stopped when Saffron couldn't hold back his laughter.

"Oh, this is funny, is it?" Cylvan asked, grabbing and turning Saffron around to face the threat, using him as a shield. Saffron tried to bite back more laughter.

"Seeing as I've been assaulted, I think I need to go to the healer. What if I lose an eye, thanks to that watery tart? Where's the sword you promised me, lady of the lake?" Cylvan went on dramatically, ducking when Nimue hissed and spit another water-arrow at him.

"Walk with me, beantighe, will you? I'm feeling faint," Cylvan went on, putting a hand to his forehead and pretending to swoon.

Adelard let out a cry of alarm, grabbing Saffron's sketchbook from the dock and pushing it into Saffron's hands while encouraging him to *hurry! Hurry!!*

"God, *alright*," Saffron sighed, tucking the sketchbook and empty charcoal tin away, playing the role of concerned servant and propping Cylvan up as he said his goodbyes to Letty and Adelard.

"Why are you limping?" Saffron muttered as they made their way back to the main walkway, but Cylvan just smirked as he groaned and moaned and flopped over Saffron's shoulders more. Saffron nearly lost his footing, but couldn't resist laughing more. Cylvan's back, his shoulders, his waist were all firm under Saffron's hands, and he was reminded of how heavy Cylvan was despite his lack of obvious girth.

"I think I've lost an eye, beantighe. She shot it right out of my head," Cylvan went on miserably, as if Saffron hadn't babied him enough. Sighing, Saffron paused as they rounded one of the lecture halls and slipped into the shadows. Tugging Cylvan down, he pressed a few fingers below the eye in question, dusting his touch over the mole below his dark lashes.

"It's a little red," Saffron agreed. "But definitely still there. Do you really need to go to the healer?"

Cylvan smiled. "Perhaps not, if you think I'll live."

Saffron disappeared into the color of the prince's eyes before he could respond; it was hard not to, standing so close. He almost finally said something about how they reminded him of amethyst pieces—but Cylvan pulled away first, clearing his throat and pushing fingers back through his hair.

"Let's get going, then."

Saffron led the way around the lecture hall, past the greenhouse, down the side of campus to the library cast in a low orange light of the setting sun. Pulling the door open and stepping aside, he realized it was the first time *he'd* ever held the door open for *Cylvan*, and it felt so... normal. Like Saffron was just another student.

"What will you be looking into today?" Cylvan asked as they climbed the stairs together.

"Oh... I'm not sure yet," Saffron lied, knowing full well he was about to vanish into anything he could find about wolves with a taste for human blood.

"Let me know if you need any help," Cylvan offered, surprising Saffron when he reached out to tug a leaf from his hair. "Otherwise, I'll leave you to it."

"Thank you..." Saffron trailed off, but lingered, watching the prince find his normal spot at the table below Derdriu and Naoise; drop his bag on top; pull out a textbook, his bound parchment, his golden quill and ink set. He flipped a long strand of wavy hair over one shoulder and took a seat—before glancing up to Saffron's normal spot in the opulence section on the third-floor balcony, as if... looking for him.

Saffron's face went hot, bowing his head and hurrying to that exact place before Cylvan could turn and find him staring.

THE WOLF. THE LORD. THE PRINCE.

Despite it only being his third time between the books, he tossed out any thought of opulence or true names. Even if just for a few hours, he wanted to think about only one thing: the wolf.

Not wanting to tip Cylvan off, he avoided the main tome on the second floor and instead skimmed through individual registers in each section. *Music, Maps, Opulence, Philosophy, Philanthropy...* it wasn't until he skimmed over *Reigns of Alfidel* that one title caught his attention: *The Significance of King Clymeus' Wolf in The Veiled Queen's Reign and Eventual Downfall.*

His finger hovered over the words before trailing down the line, finding its specific place on the shelf and starting the hunt.

He didn't know all the details of Proserpina or her reign, only what Baba Yaga, the other henmothers, or Adelard ever talked about, as well as the occasional mention while eavesdropping on campus. Cracking open the book in question, he was immediately buried beneath more than he bargained for.

Queen Proserpina had been spurned by a human lover in the years leading up to her ascendency. So heartbroken, she shuttered every unregulated tear in the veil across the fey and human world alike, in order to better document who came and went. But that eventually mutated into *limiting* who came and went, and then went even further into closing all veils, period, except for a chosen few, allowing only the most affluent and powerful of Alfidel to pass.

Humans caught on the wrong side were killed or forced into servitude; fey caught on the wrong side were killed or dragged back. And while eventually stopped by a human named Verity Holt and her twin brother, Virtue, apparently through figuring out the queen's true name, the damage was already done, and most of the veil remained closed for good. Only those same people with affluence, or those who knew how to open their own tears like Luvon, ever went back and forth any longer.

It was also Proserpina who implemented the original rule of veils on human beantighes, covering their faces in order to show deference to fey patrons and employers, wearing white as a sign of spiritual betrothal to the edicts of the queen, a sign of wanting to become everything she thought humans needed to be to be less wicked, sinful, arrogant, selfish... Elluin's words echoed in Saffron's head. *Are you familiar with Queen Proserpina's Ten Hindrances to Human Perpetuity, beantighe?*

The significance of the wolf came in discussions of Proserpina's Harmonious King, Clymeus mac Dela, who the author asserted was the one to drive Proserpina's grief into bloodthirsty madness. With King Clymeus able to shapeshift into the beast, it wasn't unusual for Proserpina to be found weeping into her king's fur, riding on his back through the gardens, pressing her face into his snout when grief became too much to bear. But when he wasn't doting on his wife—he was chasing down humans to rip apart or arrest.

Saffron's hands shook as he found the chapter discussing Clymeus' role in gathering *humans in flight*, having to snap it shut before he couldn't swallow back the anxious bile. Hurrying up the ladder, he shoved the book back into its spot on the shelf, pausing a moment to press his forehead into the wood, undoing the top few buttons of his collar as he felt warm. But taking his first step down, his boot slipped on the carved rung, nearly crashing to the floor—only for a pair of hands to grab him by the waist, propping him upright again.

"P-Prince Cylvan!" Saffron exclaimed, and Cylvan kept his hands on Saffron's waist a moment longer. "Sorry, I didn't see you—"

"What is it with you and ladders?" Cylvan teased, finally letting Saffron go, though his fingers hovered for an extra moment. "I just came to see how you were doing... and ask how you've been feeling lately."

"Oh... much better," Saffron nodded with a self-conscious smile, wondering if Cylvan was going to mention Cloth's death—but when he didn't, he wondered if Cylvan didn't know, or just... didn't want to talk about it.

He almost wanted to ask—but watched as Cylvan's gaze lingered on his unbuttoned collar, the high-waist of his pants, his legs. Saffron shifted on his feet before deciding against it.

"Did you need something else, my lord?"

"Oh, right," Cylvan snapped out of it, pulling a bundle of something from his blazer pocket. Unfurling in his hands like a blooming tea, Saffron gasped at a cluster of apple slices.

"Those are—! Prince Cylvan!" he tried to snatch them away, but Cylvan jerked the offering out of reach with a sly smile.

"I won't break out in hives just holding them, beantighe. They're for you."

Saffron blinked, gazing down at the cut fruit in uncertainty.

"Me?" he asked. "Why?"

"There were a few left in the icebox back at Danann House. I think it might be extra from Luvon's wines when he visited on Imbolc. I thought about throwing them away, but... I ate the plums... and then the berries, and the pears... and they were all admittedly very good, so I thought... I shouldn't let the apples go to waste, either."

"Oh..." Saffron said thoughtfully, taking the bundle as it was offered again. Cylvan looked like there was something else he wanted to say, but just cleared his throat and straightened back up again.

"Alright, get back to work. No more breaks. Ostara will be here sooner than we think. Tick tock, púca."

Before Saffron could protest, or say thank you, or anything else at all, Cylvan was gone again. It left him feeling a little disoriented, like he'd just been sucked up in a water cyclone and dropped off somewhere new. Frowning down at the apples, he pressed one into his mouth and sighed at the taste. It was definitely one of Luvon's. Did Cylvan really... think of him? Cut it into pieces? Wrap it in wax paper, then carry it all the way across campus?

Thinking about it like that made it sound so much more burdensome than just a few pieces of fruit—but Saffron struggled to imagine Cylvan with a knife slicing away in Danann House's kitchen, thinking about Saffron the whole time. Removing the core and wrapping it in paper. Remembering to put it in his bag. Keeping it from getting smushed under his books. That was—too many steps for one prince.

The prince.

He bit another slice, the snap of it loud between the shelves.

The prince. He couldn't avoid it, the image of Cloth's body, the blood, her gray eyes unspooling like the apple slices did in Cylvan's hand.

Why hadn't he mentioned her? Surely Cylvan would have found out, somehow? Surely he'd... seen something?

Why else would Cloth have mentioned him, unless he really did know something about it?

Snap. Saffron nearly bit off one of his fingers that time, but tasted only apple when he chewed.

Clymeus... had been a king. Proserpina came from the Tuatha dé Danann family line. Was there any chance... was there any connection at all?

The wolf. The lord. The prince. The fruits.

Arrow had said the fruits were for the wolf—but could they be for the lord, too? Or for the prince?

Then—had the wolf asked for them? Or the lord? Or the prince?

Did any of them know the other was involved? Or was Saffron missing more of the pieces? Pieces he didn't get from Arrow, pieces he couldn't get from Cloth?

Gazing down at the apples, he tried to picture Cylvan taking the time to slice and package them for him, again.

Cylvan... couldn't have been the one to kill Arrow, since Saffron was with Cylvan on Imbolc when Arrow was attacked. And surely Arrow would have mentioned something other than *the wolf* if it had been the prince seeking blood.

Saffron didn't know when exactly Cloth died—but she'd apparently gone missing days earlier, the same day Saffron wandered off with his fever and met Cylvan at the library. Maybe Cylvan could have attacked and killed her while Saffron was out of it... but why would he keep Saffron close in the meantime? Why would he invite Letty and Hollow into Danann House in the meantime?

Snap.

Saffron could just ask him. Saffron *should* just ask him. Even if Cylvan had nothing to do with it, he was perhaps the only person on campus who might not only *care* to hear about a wild animal killing human servants, but who would have the power to force Elluin's hand before a third body showed up...

Snap.

Saffron knew why he didn't want to mention it.

A part of him—didn't want to know if Cylvan was aware of

the wolf. He didn't actually want to know if the prince was turning his back on Saffron's friends being killed.

Because Cylvan was... a breath of fresh air. With no talk of the wolf at all. There was a strange comfort in having just one person who wasn't aware of the violence. The grief. The fear. Was it selfish for Saffron to want to revel in that peace just a little bit longer?

Saffron ate another piece of fruit. *Snap.*

Perhaps he could... skip two stones with one throw.

15

THE QUEEN

Carrying another apple slice in his mouth, Saffron made his way to the balcony railing where, down below, Cylvan was completely unsuspiciously poking through the pages of Saffron's sketchbook. He jumped and banged his elbow on the table when Saffron cleared his throat.

"Yes, beantighe, what do you want?" the prince asked tightly, leaning over the table in an obvious attempt to hide his thwacked funnybone.

"Do you know a lot about the veiled queen?" Saffron asked.

Cylvan straightened up, shaking out his arm. He smiled, then hid it. He responded with cat-like indifference, leaning back in his chair and crossing his arms with a sigh.

"Ah, yes—great-grandmother Aryadna, of *course*. I know plenty about her, perhaps more than any historian who's ever written a silly book..."

"Who?"

Cylvan huffed, clacking the chair's front legs back to the floor. "Just—come down here, púca."

Saffron skipped down the stairs, hand gliding across the banister as he went. He walked a little too quickly to be casual.

"Is that her true name?" he asked, claiming a seat at the table as Cylvan moved his own bag from the chair.

"What? Of course not—even I don't know that. Aryadna is her civil name," he explained, and then closed his textbook, turning to face Saffron fully in a way Saffron wasn't really expecting. He seemed —eager, for some reason, though whether it was to discuss Proserpina, or simply to have a conversation at all, Saffron didn't know. He just crossed his legs on his chair and nibbled on another slice of apple.

"You don't know her true name? Why not? She's... dead." He paused with the piece in his mouth, watching Cylvan closely. "Isn't she?"

Cylvan smiled in a way that made Saffron's inside squish.

"One day when we have time, I'll tell you about *tapestries*, alright?" He offered with a sly smile. Saffron nearly broke and demanded he speak about it *immediately*, but bit it back to try and focus. He was there to ask about the wolf. About Clymeus. About...

"Are there still people who... worship her?" he asked, avoiding Cylvan's eyes. "People who... who think she had the right idea, or something? I was reading a book about her and King Clymeus just now, and it was... not a particularly pleasant experience, but it made me wonder, since... well, Verity Holt defeated her using her true name, right?"

He made the tenuous connection to their geis so Cylvan wouldn't know he'd been sidetracked, as well as so he hopefully wouldn't catch on to Saffron trying to nudge the conversation toward *big, black wolves with a taste for human blood*, just in case he really did know more than he put on.

"Well..." Cylvan gave Saffron a hesitant smile, like he wasn't quite sure how to answer. "It's a complicated relationship most high fey have with the veiled queen, but... the simple answer... yes. There are many who agree with some tenets over others, and even fewer full-blown zealots, but... yes."

"Did humans and high fey get along before she came?"

Cylvan gave him another weary smile.

"You're posing some extremely nuanced questions, here. None of these I can answer simply. But—I suppose humans and high fey got along as well as any people with different lifestyles could. There was more peace than tension, but obviously with the opposing, erm... occult systems, and differing needs for survival, as well as the crossover of cultures and traditions..."

"Occult systems?" Saffron caught the thing that made Cylvan stumble, thinking immediately to Baba Yaga's teacups. "Do you mean, like—magic? Like opulence?"

Cylvan clamped his mouth shut, before smiling awkwardly again.

"Sort of, I suppose... Proserpina did a fine job wiping most written history of the details of her reign, so who knows *exactly* what it was or how it worked, I guess... Ah, but humans have a myriad of traditions with folk magic on their side of the veil, so I would also keep that in mind..."

"Oh..." Saffron trailed off in a strange disappointment, before realizing he was losing the path of conversation again, wanting to direct it back toward the wolf king, but—"Why did Proserpina wipe her own history?"

"Her reasons... aren't clear, either. There was a purge of more than just history once Verity Holt came into the picture and the queen knew she might be done. Personal letters, journals, historical essays... she was also quite particular about the people she kept close, so her reason for a lot of things was never quite clear, except that she insisted it was necessary."

"What sort of things did she say to justify it?"

"Ah, hold on, let me get into character." Cylvan pulled a handful of black hair forward, draping it over his face before engaging in a dramatic monologue:

"Humans are a curse on our land and our heritage; never again shall an iron-yoked moon-ear cross into this world and force a single commanding word upon any fey, whenst they claim only a blink of life compared to our blessed eternities... May Danu bless

our silver-blooded roots...' Ah, damn, I never remember the next part. It was something like this: '*Adone, that treacherous, licentious, unloyal son of a bitch, never again should a fey of stature trust anyone of arid, iron-veins...*'"

Saffron feigned applause when Cylvan flipped his hair back with an embarrassed smile. He cleared his throat and continued as Saffron stretched up to help unwind some strands from his horns.

"Never thought memorizing those edicts in class would come in handy like that... Sorry for using such nasty words. It was for educational purposes."

"So Proserpina—really only did it because she hated Adone that much? That was her human lover, right?" Saffron asked, fixing Cylvan's hair more before plopping back into his seat.

"That's them, yes. I wouldn't say it was *only* because of them, but..."

"Is it true that... King Clymeus made it worse? That's what the author of the book was saying. Something about—Proserpina might have just been a bitter queen if Clymeus hadn't pushed her to action."

"Ah..." Cylvan's smile wavered. "It's... hard to know Clymeus' intentions, either. His family... historically has issues with humans passing through the veil, and vice versa. I wouldn't be surprised if he used Proserpina's grief as a means to an end."

"The end being—shuttering the veil. Erm, as much as they were able," Saffron clarified, and Cylvan nodded, before plucking one of the remaining apple slices and nudging it between Saffron's lips. Saffron accepted, taking a bite while lost in thought.

"Luvon probably visits the human world every few months or so, even when he's not making changeling deals..." he considered out loud. "He has lots of friends on the other side, both human and fey... but he also doesn't talk about it openly, like he pretends he doesn't know how. But passing through the veil isn't illegal anymore, is it? So why do people still pretend like it is?"

"Well..." Cylvan trailed off again. Saffron almost expected another monologue, but he just sat back in his chair in thought.

"The veil… doesn't work like it used to. At least from what I've read. You see—if you lay a map of the fey world over a map of the human world, they don't line up, but—before the veil was tampered with, passing through was more or less a direct hop from one map to another. Like poking a needle through. You could anticipate where you ended up.

"But… as natural tears were found and closed on both sides, it was like one map shifted—and then never stopped shifting. So unless you have someone on the other side to anchor you, there's no telling where you'll end up. I think most fey just consider veil-hopping dangerous and irresponsible, now. And, in general—bad luck, since it's so associated with the queen. Maybe they're afraid of getting trapped in the human world, too… There are plenty of reasons."

Saffron nodded. He recalled the only time he went with Luvon to the human world, how they had to hike to a specific point in Amber Valley and wait for a specific time of day in order to pass through and land exactly where Luvon wanted. Somewhere called… Cardiff? On the back of a… whale?

"I wonder if opening the tears back up would fix things?" Saffron muttered. "Aren't there still people who keep closing them? Why?"

"I think… many people are afraid of what might happen if we suddenly let the veil burst again," Cylvan shook his head. "There were enough consequences when it was closed, there's fear that letting it rent apart again would be even worse."

"What kind of consequences?"

"Well—did your book mention anything about Ashen Periods? Depending on the proximity of a fey town to a tear in the veil, how big the tear was, and how long they'd lived near it—once it was closed, the people living there would lose their opulence altogether for any number of years. For some, it came back within a few months—but many others lost their ability to do magic at all. There's actually a whole class here at Morrígan that discusses how Proserpina used anticipated Ashen Periods of big cities in her spread to conquer Alvénya across the sea... ah, sorry, I'm getting ahead of myself."

But Saffron shook his head, a new curiosity-fox jumping and spinning in his mind as he had to resist chasing it. The wolf. The wolf king. Stay focused—

"What happened on the human side when tears were closed?"

"Ah—it's actually hard to say. What didn't get purged about opulence is why we know what we do, but I don't know if anyone ever thought to observe the effects on arid—erm... the human side."

Saffron heard how Cylvan's words snagged again, but the prince quickly changed the subject like he saw Saffron's mouth twitch. "Do you... know the origin of Proserpina's name? It's based on a human myth."

Ah—another curious fox bolted, and that time, Saffron took chase.

"R-really?" he asked with eyebrows raised, thinking about how Baba Yaga was nicknamed after a human myth, too. "Are there a lot of human myths?"

"Of course," Cylvan grinned. "Great-grandmother Aryadna got the name *Proserpina* from humans, actually. She hated it at first, but eventually leaned in."

"Do you know it? The myth? Will you tell me?"

Cylvan reclined with a smug smile, twirling a piece of hair around a finger.

"Alright, alright, give me a moment to remember. It was actually one of my favorites before Naoise and Derdriu came along."

Saffron grinned, scooting in his seat in anticipation.

"Humans renamed her Proserpina, but in the myth, she was better known as Persephone..." he began, and regaled Saffron with the story of the goddess of spring and her husband of the underworld, a tale of dubious romance and trickery and pomegranate seeds and deals gone awry. By the end, Saffron was on the edge of his chair, mouth open as the world had narrowed to only Prince Cylvan in front of him. Prince Cylvan with his long hair, his sharp nails, his dark horns, his tempting mouth... like a Hades of Saffron's own.

"There's so much crossover between them and the veil," Saffron whispered, Cylvan smiling as if hoping Saffron would notice. "The pomegranate seeds are like fairy fruits... the underworld is like Alfidel—"

"Erm, obviously the underworld is the human world. Alfidel is the land of beauty. That's why even Oisín calls it *Tír na nÓg*, beantighe."

"Um, *alright*," Saffron rolled his eyes, smiling when Cylvan laughed. "Then... why did humans call her Proserpina?"

"Well... before she became queen of Alfidel, she lived in the human world with Adone. She was third in line for the throne, so she never expected to be crowned. But her parents and sisters died in a failed coup by another Sídhe family, and she was pulled back to take the reign. And then all that drama between her, Clymeus, and Adone happened, and the rest is history."

Cylvan sat forward until their faces were only a foot apart. Saffron smiled at the curious look in his eyes.

"How do they compare to Naoise and Derdriu?"

"Hmm," Saffron considered with emphasis. "I don't know... I quite like the intrigue of Hades and Persephone's love, but I think I prefer the consensual romance of Naoise and Derdriu from the beginning."

"Fair enough," Cylvan smiled. "I quite liked that about them, too."

He let the words linger, lips parted slightly as he considered the next thing he wanted to say. "You... really enjoyed that book of mine, didn't you?"

Saffron shifted awkwardly in his seat, smiling and self-consciously tucking hair behind an ear.

"Yes," he finally nodded. "It's the only book I couldn't bring myself to burn once I was done. Even though it would have gotten me in trouble if anyone found it. I read it over and over again, and every time it was like I found new details that I hadn't spotted before... Your annotations also helped me understand the stories, and I came to know them almost as well as I knew the myths they commented on..."

"I'm glad I could help," Cylvan chuckled. "How did you even teach yourself how to read? All on your own, with stolen books?"

"Luvon has five daughters," Saffron said with a weary smile. "I used to read their old school books when they were sleeping. I used them to learn letters and basic sentences..."

He laughed softly, shaking his head.

"They weren't perfect, though, especially when I faced old-Alvish spelling of names. I thought Naoise was pronounced like it was spelled for a long time. I called Niamh *'Naiam'* until I realized there was a pronunciation guide in the back glossary... And I only learned that Derdriu is modernly spelled like *Deirdre*, because... well, you left a sarcastic note on the page. You probably don't remember, but..."

"Oh, I remember," Cylvan smirked. "I have a personal vendetta against all old-Alvish spelling. It started when I was learning the Tuatha dé Danann family tree and had to memorize the spelling of all past kings and their children. Once someone dies, their name is recorded in old-Alvish, you know, even if it was spelled differently while alive."

"Oh?" Saffron blinked. "I didn't know that. How will they spell your name?"

"Oh, hmmm," Cylvan leaned back, gazing up at the ceiling and mouthing something as he thought about it. "S-I-L-B-H-A-N, I believe."

"I like it."

But Cylvan didn't sit forward again right away, chewing on his lip as he continued to gaze at the mural of Naoise and Derdriu overhead. When he did finally straighten up, he looked a little apprehensive.

"Would you... like to see them up close?" he asked. Saffron glanced upward, then back to Cylvan in confusion. The prince suddenly grinned like he had another big secret to spill. "Come on, come here."

Getting to his feet, Saffron cautiously followed, all the way to where the table ended and Derdriu and Naoise gazed down at them like ants on the floor. Cylvan turned with a regal sweeping motion, standing up straight.

"I'm going to give you an up-close-and-personal lesson in opulentology, so count yourself lucky. Few humans know my secrets like this."

Saffron's eyes went wide, nodding enthusiastically. Cylvan gave him a haughty, satisfied smile, holding up his right hand and motioning to a single ring nestled on his smallest finger. Saffron stepped in closer, the prince offering his hand for observation.

"Is that an access ring?" Saffron asked, thoughtfully touching the shiny gold band set with an equally shiny, faceted, yellowish stone on top.

"It's not an access ring, but I'm required to wear it on campus," Cylvan told him, before wiggling it off and dropping it into Saffron's hand. "The stone is called *citrine*. It's clear quartz with iron inclusions that turn it yellow."

"Iron?" Saffron blinked, appreciating the sparkle in the low light through the windows. "Doesn't it hurt?"

"At that size, I hardly feel it at all," Cylvan said. "I'm one of only two high fey on the whole campus who has to wear one. Do you want to know why?"

"Of course," Saffron laughed. "You could have guessed that."

"You're right, but I like to hear you admit it. So," Cylvan plucked the ring from Saffron's fingers and left it on the nearby table. "Here is your lesson for the day: Families with the oldest, longest lineages are more opulent than others, meaning they have more magic in their blood... specifically, Sídhe families like mine."

Saffron recalled Cylvan mentioning a Sídhe family attempting to overthrow the throne, but then also recalled another moment he'd heard the word that day. "That's what Nimue called you, isn't it?"

Cylvan smirked, but nodded.

"There are six Sídhe families in Alfidel, seven including mine, considered the oldest and most opulent. Descendants from these family lines have special gifts that not even the most learned high fey can compete with. In order to attend school with non-Sídhe students, Sídhe fey like me are required to wear citrine to suppress our abilities. Mostly so we don't bully the other students."

"You bully me well enough," Saffron muttered as Cylvan took his hands.

"Would you like to see?" Cylvan went on in a low voice. Goosebumps flushed Saffron's arms. "But only if you swear not to report me to Elluin."

"Of course," Saffron smiled, squeezing Cylvan's hands. Unable to hide the growing anticipation in his voice, he hopped back and forth between his feet. "Show me!"

"Alright, just stay where you are." Cylvan took a few steps back, holding a thoughtful hand under his chin. "Hmm... untuck your blouse. Pull your veil over your face. Alright, good. Are you ready?"

Saffron was embarrassed to look so undone, but then Cylvan raised a finger, and a rush of air swept from the floor to whip the bottom of his shirt, blast the veil from his eyes, and suck a breath right out of him. Saffron gasped before laughing wildly, pushing his newly fluffed hair from his face again.

"Wind!" he exclaimed. "You can move the—!"

Another gust swallowed him, making him laugh more and put his hands out to defend himself. Cylvan smiled the whole time, flicking his finger, twirling it, summoning mini-gales from every direction that had minds of their own. Combing through Saffron's hair, traveling under his blouse and revealing his stomach, nearly pushing him off his feet. When he inevitably stumbled into Cylvan's arms, he couldn't stop laughing, attempting to flatten down his messy hair. Cylvan just ruthlessly messed it up again.

"Are you impressed?"

"It's amazing!" Saffron exclaimed. "I've never...! Not even in books! Are you part nymph? Is all Sídhe magic elemental? Who is the other Sídhe lord on campus? What can they do? Do you think they would show me, too?"

Cylvan grimaced. "Why don't you pretend to be captivated by my magic alone, for now?"

"Oh—I don't have to pretend!" Saffron promised, hopping on his toes a little more. "Will you show me more?"

"Alright. Give me your hands again."

Saffron settled his palms into Cylvan's between them. Another swirl of wind overtook him—and lifted his feet from the floor.

Saffron lunged in surprise, clinging to Cylvan as together they hovered a few inches off the ground. Traveling slowly upward, the ruffles on his blouse, his veil, his hair floated as if gravity had been turned off, lungs fluttering in his chest. He tightened his grip around Cylvan more, until Cylvan's arms wrapped gently around Saffron's back and pulled him in closer.

"I won't let you fall, Saffron. I promise," Cylvan whispered, making Saffron's breath catch. "Go on, look up."

Saffron gulped, allowing his eyes to trail upward, and his mouth dropped open. Derdriu clutching Naoise—Saffron could reach out and touch them. He could see the individual brush-strokes, as textured and vivid as the day they were first painted; he counted Derdriu's eyelashes, even followed the little stray hairs caught in the wind around her.

"What do you think?" Cylvan asked, drawing Saffron in slightly more until their chests and stomachs fully touched, legs tangling up in one another. One of Cylvan's arms slid down to brace the back of Saffron's thighs and prop him up a little higher, and Saffron stretched upward, brushing his fingers down Derdriu's face as if attempting to comfort her sorrow. "Are they as beautiful up close?"

Saffron beamed, wanting to tell the prince exactly how beautiful they were—but the words caught on his tongue as he gazed down and met Cylvan's eyes again. Like indigo petals, colorful even in the low light; his features, somehow both soft and sharp; his eyelashes dark and feathery as they gazed up at him. Saffron saw the beauty mark beneath the prince's eye, the leaves and vines carved into his horns, the gold jewelry in his ears, the perfect shape of his mouth... all things he recognized of the fey prince, but had never appreciated so intimately until that moment.

"They're... perfect," Saffron whispered, butterflies blooming in his stomach as Cylvan's enchanting lips quirked upward.

"I..." Saffron went on without thinking, not knowing what words would come next, just... wanting to say *anything*. Wanting the prince's eyes to stay on him a bit longer. Wanting that moment to last a bit longer.

When no words came, Cylvan smiled smugly, asking if his incredible abilities had left Saffron speechless. Saffron didn't know how to explain the ways Cylvan did far more than that to him.

16

THE SILENCE

At opposing ends of the nave, Cylvan could windblast hard enough for Saffron to feel a breeze all the way across to where he stood. He could make a book hover for three minutes before getting tired. He could summon gale-force winds strong enough to knock Saffron off his feet, while Saffron laughed the whole time. At the peak of his arrogance, Cylvan even jumped from the upper balcony and blasted a wind-cushion to catch his fall, but still grunted on impact. Saffron had never laughed harder in his life, kissing the underside of Cylvan's wrist as the prince complained about it hurting.

While Cylvan showed him how he could even create tiny rain clouds and mimic the sound of thunder, Saffron's eyes caught the light of the prince's palm-sized lightning storm on his horns. Vines tangling and weaving over one another, hollowed out in the center in a way Saffron hadn't noticed before.

Saffron wanted to ask if he could touch them—but Cylvan distracted from the temptation when he asked about Saffron's drawing things on the dock, and where Saffron normally got his charcoal from.

"I make it myself using dry branches."; and then how often he added new pages into his sketchbook—*"Whenever I have a book*

to steal paper from. "; What his favorite thing to draw was— *"Any of the wild fey in the woods."*; If there was anything he'd always wanted to draw, but could never find— *"I've always wanted to see a real nymph. I would actually love to see all kinds of nymphs, one day..."*

An hour after midnight, Saffron dozed off as Cylvan read to him from a book about locating and making nice with nymphs for Saffron's future reference. When the prince's speaking voice slowed to a stop, and Saffron felt fingers touch his shoulder, he lifted his head sleepily and apologized.

"Why don't you stay the night with me again?" Cylvan teased.

"Hmm," Saffron smiled drowsily, rubbing his eyes. "That's very tempting, but... beantighes are being accounted for more than ever. I really shouldn't be away all night."

"Fine," the prince complained. "But I will at least walk you to Agate Bridge."

Gathering their things, Cylvan asked if he could join Saffron the next time he made charcoal on his own. In exchange, Saffron jokingly asked if Cylvan could float to the tops of trees to find better branches.

"No problem," Cylvan answered. "You only got a peek of it tonight, but I'm actually quite good at flying."

"Can you fly far? For how long?" Saffron asked as the curiosity hit him again. "Can you go very high? I've noticed at the top of the mountain it's always a little harder to breathe—is it the same in the sky?"

"Why don't I show you sometime?"

"Oh!!" Saffron practically leaped. "Really!"

"Why not? Perhaps on your next day off. What if I flew you into Connacht and just bought you some charcoals from a shop?"

Saffron nearly shrieked with giddiness—but the second they stepped outside, voices came laughing from the darkness, and Saffron immediately froze. In the campus' center, a group of students were busy sword fighting, movements exaggerated and sweeping while they slurred playful threats at one another. It wasn't unusual for high fey to get drunk and mess around, no matter the time of day—but the thought of being spotted leaving the library, especially with the prince, was nerve-wracking enough. The fact that Saffron recognized one of the drunken voices as Kaelar's only made Saffron's nerves heighten more.

"Oh..." he said nervously, taking a step back. "I should..."

Before he could take off like a rabbit, though, Cylvan was already adjusting his shoulder bag and stripping off his jacket. He wrapped it over Saffron's shoulders, Saffron barely asking what he was doing as he crossed his bag back over his body—and then scooped Saffron into his arms, taking off into the sky.

Saffron released a sharp scream of surprise before clamping his hands over his mouth. Cylvan just laughed, pulling Saffron closer as they reached the peak of his arc high above the buildings, the trees.

"Look, púca!" he called out over the wind. Saffron nervously pulled his face from the side of Cylvan's neck, heart leaping at the sight of the illuminated buildings below, the fog rolling through the Agate Wood and Obsidian Valley in the distance. It made him breathe fast and hard as his whole body screeched with fear, but not a single noise of fright left his mouth. In fact, with his arms looped around the back of Cylvan's neck, his back and legs supported in Cylvan's arms, the newly familiar weightlessness blooming in his chest... Saffron felt completely safe. There was nothing there to frighten him at all.

He burst out laughing, pulling himself closer to Cylvan as he nearly lost his grip. Flailing his legs like an excited cat, he just appreciated the view, commenting on the buildings below, how he could see Connacht in the distance, the beautiful way the fog claimed the mountainsides and made the horizon look like a silvery ocean.

Wrapped up in Cylvan's jacket, carried in his arms, embraced by the fresh air high above the school, the woods, anything at all that could hurt or scare him—emotion welled up in the back of Saffron's throat, and he couldn't stop smiling again.

"Cylvan!" he exclaimed, like he finally knew what he wanted to say. Cylvan gazed at him, unable to resist his own smile as Saffron grinned. "I think you're incredible!"

The words appeared to catch Cylvan off guard. He just looked at Saffron with sincerity, before laughing.

"Only for you."

"Then I will consider myself lucky!"

Cylvan laughed more, before the wind shifted and they began their descent toward Beantighe Village within the trees. Lighting down on one of the roads outside the iron fence and rowan trees, Cylvan let Saffron down gently, but kept one hand on his back.

"Will you be alright on the way home?" Saffron asked, removing the coat and returning it. "You aren't too tired?"

Cylvan shrugged the coat on, nodding and pulling hair out from the back.

"I'll be alright... unless you're offering me a warm place next to you, instead." He paused for effect, before laughing at himself. "It's not too far once I get up there. Can you find your cottage from here?"

"Oh, yes, I know exactly where we are," Saffron sighed, having drifted slightly at the thought of Cylvan entering Cottage Wicklow with him, climbing into the tiny bed, wrapped up close and keeping one another warm... he shivered, shaking the thought away as his whole body tingled.

"Um, I had a lot of fun—erm, I mean, I *got a lot of very serious studying done* tonight."

Cylvan smirked. "I had a lot of fun, too."

Saffron opened his mouth to ask the same question he always did, and Cylvan's smile softened as he anticipated it.

"Will you be at the library tomorrow night, your highness?"

"Unfortunately... I'll be attending a party in Connacht," Cylvan admitted, though sounded disappointed. "Sorry, beantighe. Try out that ring on your own, will you?"

Saffron smiled weakly, nodding. The emotion swirling in his chest was two-fold—relief to know he would still be able to go

into the library at all, and... a slight pinch of his own disappointment that he would do it by himself.

"Be careful on the rest of your way home, alright?" Cylvan
went on.

Saffron nodded. "You too. Maybe I'll see you on campus
tomorrow, before your party..."

They smiled at each other until Cylvan gently tugged his arm,
unknowingly clutched in Saffron's hands.

"You'll have to let me go, eventually."

"Oh!" Saffron jerked away in embarrassment. "I'm sorry! I
just—"

Cylvan interrupted, pressing a kiss to Saffron's cheek. It made
Saffron flush, touching the spot as Cylvan pulled away again with
a smug look.

"Don't worry. You'll have plenty of opportunities to touch
me more tomorrow."

"O-oh," Saffron squeaked, and Cylvan just laughed again,
wishing him good night and taking off like a raven to the sky.
Saffron watched him go for as long as he could, smiling to himself
as his heart raced—before taking off on his own for the fence
before any stalking wolf came to grab him.

WHEN MORNING CAME, SAFFRON WAS UP AND DRESSED
before anyone else, taking time to brush his hair down, align his
veil perfectly, tuck his blouse into his pants, and even check for
wrinkles in his slacks and scuffs on his shoes. Even Baba seemed
to notice his attention to detail, narrowing her eyes suspiciously
as he just planted a kiss on her cheek and hurried out to the
road.

At first, the prince was all Saffron could think about—until
he fell victim to one of Fleece's heated debates and pushed up his
veil to argue. To claim there were no such things as *actual ghosts*
like in stories Baba told on Samhain meant Saffron had no choice
but to *insist* there was no way to know—and who was to say

ghosts weren't just some sort of wild fey thing? Or an opulent trick?

They all looked at him curiously when he used the word *opulent* so casually, making him blush and divert his attention again.

Letty took Saffron's side and posited that maybe only humans could see ghosts at all. But according to Fleece, that implied humans either had magic sight while alive or magic bodies that allowed them to wander even after death. Saffron argued that no one ever said it had to be explained by magic, and then asked what the fuck "magic sight" was supposed to mean—

"I'm sure you're very familiar with magic by now, aren't you, Saffron? Fucking a high fey and all," Berry interrupted, and the enthusiastic debate quieted down. Awkwardness tasted like rotten fruit that morning, Saffron gaping a little as Fleece muttered something and took Berry's hand. Berry frowned, furrowing his brows before aggressively kicking a pinecone that was in his way.

"Sorry," he grumbled.

"Um... that's alright," Saffron answered, trying to laugh it off, though it caught in his throat. "I'm genuinely... not fucking any fey lord, though..."

But Saffron knew why Berry said it. From Saffron's coy comments while washing Arrow's veil in the lake, to spending days at a time away from the village, to coming home late flushed and giggling. And none of that even touched what others whispered about when they thought he couldn't hear.

From what he gathered, no one really thought he was the one who killed Cloth and Arrow, but the hushed consensus remained that Saffron knew *something*. And they weren't *wrong*, but not for the reasons they thought. Perhaps Berry had formed some sort of relationship between those two accusations, after all...

Saffron cleared his throat, coming up with a simple stretch of the truth while pinching his dirt-stained library ring.

"I was actually thinking about talking to Professor Adelard today," he announced, glad when even Berry lifted his head. "He knows a lot about local fey, so maybe he knows something about wolves, too. And how to stop them, or at least get them to go somewhere else..."

"Yeah, like onto campus," Letty said, and a wheeze left Saffron. "I mean, not like I want it to go and kill students—"

"Why not?" Berry argued. Saffron attempted to clear the lump in his throat. Letty just sighed. Then shrugged.

"What I'm *trying* to say is the only reason Cassila, and by extension Elluin, are putting off doing anything to help is because the students somehow haven't noticed yet. Or just aren't talking about it because they don't care enough... And until the students speak up, no one's going to care about us."

"Right. Sic the wolf on some students, and it would be gone by the next morning," Fleece agreed bitterly.

"Maybe if the next beantighe to go had a patron who gave a damn," Letty mumbled sarcastically. "Hm. Like you, Saffron."

"Gee, thanks," Saffron huffed. "But don't you think the foundling thing could just be a coincidence? There are plenty of foundlings working here, right?"

"Sunbeam wasn't a foundling," Berry interjected, and they all looked at him again. He immediately puffed up, face going red. "Damnit, has everyone completely forgotten! There's still someone else missing! Just because we haven't found a body doesn't mean—!"

Letty took Berry's opposite hand. Fleece squeezed the one they already held. Berry just restrained himself and blinked back angry tears as Letty whispered condolences to him.

"Sunbeam and Cloth were friends, right?" she asked. "Maybe she just went looking before Cloth was found. It's possible the wolf has no idea about her, and she's just lost. She'll be back in no time."

Berry didn't answer, but his eyes lifted sharply to Saffron, who kept his gaze for a moment before having to look away. It spoke volumes, but Saffron couldn't quite make out the words.

The conversation ended as they reached campus, Berry

pulling his hands from Fleece and Letty's and entering the assign-ment building alone. The others just followed behind in silence, unable to find the same energy again.

Assigned to replace linens in dorm rooms was an inherently tedious and miserable job, especially so early in the morning when so many students were supposed to be out of bed but preferred to argue instead—but the singular saving grace was the competitive nature of it, two beantighes assigned to each floor racing to see who could strip and flip every room the fastest. Partnered up with Cricket from Wicklow's Maple Room was also particularly thrilling as they were considered the best and the fastest, more than once tangling Saffron's arms in the sheets as Saffron couldn't keep up.

After an afternoon scraping ponds in the Elathan Gardens, the sun finally set, and Saffron walked all the way back to Beantighe Village with the others—only to turn right back around again when no one was looking and hurry back for his night amongst the books.

He knew he would be by himself that night, but he didn't realize how *alone* he would be, feeling the lack of Prince Cylvan like something forgotten. The small sounds, the long sighs while studying, his sarcastic comments, Saffron never thought he'd miss them until he didn't have them.

He tried to focus, but glanced up whenever he heard a sound. He wandered between the shelves like one of the mice that scurried across the floor looking for something to snack on. He never thought it would be possible to find *nothing* in an entire library that could hold his interest. He didn't even know where to start looking, as his mind scrambled with a hundred different things he wanted to know more about all at once. Perhaps Cylvan had been mentally influencing Saffron's search whenever he sat at the tables below? Was that a thing opulence was capable of? Or did their conversations just—make the research more exciting?

His mind drifted, and he wondered what a party in Connacht

was like. What Cylvan was wearing. Had he put on makeup? What did he do with his hair? Was he having fun?

What if... Saffron had joined him, like he once requested?

Would he have sat perched between Cylvan's knees all night again? Would they have spent the night commenting on the other partygoers and their outfits? Would Saffron have fed him more fruits, feeling the way Cylvan's tongue trailed over his fingers every time?

He dropped the book in his grasp when he thought about it.

Maybe he would sit on Cylvan's lap, instead. Like a real cat. Pull his legs up and nestle against Cylvan's neck. Cylvan's finger would still curl along that piece of skin below his ear, and Saffron would still feed him strawberries. And...

Oh—did he have another fever? Why did he feel so warm?

He was about to stuff the book in his hands back on the shelf as midnight quickly approached and he'd gotten exactly nothing done—but at the last second, his eyes skimmed the words *"arid magic"* within the text, and a familiar curiosity-fox poked its head from the den in his mind. Hadn't Cylvan used that word while discussing the veil? Hadn't the word "arid" been one that'd made him stumble, as well as "occult"?

For the first time all night, the warm fantasies popped, allowing Saffron even a brief moment of actual focus.

Like in all of Saffron's readings on opulent magic, *arid magic* was never outright defined in the paragraph where it was mentioned, only a comment on the date its practice, teaching, and discussion was made taboo—which was right at the beginning of Queen Proserpina's reign. However, searching the rest of the page, and a few pages after that, and then the index in the back, there was no other mention of arid magic in the book at all.

Snapping it shut, he returned it to the shelf. He briefly skimmed the titles of the books next to it, before leaving to head down to the main floor where the register tome sat.

Searching pages of the Opulentology section with no luck, he then skimmed the tabs along the edge for anything that resembled *arid magic* or *occult magic* or even *folk magic,* the whole time reminded of when Cylvan first showed him how to use the tome at all. Saffron wondered if the prince was impressed at how much he'd learned, smiling sarcastically to himself.

Finally, at the very bottom of the edge in a tab colored red, he found the word "Aridology." Pulling back the sheets, he nearly ripped the tab clean off with the weight of the other thousand pages it lifted—only to be disappointed when the entire section was blank, save for one line in the middle of the page:

Aridology Collection Archived on Grounds of Condemnation, est. Night of Proserpina, Spring, Wheel 2. Avren Nat'l Collection, ΨARC;016. See proctor for special access.

Not knowing what "proctor" meant, but having an idea about "Avren Nat'l Collection," Saffron just grumbled and plucked a piece of parchment next to the book to make a note. From there, he accepted defeat, and returned all of his things.

Sneaking from the library, Saffron crossed the dark campus for Agate Bridge, pausing for a moment to gaze up the rest of the walkway where the path to Danann House split off. He wondered if Cylvan was still in Connacht, or perhaps already back home in bed—and more indulgent thoughts crept up and knocked on the door of his mind.

Considering the long walk back home and the wolf-shaped nerves prickling under his skin, he decided to let them in to keep him company.

He fantasized about... going to Danann House instead of crossing Agate Bridge. What if he asked Cylvan for a flight back to the village, because he was just *so tired* from all the walking, and there was something stalking around in the woods, and he was just so *frightened* and *scared*...?

Cylvan would scoop him up right away. Sweep him through the window and into the night sky, holding him close and warm while Saffron took the chance to gently interrogate him about what a *"proctor"* was and demand a trip to the library in Avren. Cylvan would laugh and shake his head like he always did when

Saffron was being demanding; he would smirk and sigh; he would threaten to cut out Saffron's tongue for daring to speak of *taboo magic* to the Prince of Alfidel... Oh, maybe he would demand Saffron's silence, but when Saffron refused, maybe he would—would k-kiss him, to silence him...

Saffron's heart raced. He felt feverish again. He couldn't stop giggling as he pictured it, and then tried to push the thoughts away, only for others to swarm back and take their place. He gave in once more, following the romantic thread, the sound of Cylvan's voice, how he smiled while holding Saffron close to his chest...

Oh—perhaps, one day, if Saffron wasn't able to solve their geis after all... instead of cutting out his tongue, or letting Luvon push him through the veil, Cylvan would just... carry him far away. Drop him off somewhere no one would find him, where he wouldn't be able to use Cylvan's true name at all. Maybe in the snowy mountains, or near the ocean, where he could live quietly, never seen by anyone ever again...

And then—the prince would come to visit. What if he arrived unannounced just to say hello, to make sure Saffron was doing alright? To use his wind to clean the rafters, to bring more books for Saffron's little library? To compliment Saffron on his sketches and all the reading he'd done?

Oh, no. He pressed his hands to his warm face, biting back a small noise of giddiness. It wasn't good, or safe, or healthy to think about things like that, not when Saffron was a beantighe and Cylvan was a prince. But—perhaps there was no harm so long as Saffron knew they would only ever be fantasies. If he never let those thoughts loose into reality.

He was still battling himself internally when something claimed his attention off the trail, making him stop short and turn.

When the shadows remained silent and unmoving, he decided he'd only imagined it, and continued ahead—until another sound came, like moving feet. He paused again, but didn't come to a full stop, hurrying his pace instead. He tried to think of his cabin by the ocean more, about Prince Cylvan swooping in. Saffron would bake him pastries and pot roast with vegetables from his own garden. It would be peaceful. And lovely, and romantic—

Another sound made him stop. That time, he puffed up his chest and called out to whatever it was.

Silence—and then more moving feet, as five shadows suddenly emerged from the darkness and rushed him.

Saffron stumbled back, a partial scream of surprise erupting from his mouth as he turned and ran. His heart slammed in his chest, swelling into his throat as he raced as fast as he could, considering leaping into the woods to lose those in pursuit, or maybe grabbing a branch to fight them off—but Beantighe Village wasn't far. If he could just make it past the rowan tree sentries, the iron gate, he would be out of their reach. High fey would never cross into village territory just for a prank.

But upon cresting the boundary of the village, he watched in horror as the five pursuers stormed through behind him.

Too faintly illuminated by the lanterns glowing outside each cottage door, Saffron couldn't make out their faces. Before he could say anything, do anything else, they grabbed and threw him to the road.

A fist met his mouth, and then his eye, crushing him into the dirt until gravel crunched between his teeth. Gasping for breath, attempting to fight back, his ears rang from the collision of fists. Blood mixed with grit on his tongue and dripped in thick strings onto the road, just attempting to push himself back up again, only to be grabbed by the hair and dragged.

Clawing at the hand that held him, his thoughts raced—was it Kaelar? Taran? Elluin? How did they cross the gates so easily, without even a flinch? Had they been waiting for just anyone to pass?

But then—Saffron recognized one of their voices, and his legs gave out again. His kneecap slammed against a worn cobblestone, making him cry out as he attempted to follow where they took him.

"B-Berry," he begged, voice crackling. "Why—"

"I know you've been running around with the fey prince," Berry growled, tugging on Saffron's hair again when Saffron lost his balance. It made Saffron choke, eyes watering as his scalp burned. "You were our Brìghde this year. You swore to protect us —and yet you're the one hurting us, aren't you?"

"What?" Saffron pleaded, the road giving way to grass as they dragged him across the bonfire field. "I haven't—hurt anyone, Berry!"

"You haven't protected anyone, either. Arrow needed your help. Cloth needed your help. Sunbeam still needs your help— but you're too busy fucking that high fey to give a shit, right? So I thought—if we need a third victim for Elluin to care about us, why not Brìghde, who swore to watch over us?"

"Berry, please—" Saffron attempted to pull himself free again, searching through blurry, wild eyes to find the faces of the other humans behind him. Thread and Leaf from Cottage Wicklow, Cache from Monaghan, Branch from Dublin. None of them met Saffron's eyes, just hurrying to keep up as Berry pulled Saffron toward the fence.

Using the two layers of his veil, they pinned him facing the woods and tied his wrists to the iron posts. Saffron just begged Berry to listen, to just *look* at him. He kept apologizing for Arrow and Cloth and Sunbeam, swearing he had nothing to do with them—but it soon became harder and harder for him to believe it himself.

Arrow had asked Saffron about the fruits in the woods, and Saffron let them leave. Saffron never even told anyone they'd gone.

Saffron had been spending his nights on campus, in the library with Prince Cylvan, completely neglecting his friends, his village chores, and anyone else who might need him. Cloth had gone into the woods by herself because she wasn't able to get his help.

Sunbeam was still missing, and Saffron, despite knowing the woods best, never offered to help Berry or anyone else search more because he was too busy with his own fey deal.

And Saffron—had grown closer to Prince Cylvan. Close enough that he could have been more forthcoming about the wolf and whether Cylvan knew anything about it. Whether Cylvan was behind it, or knew what to do to stop it, or knew *anything at all*. Saffron could have asked Cylvan to insist Elluin do something sooner, instead of waiting for a third victim to come and hoping she might address it, then. But instead—he decided to cling to the simple peace Cylvan offered him, by never discussing the wolf at all—and potentially dragging out the danger for everyone else.

Maybe—it really was his fault. Maybe the words on his back weren't so out of place, after all.

Another angry fist slammed into his stomach. Another found his jaw. He tasted only blood and spit and bile by the time Berry and the others left, tied off and vulnerable for any wild animal to come and drag him away for dead.

Selfish. Selfish. Selfish. Selfish.

17

THE RAVEN

aba Yaga found him before the wolf did. Apparently, Saffron had left a trail of blood all the way from the front gates to where he dangled from the section of fence hidden behind a garden wall. She screamed when she spotted him, though Saffron barely heard it, mind nothing but a buzz as his head dangled from his shoulders.

When asked who attacked him, he told them fey students.

He couldn't blame Berry. Or Thread, or Leaf, or Cache, or Branch. Everyone was just scared. Berry was just worried for Sunbeam, who he cared about. Saffron couldn't blame them for that, not when, in many ways... they were absolutely right. Saffron could have done more. All Saffron had done, until that point, was ignore the cries for help as he focused on himself. He'd walked as Brìghde then turned his back the second they blew the candles out.

The next morning, Saffron asked Baba Yaga to specifically request him for chore assignments in Beantighe Village for the week. It meant walking all the way to campus to be marked for attendance and then walking all the way back again every day, but it allowed him to more easily hide from any student who might see his battered face and make a scene. It also gave him a chance to prove to Berry and everyone else that he did want to be there with them, helping them. He wanted to be with his friends, his human family, and show them where he stood.

On the first day, he helped Baba Yaga catch up on all the things he'd missed while skipping his normal village chores.

On the second day, he searched the woods for any trace of Sunbeam or where she might have gone, but inevitably came up empty. Though in the process, he also found a set of giant paw prints through the undergrowth, and held his breath the entire time he followed in fear of turning around the next tree and coming face to face with the rot-smelling beast. And then—he noticed the footprints that seemed to walk alongside them, either human or fey by their shape, and it made his insides tangle more like vines.

The lord. The prince.

When he wasn't tracking in the woods, he played card games and gambled river stones with his friends in the evenings, like he used to. He hunted for wild tobacco and marijuana to give as gifts, and then helped Silk replenish her medicinal herb collection, even taking the time to cut, bundle, and dry the sprigs while she did her own chores on campus.

Saffron helped Hollow find new branches they could carve into wooden swords, as Blade had accidentally snapped his a few days prior when she went too hard during practice. He then offered to help try them out, only to leave with bruises up and down his legs and a promise from Hollow to teach him better tricks next time.

He combed knots out of Letty's hair while she told him about Nimue, and how she and the undine had been meeting to chat every morning. She talked about how Nimue named herself after a human myth, how she'd swam all the way to Lake Elatha from the ocean—and how they already kissed once as the sun was setting, and when Letty admitted it was her first, the undine actually looked embarrassed.

Throughout all of it—Berry still wouldn't speak to him.

Wouldn't look at him. He apologized for what they did, and thanked Saffron for not telling Baba who really attacked him—but otherwise, treated Saffron like the ghost Fleece once claimed didn't exist.

Despite everything, Saffron still wished every night he could visit the library again. Staring up at the ceiling in bed, in the dark, watching the orange cat-that-wasn't-a-cat bumble around in the rafters, he thought only of the books; he thought only of Prince Cylvan. He *dreamed* only of Prince Cylvan. The devouring want to go back, mentally working through possible excuses for any reason he could escape for the evening just to have another chance to read, another chance to maybe bump into Cylvan studying at the table—it all made him swirl with guilt. Guilt for wanting to abandon his friends again—and guilt for actually abandoning the prince without warning.

But, most of all, guilt because he missed Cylvan more than he should have.

Four mornings passed before the prince finally caught Saffron marking himself in attendance and turning back for the road. Grabbed by the arm, it made Saffron jump, lost in his own thoughts and not noticing the shadowy raven swooping in on him. He didn't have a chance to even chirp out a greeting before the prince towed him off the side of the path to ask if everything was alright. Saffron just kept his veil down, not wanting Cylvan to see his split lip, the bruises across his jaw and cheek, how one of his eyes was still swollen.

But the sun was apparently bright enough to render Saffron's veil useless, or maybe Cylvan was just looking close enough to see, because he soon pushed Saffron's veil up without warning, revealing every inch of him.

"What..." Cylvan started, making Saffron flinch when his fingers gently brushed along his sore cheek. Saffron just kept his eyes down, biting his lip as Cylvan's voice turned venomous. "Who did this to you?"

Saffron shook his head. He averted his eyes more.

"It was my own fault," he whispered, surprised when Cylvan grabbed his shoulder and made Saffron meet his eyes again. Saffron's blood went cold at Cylvan's expression contorted into fury, amethyst eyes sharp as they scoured Saffron's face over and over again.

"Tell me who did this," he repeated tightly, "so that I may tear them apart with my own hands."

Saffron jumped, turning his eyes down again and touching Cylvan's hand on his shoulder. He shook his head, stiffening when Cylvan hissed a demanding *"why not?"*.

"It doesn't matter," Saffron answered quietly, shaking his head more. "I don't want to talk about it. You don't have to worry, either, Baba assured me nothing will get infected, it'll all heal normally—"

"That's—!" Cylvan interrupted, making Saffron flinch again. Cylvan swallowed back whatever he was going to say, letting out a soft breath. He touched Saffron's black and blue cheek again with fingers gentle enough to hold smoke. His hand shook like it was difficult for him to hold back, but Saffron didn't know what else to say. "Saff—"

"What's up, Cylvan?" a voice called from the walkway, making Saffron jump. He turned to look, before quickly glancing away again as soon as Kaelar came into focus. He was joined by Eias and Magnin, all of them looking at Cylvan with curiosity. Cylvan's hands pulled away without a sound, and he tucked them casually into his pockets.

"Nothing, really," Cylvan responded with cool arrogance, clearly theatrical for the new audience. "I just watched this clumsy beantighe eat shit on some stairs in Nemain Hall. Couldn't help but feel bad for them."

"Is that the same one that poured wine on Lord Taran?" Magnin asked, and frustrated tears immediately burned in the back of Saffron's eyes. "Are you sure you didn't push 'em down, just for the thrill?"

"Nah," Cylvan laughed. "I think beantighes just don't know how to tie their own shoes."

Saffron turned and hurried away. The embarrassment made his skin tingle like air before lightning, frustration spilling over and dripping down his swollen cheeks once he was clear of witnesses.

THE NEXT DAY, WHILE DUSTING THE RAFTERS WHERE Hollow had done a lazy job on Imbolc, Saffron made conversation with the orange cat as it floated and swatted lazily at bugs scurrying by. Wiping down the colored glass in the parlor, he dug centuries-old dirt from the cames between the panels like hard candy. Outside, rain pattered like knocking hands of a million pixies—and then a handful of pixies actually did show up, and Saffron let them in if they promised to stay out of Baba's way. They didn't, and Baba sent the cat after them.

When the rain let up, Baba sent him to gather reeds for a new broom, though a part of him knew she just wanted him out of the house. She wasn't used to an incessant fox terrier following her around day after day asking for something to do. He took his sketchbook and found scraps of charcoal to keep him busy.

Wearing his short cream-colored cloak, the air was humid but not particularly cold, rain only tapping occasionally as clouds shook off the extra weight. Leaving through the gate behind Wicklow, Saffron trailed his fingers down the shimmering posts of the iron fence, along the trail beside the rowan sentries, to the back road where he walked for a few minutes before branching off onto an invisible path only he knew. The crisp smell of fresh grass, moss, ferns, trees, wildflowers filled his nose and swirled in his chest, every sensation emphasized with a little petrichor in the air. He hoped that emphasis would apply to wolves, too, just in case. He was glad he brought his knife.

Dodging the largest puddles to keep his socks dry, his hood eventually grew crowded as pixies found him and took refuge from the heavy air. A few sprites even joined in, and then two entire robins ridden by pixies like horses. It was when a toad leapt onto his shoulder and tried to wriggle inside as well that Saffron finally wrenched his hood back and shook out his hair. A thousand screeches of protest buzzed from the cloud of creatures in response.

When another robin landed on his head and tried to get his attention, he snatched it out of the air like a frog tonguing a fly—but to his surprise, it wasn't a robin-steed, but a messenger bird. Apologizing, he hurried to the nearest crook in a tree and released it, apologizing again as it fluffed its wings and chirped at him in annoyance.

Taking the offered scroll hesitantly, he wasn't quite sure what to do. He'd never received a letter before, at least not directly. Whenever patron-families wanted to send something to a beantighe, it would usually go to their henmother and they would read the message for whoever it was addressed to. Despite being familiar with day-robins meant for campus messages, and ravens used for long-distance messages and parcels, Saffron didn't actually know how they worked or how the messenger tokens were meant to be used. Was it some sort of mistake?

GOOD MORNING. HAVE YOU EATEN BREAKFAST TODAY?

He recognized the handwriting instantly, mouth gaping before instinctively looking around to search the sky—but there was no additional giant raven swooping down to get him. His stomach growled at the word *breakfast*.

Eyes returning to the robin, he held the note out slightly.

"What do I do?" he asked, crying out when the bird chirped again before flying away. He watched it go, gazing back down at the note again in a panic. "What do I do!" he called after it, but it disappeared over the trees.

Would Cylvan realize the bird left before Saffron could

respond? Or that Saffron fundamentally *didn't know how* to respond? Did he just have to roll up another note and the bird would know where to take it? How? If it was so smart, why did it fly off the second he spoke to it?

"Morrígan birds are dull compared to you," he later said to a wild robin standing defense in its nest, shocked to wake up and find a human at the top of its tree stripping away old branches. Throwing them to the forest floor below, Saffron just kept complimenting the little bird bitterly, explaining that he wasn't there to steal her eggs, he was just trying to get some branches to make new charcoals since he lost his old ones in the lake. *"Do you know about undines?"* he asked as she peeped at him. Two pixie companions soon found him again after getting lost chasing a snake in the grass, and the robin went wild trying to scare them off. He snapped at them to leave the bird alone and go back to hunting snakes, or maybe bees, or to go find a student to rob—

"How did you ever get up this high?"

Saffron jolted, grabbing a hollow branch that snapped under his weight. He tumbled at least ten feet before hands grappled for him, more dead branches and pine needles raining down over his face and hair as he clamored for something solid to hold on to. Clinging upside down to Cylvan's thighs, the prince clung to his waist, and Saffron's face went red as he flailed his legs in embarrassment.

"P-Prince Cylvan!" he exclaimed. "Wh-what are you doing out here!"

"What are *you* doing out here!" Cylvan argued, adjusting his grip. It made Saffron blush and squirm more at the thought of a royal face pressed between his thighs. "Stop—climbing tall things when you're so—damn—clumsy!"

"You—! You think I was prepared to hear a voice in the middle of the fucking woods?" Saffron squeaked, adrenaline controlling what words left his mouth. "God—I thought you were a-a sluagh, or something—*Ériu's plucking harp*, I thought I was done for..."

"You're not allowed in the woods anymore! No ladders, no trees! Nothing!"

Saffron laughed—but then Cylvan lost his grip, and he tumbled another few feet before grabbed again by the wrist. He couldn't help another wheezing chuckle as Cylvan looked like he'd lost a hundred years off his life.

"You really are a handful, you know that?"

"Ha, ha," Saffron mumbled, straining his arm and throwing out his other hand to grapple for Cylvan's shoulder bag, then his doublet. Hooking his arms under Saffron's, Cylvan pulled Saffron into his chest as if he weighed nothing, pinning them together as his hands locked back around Saffron's waist. The sudden closeness made Saffron self-conscious, turning away when he recalled the state of his face.

"Th-thank you," he finally said. He glanced down to the forest floor where his body might have splattered if Cylvan hadn't caught him, considering the distance and muttering: "... I probably would have been fine."

"Seriously?" Cylvan asked flatly, and Saffron smiled.

"I've fallen from higher."

"Oh—you're *definitely* not allowed up any more trees."

Giggling, Saffron pulled pine needles from Cylvan's braided hair, then from the creases of his black suede doublet and the laces of his black tunic underneath. Soft, expensive fabrics that made Saffron grimace when thinking about his own worn wool doublet and cloak in comparison.

"I'm sorry I didn't respond to your note," Saffron finally said, digging a particularly stubborn needle from a dark plait of Cylvan's hair. "I've... never gotten a letter before. I didn't know how. And then the bird flew off before I could figure it out..."

"That's alright," Cylvan smiled. "I'll show you how to respond to a message for next time. In the meantime, I, ah... brought... breakfast."

Saffron blinked at him with eyebrows raised. "You what?"

"Erm, you haven't been on campus for a while, and I haven't

seen you at the library, and last time you ran off before I could finish talking to you, so... I figured I would... hunt you down. Make sure you hadn't fled the country." He cleared his throat, gazing off toward the horizon before smiling awkwardly—and Saffron realized with a thud of his pulse, the prince was... nervous? "I don't have class today, either, so I thought we could... eat together, if you'd like..."

"O-oh! Sure!" Saffron exclaimed, accidentally yanking on the back of Cylvan's neck. "Sorry, if I'd known you were coming I would have waited closer to the road, or—erm, *on* the road..."

"That's alright," Cylvan's uncertain smile flickered into relief, and Saffron couldn't help but mimic it. "I rather enjoyed searching for you without any hints. Like finding a sprite in a meadow. Speaking of—there's this pond I overheard some other students talking about, on the other side of the mountain. It's supposed to be nice, and no one will bother us... Does that sound familiar? Since you love tromping around in the mud all day..."

"On the other side of the mountain?" Saffron shook his head. "I'm never able to get very far on my days off, since I can only walk."

"Well, no walking today," Cylvan grinned, tightening his arms around Saffron's middle. "Hold on tight."

A shrill laugh escaped as Saffron clung to Cylvan's shoulders, shooting into the sky like a geyser. Pulling his knees close, he buried his face in the crook of Cylvan's neck as his stomach flipped and danced, Cylvan's hands flexing on Saffron's back and under his knees. When Cylvan nudged him to open his eyes, Saffron nervously blinked against the wind, grinning at the sight of Obsidian Valley, trees like fibers of a carpet; the Three Crone Peaks far off in the distance, sun hanging directly over the middle point as it crept up into mid-morning. The Connacht river snaked all the way to the horizon, twisting and branching off into Quartz Creek that cut through the Agate Wood, twirling like a ribbon past Beantighe Village's tiny clearing amidst the trees, and a little further away, Morrígan's campus on the edge of Lake Elatha.

Breathing in the fresh air, he accidentally grabbed one of Cylvan's horns when a sudden gust caught him off guard and wrenched his shoulder bag like a kite. Apologizing, Cylvan just shook his head and laughed, pulling Saffron in closer to protect him. Saffron couldn't help it—he pressed himself into Cylvan's neck again, using the windchill as an excuse when really, he just wanted to feel the warmth of his skin. Smell his perfume. When he accidentally slid fingers up the nape of Cylvan's neck, Cylvan chuckled and touched his mouth to Saffron's hair.

"Are you cold?" he asked like he knew exactly what Saffron was doing, making Saffron pull away again quickly.

"I'm alright!" he assured over the wind, yelping when Cylvan's braid suddenly smacked him in the face. Cylvan howled with laughter, before crying out dramatically when Saffron grabbed the braid and yanked on it.

"I'll cut this off!" he threatened. "My knife remembers the taste!"

"Don't you dare! That's Alfidel's hair!"

"I'll cut it off and I'll eat it!"

"I'll eat *you!*" Cylvan chomped on the curve of Saffron's neck, making Saffron shriek and flail his legs. Cylvan pretended to lose balance in the sky, tumbling then catching himself, dipping to the right, the left, like a drunk man trying to walk. Saffron laughed the whole time, clawing at Cylvan for safety as he begged for forgiveness and swore not to do anything at all to *Alfidel's hair*.

On the other side of the mountain, Saffron spotted the pond Cylvan referred to, holding his breath as a wide clearing came into view. Speckled with more purple lavender than Saffron had ever seen, a body of water like the rim of a huge mirror claimed the land at the bottom of the grassy slope. He nearly complimented it, but then spotted something else in the water, and his mouth dropped open entirely.

"Cy-Cylvan!" he cried, punching Cylvan's shoulder and

nearly leaping from Cylvan's arms. "Th-th-there's—! There's—!! In the water, Cylvan!!"

People—

No, not *people*—

The way they moved, swam, draped over the rocks and braided their hair, glittering in the sunlight, weaving flowers and grass into crowns—

It—They were—

"We can't get too close, or else they might try to drown us," Cylvan said. "Do you promise?"

But Saffron couldn't think straight enough to speak. Those were—*nymphs!* Water nymphs! Saffron's mouth dangled open as they landed a safe distance from the pond, the beautiful creatures barely giving them a second glance as they just continued washing their hair, swimming around naked, kissing one another. Saffron stood like a statue amongst the grass and the lavender, unable to move or think or hardly breathe at all.

"Come here, púca," Cylvan prodded through the thrilled, echoing nothingness in Saffron's brain. Without taking his eyes from the water, he sidestepped to where Cylvan was, a hand sliding into his to gently tug him down. Saffron still couldn't pull his eyes from nymphs, even as he landed ungracefully in the grass. He could have faced the wolf itself, or Elluin with her silver needle, or King Ailir demanding his full attention, and Saffron still wouldn't risk looking away for even a moment.

"What are you thinking?" the prince poked Saffron in the cheek, before nestling some food Saffron barely tasted into his mouth. "Chew before you swallow."

"They're... beautiful," Saffron said with his mouth full, suddenly overcome with every emotion a human could feel. "They're just so... beautiful."

"... Are you crying?"

Saffron sniffed. "Y-yeah," he said, right as tears dripped down his cheeks.

"I think I suddenly understand how nymphs kill humans so

easily," Cylvan muttered, using a thumb to gently wipe the line of tears from Saffron's cheek closest to him. It forced Saffron to finally pull his eyes away, turning to the other most beautiful person he knew. His chin quivered more when he realized gazing at Cylvan made his stomach do the same little flips as when he watched the nymphs.

"Did you know they were here?"

"Hmm~ What? No~ of course not..." Cylvan bit into a strawberry with poorly feigned ignorance, and Saffron hiccupped with more emotion. He turned back to the nymphs on the water, and then back to Cylvan. He sniffed again.

"As an air nymph, y-you're at least as beautiful as they are, your highness."

"Oh, stop it. You don't have to grovel."

Saffron finally laughed, wiping his eyes and his nose before digging around in his bag.

"Do you mind if I draw them?"

"I thought you didn't have any charcoals?"

"I found some nubs under my bed," Saffron said, digging through his bag, past the rocks, the random papers, the feathers, the various pixie gifts.

"... *Oh*," Cylvan sighed in disappointment, reaching into his own bag and removing a thin wooden box that clacked with every movement. "Then I suppose you won't be needing these?"

Saffron stared at him for what had to be the third time that morning, hesitantly reaching out to take the box for himself. Inside were true artist-grade charcoals with dark velvety surfaces, a whole pile of them, nestled like black sugar cubes in the pine container. Compressed into hard sticks that wouldn't break with too much pressure, that might give him the deepest blacks he only got from the thickest twigs he burned himself.

"P-Prince Cyl-Cylvan," Saffron blubbered more, and Cylvan smiled in satisfaction, flipping his braid as if to congratulate himself for a job well done.

"I thought of you when I saw them in Connacht the other

night," Cylvan went on. "They're the same charcoals Nemain students use in art classes, so they should be fine quality. But I would still like to watch you burn your own sticks someday, as I'm intrigued—" Saffron cut him off with a sudden hug, making Cylvan chuckle and ask if he liked them. Saffron couldn't respond, just throwing his sketchbook open, moving so fast he nearly tore the pages.

He nearly swooned while applying the first stroke of pigment, then sighed in delight after sketching another. And then another, and another, momentarily distracted from both the watery creatures and the handsome fey as an additional beautiful thing was within his reach.

"Are they nice?" Cylvan asked, and Saffron beamed and nodded, demonstrating by quickly sketching a nearby tree and filling in the leaves. Cylvan smiled the whole time, though never actually looked at the page until Saffron insisted. His purple eyes just kept lingering on Saffron's face.

No matter how hard Saffron tried to keep his composure, he silently cried the whole time he sketched the nymphs, the lake, the lavender field. Not sobbing or wailing, just sniffing, dripping tears, having to wipe his eyes and nose on his sleeve so he could focus on the work in front of him.

Even at a distance, he could still capture the shimmering creatures' movements, their patterns, their characteristics. They all had long hair the color of light flowers. They could dive beneath the water and remain there for an unnatural amount of time. Sometimes, their limbs wobbled and turned transparent, as if returning to a watery form. They kissed and sang and pleasured one another right out in the open, but none of it made Saffron blush, only made him gasp slightly in interest, scribble faster, write little notes when they did anything particularly curious.

Cylvan regularly tucked things to eat in his mouth, chuckling every time Saffron barely acknowledged him. Peeled oranges, plums, bite-sized pieces of sandwich, a sip of mimosa, toast. When the taste of cake with whipped cream and strawberries touched Saffron's lips, he finally sat up with sparkling eyes, and Cylvan laughed more before handing the rest of the cake over. Saffron was too busy eating and watching the nymphs to notice how Cylvan had taken his sketchbook and was flipping through it, making Saffron jolt and snatch at it in embarrassment.

"Is this in the Winter Court?" Cylvan asked, referring to some landscape sketches from a few months prior. "It looks familiar."

"Um... yes." Saffron sighed in defeat, sitting back again and taking another frustrated bite of cake. "There's a trail from Luvon's Winery up to Lake Corsecca. Whenever I visit for Yule, I like to go and listen to the ice cracking. It's like... when you dry fire a bowstring."

Cylvan nodded with a sentimental smile. "My mother has a house on Lake Corsecca, but on the other side. Ahh... right here, actually." He pointed to a distant spot in Saffron's drawing. "I spent the last year there, as well. How funny—I wonder if we ever crossed paths in Amber Valley?"

Saffron couldn't fathom crossing paths with the prince while wearing his triple-wool doublet, long johns, boots with three pairs of socks, knitted hat with earflaps, and scarf wrapped tight enough around his mouth that his cheeks bulged.

"I worked in Luvon's wine shop for a few days," he said anyway. "Perhaps there?"

"Hmm," Cylvan considered, before shaking his head. "I don't think so. I certainly would have remembered you if I had."

"I'm not sure about that."

"I am," Cylvan went on with a coy smile, closing the book and handing it back. Saffron tucked it into his lap, strumming his fingers on the worn cover.

"You said *mother* just now..." Saffron started curiously. "Do you mean King Tross? I don't know how he identifies himself, so I'm sorry if that's rude—"

"No, no, not rude at all," Cylvan smiled, stealing the last bite of cake and licking whipped cream from the wrapper. "I was referring to my birth mother, Naoill, who lives in the Winter Court. That's where I was born, actually."

Saffron smiled sarcastically. "Me too, sort of. Did you grow up there too?"

"No, I grew up in Avren with my fathers."

"So you have three parents? That's not fair."

"Don't you technically as well, changeling-baby?"

Saffron grimaced, then scoffed, then scowled.

"No! It's not the same. Why doesn't your mother live in Avren?"

"They prefer the cold and the dark," Cylvan smirked. "They also hate frivolous socializing like I do, and living in the Winter Court means they don't have to deal with many fete invites."

"Did you get these from them?" Saffron teased, poking a finger into the point of one of Cylvan's horns and wobbling him a little bit

"Oh, yes. Also their hair and eyes, in case my complete lack of resemblance to sunny, blonde, tan Day King Ailir wasn't clear enough."

"And your iciness?"

Cylvan feigned insult, and Saffron laughed.

"After all the kindness I've shown you today, beantighe? Perhaps I should throw you to the nymphs after all. Then we'll see if you call out to this icy prince for help."

Saffron laughed more, tugging back when Cylvan jokingly claimed his hand.

"Nooo, please, icy Prince Cylvan, I'm sorry, I didn't mean to offend you~"

"Unlike yours, *my* forgiveness is for trade—and I insist you sketch me along with your nymphs. Come on, a prince always remembers his debts owed, both by him and to him."

"Oh!" Saffron grinned. "I would have done that anyway. Just —I'm not used to drawing faces up close, so don't get upset if I make you look uneven, alright?"

"No, not alright," Cylvan responded flippantly, already

settling into a pose. "You will draw me again and again until you get it perfect, even if it takes a lifetime."

"Fair enough. Anything for my unseelie ice prince."

Cylvan playfully snapped his teeth as Saffron adjusted how he sat. Flipping to a fresh page in his sketchbook, he waited as Cylvan adjusted his posture, situating himself on his side, arm bent over his hips, legs out long as his perfect face gazed dramatically off into the distance. Saffron took a moment to adjust his snakelike braid, fix his bangs to hang clear of his eyes, and even set some of the decadent treats around him.

"I have a feeling this isn't the first time you've posed for a portrait," Saffron mumbled as he took in Cylvan's effortless appearance. Just a lovely prince appreciating the nymph-faunae on the lake, interrupted by a curious human looking for pretty things to draw.

"I've posed for official portraits since I was a baby," Cylvan answered without moving. "And the royal family takes it very seriously."

His eyes moved to where Saffron was lightly sketching his shape.

"Are you sure you'll be able to properly capture my elegance? I heard you're only the royal painter's apprentice."

"I swear to do my best, oh mighty Ice Prince Cylvan," Saffron answered as best he could, focusing hard on his lines. "Though you might... come out with the proportions of a pixie, if I'm not careful. With their gangly limbs... and bug eyes..."

"Don't you dare," Cylvan hissed, and Saffron finally flickered his eyes up to smile.

Dabbing black pigment into Cylvan's sharp fingernails, his dark doublet and tunic, shading the delicate leaf and vine carvings in his horns, aligning the point of his ear with the corner of his eye, the concentration allowed for unwanted thoughts shaped like wolves to creep into Saffron's mind. With nothing else to distract him, sinking into the mental silence that came naturally while he sketched, he couldn't stop them from pinching. It would be the perfect time to ask. Cylvan was in a good mood, he was being chatty, and if Saffron phrased it right, it might not even come across as anything serious...

"C-can I ask you something else, your highness?" he asked, fighting to keep his voice calm and casual.

"You wait until I am trapped in a pose first?" Cylvan responded, voice remaining playful. "Should I be worried?"

"A-ah... well..." Saffron trailed off, cursing when the stick of charcoal popped between his fingers beneath the pressure. He scrambled before it disappeared into the grass, lifting his eyes to find Cylvan watching him with sudden concern. Saffron gulped. He motioned for Cylvan to get back into position and returned the charcoal to the page.

"Do you... do you happen to know anything about the wolf attacking beantighes?" he managed, voice wavering, mouth going dry and trying to cut him off. But to his relief, while Cylvan's jaw tightened slightly, he otherwise remained calm.

"I do not," he answered simply. "I thought I overheard something about it the night your friend died on Imbolc, but nothing else since then... Should I be worried? Wait—weren't you just wandering alone in the woods?"

The wolf. The lord. The prince.

Saffron gulped. "I'm... I'm sorry, but would you be willing to-to declare it? I know I have no right to ask someone like you, but—"

"Relax, púca," Cylvan interrupted with an easy smile, before continuing with intention: "I do not know for sure how your friend died on Imbolc. I also do not know the details of any other deaths that might have come after."

Saffron nodded, feeling a weight lift off him. He allowed a relieved smile to twitch at the corner of his mouth. "Thank you. I'm sorry."

"Don't be," Cylvan said calmly, gazing back across the landscape. "Thank you for asking, instead of just assuming."

"Oh..." Saffron laughed awkwardly. "You don't have to say that..."

But something about the way Cylvan said it rubbed Saffron the wrong way. He tried to focus on how Cylvan's long braid draped over his shoulder and curled in the grass. The shape of the individual plaits, the loose hairs, the ribbon tying it together—

"Do other people not treat you kindly?" he blurted, before clamping his mouth shut and furrowing his brows. "Sorry—"

"What makes you say that?" Cylvan asked, but it wasn't teasing. It wasn't mocking or accusatory, either. Curiosity dusted the words like powder on faux fairy fruit. As if Cylvan meant it to come across as merely conversational, but a pinch of honesty crept through. Saffron nearly snapped the charcoal piece in half, but clenched his stomach to keep the emotions down.

"May I speak out of turn, your highness?" he finally asked.

"Of course."

Saffron scribbled on the page more aggressively, fighting to get Cylvan's horns as black as he could because otherwise, he thought he was going to explode.

"Well... it's just... for what it's worth... I wish Lord Taran, specifically, treated you with more respect." He said through clenched teeth, trying to keep his tone objective. "He always grabs you so roughly... and he never even says good morning... He never smiles at you, or helps you pick up your books... and people always say hello to him first, and then wait like they need permission to speak to you, next, and I have never understood it... and of course, the way he follows you around campus, the way he searches for you like he wants to punish you for something... sometimes, when you come to me to get away from him, I'm afraid to leave you alone again because I worry why Taran is so angry in the first place. He treats you like a pretty bird he's trying to keep in a cage, or something... and it just... I will admit, you can be moody, and demanding, and a know-it-all, but I have never seen you treat Taran or anyone else in the same way in return. Even me, who deserves none of your respect, even when you didn't know me at all... you weren't always particularly kind, or polite, but... the times you're less than agreeable, you apologize, or at least show remorse. I don't know..."

He rambled on and on, sanding down his stick of charcoal into nothing but a nub and a pile of soot on the page as he just fought to keep it together. But by recalling every moment, additional memories came to light, only making him angrier. Cylvan said nothing for a long time, which soon replaced Saffron's bitterness with apprehension, wondering if he'd gone too far. He was about to apologize, when Cylvan spoke first.

"Taran is my fiancé."

Saffron's mad scraping slowed to a halt, but he couldn't bring himself to lift his eyes. He just nodded slowly, letting out a scant breath. Why did those four words squeeze him like one of Elluin's thumb screws?

"I'm... sorry for speaking so ill of him, your highness."

"No, don't be sorry," Cylvan asserted, and Saffron finally lifted his eyes. Cylvan was gazing off into the distance still, but his expression was newly intense. The muscle in his cheek twitched as he clenched and unclenched his jaw, eyes focused on something Saffron knew wasn't anything in sight.

"Technically... we aren't *formally* engaged, but courtiers consider us as much," Cylvan went on. "All of Alfidel expects an official announcement soon, whether I want it or not."

Saffron bit his lip. He returned to his sketch, not wanting Cylvan to feel pressured by his gaze. He skimmed the charcoal gently across the page that time, letting it swirl like his emotions.

"Do you..." Saffron finally said before realizing. He closed his mouth again, shaking his head and kicking himself. But Cylvan's attention found him and waited.

"It... would be inappropriate for me to ask," Saffron tried to escape his misspoken words. "Let's pretend I didn't say anything at all."

"Tell me."

Saffron shook his head more. When Cylvan touched his hand

holding the sketchbook, Saffron finally met his eyes again with a clutch of his heart. The Cylvan gazing at him was no longer the arrogant, self-assured, confident prince Saffron had come to know. Suddenly, his amethyst eyes were filled with uncertainty. With stormy restlessness. It almost brought more tears to Saffron's eyes, but he frowned and blinked them away. Shaking his head, he apologized under his breath before asking: "*Do* you want it? Do you... do you love him?"

Cylvan's expression didn't change at first, before he smiled wearily, shaking his head.

"I do not have to love him," he said, but the words were practiced, as if he'd repeated them under his own breath every day for years. "My future Harmonious Partner is only meant to bring balance and a second perspective to my rule. They do not have to be a lover; they don't even necessarily have to be a friend."

Saffron bit his lip. Those words were like a knife in his chest—and Cylvan said them with so much and so little emotion all at once, as if there were a thousand other things he wished he could add. Words spoken like he'd repeated them his whole life, whether to other people or just to himself. And something about them... made Saffron anxious, like Cylvan was going to suddenly take off into the sky and leave him there. But Saffron was less concerned about being left alone—and more about Cylvan feeling like he had to run at all.

His suspicions were confirmed when he noticed Cylvan picking at the grass beneath his hand. Picking, tearing, twisting in agitation, veins popping over his knuckles.

Saffron closed his book slowly. He lifted his fingers and pushed hair from Cylvan's eyes, before growing slightly bolder and silently coaxing the prince's head into his lap. To his relief, Cylvan went without protest, closing his eyes as soon as he sank against Saffron's crossed legs.

"My henmother always pulls me onto her lap when I'm feeling anxious," he explained softly. Cylvan opened his mouth to refute his own obvious emotions—but then Saffron gently tousled his hair some more, and his mouth slowly closed. Saffron took it as a sign to continue.

"I read a little about Harmonious and Primary rulers," he breathed. "It was... in the context of Proserpina and Clymeus, but I think I understand..."

His next words trailed on his tongue. He moved them around in his mouth, tasting them, unsure if he was really ready to ask. But at the sight of Cylvan's closed eyes, resting as if it was the first time he could in years, Saffron couldn't stop himself.

"Can I ask? Um, is there a-a reason? Why you haven't formally proposed?"

Cylvan's eyes flickered back open, and Saffron realized his mistake. He nearly apologized, but Cylvan just let out another long sigh and closed his eyes again, reaching out his arms and wrapping them around the small of Saffron's back. Locking Saffron down, so that he might never leave from being Cylvan's safe place to rest.

"A myriad."

The answer was simple, but made Saffron's heart pound. He wanted to ask more, wanted to know every reason, especially if they were what caused Taran to treat Cylvan so poorly—but then realized the serenity on Cylvan's face was far more valuable. He kept the prodding questions to himself, gently smoothing black hairs behind the prince's pointed ear.

"Well... why does everyone expect you to marry him?" Saffron went on. "Could you just... ignore the courtiers? And marry who you want, instead? All they do is gossip, anyway... how serious could it be?"

"That's... a long story," Cylvan breathed, turning and nestling his face slightly deeper into Saffron's lap. "Taran comes from a very old, powerful, well-respected family... He's always been top of his class, never gotten in trouble... Unlike me, who seems to always find trouble wherever I go. Especially since Taran and I were friends when we were young, many people think our engagement will allow him to… erm, rub off on me, I suppose. Tame my *wild nature,* as they put it…"

"Wild nature," Saffron mumbled, but held up Cylvan's sharp, clawlike nails when he did. Cylvan chuckled with a little more life. "You say he comes from a powerful family… Does that… Is Taran the other Sídhe lord you mentioned in the library?"

"You catch on far too quickly. I wanted that to be a big surprise."

"Hmm," Saffron pouted. He pressed one of his thumbs into Cylvan's claws, making his fingers bend. "Would Taran treat you better if you finally proposed to him?"

Cylvan continued with that calm, weary smile, and Saffron combed more hair from his eyes.

"I imagine it would… ease some of the pressure, yes," he breathed, closing his eyes again and furrowing his brow, as if reaching a point where he wasn't sure he wished to continue. But Saffron didn't say anything, didn't offer him an out, just waiting to see what Cylvan would decide. "I… worry what he might do once he's my Harmonious Partner and I'm expected to rely on him. But—I also know I'm running out of time. I've been putting it off too long. He was actually expecting it to happen on Imbolc, you know… and now I worry he might do anything at this point for a proposal."

"Does…" Saffron caught himself, frowning and ripping up a bunch of grass of his own before finding the courage to say it, knowing Cylvan would only pester him again if he didn't. "Does Lord Taran love *you?*"

Cylvan smirked. "I do not even try to guess what Taran really thinks of me. But I do know one thing—his family certainly has some influence on him. I would not be surprised if the reason he is so insistent on an engagement is to partially get them off his back, on top of, you know—being promised half of my kingdom."

Saffron huffed in growing frustration. He busied himself with digging little flowers from his ripped grass and sticking them through the hollow spots in Cylvan's horns. Cylvan, meanwhile, closed his eyes again, drifting away into peaceful loveliness as Saffron's insides swarmed like bees. He wondered if Cylvan could hear them.

"Prince Cylvan, I..." Saffron started when the bees rushed up the back of his throat, voice trembling again. Cylvan's eyes cracked open once more, but didn't lift. They just stared across the field, across the lavender flowers that matched the color of his eyes. "I... care about you. Every moment I spend with you, I care about you even more. It... frightens me a little bit, especially when I consider who you are, and who I am, but..."

"Who are you?" Cylvan asked without emotion.

"Well... it's... like a pixie caring for a raven, isn't it?" Saffron smiled softly. "Someone insignificant like me, thinking I can do anything at all for someone as big and grand and free as you are. But, I guess... perhaps, while the pixie cannot help with raven-sized problems... it can at least share the little treasures it steals, because it knows the raven likes shiny things, too..."

"... A *raven?*" Cylvan finally chuckled the more he thought about it. Saffron laughed, too, embarrassed by his analogy. But then Cylvan sat up, and suddenly they were very close, making Saffron's breath catch. Cylvan plucked a piece of grass from Saffron's hair, twirling it between two fingers. "Perhaps the raven cares for the pixie as well, but worries its squawking and sharp talons and... *reputation* will scare it away. What then?"

"I would... tell the raven that pixies aren't afraid of anything, really... They're small enough that not even rowan or iron can hurt them. And... once the pixie saw past the beak and claws, it would see how pretty the raven's feathers are. And how its ability to fly is actually very fun on nice days..."

He laughed as it got away from him even more—but was interrupted when Cylvan suddenly pressed their mouths together.

The movement was gentle enough that Saffron's eyes closed, unable to stop his fingers from floating to touch the curve of

Cylvan's jaw. Warmth washed through him from the place their lips touched, and his breath left him in a soft exclamation of pleasure.

When Cylvan pulled away again, it took Saffron a moment to open his eyes, forgetting where he was.

"Prince Cylvan?" he asked in uncertainty, but Cylvan just touched his face and kissed him again. Saffron let out another breath as he was coaxed back into the grass, releasing another soft sound as Cylvan's fingers caressed his bruised skin gently, as if worried his touch would leave marks of its own. They curved under Saffron's ears, into the hair at the nape of his neck, and Saffron shuddered at the sensation. His own hands fell to Cylvan's neck, and then his shoulders, wrapping over the muscles beneath his doublet.

"Cylvan," he attempted one more time, but less in question. In—request. More, more—Saffron wanted to kiss him *more*. Just to taste Cylvan's mouth filling every gap where Saffron swallowed back unspoken words of affection.

"I care for you as well, Saffron—enough that I finally understand why people worship a Day Court," Cylvan confessed between their mouths. "I want to fill your life with light, and joy, and peace, and safety..."

Saffron's heart raced, finding it difficult to open his eyes whenever Cylvan pulled away. Saffron just kissed him again every time, wishing Cylvan never needed a breath at all.

"You are more than just a pixie," he went on. "If I am indeed a raven—then you are the treasure I wish to spend all my days appreciating."

Saffron wrapped his arms back around him, pulling Cylvan in more. There were a thousand things he wished to respond, but one stuck out the loudest:

I wish to always be a safe place for you to close your eyes and rest.

18

THE LORD

While returning to campus assignments meant Saffron saw the prince regularly again, their shared nights in the library were still few and far between.

But at least they could cross paths, sometimes fleetingly, other times more meaningfully, other times just in glances. Occasionally, to even be pulled into a dark hallway, where Cylvan held Saffron's face and kissed him like it was the first time.

Sometimes Cylvan kissed him longingly—other times he was more demanding, pushing Saffron's veil off and caging him on his back against the vacant stairway, leaving marks on his neck before apologizing as Saffron overheated between shrill bouts of laughter. And Saffron couldn't get enough of it—he wanted more, more, more, constantly wishing Cylvan never had to leave at all.

The only respite during longer stretches of loneliness came in Cylvan's letters, delivered by robin or nightjar depending on the time of day, adding to the stack Saffron secretly kept bundled in his drawer under the bed. After a list of written instructions on how to respond, Saffron even sent his first ever letter back—and Cylvan's returned words of confirmed delivery and congratulations were enough to make him jump up and down in excitement.

Saffron sent notes from the library with all the words he

didn't know, any interesting facts he learned from the pages he poured over. Other times, he sent a little sketch of something when he had nothing else to say, or talked about what he was doing in Beantighe Village with the others. And every time, Cylvan replied, sometimes within moments. Sometimes soon enough that Saffron hadn't even turned the page on his lap.

But as another week passed, interactions with the prince grew even fewer, less intimate, until soon they were hardly more than acknowledgements in hallways, on campus walkways. Nods of greeting, occasionally with a smile.

Saffron might have taken it as a sign of Cylvan pulling back, deciding he wanted nothing else to do with Saffron and his neediness, had the letters not continued. Had there not still been a robin coming for him every evening the prince remained missing from view.

LIBRARY GHOST—WHAT DO YOU INTEND TO STUDY TODAY?

xx MORRÍGAN'S AIR NYMPH.

Hansome wind nymph, Today I am reading about human blood. Aparently it contains iron, (like the metal), and that is why we canot performe opulent magic. Is'nt that interesting? I always thouht I was just dull. Do fey really have silver blood too?

Library Ghost.

IRON BEANTIGHE—YOU MAY BE DISAPPOINTED THAT FEY DO NOT HAVE VISIBLY SILVER BLOOD—THOUGH THERE IS ALLEGEDLY SILVER *IN* OUR BLOOD. IT IS MOSTLY ONLY A METAPHOR (A FIGURE OF SPEECH) FOR OUR OPULENCE. HUMANS ARE IRON-BLOODED, FEY

ARE SILVER-BLOODED, AND SÍDHE FEY ARE GOLD-
BLOODED. UNFORTUNATELY I DO NOT BLEED GOLD
WHEN CUT, EITHER, SO DO NOT TRY. THOUGH I
WONDER IF WOODLAND-LOVING IRON BEANTIGHES
LIKE YOU BLEED MOSS? I WILL HAVE TO EXPERIMENT
SOON.

xxx YOUR GOLDEN HIGH LORD.

---

*Golden Lord, I do not bleed moss. But do you think fey like Lord
Kaylar bleed swamp water? Perhaps we can find out together.*
Iron Beantighe (with a knife).
p.s. I keep forgeting to ask. What is a "proctor"?

SAFFRON COULD BE PATIENT. SAFFRON KNEW LITTLE
about royal engagements, or Lord Taran, or what exactly Cylvan
was dealing with outside of classes and in the walls of Danann
House, but he could be patient. The regular letters meant Cylvan
wasn't totally tired of him. They even helped spark his inspira-
tion, reading more about opulence, about the fantastical myths
where true names were a conflict, about how human and fey lived
with one another before Queen Proserpina closed the veils.

Sitting on the edge of the lake one night while waiting for
curfew to pass, Saffron finally introduced himself better to Nimue
and her sisters. According to the undine, Letty had told her all
about Saffron and deemed him a friend to chat with, so he had
special privileges—and that made him strangely proud, and then
grateful, even pulling out his sketchbook to draw her in appreciation.

One by one, all of the lake-sisters requested sketches of their
own, at one point grabbing Saffron's sketchbook and carrying it
out into the water, him just begging from the shore that they
please, please, please, *please not get it wet!!*

When curfew passed and it was safe to head to the library, he offered the undines a bow of thanks and promised to return soon, tugging on his shoulder bag and hurrying across campus.

When no little robin came looking for him that night, he lingered a bit longer outside the front doors, wondering if Cylvan was too busy to write to him, or perhaps he intended on coming in person... but as the sun sank into full darkness, and still no bird arrived, Saffron had no choice but to begin work on his own.

Fairy fruit. The wolf. The lord. The prince.
Foundlings. The old king. Proserpina. The veil.
The crone. Arrow's veil. Coffee beans?

Saffron searched his memory for every single strange thing since Arrow's death, even those that might have just been random happenstances.

Silver needles. Proserpina's Silver. Hindrances. Undines.
Fern rings. Rule of threes.

Saffron groaned, scrabbling nails through his hair in frustration and hunching over his book again. He wished Cylvan was there. How long had it been since they'd seen one another? Maybe no more than a few days, only because they met eyes once when passing on the walkway. But to speak to one another out loud, rather than just in letters? To have a moment alone? Had it been a whole week? More?

Moving his finger in the light of his single candle, he appreciated the golden glow of the fern ring, his biggest reminder of the prince. He pulled it off and scrutinized it for the hundredth time, appreciating every little artisanal mark on the leaves, the diamond in the center. It shined even brighter than the gold library ring, though equally as bright as Luvon's gold patron ring on his thumb, with its circular face donning Luvon's family crest of a stag over snowy mountains. He'd memorized that emblem after years of appreciating the design when he was bored, sketching it from memory, touching the wooden plaque over the front door of Luvon's estate whenever he went home. The stag, the moun-

tains, the decorative circular frame, embellished with lines like...
cracked rings in a tree.

Like—

He held his breath.

Like cracked rings in a tree?

Pausing for just a moment longer, he then dug into his sketchbook, flipping through the pages until he found Baba's teacup
folk circles. Lying them flat on the floor, he pulled the candle in
close again to observe the markings on his patron ring.

Grabbing a piece of charcoal next, he carefully recreated the
embellishment on the page, hand shaking a little as he did. Didn't
Cylvan say—the fern ring was supposed to work like a patron
ring, but reversed? Saffron had never actually considered what
made patron rings magic in the first place, what allowed them to
protect the human wearer from being compelled... but then he
thought about his conversation in Adelard's office, and how the
professor talked about how true names worked by focusing a fey's
vulnerability to enchantment into a single word... So perhaps
patron rings functioned similarly? To focus a human's vulnerability to enchantment into a single object... or a single word, as
well?

He glanced at Baba's folk circles again, how they varied from
one another and were labeled with single-word intentions. *Sleep,
wake, pain, fever, fright, illness, antidote, strength, truth.*

He examined the similar circle copied down from Luvon's
patron ring. Could... the markings on the ring be similar to how
Baba used her teacups? Could the unique design spell out a word,
too? Like how fey used true names? Protecting the human wearer
from being compelled...?

But why would a fey-made patron ring have human folk
circles carved into its front in the first place?

Glaring at the markings in frustration, he searched and
searched his memory again for anything he might have missed.
Opulent magic? Folk magic? Occult magic? Arid magic, Aridology? He couldn't claim it was the markings that charmed the

patron ring with certainty—but there had to be some sort of significance, didn't there? Unless Saffron was trying to find answers where there were none?

Scratching his nails through his hair again, he felt—on the verge of something. Something, something, *anything.*

Cylvan claimed the magic ring was supposed to be a patron ring, but reversed—surely he knew how patron rings worked, then, right? Could he explain what the markings meant, or if they actually meant anything at all?

"Ugh," he hissed. "Why couldn't you have come tonight, you stupid prince?"

The words lingered, and Saffron closed his eyes, furrowing his brows in more frustration—before feeling vengeful, and gathering his things. If Cylvan wasn't going to come to him, then Saffron would go to wherever he was.

But upon leaving the library for the dark campus, before he could race off to Danann House in search of his raven, he spotted another familiar figure sweeping the walkway right outside. He nearly called out to greet him—but then saw the heaviness in Hollow's body, the way he swept the same spot over and over again as if lost in thought. Smiling to himself, Saffron hurried up in silence.

"Hollow?" he asked, attempting to spook him—but Hollow just turned slowly. Even hidden behind the veil, Saffron could immediately tell something was off, and his excitement petered slightly. "Everything alright?"

"Hey, Saffron... wait," Hollow snapped to attention. "What the fuck are you doing here? It's the middle of the night! You— you literally woke me up for my shift—did you walk all the way back here? Saffron!"

Saffron smiled mischievously, nudging Hollow's broom with the toe of his shoe. "Don't worry, I was just heading home... sort of. You looked like you had something on your mind, so I thought I'd come and say hi, first."

Saffron meant the teasing to be lighthearted, but Hollow's

drawn-out silence made him reconsider. He raised his eyebrows in encouragement, and Hollow shifted awkwardly on his feet. He thought about whatever it was for another minute before finally speaking in a low voice.

"I was... approached by Lord Taran earlier tonight," he said, and Saffron's playful smile dropped in an instant. "He... he asked me... if I know anything about, um, wild fairy fruit."

The world went silent.

"Fairy fruit?" Saffron heard himself ask over the low ringing in his ears.

"Yeah..." Hollow said considerately, sweeping his broom again. "He said... he needs it for... for the wolf, Saffron."

Saffron stared at him. The ringing tumbled into a high-pitched noise filling Saffron to every edge of his mind. Hollow cleared his throat. He swept a little more.

"He said... he's been able to keep it away from campus, but not from Beantighe Village, which is why it's been attacking us instead... But if he gives it wild fruits, he can compel it into submission..."

It was a long time before Saffron recalled how to speak.

The wolf. The lord.

"Did he say... why he needs you to get it for him?"

Hollow nodded slightly. "He said... it's behind an iron gate in the woods. In some old ruins."

"He didn't..." Saffron breathed. "Say anything about Prince Cylvan, did he?"

Another silent sweep of the broom.

"Erm... he said... Prince Cylvan has something the wolf wants, but that... it would be better for us all if Prince Cylvan doesn't find out..."

The prince.

"And..." Saffron's heart pounded cracks into his ribs. "What did you say, Hollow? You didn't—You didn't agree, did you?"

Another sweep.

"I asked him why I should believe anything he says," Hollow

exhaled a low breath. "And he asked me... if I've seen it myself. The wolf, I mean. When I told him no, not technically... he said... if I had, I would trust anyone at all just to get rid of it."

He was quiet for another moment.

"He also said... the few beantighes it's killed are only the start, and it's going to just keep getting angrier, until..."

He shook his head. Saffron's heart pounded even harder.

"What am I supposed to do, Saffron?"

"You—!" Saffron wanted to shout "*you never cross paths with Taran again!*" but—

What if it was true?

What if Taran had made that same request of Arrow first? And then Cloth? And now Hollow? What if the wolf killed them because they weren't able to find the fruits needed to quell its rage?

What if that was why Taran was so possessive, so controlling of the prince at all? Because he was trying to protect Cylvan without scaring him?

Saffron's breath caught. He snatched Hollow's broom and threw it to the ground, unable to take the sound of scratching bristles any longer.

"Hollow, just—just don't do anything tonight, alright? We know the wolf won't attack on campus, and it won't attack if you're in a group, so just—"

"Yeah," Hollow's voice cracked with a weary smile. "I almost sprinted right back to the village before I realized... Never thought I'd be so grateful for chores..."

Saffron wanted to scream, but he smiled desperately instead. His hands shook, taking Hollow's and squeezing them.

"Good... good... just stay on campus for now... head back to the village with everyone else in the morning..." he gulped, pulling Hollow's hands to his forehead as he tried to think. "I... I think I want to go check on Prince Cylvan, too, if that's... I asked the other day if he knew about the wolf, and he said no, but I just..."

"Yeah," Hollow agreed. "I understand, Saff, it's alright. In fact

—I think I would prefer that, if it keeps you from going home right now. Just—don't go into the woods by yourself, either, alright? Head back in the morning with the rest of us. You can come hang out with me if the prince doesn't preoccupy you."

Saffron wasn't sure if that was teasing or not, thoughts far too scrambled to be sure of much at all.

"Alright," he said, squeezing Hollow's hands again before pulling him into a frantic hug. "I'll take tomorrow off from assignments. We can figure something out, alright?"

"Yeah. That sounds good. Be careful."

"Don't let Taran speak to you again."

"I won't. I can promise that much."

Saffron offered his friend a weak smile, kissing his veiled forehead before turning and running across the dark campus.

Prince Cylvan has something the wolf wants.

Saffron pushed his legs faster, flying past the buildings, the lantern-wisps. He tried to think what that could possibly be—but it was quickly overwhelmed by worry for Cylvan, period. Saffron had seen what the wolf did to beantighes, who had nothing— what would it do to someone who had something it wanted?

19

THE CIRCLES

To Saffron's relief, the prince's Aon-adharcach suite was illuminated from the inside, bright with what Saffron guessed was the fireplace burning. Proof that Cylvan was home. Cylvan was home. He was safe.

Only needing an access ring for the actual door, Saffron hopped over the exterior garden gate. He found the stiff wood latticing against the facade that would take him up to the suite's balcony next, hooking fingers through the makeshift rungs and pulling himself off the ground. Up and up until he could peek through the balustrades around the balcony's edge and peer through the open doors, spotting the horned daemon by himself on the other side.

The prince held his violin tucked into the curve of his neck, bow sliding across the strings though no music escaped the soundproof barrier, even with the balcony doors cracked open. Swaying to the sound of his own mysterious hymn, Cylvan paused occasionally to whisper something to himself, to swallow back half a glass of wine, to pour himself more, to toss hair over one shoulder. His hands moved with expertise, clutching the bow with both delicacy and commanding firmness, and Saffron wanted to know what notes spilled from the dark instrument.

Kicking his legs over the railing silently, Cylvan didn't notice —but the moment Saffron's feet touched, the faint sound of music fell over him. As if nestled right within the cottony shell of the barrier, allowing him a peek through the other side.

Despite being muffled—it was absolutely hypnotizing. Long notes swelling and fading, chasing high-pitched companions before descending into another dark monologue. It was nothing like the music Hector, Dublin's henmother, played on the fiddle on holidays. It didn't make Saffron want to get drunk and dance —it made his heart creak to and fro as if it debated breaking or spilling.

He managed to pull himself from the enchantment long enough to knock on the window, and Cylvan jumped on the other side, nearly dropping the violin in surprise. Saffron hid a laugh behind his hand, before smiling and motioning to come and let him in. A relieved smile stretched over Cylvan's mouth, approaching with the violin still in one hand, pushing the glass open further with the other.

"It's so strange," Saffron smiled as the muffling barrier popped. "I heard this song, my lord, and felt compelled to follow it here... you aren't one of those fey who lure humans with music, are you?"

Cylvan smirked.

"Only one human," he promised bewitchingly, taking Saffron's hand and pulling him into the room. Stepping into the warm suite, past the final edge of the silencing barrier, Saffron heard the crackling of the fireplace, the ticking clock, the sound of Cylvan's bare feet as he went to the wine cart and poured another glass.

Tucking it into Saffron's hands, Saffron was distracted by the prince's toes, and Cylvan wiggled them.

"I wondered if they would be claws, too," Saffron said. "But they look just like mine."

"Do they?" Cylvan asked, bending suddenly to hook his arms around Saffron's knees and toss him back on the couch. Saffron fought to keep the wine glass from spilling as the prince curled him in the cushions and proceeded to unlace his derby boots.

"W-wait!" Saffron laughed, but Cylvan popped off Saffron's shoes, tossing them back toward the balcony window.

"Now you'll stay," Cylvan smiled. "Humans take off their shoes when they're staying a while, right?"

Saffron's words caught. He suddenly couldn't remember why he'd come to the prince's suite at all, as if he really had just followed music he didn't know he could hear.

"Y-yes," he smiled as his cheeks went warm. "I'll stay a while."

Sitting on the edge of the couch, Saffron sipped his wine, watching in rapt admiration as Cylvan reclaimed his violin and the song continued. No longer wailing and melodic, it grew into something lush and tempting, warming him like the fireplace warmed the room.

Beneath him, no one had cleaned up the blankets from when he'd stayed weeks prior while sick, and something about that made him smile more. He ran his fingers up and down the fur on the cushions, sipping more on the wine and even leaning back slightly to close his eyes and just... float. On his empty stomach, the alcohol prickled him quickly, combined with the intoxicating sounds of Cylvan's fingers over the strings. Perhaps he was an alluring leanan sídhe of the violin, after all, and Saffron had fallen for the melody without a moment of hesitation.

When the music's tempo increased somewhat, Saffron opened his eyes again and couldn't resist asking, "Do you know how to stepdance?"

Cylvan raised his eyebrows in a way that said *"Obviously?"* and flourished his feet a little. It made Saffron burst out laughing, covering his mouth to hide it, and Cylvan threw down his violin in mock insult. Grabbing Saffron's hands, he pulled him to his feet to square off.

"No, no! I'm not drunk enough for this," Saffron insisted, and Cylvan turned the glass still in Saffron's hand toward his mouth, making him drink more. Saffron gulped it down, letting out a breath and wiping his mouth on the back of his hand.

"Won't someone hear us?" he asked, cheeks flushing as the alcohol settled in deeper, gripping him like a summer heat. Cylvan shook his head with a coy smile, pulling Saffron in closer until their chests nearly touched.

"The Aon-adharcach Suite is enchanted to keep most inside noise from getting out—unless you're a human falling victim to my music, it seems," he promised. "Now, go on. Show me how humans dance."

"Um... alright," Saffron laughed, stealing another sip of the wine before setting it on the nearby table.

Taking Cylvan's hands, his feet wobbled as he showed the prince the steps to every beantighe dance he knew, explaining those performed around a raging fire, others barefoot in the grass with flower crowns, others when two humans wanted to bind themselves together forever even in places as disheartening as Morrígan Academy. By the end of it, he had his sleeves pushed up and his collar unbuttoned from the effort, giggling constantly as the wine claimed every inch of whatever Cylvan didn't already own of him.

Cylvan taught him courtier dances in trade; something called the Waltz, something called the Allemande, and then the Minuet, explaining how so many high fey dances were inspired by human ones, how even many courtier fashions were inspired by things pulled through the veil... and Saffron found that fascinating, especially in his drunken heat.

When Cylvan asked what he was thinking after going silent for a long time, Saffron just smiled at him.

"I think... I wouldn't mind seeing human dances... in person, one day," his voice shook as he admitted it, squeezing Cylvan's hands tighter. "If I could see them with you. And—and you promised to bring me back, after."

Cylvan regarded him for a moment, before a gentle smile showed on his mouth.

"Alright," he said. "I haven't visited the human world in a while, anyway. We'll bring Eias with us—they're obsessed with all things human, so they would have the best recommendations. I'm sure we would have a great time."

Saffron grinned more, hopping up and down excitedly—before losing his balance and tumbling back to the couch with a laugh, accidentally dragging the prince down with him. He tried to sit up again, but Cylvan chuckled and gently nudged him back. Saffron slumped into the cushions with a lazy smile as Cylvan sat between his knees, crossing his arms over Saffron's legs and resting his head. Saffron's fingers found his soft hair, brushing through it —and suddenly they were back in the valley with the nymphs, the prince's head on Saffron's lap as if it was the only safe place in the world. It made Saffron's heart thump, and he cracked open his eyes to gaze at the coffered ceiling, finding the line of Cylvan's ear and tracing it.

"Is everything alright?" he finally asked. "You haven't been to the library in a particularly long time..."

Cylvan didn't answer right away, but Saffron didn't pressure him. He just closed his eyes and trailed his fingers up the prince's pointed ear, his temple, around his hairline.

"Taran has gone mad, recently," Cylvan finally breathed. "I've been on my best behavior in an attempt to appease him. That's all."

Saffron's hand in his hair came to a halt, but Cylvan didn't open his eyes, just sank deeper into Saffron's lap. His hands reached out and looped around Saffron's back, pulling in closer.

"Don't worry about it," he breathed. "I've suddenly forgotten about it entirely."

Despite how badly Saffron wanted to insist, he clamped his mouth shut. Closing his eyes, he returned his hand to brushing through Cylvan's loose hair, combing it out of his eyes.

He wanted to bottle that quiet moment. Let it ferment like the wine in his blood, so that he could sip it whenever he wanted. Him and Cylvan in the quiet room, warmed by the fire, warmed by the wine, warmed by dancing and laughing with one another. A brief moment of peace for his troubled prince to rest his head, where Saffron could protect him in his own way. He wished Cylvan didn't need protection at all, he wished Taran would just show Cylvan an ounce of kindness, even if he really was trying to shield the prince from the wolf—but if he wouldn't, Saffron was happy to be there to show Cylvan he still deserved it.

When Cylvan spoke again and asked what sort of trouble Saffron had been getting into in the library on his own, it came like an ocean wave crashing over him. Sitting up, he reached for his bag on the floor by the couch, giggling when Cylvan whined and complained like a lazy cat for being moved around.

Pulling out his sketchbook, he flipped through the pages until he found Baba's teacup folk rings, as well as the sketch of the markings around his patron ring. Considering it for a moment, he prodded Cylvan's head and urged him to sit up and look.

"Um, so my henmother—"

But Cylvan jolted, wrenching Saffron's sketchbook from his hand. He slammed it shut with wide eyes, before turning to Saffron with an expression Saffron couldn't read. Shock, betrayal —and Saffron just stared at him with his mouth hanging open, heart pounding in his throat.

"Prince Cylvan?"

"Why did you bring this here?" Cylvan asked tightly. "Why did you show this to me?"

"Wh-what?" Saffron asked in surprise, jumping when Cylvan dropped the sketchbook and got to his feet suddenly. Saffron scrambled to grab it before it hit the floor, just watching in silence as his prince ran fingers back through his hair, took a breath, then poured and downed another glass of wine.

"What's... wrong?" Saffron asked in uncertainty as Cylvan took another deep breath, and then another gulp of wine. When he still didn't speak, Saffron's nerves fluttered higher, like ice in his alcohol-warmed veins. "I'm—I'm sorry—I just..."

He frowned down at his book, suddenly—embarrassed?

Ashamed? Annoyed? He didn't quite know, a myriad of emotions twisting through him as that wasn't the reaction he was expecting. It overwhelmed him with frenetic energy, though, like Cylvan had injected bugs under his skin.

"Do you want me to leave?"

He said it flatly, trying not to show his mix of emotions. Cylvan closed his eyes behind another gulp of wine, before pulling the glass away with a breath. When he still didn't answer, Saffron just silently tucked his sketchbook back into his bag. Pulled his veil on. Made his way for his shoes by the balcony door—

"No... no, I'm sorry. I don't want you to go," Cylvan's hand reached out, taking Saffron's sleeve. Saffron frowned at it, before frowning at Cylvan, who let out another breath.

He hooked fingers under the strap of Saffron's bag and returned it to the floor. He took Saffron's hand and pulled him back to the couch, coaxing him down where he sat originally, then took a seat next to him. Saffron moved stiffly the whole time, as if Cylvan's words had sobered him in an instant and forced his ease to shutter away in the back of his chest.

"I'm sorry," Cylvan said, taking Saffron's hand on his thigh and kissing the back of it. "You just caught me off guard."

"What did I say?" Saffron asked after swallowing the lump in his throat.

"It's..." Cylvan tried to smile, but it was awkward. "Do you... know what those are? Those circles in your book."

Saffron frowned. He shook his head, wanting to insist *"that's why I brought them to you in the first place..."*, but remained silent.

"These are... forbidden magic, Saffron. Illegal. Highly taboo. Even just having them drawn in your book—if anyone found you with them, they would execute you on the spot, and investigate every single other person you've ever spoken to."

Saffron's eyes finally snapped to him, going wide in fright. Blood rushed to his legs as his instincts screamed for him to flee, but Cylvan must have sensed it, because his hand slid to Saffron's thigh, gently squeezing.

"Don't worry, it's alright—I'm certainly not going to tell anyone."

But Saffron still didn't relax. That—didn't help him feel any better, not when his first words had mentioned his henmother—

"I didn't mean to frighten you, I'm sorry," Cylvan repeated when Saffron wasn't immediately abated. "Like I said, I was only surprised, that's all. Just promise me—you'll keep them hidden. I'd rather not see them again, in case anyone ever wades through my memories looking for something to get me in trouble..."

He laughed awkwardly, and Saffron's panic ebbed just slightly. He bit his lip, but nodded, and Cylvan smiled a little more. He kissed Saffron's hair, and then his cheek, nudging him to perk back up. Saffron just stiffly adjusted the patron ring on his thumb. Even if he couldn't discuss the markings directly, he still had questions to ask, and hoped Cylvan wouldn't mind.

"So the reason..." he started, clearing his throat as his mouth was dry. "Well, you once said... the fern ring was supposed to be like a patron ring, but reversed... so I was examining my own patron ring in the library, and I saw these markings around the edge..."

He motioned to the encircling hatchmarks, and Cylvan took Saffron's hand to examine the ring more closely. After a moment, he nodded.

"I haven't looked at any patron rings closely, recently, but... you're absolutely right..." he whispered, less to Saffron and more to himself. When he let Saffron's hand go again, Saffron fidgeted with the ring one more time before continuing.

"So then I wondered if, maybe... what if the markings on my patron ring work the same way as... those circle charms do," Saffron attempted to skirt more, frowning and huffing in frustration, but Cylvan's hand floated to hold his, again. "And all we have to do is... find the right combination for the fern ring, like the one on my patron ring, and then... that's it, I guess..."

"Ah," Cylvan breathed, squeezing Saffron's hand in encouragement, curling a finger under his chin with the other in consideration. "I think... you might actually be on to something, when you explain it like that... Makes me even more embarrassed for my reaction."

Saffron smiled weakly, partially in relief and partially with a tiny flash of pride. He appraised his patron ring again.

"Then... the markings really are that kind of taboo magic?" he asked in a secretive voice. "But why would a patron ring have illegal magic right on it like that? It's not—it's not just Luvon's, is it?"

"Patron rings are enchanted by oracles, and the process is kept secret... for good reason, I'm sure you can imagine," Cylvan laughed under his breath. "If people knew how they were charmed, there would be nothing stopping them from developing a counter-charm, you know?"

Saffron just kept gazing down at the ring. Then—even if the magic was taboo, it must have only been taboo for non-oracle fey to perform it. But was it only so that things like patron rings couldn't be made, or counter-charmed, like Cylvan said? Or was there a different reason?

"Is this..." he trailed off, bracing for another reaction, just in case. "Is this kind of magic, arid magic? Or a different kind? Are there lots of taboo magicks? I wasn't able to find much about arid magic in the library, except that it was made illegal when Proserpina came into her reign..."

But Cylvan had seemingly stopped listening, goosebumps flushing down Saffron's arms when fingernails tucked some of his hair away, and a mouth found the side of his neck.

"Cy-Cylvan," Saffron laughed weakly.

"I'm listening," Cylvan promised, breathing against Saffron's skin. "Keep going."

"Um, w-well," Saffron attempted. "If this *is* the same magic Proserpina outlawed, ah, since..."

The words were too light on his tongue, floating away before he could speak them. Cylvan's hand on his knee crept up his thigh, making Saffron go hotter as a mouth still tasted below his ear.

"Tell me more," Cylvan encouraged breathily. "Tell me about how you're going to perform... forbidden magic for me, púca."

Saffron managed to laugh a little bit again, inhaling sharply when the hand on his thigh reached the inner crux of his leg and teased him. "I—I thought you wanted to hear about—what I've been researching."

"I do," Cylvan purred, kissing his neck again. "Keep going."

"Erm—well, I—I tried to find some books about... about arid m-magic, but, ah—they've all been moved... to Avren, I think... so I don't know... where to go next," Saffron stammered as his face flushed hotter, the hand on his thigh trailing up to tuck under his ear. "Cylvan..."

"Why don't I take you to Avren, then?" Cylvan smiled, tucking Saffron further into the couch cushions. "Until then—I have so much catching up to do."

"Catching up?" Saffron asked weakly, clutching at the fabric of Cylvan's shirt. "On what?"

"On appreciating my treasure," he breathed, finally pressing their mouths together. It drew every breath from Saffron's lungs, and he melted entirely into the couch. "Would that be alright?"

Saffron kissed him back, holding Cylvan's face in his hands. Flattened beneath his weight, Saffron wrapped his arms around Cylvan's shoulders to hold him where he was. The prince slid a knee between Saffron's legs, making him gasp slightly, the break in their mouths allowing Cylvan's mouth to trail down his jaw.

"Is it alright—if I keep going, Saffron?" Cylvan asked one more time, fingers undoing the top button of Saffron's collar, and then the next. Saffron could hardly keep his thoughts straight beneath the heat of Cylvan's mouth, let alone put words in his own.

"Y-yes," he finally managed, tangling fingers in Cylvan's hair as more buttons came undone down his chest. Cylvan's mouth followed the line, kissing the base of Saffron's throat, his collar-bones, tucking his shirt open and finding one of his nipples. It made Saffron shiver, a breath of laughter escaping Cylvan's mouth.

A hand slid between Saffron's back and the couch, cupping the back of his head. Cylvan kissed him again, fingers trailing down the center of his stomach and making him clench as they teased the top of his waistband. Cylvan kissed his forehead, then his hair, and then touched their lips again.

"Like a raven over his treasure," a foxlike smile crossed his lips. "I want to memorize every beautiful, forbidden thing about you."

20

THE NIGHT

To be memorized was to be devoured. It was invigorating, overwhelming all at once, and Saffron vanished into it easier than he vanished into the woods. The way Cylvan tasted and tasted him, the sound of his breaths, the pounding of his pulse when Saffron's fingers brushed his neck, caressing his face.

"Mmh—" Saffron moaned softly when Cylvan's mouth returned to his neck. It made the prince's hands on his waist tighten, burying nails into Saffron's skin.

"Make that sound again," Cylvan's words smiled.

Saffron giggled breathily, pressing his fist back into his mouth as he couldn't stop more pleasured noises from leaving him. With his pounding heart in his throat, making his voice shake, he wasn't sure he'd be able to speak at all soon enough.

"*Cyl—van,*" he gasped, goosebumps flushing him when the prince's warm hands found the top button of his slacks, slowly easing it open, followed by the next, and the next. Cylvan asked again if he could do more—and Saffron hesitated only long enough to swim through the feverish haze of want and wine to answer.

"Yes," he whimpered. "Cylvan—please, do more to me, please..."

A mouth found Saffron's chest, tongue swirling delicately over his nipples, a hand sliding down his center to tease between his legs again. It made Saffron squirm in desire, emboldening Cylvan even more, biting down on the side of Saffron's neck and making him cry out as a hand simultaneously slid beneath the waistband of his braies. Fingers teased him, skin to skin, and Saffron shuddered, throwing his head back. His hands grasped Cylvan's shoulders, then the back of his neck, then his arms, not quite knowing where to go.

"I want to know how you sound... when it's too much to handle," Cylvan's sly voice returned, Saffron's nails clawing at Cylvan's back as fingers teased and then gently stroked, breaths melting into another gasp as Cylvan's mouth returned to his and demanded every movement of his lips.

"Cyl—*ah! Mmh!*" he gasped, clutching at the cushions as one of Cylvan's fingers explored further, making Cylvan laugh softly and kiss him again.

"If this is how you respond to my hand, púca—I can't imagine the noises you'll make when I use my mouth."

"Oh—" Saffron choked, before gasping when he was lifted from the couch. Meeting Cylvan's mouth again, Cylvan stumbled through the clutter on the floor before collapsing on top of Saffron on the bed, making Saffron laugh until he was silenced with another demanding kiss.

Cylvan's mouth tasted his chest and stomach next, hands firmly clutching Saffron's waist and sliding his body further up the dark sheets until Saffron's hair splayed out against the pillows. Before Saffron could say anything else, the demanding mouth returned and trailed down his center, leaving lines of fire in its wake.

When a tongue tasted the skin beneath his navel, Saffron pressed his hands to his mouth to stifle the sound of delight, laughing weakly when Cylvan purred and cooed at him in reaction.

"Just say something if you want me to stop," he whispered, finally pulling Saffron's slacks from his legs and unlacing his braies. Hands traced the inside of his already-trembling thighs, and Cylvan kissed a line of tempting gifts from Saffron's knee to his hip, only making Saffron's breaths shake all over again.

"Is this—alright?" Saffron asked weakly. "If you want —instead—"

The thought of the Prince of Alfidel going down on him embarrassed Saffron in more ways than one. He wasn't anything special; he wasn't particularly beautiful; he had scars and hair and imperfections that probably didn't exist on fey partners Cylvan had had in the past. It made Saffron suddenly self-conscious, suddenly hyper aware of every single flaw, the scars on his back, his arms, his legs, his face; the stretch marks on his hips and thighs and stomach; the acne; the patches of dry skin; the birthmarks; the uneven tan lines—

But Cylvan kissed the soft places on the inner curves of his thighs, trailed his tongue over creases of skin, pressed his lips reverently to every imperfection Saffron displayed.

"This is everything I want," Cylvan breathed. "To devote my mouth to every inch of these legs I'm obsessed with, and find other parts of you to worship."

Cylvan kissed the base of Saffron's length, making Saffron's body flush even hotter.

"Is this alright?" Cylvan mimicked the words. Saffron managed an overheating, whimpering *yes*, before his back arched as Cylvan curled his lips, taking every inch of Saffron into his mouth. Stroking him with heat and a knowing tongue, Saffron writhed in pleasure he didn't know what to do with, gasping and curling a pillow into his mouth to stifle his moans. Fingers teased other places between his legs, and Saffron could only grasp weakly at fistfuls of Cylvan's hair, one of his horns, the pillow behind him, unable to keep himself still. Unable to bite back sounds of

pleasure and overwhelm like he could with Hollow or anyone else
—the way Cylvan's mouth learned every inch of him, the way his
fingers knew all the soft, sensitive places to stimulate, the sounds
he made every time Saffron shivered, bucked his hips, arched his
back, cried out against the pillow pressed into his mouth—

Saffron was going to tear apart.

When the base of his stomach twisted like ribbons and
captured sunlight, when his legs trembled in climbing delight, he
attempted to push Cylvan's mouth away—but the prince just
pressed Saffron's hips down, swallowing what Saffron released
into his throat. It made Saffron's entire being boil into steam. The
crown prince—of Alfidel—just—swallowed a mouthful—of
Saffron's—

"Saffron," Cylvan's voice was close again, Saffron rushing
back to reality and gasping for breath as he spotted the prince
leaning over him in the low light of the fire. Saffron didn't know
when Cylvan had sat up—had he passed out? Did he cross
through the veil? Was he even still in his body? Cylvan saw the
swirling glow in Saffron's eyes, making him chuckle. "Are you
alright, púca?"

Unable to find the words, Saffron just pulled Cylvan down to
meet his mouth once more, practically attacking him, devouring
him, wishing to feel him all over again.

"More," he begged. "I want more of you, Cylvan, please, I
want everything—"

Cylvan kissed him again, pushing sweat-damp hair from
Saffron's face. "Are you sure?"

Saffron could only nod in near heat-exhausted desperation,
making Cylvan laugh under his breath again. He kissed Saffron
again, grinding between his legs and making Saffron throw his
head back and moan. His hands clumsily clawed at the fabric of
Cylvan's tunic, attempting to pull it off over his head. When he
couldn't untangle it from the prince's horns, Cylvan finally sat
back and stripped it off, himself, providing Saffron with a full
view of his torso, elongated with the movement of his arms

stretched upward. Saffron's hands extended to touch him, sliding up the slight dips in his stomach, his chest, over the gold bars in his nipples, curving against his shoulders, only to sigh into Cylvan's mouth when he bent forward to kiss him again.

"Everything about you—" Saffron gasped. "Is—perfect, your highness."

"I was going to say the same about you," Cylvan responded coyly, still kissing while clenching his muscles and undoing the buttons on his own waistband. "Do you know—that you taste of strawberry cake?"

"Strawberry cake?" Saffron laughed, then squeaked when Cylvan collapsed on top of him while struggling to undo his pants fast enough. Saffron offered to help, but Cylvan swatted him away, as if his battle against the buttons was a personal rivalry. It made Saffron laugh more, only to be silenced by another command of the prince's mouth on his.

Finally kicking his pants off, Saffron flushed and released a sharp breath at the size of him, looking back up at Cylvan as his insides curled excitedly.

"Still perfect?" Cylvan asked, pressing Saffron back down into the bed, but Saffron couldn't answer as Cylvan stroked between his thighs and reduced Saffron's mind to a thunderstorm of frenetic anticipation. Pressing and rolling his hips into Cylvan's impatiently, Cylvan made a sound of matched wanting, taking one last moment to grab the open lapels of Saffron's blouse and push it off over his shoulders, and then his arms—

Saffron suddenly panicked, recalling the unsightly scars on his back.

"W-wait," he gasped, and Cylvan pulled away in an instant. He might have leapt off the bed entirely had Saffron not snaked his legs around Cylvan's waist and locked him down. Saffron just gulped, hating the instant concern in Cylvan's eyes, worried he might have ruined the moment—but the thought of Cylvan seeing the scars on his back in a flurry of intimacy made Saffron's heart sink. Even if Cylvan knew they were there, even if he'd seen them before—for them to be visible while being so vulnerable in every other way, Saffron's stomach twisted in humiliation.

"Can we... put out the fire?" he asked quietly. Cylvan spun and windblasted the flames into an early grave, making Saffron choke on a laugh. It sank the room into immediate darkness, but not enough to quell his anxiety.

Still, Saffron tried to kiss him again. Tried to push the thoughts out of the way and stay in the moment, telling himself Cylvan already knew about all of Saffron's imperfections. He clearly didn't care, so Saffron shouldn't either, but—

"Saffron," Cylvan pulled away, and Saffron's heart pounded. "What's wrong?"

He couldn't find a way to explain, mouth just hanging open and then closing, again and again as he desperately searched for any words at all. Nervously pulling his discarded shirt back up over his shoulders, he finally whispered, "I'm... sorry, I'm sorry..."

"What? Saffron..." Cylvan whispered, cupping Saffron's cheek and kissing his hair. "Do you want to stop?"

"No!" Saffron insisted again, shaking his head and frowning at the spot between Cylvan's collarbones. "No, it's just..."

He closed his eyes tightly. He swallowed against the lump in his throat.

"I just... don't want you to see," he whispered, though it sounded pathetic. His nervous hands clutched the fabric of his shirt closed again, tangling it like grass he wanted to pull apart. "My... my back. I don't want you to see it. They... the scars didn't heal all the way, and I... don't want you to read them... It's embarrassing..."

He sniffed, shaking his head and apologizing again. Cylvan just hesitated another moment, before kissing a tear from Saffron's cheek. When he pulled away suddenly, Saffron reached out to grab him—but Cylvan just kissed his forehead again and told him to hold on.

Searching around the messy floor, he returned with a bundle of baggy linen that Saffron recognized as the same black shirt he'd been wearing before Saffron pulled it off. Saffron's heart sank, thinking Cylvan was getting dressed again—but then Cylvan yanked it on over Saffron's head, instead. Looking at him in confusion, Cylvan just smiled, searching for Saffron's arms within the tent and coaxing his hands through the oversized sleeves.

"This will be more comfortable than your blouse," Cylvan said matter-of-factly, the black shirt dangling over Saffron's body enough to cover his torso and partially cover his hips. The sleeves were long enough to swallow his hands, collar wide enough that it slipped off one of Saffron's shoulders.

Cylvan then kissed him more gently than anyone ever had before, and Saffron had to bite back the sudden rush of blubbering emotion as Cylvan pulled back and pushed hair from his eyes.

"You don't have to show me anything," Cylvan told him. "Is this alright? Do you want to keep going?"

Saffron rose to his knees and kissed him back. He pressed himself into Cylvan's chest and stomach, Cylvan's hands trailing softly up his back to caress him. A few more relieved tears dripped over Saffron's eyes, and Cylvan kissed them from his cheeks.

"I want to keep going," Saffron said again, kissing beneath Cylvan's jaw and coaxing him back down onto the bed.

Pinning Saffron's wrists into the pillows, Cylvan pressed between Saffron's legs, grinding against him until Saffron couldn't take the teasing any longer, wanting to know exactly how it felt to be fully appreciated by his unseelie prince.

Using his own fingers to warm himself, made slippery with massage oils Cylvan kept in his nightstand, Cylvan just kissed and teased him more, drawing lines down his stomach with sharp nails as a reminder of why Saffron didn't want the prince's fingers anywhere near where his own fingers buried themselves. It was... funny. Something about it was even charming. It made Saffron laugh, which only made Cylvan laugh, which was—more of a turn on than Cylvan's own fingers would have been.

Saffron finally reached the point of begging, pressing himself into Cylvan's hips as Cylvan spread his legs open—and then pressed himself inside. Slowly, at first, sliding deeper with every thrust as Saffron's back arched and he silently gasped, quivering and moaning, arm crossed over his face and clutching the sheets beneath him.

Even deeply buried between Saffron's legs, Cylvan was thoughtful, regularly asking if Saffron was alright. On his back, pressing the end of his sleeve into his mouth to muffle his moans, Saffron slipped in and out of reality as every kiss, every touch, every thrust, made him feel like he was drunk on fairy fruit. He never knew—the taste of any fey lord could intoxicate him so intensely, reduced to a simpering, giggling mess, begging for *more, more, more* of every touch without a taste of magic dust on his lips. Like a sweltering wildfire, like lightning, like the sweet, tickling caress of rye whiskey on Imbolc, Saffron shuddered with rolling pleasure again and again until he thought he might never wake up again.

On his back, on his knees, over the edge of the mattress, biting at pillows and raking fingers as his body jarred with every thrust. Gasping as sweat dripped down his spine, tasting Cylvan's skin while pinned to the blankets, time passed like smoke through his fingers.

Pushing Cylvan down into the pillows, Saffron slid himself back on top with a small sound, Cylvan's sharp nails gripping him as Saffron rotated his hips. Saffron wanted to coax out that same simpering, vulnerable desperation on Cylvan's face that he himself had worn all night. Moving on him rhythmically, Saffron bit back a smile as Cylvan's hands puckered the skin of his thighs, the prince's strong body rendered nearly petrified with no magic at all—only Saffron's legs, his rolling hips, his hands trailing up the center of Cylvan's stomach and chest, muscles swollen and warm beneath Saffron's touch.

"You can have my kingdom. Anything you'd like," Cylvan moaned in a low breath, making Saffron laugh. His head arched back, gasping for breath, clenching his teeth in tandem with his stomach muscles going tight. Closer and closer, until Cylvan's body locked, fingers digging harder into Saffron's thighs. "Just keep—Saffron, *mmh*—! Yes, like that—!"

"You're all I want," Saffron whispered as Cylvan's pointed nails left marks on his skin. They trailed up to Saffron's waist, making Saffron gasp as Cylvan reclaimed control over the movements, Saffron's body curling against another rush of demanding thrusts.

All of Cylvan's defenses crashed as he peaked, Saffron's heart racing as an intensity flashed over the prince's expression, and then a softness, and then—a gasping, smiling serenity, as he collapsed back and ran fingers through his hair. Breathing heavily, Saffron carefully pulled himself away, before flattening down flush against Cylvan's warm chest and stomach to kiss him more across his collarbones, up the side of his neck. Just wanting to continue tasting him, feeling him, sensing his heartbeat beneath his hands.

Cylvan was somehow even lovelier with his hair sweaty and clinging to his face, cheeks flushed, mouth kiss-bruised and trembling as he fought to catch his breath. Saffron couldn't help but just smile more, crossing his hands over Cylvan's chest and resting his chin on them.

The prince smiled, combing fingers through Saffron's hair a few times before settling within the strands, and then trailing a thumb across Saffron's cheek. Saffron knew it was the place he had the biggest scar, the white line that stretched almost all the way to his ear.

"You're... like nothing I've ever had before," Cylvan breathed. It made Saffron's heart flutter, smiling in embarrassment and shaking his head. But Cylvan kept smiling, too, just touching Saffron's face gently.

"I was careful not to leave any marks on you..." Saffron said next, trailing fingers down the side of Cylvan's neck. "Since you, erm... probably don't want anyone to know..."

"Oh," Cylvan said with a sarcastic grimace, tugging on the

collar of Saffron's borrowed shirt. "Whoops. Didn't know we'd agreed on that."

Saffron laughed, rubbing his neck where he'd already assumed himself to be littered with love-bites on top of *actual* bites. "Don't worry. It's not really unusual for beantighes to display their nightly rolls in the hay."

"Ah, right—you all fuck like rabbits, right? That's what other students say."

"They're... not wrong. Sex is a very good stress relief."

"Do you have a favorite?"

"Do you really want to know?" Saffron asked, and Cylvan narrowed his eyes suspiciously. Saffron laughed weakly, pushing more sweaty hair from his eyes. "Well... Hollow and I have been bedmates for a few years now. He's generally my go-to. I also don't really have *favorites*, since everyone does it differently..."

"Hollow??" Cylvan scoffed, though the feigned jealousy sounded a little genuine. "*Hollow,* your friend, that brute? With his jawline? And arms?"

"That's him," Saffron grinned, and Cylvan groaned dramatically, collapsing back into bed as if Saffron had just given him terrible news. He giggled, stretching forward and kissing Cylvan again, before whispering: "You kiss me differently than he does. I think, after tonight, I may no longer like rabbits at all... I was recently taken by a raven, who is more of my type."

He poked the tip of one of Cylvan's horns with a coy smile, and Cylvan dragged his talons down Saffron's shoulder, grabbing his wrist and burying teeth into his skin, making Saffron squeal.

Sinking off to the side, tired laughs wouldn't stop rolling out of him, resting his head on Cylvan's chest as it rose and fell from the effort. He just quietly touched more of Cylvan's shoulder, his stomach, pinching his pierced nipples and grinning when Cylvan made an intimate sound, drawing lines between the muscles of his abdomen, the v-shape on his hipbones... until his eyes lingered on a silver cuff on Cylvan's right wrist. Shaped like two hands embracing, Saffron touched it gently.

"What's this?" he asked, and Cylvan lifted his arm to look, before sighing and dragging his hand down his face.

"Ah... one of Taran's tricks. And the real reason I haven't been able to visit the library lately," he muttered, glaring at the bracelet. "Proserpina's Silver comes in many forms, and was traditionally used to control wild beantighes. This particular piece... traps me within a certain boundary, unless the owner of the spell gives me permission otherwise. I have been lovingly relegated to Danann House at night, and my classes during the day, where Taran is by my side at all times..."

New anger sparked in Saffron's body. He grabbed the silver cuff and looked over every inch of it, but couldn't find a seam. He hooked fingers under one of the ends and rattled it, though it barely shifted. Cylvan just watched with a tired smile.

"Can't you tell someone?" Saffron asked. "Can't you send a robin to Elluin? Or King Ailir? You shouldn't be treated like this!"

"Elluin... is snugly under Taran's wing; she does whatever he says. And Taran would notice if a raven was missing," Cylvan said like it was something he'd already come to terms with. "Even if I could send a letter to my father... I'm not sure he would be quick to my rescue, anyway."

"Why not?" Saffron insisted. "This is too much—you haven't done anything wrong."

"Not according to Taran," Cylvan smiled bitterly. "According to him, I've been spending *far too much time unaccounted for*, and it's making him worry what nasty things I've been getting up to."

Saffron couldn't help but think of their day with the nymphs, specifically, feeling an ounce of guilt. Returning his chin to Cylvan's chest, Cylvan's hands trailed lines up and down Saffron's back, gazing at the ceiling while deep in thought.

"You're familiar with... Alfidel's Courts of Expectation, aren't you?" Cylvan said without prompting, and Saffron propped himself on his elbows in question. "It's the tradition of... determining the welfare of Alfidel through oracle readings, whenever a new ruler steps into power."

"A little bit," Saffron nodded. "Mostly that King Ailir is a... Day King? A Day Court? It means things are good for Alfidel right now, right?"

"Correct," Cylvan smiled, petting the back of Saffron's hair. "An upcoming ruler's Court isn't formally determined until after they've married their Harmonious Partner, so, while technically, there's no telling what *my* future Court of Expectation will be... everyone already believes... I am destined for a Night Court. The first one to come since Queen Proserpina. A new Night Prince, rising to the throne."

Saffron frowned, scooting in closer as Cylvan's brows furrowed in frustration at the ceiling. "What for?"

"Well... we already talked about a few of the reasons. Sharing my mother's cold, cruel, icy demeanor doesn't help," Cylvan chuckled, but Saffron didn't. "The complete opposite of Day King Ailir, who is charismatic, well-liked, lights up a room with his big laugh... I'm simply... nothing like him."

Cylvan said it like it was the first time those words managed to escape his tongue, despite living there for centuries. It reminded Saffron of the way he explained his forthcoming engagement to Taran in the valley with the nymphs, and his insides twisted. He delicately brushed hair over Cylvan's forehead, silently encouraging him to continue, if there were additional things he needed to exorcize.

"Growing up, I did everything I could to be more like my father," Cylvan whispered. "I filed down my horns to nubs, tried to smile all the time, tried to be friendly and charismatic, too. But... it never mattered, because I was still my mother's son. In reality, I cried and threw tantrums all the time. I was a brat. I was competitive to a fault. I was always trying to prove myself the best, wanting people to think I was someone they didn't have to be afraid of, but instead it all just made me look... selfish. Cruel. Unlikeable. When my next sibling, Asche, was born—they had my father's blonde hair, golden eyes, charming laugh. Even though we have the same mother, Asche was blessed with those cheerful features. Even though they also have our mother's horns, well... it only made me look worse. And those perceptions just keep growing, evolving more and more, and now... even if I received a Day Court declaration, I wonder if people would actually believe it..."

"Well... I rather like your horns," Saffron whispered, despite knowing it wasn't helpful. "I think they're beautiful. Even when we first met, and you accosted me in the woods, it wasn't your horns that intimidated me."

"No?" Cylvan returned a weary smile.

"Your eyes are very intense," Saffron whispered, brushing his thumb below Cylvan's bottom lashes. "And sometimes you smile this wicked grin, and I wonder if what you're thinking involves bloodlust."

Cylvan chuckled.

"But," Saffron continued encouragingly. "I've also seen... the sunnier parts of you, too. Like your wind magic, your dumb jokes, your messy bathroom counter. And of course... what made me like you so much in the first place—the way you talk about romantic stories. None of those things are very *Night Prince*, in my opinion."

"How can I get you on the front of every gossip pamphlet?" Cylvan teased. "Perhaps you alone can change the minds of all of Alfidel."

Saffron grinned, sitting up more. "You could dress me up in silk bows and sparkly things and let me hang on your arm wherever you go. The prince's little beantighe pet, who only speaks of how nice and lovely and sunny he is whenever someone asks."

"Oooooh," Cylvan pulled Saffron back down onto his chest with a sharp laugh. "My little beantighe pet! I'll have to wash the creek water from your hair first, scrub the calluses off your feet, clean the charcoal out from under your nails—my own prized little rabbit to show off to the public, and devour in private."

"Imagine what I can *really* do with your true name on my tongue," Saffron hissed mischievously. "And a magic ring that keeps anyone else from using it."

"You wouldn't be the first to think so," Cylvan smiled darkly, kissing him again. "Perhaps I'll take you away to Alvénya, and we'll disappear into the countryside. I will not need to protect my true name at all if I never propose to Taran."

"What?" Saffron asked in surprise, but Cylvan kept kissing him, down the side of his neck, hands trailing to sensitive places all over again. Saffron just bit his lip, not needing any more explanation to suddenly understand—the magic ring Cylvan needed was meant to be worn by Taran.

Every emotion to come with that realization bundled and crested in Saffron's stomach, his chest, his mouth—and he kissed Cylvan harder, willing everything swirling inside of him to be spoken without words. When it still didn't feel like enough, he pulled away an inch, holding Cylvan's face.

"I'll figure out the right spell for you, even if it's forbidden," Saffron swore, pressing their foreheads together. "Even if you have to get engaged to Taran, or anyone else in the meantime—I'll keep trying until the day I die. And until then..."

Saffron closed his eyes, but the desperation was clear in his words.

"I... I'll stay with you, Cylvan. For as long as you need me. As your beantighe, or your pet, or your friend, or your lover, whatever you need—I'll stay with you, to always be there when Taran treats you unkindly."

Cylvan was quiet for a long moment, before fingers trailed down Saffron's cheek.

"You promise me?" Cylvan asked in a breath. Saffron pulled him closer, burying his face into the side of Cylvan's neck. Cylvan wrapped an arm around his back, holding him there, both of them sinking into one another's warmth in silence.

"Will you do me a favor?" Cylvan's voice returned first, barely more than a whisper. "In my wardrobe, there's a gold jewelry box. Will you bring it to me?"

Pulling away, Saffron nodded. The bottom of Cylvan's tunic unfurled over his hips as he climbed from the bed, kicking his strewn clothes out of the way as he crossed the room. Digging around in the wardrobe, he found the box in question and returned to the unseelie prince draped over the pillows, making Saffron squeal when he was grabbed and dragged by the knee across the sheets. Cylvan then snagged the box for himself, opened it, hunched over it like a goblin hoarding treasure, and finally removed something hidden within curled fingers.

Taking Saffron's hand, he opened his palm upward, pressing a kiss to the center before tucking what he held into the curve of it. Saffron knew what it was the moment it touched him, but his mouth dropped open slightly when Cylvan pulled his hand away and revealed a ring of the royal family.

"Saffron," Cylvan said, pressing his fingers to the ring for a moment. "In all ways of safety, protection, and companionship, for as long as you wish it... I swear to patronize you until we both shall die."

Saffron stared at him, and then down at the ring, and then back at Cylvan, who just smiled. He appreciated how the emblem shined even in the low light, a barn owl surrounded by fern leaves and thorns, two crescent moons flaring like wings from a sun motif at the top, *Tuatha dé Danann* printed in script around the edge. Saffron's heart fluttered like there was a pixie caught in his ribcage

"Really?" he asked in a tiny voice, unable to believe it.

"I swear to watch over you, protect you... kiss you, make you laugh, surprise you with more nymphs when you least expect it..." Cylvan trailed off into a smile, before squeezing Saffron's hand again and kissing where the ring sat in his palm, "and give you all the books, tutoring, and endorsements you could ever want. Let me patronize you."

He pressed another kiss to the underside of Saffron's wrist, hand trailing to cup Saffron's elbow, then over his shoulder to hold the back of his head. Pressing their foreheads together again, Cylvan took in a breath.

"Stay with me, Saffron," he beseeched once more. "As my treasure. As my one, simple peace, so that I may always know there is at least one person who cares for me."

More tears spilled from Saffron's eyes despite the attempt to keep his composure. He threw out his arms, knocking Cylvan back to the bed with a full-bodied hug. Saffron kissed him long and hard until he couldn't breathe.

"Y-yes!" he finally exclaimed. "Yes, of course! Cylvan, of course—!"

Cylvan grabbed and kissed him one more time. As if to form another geis—one that would bind them forever.

21

THE MEMORIES

Once more, twice more, Saffron disappeared into the mouth of the Night Prince. Disappearing into his silk sheets and velvet words, hands like wind through mountain valleys and mouth like moonlight across fields of grass, until Saffron was drunkenly begging for the Night to come for him again and again.

When even the Prince of Darkness was conquered, Saffron couldn't bring himself to close his eyes and sleep. He was too busy listening to the soft sounds Cylvan made, trailing fingers down his arms and chest, tucking hair from his eyes, touching the carvings of his horns, watching his eyelashes flutter in exhaustion.

Kissing his shoulder, Saffron finally slid from the bed—momentarily losing the ability to walk as a bolt of soreness shot up the backs of his legs and spine—and made his way into the prince's bathroom to draw a shallow bath and clean himself off and out. Wiping down every inch of himself with warm water and a soft towel, he sighed and smiled to himself the whole time, trying to memorize every sensation. Trying to imprint every memory so he wouldn't lose it, no matter how much time passed.

Saffron had never truly known what it meant to live in a Day Court—that propaganda was reserved for the fey who benefited at all from power and affluence. He'd never personally known the difference between a Day and a Night Court, either, except in comparisons between Ailir and Proserpina—but Cylvan was nothing like either of them. Nothing from Cylvan's hands frightened Saffron at all any longer, so even a coming Night couldn't bring him to worry.

After his bath, Saffron got dressed in Cylvan's baggy shirt again and tucked the hem into his slacks. Folding his uniform blouse and stuffing it in his shoulder bag, he then found a thin chain in Cylvan's jewelry nest and looped it through the royal crest ring to wear as a necklace. While the ring didn't have the protection charm Luvon's did, didn't have the forbidden magic circle carved around the edge, somehow Saffron thought just keeping it close would protect him from anything at all. Tucking it beneath his collar, the gold was a cold kiss against his bare skin, making him smile every time it touched.

He then couldn't resist lighting a candle and sneaking more around Cylvan's room, touching all of his things. He ran his fingers through the lovely garments hanging in the wardrobe, then picked up most of those tossed on the floor; he appreciated every other piece of the prince's jewelry, his array of shoes, his schoolbooks and stacks of parchment weighed down with written assignments both finished and upcoming. When he found a familiar handful of dirty quartz points in a little bowl, he grinned, feeling warm and tingly all over again.

He spent an hour reading an essay Cylvan wrote regarding an Alvénian philosopher, discussing their books on *The New Ethics of Changeling-Human Practices in Post King Elanyl's Evening*, to which Saffron had some thoughts he tucked away to discuss later. A part of him wondered if Cylvan thought about him at all while writing it.

He was perusing the prince's bookshelves and taking initiative to reorganize them, some turned on their sides, pages smashed with others shoved next to them, more stacked on the floor as Cylvan seemingly didn't have time to find homes for them on the shelves—when Saffron found a thick book flat against the back of the shelf, hidden by the others stacked over it. At first, Saffron thought it might be another haphazard attempt at organizing, before he read the title, and his heart did a little flip.

How Opulent and Arid Systems Complement One Another Within and Across the Veil, by Fleur de l'Authier *(translated from its original French)*.

Never having heard of *French* before, Saffron cracked it open, relieved to see the words inside were at least in Alvish that he could understand—in theory, at least, as the vocabulary within launched directly over his head like a magpie swooping for something glittery on the ground.

> *While many authors (see: Svedana de Borre, Wittrock av Thomassin, Géirchud of Alvénya, etc.) will argue that arid and opulent magicks are two wholly separate beings that only coexist in the way of a human-person and a fey-person shaking hands, many more are coming to the understanding that the very "handshake" at the center of this argument does not actually exist one without the other. In this text, I will further declare that the thoroughly debated, thoroughly challenged metaphor of the arid-opulent handshake is, in fact, the means allowing the veil to flow and flirt freely at all. One can begin to understand the necessity of the two intertwining with one another as a means of all magick users reaching their highest ironick or silverick potential...*

None of the words made an ounce of sense to someone still trying to understand the basic definition of *opulence*, but Saffron grinned when, in the margins of the page, he found a familiar sight.

In France (human, spoken French), intentional veil openings are called "handshakes", while in Alvish they are "knocks" (or, in Proserpina's Night, they were "tears", implying a violent

RENDING OF THE VEIL). ARID HUMANS CONSIDER THE
PASSAGE A JOINT ENDEAVOR WHILE OPULENT FEY
CONSIDER IT INDIVIDUAL ACTION. CHARMING.

The phrase *arid humans* made his heart skip—but before he
could read more, inserts from further pages suddenly fluttered
out. Loose leaf papers cascaded across the floor, making Saffron
curse as he glanced to make sure the prince was still asleep.
Kneeling to gather them up as quickly as he could, he nearly
folded them right back into the pages to return it to the shelf, but
stopped short when he saw what was drawn on them.

Pulling the candle closer to get a better look, sure enough—
hatchmark lines gazed back at him, drawn and labeled all in
Cylvan's handwriting. Lines and circles and other shapes, some
complicated, others simpler. More unlabeled, others tagged with
words like *silence, confusion, forgetfulness.* On another page, what
appeared to be an alphabet labeling each cluster of strokes into
individual Alvish letters and sounds. At the top, the page was
titled:

LINGUISTIC BASICS OF THE BEITH-LUIS-NIN,
FEDA WRITING SYSTEMS OF ARID PRACTICE

Cylvan had reacted so intensely when Saffron briefly showed
him the circles in his sketchbook—but right there in front of him,
Saffron held pages and pages of Cylvan's own notes and research
with similar shapes drawn in ink. He even had a whole alphabet of
what each line meant and how it corresponded with the Alvish
alphabet—so why had he reacted like that when Saffron showed
him his own discovery? Why had he responded as if Saffron had
brought a venomous snake into his room?

And if Cylvan already knew arid magic was what he needed to
charm the ring—why did he make a geis with Saffron at all? Just
to spend a month waiting for Saffron to re-discover everything he
apparently already knew?

Arid-opulent handshake.

Arid humans; opulent fey.

Did Cylvan... need a human to perform it?

Then... humans really could do magic?

A tiny wind snuffed his candle, making him jump. He watched smoke curl from the smothered wick before turning slowly—finding Cylvan standing over him. He was expressionless, fists clenched at his sides and shaking as if it was everything in him not to react on instinct.

"I need you to put all of that away, Saffron," he said with forced calm in his tone. But Saffron didn't move, just gazing up at the prince in silence.

"Is this... is this human magic, Cylvan?" Saffron asked with cautious optimism.

"I said put it away. Please."

Cylvan put a hand out. He took a step forward, and Saffron rose to his feet, but pulled the book into his chest.

"Why didn't you tell me you'd already done all this work?" Saffron smiled hesitantly. "We could have saved a lot of time, don't you think?"

But Cylvan didn't smile. He didn't smirk or laugh or shake his head or look impressed with Saffron any longer. His eyes remained pointed, dark.

"I'm a little surprised I actually figured it out on my own," Saffron attempted again to lighten the mood. "Were you impressed with me? I was right, wasn't I? We just need to find the right combination of..."

But Cylvan still didn't answer. His eyes pierced Saffron as if suddenly questioning everything, as if trying to peel Saffron away by his skin and muscle to determine if there was something he'd missed in his heated appraisal hours earlier. Why did that make Saffron's blood turn cold?

"Cylvan," his voice cracked. "Please... say something."

"Give me the book."

"Why?"

"I said give me the *fucking book*, Saffron!" he shouted, and Saffron flinched, stumbling backward into the shelf. All warmth snuffed from Cylvan's expression, like his breeze had snuffed the candle, leaving only fury and ice.

"Cylvan," he begged. "Talk to me, please—"

But Cylvan rushed him again, and Saffron cried out, barely ducking out of the way. Catching his balance as Cylvan slammed into the bookshelf, Saffron scrambled for the loose pages on the floor, gathering as many as he could before leaping out of the way of Cylvan's sweeping arms again. Tripping backward, he frantically kicked himself back to his feet, staring at the prince with wide eyes.

"You were doing just fine figuring it out on your own," Cylvan pointed at the things clutched haphazardly in Saffron's arms. "Give those back. All of them. You don't need them. You're smart enough to do it all by yourself, púca—"

"Wh-what?" Saffron insisted. "What does that mean?"

"I can't—" Cylvan's voice cracked. He shook his head, flexing his hands.

"Cylvan, tell me what's going on!"

Cylvan winced, averting his gaze. He closed his eyes, a muscle twitching in his jaw.

"Saffron, I... I tried to enchant the ring myself, first," he said flatly, quietly. "I didn't... damnit, I didn't get it from someone else. I tried to perform arid magic on it, first."

Saffron stared at him, before smiling in relief. "Who cares—"

"If anyone found out I attempted *taboo, human magic* to enchant my future fiancé's *engagement ring*, Saffron..." Cylvan cut in, but couldn't finish. His expression strained. He watched Saffron desperately, but Saffron just nodded slightly in encouragement. He'd already made the connection to Taran; there was nothing to be so worried about. Cylvan shouldn't have to worry at all.

"You needed a human to do it for you," Saffron breathed

when Cylvan remained quiet, nodding a little more. "A fey can't... can't perform arid magic. Right? So..."

Cylvan's jaw clenched harder, and Saffron thought he heard the prince's teeth crack beneath the pressure. Saffron just tried to smile again in reassurance.

"Cylvan—it's really alright. I mean, this is why we're doing this, right? That's what this whole geis is about. You don't have to worry about anyone finding out—even if they did, then I would just..."

But he trailed off when a blooming realization swelled in the back of his throat.

"I'd rather not see them again, in case anyone ever wades through my memories looking for something to get me in trouble..."

"... Oh..." Saffron's mouth dangled open as he almost said something, but the nausea in his stomach overwhelmed him.

"Saffron," Cylvan prompted. His voice was soft again, edging on distress.

"You... knew you needed a human to perform it, but... you had to make sure I learned it on my own, in case a threadweaver ever searched my memories... right?" Saffron asked as understanding crept closer and closer. "So no one would think... you taught it to me? That's why you never offered to help..."

He trailed off again. In his stomach, thorns popped like knives, sinking deeper into him, writhing like snakes that would have to slither up and out of his mouth.

"Would you have... put the blame on me?" Saffron spoke the first of the sharp words leaving cuts up his throat as they climbed. "If anyone ever found out? Or suspected...?"

His stomach rolled more and more with blades that fought to escape. He would have to purge all of them to survive, but—they hurt too badly to vomit up. To speak out loud, into existence— especially when Cylvan didn't try and deny it.

"You would have let me take the blame—for trying to curse Taran?" he croaked. "The future king? Using illegal magic?

Would you have claimed I did it all on my own? Like it was all my idea? To—to curse the Harmonious King of Alfidel...?"

When Cylvan still didn't say anything, Saffron grabbed a scattered shoe off the floor and threw it at him.

"Say something, damnit!" he shrieked. "Did you talk about Proserpina so much to nudge me in the right direction? Did you blow me off so many times at first—because you thought you had nothing to worry about? If I didn't figure it out in time, would you have just given me the answers and then once you got what you wanted, thrown me to the wolves? *Answer me!*"

He grabbed another shoe and threw that one, too. Cylvan knocked it out of the air, expression going hard again as he barked at Saffron to cut it out.

"Did you mean it at all when you promised to patronize me?" he asked, voice cracking. "Or was it only because I showed you what I had? And you realized I was getting close? Was that just another trick to make me trust you? To keep me around longer as your sacrificial lamb?"

He grabbed a wine bottle next, flinging the liquid across Cylvan's chest.

"Did you fuck me as a *reward*, or something?" he asked desperately. "Or did you—did you only do it because I was trying to ask more questions? To distract me? Because you didn't want the fucking *memory threads* of answering them? Am I just—"

"No, Saffron!" Cylvan snapped, lurching forward and grabbing Saffron's arms before Saffron could hurl the entire bottle. He attempted to say something else, but more knives rushed up Saffron's throat.

"Sybil!" he cried. *"Don't touch me!"*

Cylvan reeled back with a tight breath, jaw going tight. Saffron just stared at him, finding it hard to breathe, practically hyperventilating as he—

He couldn't find the Cylvan he'd spent all night in bed with. The one he'd danced with. Who played the violin for him. Who carried him to witness nymphs on the pond, who kissed him in secret in back stairwells. The person in front of him was wild with distress and desperation and an ounce of anger, only making it more excruciating, to think someone so careful, who had caressed him, draped him in warmth, kissed him, made him feel like a treasure—did it only because Saffron was on the verge of giving him what he wanted.

"Would you have thrown me through the veil anyway?" he asked weakly. "Were you really ever going to endorse me? Or was that a lie, too?"

The way Cylvan hesitated before answering was yet another slam to the stomach. Saffron's world spun, chin trembling as he fought back more angry tears.

"I could have—been helping my friends," his voice shook. "I could have been doing anything else at all—but I've wasted the little time I had left trusting you. And now, it's too late for me to get an endorsement from anyone else—"

"I was doing you a favor," Cylvan hissed. "No one was ever going to endorse a human as old as you are."

Saffron stared at him—and a few moments passed before Cylvan's harsh expression fell, and he realized what he'd said. Saffron just clenched his jaw as more tears spilled, dripping down the front of Cylvan's shirt he wore. Finally, he used the long sleeve to wipe them away—and then pulled the library ring, the fern ring, from his finger.

He placed them on the edge of the nearest shelf.

"I really thought... the veil was the worst thing that could happen to me," he whispered weakly, but didn't look at Cylvan again. "But I think I would prefer it to this."

He let the words linger for a long moment, before wiping his eyes again and rounding the couches to find his bag. He stuffed all of Cylvan's papers, the book inside. Grabbing his shoes last, he went for the door.

"Saffron!" Cylvan finally said. He followed close, but was forced by the enchantment to keep his distance. Saffron didn't look at him the entire time, keeping his eyes straight ahead. "Saffron, wait, please!"

Saffron grabbed the door latch, but Cylvan's hand slammed it shut before he could step out. It made Saffron jump back, before squeezing his eyes shut and taking in another breath. He turned around and went for the balcony, instead. Cylvan hurried after him as his own internal thorns spilled from his tongue.

"Saffron, listen to me—I meant it when I said I wanted to patronize you! I was going to tell you everything, Saffron, please— I wouldn't let anyone hurt you. The reason I want to patronize you is to protect you, Saffron! Please, *please*, Saffron, don't go, *please!*" Cylvan pleaded, following Saffron to the balcony doors, and then outside where Saffron pulled on his shoes over bare feet and kicked a leg over the edge.

"Goodbye, your highness."

Cylvan bent over the railing, begging Saffron to please listen —but Saffron compelled himself down to the bones to keep moving. Down the garden lattice to the soft earth below. Through the plants to the fence. And from the fence—he broke into a run, desperate to escape Cylvan's pleas before he couldn't resist any longer.

22

THE BERRIES

Pulling on his veil over Cylvan's black shirt did nothing to help him blend in, but it at least hid the frustrated, frightened, heartbroken tears that streamed down his cheeks.

He hurried from Danann House right as the sun verged on rising over the mountains, reaching Agate Bridge at the same time the night-shift beantighes did. They all gave him strange looks, but he just searched for Hollow amongst them. The second he spotted his friend, he ran straight for him, throwing arms around his neck and sobbing into his chest.

Hollow didn't ask what was wrong, just held Saffron close and clicked his tongue comfortingly. Saffron embraced him for as long as he could, whispering apologies over and over again, before finally pulling away and taking his hand. They made their way back home in silence, just clinging to one another.

He barely perceived the length of the walk at all until the front gates came into view and he finally took a breath, wondering if he'd accidentally held it for the entire walk. But upon approaching, he sensed something was wrong, as there was a small crowd of people clustered right on the opposite side of the gate.

Approaching closer, Saffron's blood curdled when every

henmother and surrounding beantighe lifted their eyes across the arriving night-shifts—and then landed directly on him. He slowed to a stop with everyone else as the way through the gate didn't clear, Saffron's heart pounding in his throat as Baba locked eyes with him. He finally moved his gaze to what they held in their hands, and his mouth dropped open at the sight of his hand-drawn map of Agate Wood stained red with blood.

"Baba?" he asked nervously. But Baba said nothing before her eyes suddenly flickered over his head. Behind her, beantighes went pale and stumbled backward in alarm.

Saffron turned with the others—just in time to watch a massive wolf skulk from the shadows of the trees. From its mouth dragged a limp, bleeding Berry by the arm.

Its snout rippled, low to the ground as yellow eyes flashed across every white-clad beantighe in view, walking with its prey as if Berry weighed nothing at all. With fur dark as ink, it spiked along its back in threat, making it look even bigger than it was. The size of a horse, or a bear—with paws larger than lanterns, teeth like garden trowels, legs and hindquarters thick and muscular. It smelled of decay and wet fur and blood, just like all the other times it stalked around the perimeter of the fence at night.

People screamed behind him, shoved past one another, raced for the safety of the iron gate. Someone grabbed Saffron's arm and yanked him, too—but Saffron couldn't move. He just stared at his unconscious friend, drenched in his own blood.

Had Berry gone into the woods alone, too? Looking for Sunbeam? Using Saffron's map, when Saffron didn't offer to help?

Would Berry's blood be on Saffron's hands as much as it coated the wolf's jowls?

Someone finally wrenched him back forcefully—and at the same time, a blur raced by as Blade leapt from the crowd with a firm branch carved into a sword. Dodging a pair of snapping teeth, she slammed the rod into the bend of the animal's hind leg, a muffled *crunch* resounding on impact. The beast snarled and reeled back, releasing Berry's arm and flattening its ears with a baring of teeth all the way to the gums.

Grit from Cottage Carlow joined her, and then to Saffron's horror, Hollow shoved past him as well, all donning branches like weapons. Like practiced wasps with stingers, they slammed the wooden blades into the animal's face, its legs, dodging teeth and sweeping paws. Attempting to force it away, it wouldn't go, only ever taking a few steps back before lunging and baring its blood-stained teeth again. Dripping spit and foam, it growled and snarled every time it was battered with another branch, as if it really didn't expect retribution when it arrived.

Another blur of movement, and Silk rushed to where Berry lay on the road. Blade screamed at her to *go back*, but Silk ignored her, attempting to heave Berry up over a shoulder to move him somewhere safe.

The wolf knocked Blade away with a sweep of its giant head, bearing its fangs and hurtling toward Silk next—and that was when Saffron's legs finally moved.

Tearing a low-hanging branch of rowan from the closest tree, he raced for where Silk barely twisted to see the animal coming down on her. Saffron scraped across the gravel between her and the wolf in the last second, thrusting out his arm, clutching the berries and burying his fist, forearm, elbow, up to his shoulder down the beast's throat.

The sensation of teeth clamping down on his flesh made him shriek, dragged half a foot on his knees as the animal attempted to rip his arm from his body entirely. But Saffron just slammed a fist into the wolf's eye, focusing on his hand crushed inside its tight esophagus. He finally opened his fingers, shoving the iron-rich rowan berries down the beast's throat—and immediately, it ripped away, hacking and coughing, pink foam spilling from its mouth like vomit.

Saffron collapsed to his side when the jaws set him free, clutching his arm as blood soaked into the prince's shirt. From the wide collar, something gold tumbled out, its thin chain broken beneath fangs—a ring he forgot he still had, the gold face of the royal emblem smeared with Saffron's blood. Blinking away tears, he snatched it, scrambling back to his feet as the others raced to help Silk carry Berry back to the village.

Blade hooked an arm under Saffron's and helped him close the distance next, Saffron begging for her to take him wherever Berry went. Saffron had the book in his bag. He had Cylvan's arid alphabet. There had to be something he could do. Anything. *Anything*, when it was his fault Berry was hurt at all.

In Cottage Wicklow, henmother Salma shoved dishes off the kitchen table as Hollow dumped Berry's body on top of it, every inch of him slippery with blood. Blade attempted to help Saffron to the couch, but Saffron just pulled away and raced for the kitchen, shoving past anyone who'd gathered to look. He barely made it to the front of the crowd before Ira, henmother of Cottage Galway, was putting up his hands to force the onlookers away. Saffron struggled against him, watching as the other henmothers poured over what remained of Berry's wounds, going pale at the renting of his flesh, just like Saffron had found on Arrow—

"I can help!" Saffron begged, but Ira attempted to push him out, too. Saffron swore through his teeth, forcing his way into the kitchen as Ira gave up and focused on the others.

Rushing to Baba Yaga, she attempted to remain polite, commanding him to go outside, there wasn't anything for him to do, it wasn't anything for him to see—but she was already wiping the extra blood from Berry's chest as Salma drew a wide circle around his wounds in wet charcoal—and then around the rim, drew accentuating hatchmarks.

Arid magic. *Feda marks.* Just like in Cylvan's notes. Just like on Baba's teacups. Then—Baba knew all along what those marks meant. All of the henmothers did.

Behind her, Hector stripped red rowan berries from a branch not unlike the one Saffron used to poison the wolf—and shoved them into his mouth. More and more until the juices spilled over his lips. By then, Baba and everyone else had forgotten about Saffron standing paralyzed in the corner, watching as the humans in front of him—performed magic.

They didn't hold bandages or needles and thread to sew up Berry's wounds, only wet charcoal to draw on his skin whenever fresh blood cut through Salma's original ring. They held herbs to stuff inside the gaping injuries and passed around handfuls of rowan berries to one another to eat. Ira used Berry's blood to paint another glaring red circle around him on the table, decorated with more marks like those on his chest.

As soon as the flowing blood slowed enough that it no longer interrupted Salma's charcoal circle, the moment she could add the last hatchmark, Saffron watched in silent disbelief as the skin over Berry's wounds went taut.

It shifted and stretched, even the muscles underneath twitching and kissing where they'd rent apart, swallowing up the herbs until they dissolved entirely into his body.

When the skin couldn't pull itself together completely, it left him open in some places like a bag of rice splitting at the seams. Salma wiped sweat from her ashen forehead, asking Hector for more berries. She pressed a handful into her mouth, closing her eyes as she chewed, and then wiped the charcoal circle and did it all over again.

And again. And again. More berries. More charcoal. Wiping Berry clean and drawing it exactly the same as before. Stuffing more herbs into what remained of his wounds, closing slightly more every time Salma ate more berries, reworked the circle.

But soon, the henmother wavered on her feet—and collapsed. Drenched in sweat, she shivered as Ira and Chloem from Monaghan rushed to help her, apologizing again and again.

"My deliverance is too low—I just... don't know the right epithets. I'm sorry, I'm so sorry..." she breathed heavily, Chloem holding her face and telling her it was fine, she did her best, no one would blame her—

Clenching his fists, his jaw, his heart—Saffron dropped his bag and took her place at the table.

Baba Yaga growled at him to *leave*, but Saffron snapped right back at her.

"Let me help," he said. "This is arid magic, isn't it? Human magic? You're using feda letters to make the circle and heal him, right?"

Baba's mouth dropped open, trembling as she wanted to scold him, scream at him—but Saffron just kept his eyes locked with hers.

"Tell me what to do," he said again.

"You don't know what you're asking, Saffron—"

"I know what I'm asking!" Saffron shouted. "Tell me what to do, Baba! You know I can do it!"

Baba glared at him a moment longer—before closing her eyes and furrowing her brows.

"Hector, give Saffron berries to eat."

"Nora, we can't—"

"Do as I say!" Baba exclaimed. Hector stiffened, straightened up, held his breath—but stripped a cluster of berries from his branch and gave them to Saffron.

"Is this your first time?" he asked. Saffron took the berries before nodding. A vein popped in Hector's forehead, pinching his nose before finally conceding, too.

"The berries are poisonous, unless you eat enough to overcome the toxins and sow their ironick properties. You're going to feel like pure shit at first, and for a long time after. Just eat that amount and any more I hand over, even though they're going to taste worse than anything you've ever had before."

Saffron nodded without a word, shoving the handful of berries into his mouth—and nearly vomiting them all right back up again. They tasted like rot and rusted metal and pond scum, all at once—but somewhere beneath the agonizing flavor, Saffron swore he tasted a metallic sweetness, too. He chased after that note, eyes watering as he straightened back up again and took the offered charcoal from Baba Yaga.

He'd watched Salma's motions enough to have memorized the circle and additional marks, though he wasn't nearly as quick or elegant in the motions. Baba encouraged him the whole time— telling him to leave at least five fingers of room between the far edge of the wounds and the edge of the circle, because the magic had a natural dead space around the inner rim; she had him add the hatchmarks starting at the bottom, where he immediately placed his hand to cover it before adding the rest. As he was a novice, he wouldn't be able to "deliver asunder" like Salma could, and had to be in contact with the southernmost marking at all times in order to direct the magic from his body.

"Now," Baba breathed in a long breath. "Close your eyes, Saffron—and summon the wounds into yourself. You will not split open—but if you do it correctly, you will feel it. It will be excruciating, and it will steal your strength faster than you can keep up—but Salma has done most of the work, so you only have to close them enough that I can sew up the rest. Understand?"

"Yes, Baba," Saffron breathed, accepting another handful of berries from Hector and shoving them into his mouth. Swallowing back the bile, he focused on the bitter sweetness at the bottom again. Deep down, barely a nuance. That was magic. That was *magic*, wasn't it?

He closed his eyes. Chased it on his tongue... down his throat... into his lungs, his stomach... and then imagined what it must have felt like for Arrow to be torn to shreds.

For Cloth to be mutilated and left to die under the bridge.

For Berry to be caught searching for someone he cared about in the woods—and used as an example.

He thought about how Hollow might even come next.

Arrow's pain, Cloth's, Berry's, Hollow's that hadn't come yet —it culminated on his skin, and Saffron inhaled a sharp, shaking gasp as his eyes painfully cracked open to gaze down at himself. He searched for new blood soaking into Cylvan's shirt from his stomach, his chest—but all the blood there was from the throbbing gaps around his arm, like a halo kissing his shoulder joint. He accidentally followed that pain, instead—but Baba snapped at him to *focus*, making Saffron's eyes flicker to Berry and watch in horror as bruised pockmarks like lines of teeth manifested around the rim of the magic circle.

Squeezing his eyes shut, Saffron thought only of Berry. Cloth. Hollow.

Arrow, whose veil Saffron still wore—a reminder of the first person he'd ignored. Neglected. Failed to protect.

Sweat dripped from his face when Baba finally whispered for him to pull away, and Hector barely caught him before he collapsed. Baba asked Ira and Chloem to go find Silk and bring her back to help sew up Berry's wounds—but they barely opened the front door before being shoved back inside.

All heads lifted to find Elluin filling the doorway.

Silence fell like thick smoke as Morrígan's headmistress scanned the room, gaze lingering on Berry lying prone on the table. On his chest, a clear ring of arid magic. Human magic. Taboo magic.

"What's the meaning of this?" she asked flatly, eyes flickering to every face one at a time before stopping on Saffron, who was still partially slumped in Hector's arms. His throat was tight with fear, praying Elluin somehow wouldn't recognize what was happening—but then she turned to face Baba Yaga, the oldest of the henmothers, and motioned for Silver to come in behind her—

"It was me!" Saffron declared, shoving himself out of Hector's arms. "I did this—I performed this arid magic. None of them have any idea, they all just barely came in..."

Elluin smiled like she knew something he didn't, approaching and pinching his chin in her hands. Turning him back and forth to examine his face, she pressed a thumb into his mouth and pulled his teeth apart. She must have seen the rowan residue inside, because her smile flexed even more. Patting him on the cheek, she turned to Silver, but posed him a question:

"How did you learn about it, beantighe?"

Saffron gulped. "I... I stole a library ring, headmistress. I've been sneaking into the library every night since... since Imbolc."

"Interesting," she whispered. "That means you know how to *read* as well, doesn't it?"

Chills raced down Saffron's spine, but he couldn't deny it. He nodded, just barely.

"Did anyone teach you?"

"No, ma'am," he breathed, heart racing when her eyes lowered to his bag on the floor, and he followed to see how it'd toppled onto its side, contents poking out the top. His sketchbook containing drawings of Cylvan. The book of arid magic, the handwritten notes, both belonging to Cylvan. Even in his pocket —a ring donning the Tuatha dé Danann family crest.

A high-pitched noise rose like an avalanche in the back of his mind.

Even though Cylvan tried to trick him—connecting him to arid magic would just give people more reason to hate, fear, resent him. The Night Prince. It would give them more reason to hate, fear, and resent *humans* as well, since it was their magic to begin with—

And even if Saffron hated the prince, despised everything he'd done—

Despite everything—a part of Saffron believed Cylvan was already suffering enough.

In one movement, he ducked, sweeping his bag off the floor and slamming it into the side of Elluin's head. It knocked her into the wall, and he rammed his shoulder into her chest for good measure, adrenaline spiking in wicked thrill at the wheeze it crushed out of her.

Silver drew their sword, blocking the front door—but Saffron grabbed a copper pan from a hook and cracked their skull with it, a loud *clang* ringing through the kitchen. Baba shouted his name, and he turned—seeing her face, a thousand emotions on it. Time slowed, sinking like honey around them as for a moment, he thought he knew every single thing she was thinking. There was pride, fear, hope, regret—all of it culminating into one word:

"Run," she begged.

Racing down the hallway, he crashed through the back door, launching straight off the stone steps into the garden below. Grunting, he tore back to his feet right as Silver exploded out after him, calling out for him to *stop*, attempting to compel him—but Saffron ripped through the vegetable patch, streaking for the rickety bridge, the back gate, throwing it open and sprinting into the trees.

23

THE RIDGE

Iron in human blood makes them theoretically incapable of opulence, just as silver in fey blood makes them theoretically incapable of aridity...

You wait ten chapters to tell me this? Why not say so earlier and save me the trouble? What of golden sídhe blood, then?

Opulence is cerebral, aridity is tangible...

Fey: all in their head; humans: nothing in their head. Is that why some people call them "stone-ears"?

Aridity may exist without opulence, and vice versa—but high fey and humans have become so betwixt with the magic of the other, to separate them would be to separate spring and summer, winter and fall.

HAYFEVER SPRINGS AND SWEATY SUMMERS CAN
KISS MY ASS FOR ALL I CARE.

H ow could someone so smart also be so goddamned
insufferable? Did Saffron truly once find Cylvan's
inane bullshit charming? Perhaps it was easier before
he knew exactly the person behind every sarcastic comment.
While Saffron used to picture Cylvan with a handsome smile,
aware of his own cleverness as he was haughty in the margins, now
he only read bitterness and annoyance and *complete unhelpfulness.*

Fidgeting with the prince's family ring on the chain Saffron
had tied back together, he'd managed to wipe away the blood
from the smooth parts, though red still filled the engraved lines
around the ferns. Every time he wished to curse Cylvan a little
more, he glared down at the owl's face, telling it exactly what he
wished Cylvan to know.

"I will never, ever forgive you."

"A prince who remembers all debts he owes—I hope the
weight of your debt to me crushes you into dust."

"You idiot... you goddamn idiot..."

And the one thing he couldn't bring himself to say outloud:

*I... hope you're doing alright by yourself. Even though I
hate you.*

Whenever he thought back to the confrontation in Cylvan's
room, the memory was bookended by the perfect hours leading
up to it—and the image of Cylvan's expression when Saffron left
him, imprisoned, afterward. The way he begged and *begged* for
Saffron to stay, to listen... how he swore he would have told
Saffron the truth, eventually...

"Damnit," Saffron whispered.

Pixie hands attempted to snatch the ring from his fingers for the
hundredth time, always waiting until he was lost in thought to try
again. Even they seemed fed up with the prince's bullshit, smearing

mud in the corners of the book's pages and chirping insults any time Saffron cursed under his breath, offering to take the ring while giving him looks of *you really don't want this anymore, do you dummy? Let us take it. We'll hide it away and appreciate its shine in secret...*

But as tempting as the offer was, every time, Saffron just closed his eyes, exhaled through his nose, and tucked the ring back down in his shirt.

As much as he wanted to *actually* hate Prince Cylvan—a part of him knew there had to be more to it. To all of it. And while he might never forgive Cylvan for tricking him like he did—perhaps he'd meant it at the end, when he swore he was sincere in offering patronage. In wanting to protect Saffron. Maybe he really did have a change of heart...

But he wouldn't allow himself to dwell on that hope for long. He wasn't sure he'd be able to survive a third heartbreak from Alfidel's Night Prince.

He roamed the Agate Wood for almost two days by the time he made it all the way through *How Opulent and Arid Systems Complement One Another Within and Across the Veil*, attempting to take notes as he went but only growing more and more frustrated as the subject matter was far over his reading level, his baseline intelligence, his understanding of opulence, let alone aridity.

It didn't help that he'd only eaten handfuls of mountain berries, nuts, roots, and mushrooms since leaving Beantighe Village, and his arm fucking *hurt*. Even with attempts to heal himself like he did Berry, he couldn't seem to figure out how to do what Baba instructed about "keeping in contact with the southernmost marking to direct the magic from his body..." when his body was also the body he was trying to heal. He blamed the lack of red rowan berries nearby, only ever finding natural season-appropriate white bushels whenever stumbling upon a rowan tree that was meant to be his salvation.

He used his veil as a makeshift bandage around his shoulder, though the bleeding had stopped toward the end of day one. Mostly, he left it because he was worried about pulling it off and finding a new infection. He didn't have time for another infection. He also didn't know what sort of herbs or leaves to mush up and put on it. He just...

Fuck. He didn't know what he was supposed to do at all. All he knew was, if he didn't figure out something *soon*, Hollow was going to have to either go hunting for the wild fairy fruits, or fall victim to Taran's wrath, or perhaps the wolf's wrath, since it seemed to always know when someone had been approached for the hunt.

Saffron didn't want to think about that.

He didn't want to think about how the wolf only ever found and killed people Taran had made requests of.

He didn't want to think about how, the night before the wolf attacked Berry, Taran had assured Hollow he would be "quick to trust if he'd ever actually seen the wolf in person"...

Those thoughts were infections of their own—and Saffron didn't have the strength to clean them out. Not yet. Soon, but not yet.

It was early morning on day three when an energetic robin landed on the mossy log Saffron was using as a pillow, hopping through his hair and pecking at his scalp. He swatted at it, overcome with the urge to eat it whole—but then saw the scroll attached to its harness, and swallowed back the animal instinct.

SAFFRON--PLEASE TELL ME WHERE YOU ARE, SO I CAN COME AND FIND YOU. WE NEED TO TALK. I WANT TO KNOW YOU'RE SAFE WITH MY OWN EYES. CYLVAN

Saffron read and re-read the note a dozen times before the robin peeped to get his attention. Saffron yelped and grabbed the bird mid-air as it took off, before apologizing and digging around in his bag. His mind raced the entire time, not exactly sure what he was going to respond, hoping it would come to him the second there was paper to write on.

Prince Cylvan. With all due respect, go fuck yourself.

Oh. Alright. He rolled up the paper and sent the robin on its way.

If anything, Cylvan would surely be incensed enough to send another message back—which would give Saffron plenty of time to consider what he *really* wanted to say.

If he ever decided to speak to the prince again at all.

That same afternoon, while he hid from a horse-drawn merchant cart squeaking by on the road, he realized... perhaps Cylvan's royal ring alone could be what he needed. Perhaps he could just... follow the road into Hesper. Or Connacht. Ask someone there for help. Perhaps there were guards, or knights, or some sort of band of mercenaries who would love to hunt a wolf on behalf of the prince's beantighe pet.

Or perhaps Saffron could just find the wild fairy fruits, himself. According to Hollow, according to Taran—they were located in ruins behind an iron gate in the woods. And while Saffron had never stumbled upon anything like that on his own... he was the most likely person to find it. And all the same—ruins implied buildings, which implied living activity, at some point. He could just... follow the road, and find whatever came first. The nearest town, or the ruins. But he couldn't just wander in the wilderness forever. Not while Hollow was expected to deliver wild fruits.

Not while Elluin knew Saffron had performed taboo magic.

Not while he carried a ring of the royal family.

Not while a beast stalked and threatened his friends.

Not while nightmares followed on his heels, making it impossible to sleep. Not while the image of Berry's bleeding body, the sounds of Arrow's pleas, the feeling of Cloth's hand gripping him for the last time haunted him like additional infections that festered with all of the others. Every time a branch caught on the veil keeping his arm attached, Saffron felt the presence of all three of the humans he'd failed come rushing back to grab, choke, tear at him.

MORE PIXIES JOINED HIM ON THE SEARCH FOR THE road, standing out against the sky as clouds crept in from the west and rumbled with threat of rain. Saffron tied off the string at the collar of Cylvan's shirt to keep it from draping over his shoulders, making conversation with the new friends and asking if they'd like names, genuinely looking for anything to keep his mind off of what he was doing, the danger in it, how walking along a well-traveled, well-known road was like walking on tacks and screaming for everyone looking for him to hear.

"Breeze, Vine, Amethyst, Apple," he sounded off, smiling when the sparkly fairies all twirled in appreciation and reiterated similar-sounding squeaks to one another to brag. It was almost cute enough to quell the pure vomit roiling in his stomach. Almost.

The ground grew slippery as the rain picked up, leaving puddles in the wheel-ruts. He walked along the center patch, constantly checking behind him for anyone who might come up behind, regularly hurrying into the nearest brambles when a merchant or a farmer or other travelers did pass by. More than once he considered hopping out to ask for a ride, before remembering—he wasn't living a scene in a story he'd read. He had round ears and a Morrígan veil, as well as patron rings of both Luvon mag Shamhradháin and the Prince of Alfidel—none of that mentioning his bag stuffed full of notes on forbidden magic. He might as well have carried a sign that said "arrest me for treesan."

... Treisan? Treasen? Treason? Triesin...?

Following the winding incline until the trees on his right gave way to a steep, grassy ridge down below, he realized the view was familiar. He'd wandered that far only once before, it being exactly half a day's straight walk from Beantighe Village before having to turn around in order to make it back before the sun set. The recollection only made his nerves shiver more, distracting himself with the landscape stretching below the ridge, dotted with bushes, trees, rocks, before flattening out into woodland again near the bottom. The exposure made him itch with even more vulnerability, knowing he would be easier than ever to spot, especially by royal, unseelie creatures who could command the sky—grateful for the dense trees that remained on the other side of the road.

His hair thickened with humidity and sprinkling water, shaking it out whenever it dripped and making his pixie friends squeal. His fingers traced the old posts of the moss-covered fence keeping travelers from going over the edge, churning his thoughts into a thick cream in order to keep his nerves at bay.

The scenery. The lovely way rainy fog settled in the distant trees like spiderwebs. The smell of the air refreshed with the weather. Birds singing a wild chorus as if summoning more rain. How his pixie friends mimicked toads whenever one croaked from the puddles between the road's tracks.

He thought more about the arid magic in his bag. The Feda letters. He thought about how, no matter how many times he tried to draw his own and experiment on his consenting pixie friends, he couldn't seem to recreate any of Baba's magic circles to affect them. Even referring to Cylvan's copied Feda alphabet, Baba's labels didn't correlate with the spelling of the hatchmarks. But an alphabet associated with Alvish letters meant they were meant to be spelled with them, didn't it...? Unless it required a different language to perform? He wanted to rip his hair out.

Finally, he thought about... Cylvan. What he might have said in his letter, if his writing hand hadn't been overtaken with malice.

Prince Cylvan. I am folowing the road north to Hesper. There is a place at the top of the grass ridge over-looking Obsidien Vally where I will wait for you. Plese come soon. I hope you are all right. If you brake your wrist with the braclette you may be able to

*escape Danann House. Don't be a baby. But BE redy to beg for
my forgivness on your knees.*

"Hmmm," he sighed, quite liking where that was going, and
continuing with the fantasy.

Like—when Cylvan finally appeared in the sky and lighted
down on the ridge, he would embrace Saffron tightly, in desperate
relief. Saffron would apologize for leaving after compelling him.
Cylvan would apologize for losing his temper, and then reiterate
how sorry he was for tricking Saffron from the start, only to swear
on his immortal life that he truly did want to keep Saffron safe.
Protect him. Watch over him. Patronize him.

Saffron would tell Cylvan about how he physically assaulted
Elluin's face rather than allow her a chance to make any connection between them. Maybe Cylvan would even laugh. And kiss
him. And listen with pride as Saffron described his first taste of
magic in order to save his friend...

Upon reaching the top of the ridge, however, it wasn't a sky-
daemon that met him—but a raven. Donning Danann House's
messenger token with a unicorn emblazoned on the front, Saffron
paused to give it a look of question. There was no scroll attached,
nor a parcel, and Saffron briefly wondered if it had dropped whatever it meant to carry. But the bird just hopped along the fence-
post as Saffron walked, clearly following him. Clearly meant
for him.

"What is it, then?" he asked, the bird turning its head before
squawking. Saffron wrinkled his nose and continued on his way,
attempting to spook it when it hopped along on his heels all the
same. But the raven just flapped and regained its balance,
returning to the fence.

"What is it—!" Saffron accused again—but stopped short at
the sound of someone approaching along the road behind him.

Whirling, he spotted a hooded rider on the back of a black
horse. He raced for the trees.

"Saffron, wait!"

Saffron's heart leapt into his throat. He had one foot buried in the ferns, halfway gone already—but his muscles went tight. He forced himself to turn and look, watching as Cylvan's horse came to a splashing halt, barely within reach of him.

Cylvan didn't say anything at first, remaining partially hidden beneath the wide hood. Saffron could only see one half of his face, chilled by the intensity in Cylvan's expression.

The prince moved slowly, next, putting his hands up to show he wasn't holding anything. He shifted in the saddle, arching a leg over and descending to the wet road. Saffron jerked forward slightly, prepared to bolt, but Cylvan put his hands up again like he was trying to catch a frightened deer.

"Come on, púca," Cylvan finally spoke, a weary smile crossing his lips. It was—forced. Fake. Saffron could tell. "Let's head back, alright? We can talk on the way."

"Wh—" Saffron choked. "You can't be serious, Cylvan—If you think I'm going anywhere with you at all—"

"Saffron, it's alright," Cylvan interrupted, finally pulling his hood down. Upon seeing the rest of his face, Saffron's stomach sank. His prince—looked *terrible*. His eyes were swollen and red with bags underneath like he hadn't slept. His hair, braided over one shoulder, was messy. His eyes, despite being bright and vivid as ever, lacked the warmth Saffron had come to know. Saffron even swore he could see chips and cracks in Cylvan's perfect facade when he forced his smile—not unlike those he'd had the night in the library, when Saffron swore to protect him from Taran.

When the prince spoke again, Saffron jumped, not realizing how the sight had petrified him.

"I promised to take care of you, didn't I? I already have a plan. You can trust me. Come on, let's talk about it on the way back. Please, Saffron."

Saffron didn't fling himself into the woods, but he didn't step any closer to Cylvan, either. He took a mild step back, still hanging close to his curtain of escape.

"A-a plan for what, Cylvan?" he asked weakly.

"Saffron," Cylvan repeated with the return of his weary smile. "It's alright. You can trust me, púca. Come on."

"No, Cylvan—"

"Saffron, *please!*" Cylvan snapped, and Saffron jumped back in alarm. Cylvan's smile just went tighter, melting into exasperation. "Just come with me back to Morrígan, alright? We can talk on the way. Please. Come with me, Saffron. You can trust me."

"Stop saying that," Saffron told him, trying to stay calm—but the way Cylvan slowly unraveled more in frustration made him anxious. "A plan for what, Cylvan? Did Elluin say something to you? Listen, I was careful, I didn't let her find out—"

"I don't want to talk about Elluin," Cylvan insisted. "I want to take you back to Morrígan."

"Why?" Saffron insisted right back, and Cylvan's frustration crested higher. He took a step forward, hand still outstretched. Saffron took an accompanying step back—and then spotted something else between the trees, around the bend at Cylvan's back.

Saffron bolted—but Cylvan leapt in the way first, arms outstretched and blocking him. Saffron tripped back, maintaining their distance, stumbling in the direction of the fence without ever taking his eyes from the prince.

"Saffron, just listen to me. Just trust me. I'm going to take care of you, alright?"

Cylvan kept repeating those words—but the more he did, the less Saffron believed him.

"Get out of my way, Cylvan, please—Don't make me—Don't make me use your name—"

"Saffron, púca—it's *fine,* alright? This is all—this is all just according to my plan, alright? Don't you remember what we talked about in my room? But I'm going to keep you safe, just like I promised."

Saffron stared at him.

Then, Cylvan was—going to throw Saffron to the wolves, after all.

"Cylvan..." was all he managed to choke out, throat going tight and refusing to allow him any more words.

"I'm the prince. I can do anything. Do you understand? I need you to just *trust me.*"

The movement from the bend in the road—it manifested in the corner of Saffron's eye. Flashing to look, a pitiful whimper escaped him when he saw Kaelar. Approaching on a white horse, Eias followed on another behind him.

From the opposite direction—Taran and Magnin entered his vision, all of them circling behind Cylvan and trapping Saffron against the fence. Like a rabbit in a cage. Saffron needed to bolt, his muscles screamed for him to *run!*—but there was nowhere to go. Even Cylvan pinned him into the corner, looking less and less in control of himself as the moments ticked by.

Saffron took another step back, bumping into the fence.

"I don't... trust you, Cylvan," he said weakly. "Not anymore. I can't. And even if I did—"

He gulped, growing more and more frantic as the high fey closed in.

"I—I wouldn't go with you. Not when my friends are still in trouble. Hollow is in trouble, he's..."

Saffron's eyes turned to Taran, specifically, mouth going dry when he regarded a swollen black eye on the fey lord's face. Had—had he already had a confrontation with Hollow? Had there been another wolf sighting? Another attack? Was Hollow already...?

Cylvan's pale hands trembled as he slowly approached. As if Saffron was both his redemption—and the wild animal he needed to catch for it.

When he was near enough to reach out and grab him, Saffron braced for it—but Cylvan just extended his hands slightly between them, as if beseeching Saffron one last time to go willingly. As if begging Saffron to consent.

"Elluin—wants to accuse me of killing beantighes," Cylvan

said in a soft voice, low and meant for only Saffron to hear. "She's going to accuse me of being the wolf."

"Wh—what?" Saffron's hands flashed out to grab Cylvan's. He didn't mean to, he didn't even think about it—but Cylvan just grasped them gently in return, and bowed his head. Even without meeting eyes, Saffron felt his prince return to the surface, just for a moment. Just for a whispered moment between the two of them, hidden from the high fey at his back.

"I swear to you, Saffron, I will keep you safe from harm," Cylvan breathed, closing his eyes in concentration. "I will not allow anyone to lay a finger on you. I know it's my fault you're involved—but I meant it, when I offered patronage, despite everything you learned after that. I treasure you, púca, truly. And now... I need... I need my beantighe pet to please come with me... and speak on my behalf."

"But—" Saffron begged. "She saw me using magic, Cylvan— you said it yourself, they'll execute me. They'll execute everyone, everyone in Beantighe Village that I know, anyone who saw..."

Saffron squeezed Cylvan's hands. Was he going to be made to choose? Between the prince, and his friends? Baba Yaga and the other henmothers? What about Berry, who they performed the magic on? All of those people—and his prince who was breaking apart in front of him, slowly shattering like a ceramic doll beneath too much pressure? Even though Saffron hadn't forgiven him for tricking him—did he believe Cylvan deserved to be blamed for murders he didn't commit?

Saffron tried to smile reassuringly. Why would Elluin be foolish enough to do that? To make a false accusation like that?

"No one will believe..."

But Cylvan finally lifted his eyes, and Saffron's blood ran cold. Cylvan smiled wearily, just like before—but that time, it was truly exhausted. As if he'd been running, running, running from something more than just Taran, more than just his Night Court, and Elluin's accusation was the first set of teeth he wasn't able to escape.

Another crack in Cylvan's exterior. Another weight on his shoulders.

Movement over Cylvan's shoulder caught Saffron's attention. His stomach twisted up, trying to ignore it—but then he could do nothing but stare at every single miniscule detail.

Hitting the earth, Taran shook out one of his legs. He grabbed something from his saddle to drink, coughing before tucking it away again. He turned and met Saffron's eyes, then began his approach.

With every step, he limped at the knee.

One of his eyes, swollen and bruised.

An ignored infection ignited in Saffron's mind, flickering like a single candle beneath his skin. Sparking another next to it. Then another, and another—until a wildfire of flame and wax coated him.

The wolf only ever found and killed people Taran made requests of.

Taran assured Hollow he would be quick to trust if he'd ever actually seen the wolf in person.

The crunch of Blade's wooden sword against the wolf's leg.

Rowan berries eating its throat.

Saffron's fist slamming into the animal's eye.

Saffron's hands twitched in Cylvan's, squeezing them again.

Time slowed, just like that moment he shared with Baba Yaga. He felt every single one of Cylvan's emotions through his hands, and then Saffron thought he understood exactly what was chasing him. It felt like many, it felt like a whole swarm of creatures constantly nipping at Cylvan's heels, bringing his impending engagement, his Night Court, Elluin's accusation, all of it making him rush away for his own sake, but—

Maybe it really was just one thing. Just one person. A wolf shepherding him into the only corner there was, just like they were using Cylvan to shepherd Saffron.

"Elluin is snugly under Taran's wing; she does whatever he says."

"Prince Cylvan has something the wolf wants."

"Taran might do anything at this point for a proposal."

"There are only two ways to compel a high fey; with their true name, or—"

"Wild fairy fruit..." Saffron whispered, and Cylvan's eyes lifted to him in question. Saffron just stared at him as it all came together, cacophonous and silent at the same time. He offered Cylvan a tiny smile—and Taran barked Kaelar's name.

Cylvan was torn from Saffron's hands. Kaelar rushed him next, grabbing Saffron by the front of the shirt, the hair, dragging him back toward his horse.

Saffron swore and spit at him, burying his heels in the dirt and clawing at Kaelar's hand as Kaelar just laughed and cooed at him like a little bird, like a misbehaving child throwing a tantrum.

Gritting his teeth, Saffron scrambled for his bag—exhuming his knife and ripping the blade through Kaelar's arm. The fey lord shrieked, releasing Saffron in an instant—but before Saffron could lift the knife to defend himself again, Kaelar rushed him a second time, and in a fit of rage, drove Saffron straight through the wooden fenceposts, over the edge of the ridge.

A sudden gust of wind rushed his back—but came too late to sweep him out of the sky. Someone called out his name—but there were no arms to catch him.

Air whistled past his ears and through his hair as he tumbled —and all he could think about was Cylvan's face the last time Saffron nearly fell to his death. Gazing down from where Cylvan clutched him above the trees. Considering his chances.

I probably would have been fine.

24

THE UNDINE

He hit the hard grass below with a painful *thud*, wrist snapping on impact as his body ricocheted off the earth and rolled down the remaining incline. Crashing through trees, over rocks, into thorny bushes, Saffron scraped to a halt at the bottom, unable to move at first as he wasn't sure he had any bones left intact.

Grunting, he eventually attempted to push himself up, spitting blood from his mouth that dripped from his nose. He cried out through his teeth at the sharp pain that erupted up his arm from his wrist, collapsing back into the grass right as a series of concerned squeaks rushed him and nibbled on his ears.

Fuck.

He grit his teeth. Clenched his muscles. He used his opposite arm to push himself up, but mostly just flopped onto his back instead with a groan. He took stock of his injuries; despite acting as a free blood-fountain for his pixie friends, his nose didn't appear broken. His head fucking hurt. His still-wounded arm was somehow still attached to his shoulder. His wrist was broken, but he could sort of wiggle his fingers. At least his legs felt alright.

He'd lost his bag along the way—but upon sitting up and

squinting toward the path of his fall, he spotted remnants scattered like leaves after a windstorm.

There was no sound of voices or approaching horses within earshot. In fact, Saffron wasn't even sure he was within range of a road. There were no dark spots in the sky coming for him, either, which filled him with a flurry of both concern and relief. He hadn't seen what happened when Cylvan was wrenched away from him; it'd all moved too fast.

Cylvan—who was clutched in a wind stronger than even the ones he summoned with his hands and golden blood. Stronger than Saffron could even fathom, strong enough that Saffron—could even understand why he might be desperate enough to trick a human beantighe into learning forbidden magic, just for a chance at a release from the pressure that cracked him.

The engagement to Taran, that might improve his reputation as the coming Night Prince—but would also make him vulnerable to Taran knowing and using his true name against him.

Taran, desperate enough for that engagement to seek wild fairy fruits in order to drug the prince and force it, relying on beantighes to find them; only to kill them when they failed.

And when someone inevitably caught on—the fey lord had a burgeoning Night Prince to blame, to shirk the suspicion from himself. To only make Cylvan look worse. To make himself look better. To allow his claws to sink deeper and deeper into Cylvan's back as the only salvation from his decaying reputation.

"Fucker," Saffron growled, spitting more blood before wiping his nose on his sleeve again. "That absolute—fucker!"

When he found the strength to move again, he summoned blood back into his limbs by gathering his scattered things. His pixie friends helped, though it took all four of them to carry a single page of Cylvan's notes.

From the base of the ridge, he took a long path around until the decline was small enough that he could hike up it, hurrying back across the road when he was sure there weren't fey on horseback patrolling.

He couldn't go to Hesper. He couldn't even go to the ruins.

He didn't need wild fairy fruits or a band of mercenaries to kill a wolf when he knew better. When he knew—the wolf was just a Sídhe fey, vulnerable to iron and rowan and everything else any other high prick was. Saffron could manage that on his own.

Finding the edge of Quartz Creek again right as the sun set, Saffron's legs gave out underneath him, collapsing over a patch of grass made just for exhausted beantighes like him. The air grew thin and cold as the light diminished, and he risked lighting a tiny fire just big enough to warm his fingers and give him some light. He knew that even if high fey were searching for him—they were still *high fey*. They wouldn't come tromping into the wilderness. Their heeled boots and suede pants might get dirty.

Finally unwrapping Arrow's veil from around his arm, Saffron addressed the wolf's bite-barks around his shoulder. Groaning in exasperation at the familiar sight of pus and yellow skin, he found the nearest stick and chomped down on it before scrubbing with creek water and moss. It was better than nothing. For all he knew, he'd found *extra medicinal* moss, anyway, and the infection would be gone in an hour.

Besides—he needed the veil for something else more pressing, and that was wrapping a tight brace around his *snapped wrist* on the *same arm*, which he was bitterly grateful for. He'd already gotten used to being down one limb, an additional injury on the same flopping, useless appendage wasn't the worst that could happen.

Next to him, his four-fairy band of travelers collapsed in dramatic piles of exhaustion, before dunking themselves in a branching stream to bathe. Their iridescent, glasslike wings fluttered as they shook off the droplets, hypnotizing Saffron as he watched and allowing his racing thoughts to slow.

No—he didn't want that. If he allowed his thoughts to slow, if he allowed his mind to wander, it was going to overwhelm him. The only reason he'd managed to keep his composure at all until that point was because of the adrenaline, the sheer will to survive.

If he could just keep his mind busy, he could keep thinking straight, keep surviving—

But the unexpected addition of a familiar, teal pixie face made his defenses crumble in an instant, and tears filled his eyes as Dewdrop fluttered up and kissed him gently on the nose. As if breaking a dam inside of him—all he could do was pull his knees into his body and cry until there was nothing left.

PIXIES GAVE OFF A SLIGHT GLOW AS SOON AS THE SUN went down, and Saffron did his best to sketch them as they danced around the smoldering fire no bigger than a teacup saucer. It reminded him of the henmothers dancing naked on Samhain; and that just made more silent tears drip from his eyes, though he was running low. There wasn't much left in him at all, except hunger and exhaustion.

At least it wasn't his drawing wrist that had broken.

When sleep pulled too strongly, he laid on his stomach and used his bag as a pillow, watching through heavy eyes as the pixies continued dancing before moving on to him and building huts in his hair for the night.

He was just on the edge of sinking into the darkness—when the sound of splashing drew him back like thread yanked through a ladder stitch.

Jolting upright, he scrambled to gather his things, hoping the darkness would cover him just a moment longer to escape—but then a lantern light crossed his vision, blinding him. He raised his hands in defense, holding his breath at the sight of an absolutely *enormous* black horse splashing up the stream. He nearly bolted, leaving his things behind altogether—but then realized there were three people on the back of the steed, and one of them wore golden clips in her hair.

"Letty?" he tested, yelping when an excited voice screeched and leapt to tackle him to the mud. Sure enough, Lettuce cried into the front of his shirt, hugging and then hitting him, scolding him for making her and everyone else worry.

Asking how they found him, Hollow clambered down from the horse next, lifting both Saffron and Letty from the mud to hug and threaten him, too.

"Nimue helped us," Letty sniffed, wiping her nose on the back of her sleeve. She wore her favorite brown pinafore over a thick knitted sweater, nose red with emotion and from the cold.

"Nimue?" Saffron asked in surprise. "The undine?"

"That's right, beantighe," the undine's undeniable, raspy voice came from the back of the tall horse, and that was when Saffron finally took a closer look. In the light of Hollow's lantern, the horse stood perpetually drenched, dark water dripping from its soaked mane and tail. On its back sat Nimue, completely naked with humanesque legs, though her toes and fingers were webbed and adorned with scales that matched her normal tail.

"You can come up on land?" Saffron asked despite the proof standing right in front of him, slipping into curious fairy-hunter in a snap.

"Not quite," she grinned with her sharp yellow teeth. "I can follow waterways, but only on the back of my steed, here."

"It's a kelpie," Letty whispered, and Saffron nearly fainted. Everything he'd been worried about moments before melted away, shoving out of Hollow's arms and scrambling to greet the undine, her horse, asking if he could touch it, crying out in delight when the dark animal pressed a slippery, velvety snout into his palm.

"Oh... no," he whimpered. "I wish I'd known this much earlier..."

"Yeah, save it," Hollow grunted, crossing his arms over his chest. "Do you mind explaining what in Ériu's name is going on here? And why the skeleton prince, of all people, was the one to tell me exactly how much trouble you were in?"

"The—the prince?" Saffron gulped, but kept a hand on the kelpie's snout. His first instinct was to play dumb, asking: "Do you mean Prince Cylvan? Or..."

"I mean Prince Cylvan, damnit!" Hollow snapped, and Saffron gave him an innocent smile in response. Petting the horse's snout a moment longer, he flexed the opposite hand at his side, flinching when a bolt of pain shot up his arm.

"If you tell me what Cylvan said, and what's happening on campus..." he offered, "... I'll tell you what's going on."

Hollow frowned, but nodded in agreement.

Sitting in the grass, Nimue's kelpie reclined in the stream across from him, allowing Nimue to sit in the water like a maiden. Letty sat near her, and had Hollow not claimed all of Saffron's attention, he might have commented on how they held hands the whole time.

"Not sprinting into the woods after you was the hardest thing I've ever done," Hollow began, and Saffron nodded to insist he understood why Hollow didn't. "They've canceled our assignments since you left, and Elluin has almost everyone in Beantighe Village convinced you had something to do with the wolf. Talking about how you've been dabbling in dark magic, you summoned the wolf yourself to kill people, you've been taking advantage of Prince Cylvan this whole time... really just a crock of shit. Baba Yaga is inconsolable."

Saffron's arms around his knees tightened more and more, and might have snapped like an overburdened rope had Dewdrop not fluttered up and sat on his knee. He wanted to scream, to exclaim that she was trying to pin it on Prince Cylvan, too, but—!

Instead, he sucked in a breath through his nose, and asked:

"Is Berry doing alright?"

Hollow's long pause before answering was enough to make Saffron sit up in concern, but Hollow spoke before Saffron could say anything else.

"Berry... died a few hours after you left, Saffron. Despite whatever magic you did to him..." He trailed off to let the words sink in. Saffron sat back again, staring at the teal pixie swinging its legs back and forth on his knee. "I... I talked to Baba, and she told me some things about the magic... and when I told her we were coming to look for you, she wanted me to tell you... that what you did was 'perfectly done, but even with magic, we're not gods, and we cannot save those meant for the mounds'..."

Saffron sniffed, nodding and thanking Hollow quietly. Hollow waited another moment before clearing his throat and continuing.

"I wanted to wait and see what happened, because I didn't want to get you in any more trouble... but this morning I couldn't just wait any longer. Also, Letty wouldn't let me sleep, she kept pouring water on me every time, like some sort of torture."

Nimue giggled, smiling at Letty, who smiled mischievously.

"So earlier this afternoon, I went to the person I assumed would know where you were—and Prince Cylvan was a fucking mess. Just absolutely out of his mind, pacing, panicking, throwing shit. I barely got a complete sentence out of him, but eventually he told me you'd fallen from the ridge going into Hesper. I almost beat his ass—but then he begged me to find you. Said he couldn't come himself, at least not right now. Obviously I agreed."

Saffron twirled a piece of grass for Dewdrop to grapple at like a tiny cat, head resting in the crook of his propped arm. He didn't want to picture it, Cylvan being in such a miserable state, but couldn't stop the images from coming. It made his heart squeeze.

"Do students know yet?" he asked flatly. "About the wolf. And the deaths. Or is Elluin trying to blame me so she doesn't have to tell anyone else?"

"There's no talk of beantighes dying, not even students gossiping," Nimue answered that time. "Elluin has been very good at keeping it away from campus. Even I didn't know until Letty told me. No one's going to give a shit unless the students raise a fuss, which is probably why she's keeping it tight-lipped."

"She's... planning to blame Prince Cylvan, too, I think," Saffron frowned, ripping up more grass in agitation when he thought about Elluin and Taran pinning the blame on both him and Cylvan to control the narrative from every angle they wanted. Taran, to keep Cylvan docile; Elluin, so she wouldn't have to admit to patron-fey and student families that there was blood spilling on her campus. Did she know Taran was the wolf? Or did Taran feed her the same bullshit story he'd fed Hollow and the other beantighes?

"Why would Elluin have any reason to blame Cylvan?" Letty asked. "Even if he *was* doing it. I mean... he's a prince. He could just wave his hand and everyone would forget about it, right?"

Nimue chuckled a watery laugh before Saffron or anyone else could say anything. "Not as easily as you might think. Especially not when that's exactly what got him sent to Morrígan in the first place."

The undine reveled in the three looks of shock given by the surrounding humans, just basking in their disbelief and enjoying the attention. Finally, Hollow prompted her to continue with a gruff "*Huh?*"

"Ohh, didn't he tell you during your long library nights together, beantighe Saffron?" she grinned, fluttering her eyelashes. "Your dear prince... killed a human servant at his last school."

"Wh-what?" Saffron croaked, jolting enough that Dewdrop hopped off his knee with an annoyed chirp.

"Yes, that's right. Go on, now ask me how I know. Go on!" she grinned. But before Saffron could even open his mouth— "Because I'm the human he killed! Yes, I see your face! That's exactly how I hoped it'd look!"

She cackled in satisfaction as Saffron stared. Even Letty balked at her scaley girlfriend, Nimue just howling more in glee.

"But... you're a..." Saffron attempted. Nimue just kept smiling.

"Humans who drown tragically are more likely to become undines like me, beantighe. Not merrows, not mermaids..."

"How did he kill you?" Letty asked what Saffron was thinking, but was too scared to vocalize. Nimue drew hearts on Letty's thigh as she thought about it.

"He threw me in the ocean," she answered calmly. "I do not think he specifically wanted to *kill* me, though... Before I died, he and I even had... something of a rapport. Sometimes high fey just forget their strength, I suppose..."

It was quiet as the words sunk in, Saffron struggling to fight off the shivering in his bones, the fiery acid churning in his gut, melting and charring him from the inside out. Cylvan had...?

"Did you come to Morrígan looking for him?" Letty went on, and as soon as Nimue confirmed, Saffron put his face in his hands.

"Oh, yes," Nimue smirked indignantly. "I'd been searching for him for quite some time; he wasn't at his old school for a whole year. I only heard about his upcoming transfer to Morrígan when I overheard some of his peers gossiping about it. I came because... I worried he would hurt someone else like he did me," her voice shifted softer, suddenly, and she furrowed her silvery brows.

"But then... I watched you both come and go from the library. I watched him carry you from there one night, when you looked on the verge of death. I saw how he kept coming back, how he smiled whenever he walked in and left... He already knew I was in the lake, but soon started putting in even more of an annoying effort trying to earn my forgiveness, giving me gifts and bringing me snacks... I still hate him, of course. I think I always will. I don't know if I'd ever really trust him again, either, but..." her eyes lifted to Saffron's, and she nodded slightly to acknowledge him. "He seems to care for you, at least, beantighe."

Saffron ran fingers back through his hair, closing his eyes as the intensity of Nimue's words struck him. There were so many things he didn't know, and even more dark notes kept emerging. What if there was worse still buried? Could he really keep going back, and back, and back, only to be frightened again as another detail emerged from the muck? Was there anything about Cylvan to be trusted at all?

Perhaps... one thing. The value of his name. His title. His engagement. And even if Saffron wasn't sure he could trust anything Cylvan said—he was sure, above all else, that he didn't want Taran mac Delbaith anywhere near Prince Cylvan at all. Anywhere near the chance of becoming the future Harmonious King of Alfidel, either.

The future Harmonious King of Alfidel, who slaughtered beantighes in search of wild fairy fruits to drug and compel the future Night King of Alfidel into submission—and who wasn't above using Cylvan's own past mistakes to ensure it. Of course people would believe Elluin's accusation that Cylvan was the wolf, when he already had blood on his hands. But Nimue said so, herself—she didn't think Cylvan did it on purpose. He didn't do it from bloodlust. It had only been an accident.

But would the people who called him *Night Prince* care?

"I... have to go back," he breathed as determination gripped him. All eyes turned to him in question, but he just gazed down at the remnants of Berry's blood and rowan juice on the once-white veil supporting his wrist.

"I won't let Elluin blame me *or* Prince Cylvan for this—not when I know who the wolf actually is. Not when... revealing them will save more than just Morrígan beantighes, but maybe every human in Alfidel, eventually..."

He trailed off, frowning down at his wrist again, before lifting his eyes to his friends.

"Do you have veils I can borrow?"

25

THE SPIRIT

Returning to the edge of Beantighe Village, Saffron waited amongst the early morning trees until Baba Yaga came and hugged him with tears in her eyes. He kissed her forehead, and then her cheek, just like he always did before leaving for assignments. Giving her his shoulder bag, he asked her to keep it safe. Inside, Cylvan's book, his notes, his shirt, and Saffron's sketchbook. Just in case.

Wearing every campus access ring he had, it took an entire branch of red, iron-rich rowan berries to stain his new white blouse, slacks, and gifted veils crimson. The already dark gray pants turned nearly black, the once-pristine white shirt and layers of chiffon mimicking stark red roses. Blood. Rowan. There would be hardly a single fey who didn't see him.

Tucking the prince's ring with his emblem beneath his high collar, its cold-kiss reminded him to focus. He would cross paths with Cylvan on campus. Cylvan, Taran, Kaelar, Elluin—but he needed to focus. Even if it tore him apart—he couldn't break for even a moment. Not even if Cylvan begged him.

Day-shift assignments were set to begin again that morning, and he followed the cluster of white from a few yards within the trees where they wouldn't see him. Reaching campus, he remained amongst the foliage as they crossed Agate Bridge and approached the assignment office, counting his breaths and waiting for the exact moment he wished to reveal himself.

When he emerged from the trees, bright red veil trailing behind him like a bloody bride—he thought he heard the entire campus go silent in an instant. All white-clad eyes turned to stare at him, whispering his name as he passed by without a word.

He wasn't there to speak. He was there to be seen. And he would wander between every single building a thousand times, if that was what it took for every pair of eyes to perceive him. No longer could he revel in anonymity, in blending into the background, in hoping no one noticed him for even a second.

He wanted his image to burn into their eyes, like touching his rowan-drenched clothes would burn into their hands.

Passing the library, the raven paddocks, the lecture halls, the sports field, campus center, dining hall, dormitories... as first bells rang, as students spilled out in search of breakfast, between classes, on their way to meet their friends, Saffron felt their eyes float and cling to him like moths to a red candle. Following his long, bloody trail of wax, unable to wipe it away once touched. Staining and spreading every time they gazed upon him and glanced to someone else to see if they saw him, too. A streak of waxen blood unexpected, unwanted on their campus. Something out of the ordinary, unexplained—but infecting every single one of them, until they had no choice but to speak of the crimson ghost, the red bride whose chiffon trailed with every step like a wisp's smoke

"*It hurts to look at them. Why do they make my eyes burn?*"

"*Even standing too close makes me ache all over.*"

"*Someone else said they might be a rowan spirit.*"

"*But why would they look like a beantighe?*"

"*Beantighes worship rowan trees, that's why they're red year-round next to Beantighe Village...*"

Saffron's steps floated along the marble overlook edging on Lake Elatha, a sly undine gliding along below him in the water and complimenting his color. It was then he felt the intended snag of his waxen web—and he turned to find Elluin standing at the ready, but looking breathless. Silver stood behind her with one hand draped over their rapier, as if they'd coordinated beforehand in case anything went awry.

"Come to my office, Saffron," she said.

Saffron remained where he stood, letting the spring air tease his veil. When he didn't follow, Elluin snapped around and demanded louder for him to *come*. When he still didn't respond, she ordered Silver to grab him, and Saffron's eyes flashed to the weapon on Silver's hip, heart thumping as he realized he might have to face down a sword in order to get his point across—but the moment Silver lifted a hand to grab him, it was met with a beam of water sharp enough to draw blood. He bit his tongue to hide his amusement, as Nimue cackled wickedly from the water for the both of them.

"Not a single high fey will lay hands on this grieving rowan spirit," she gurgled theatrically, making Saffron smirk in appreciation.

"Look there, is that Elluin?"

"Is she trying to exorcize it?"

Elluin glanced in the direction of gathering onlookers, clinging to one another in dramatic awe as their headmistress finally confronted the red ghost-bride haunting their walkways. Amongst them, even Letty, veil pushed up to show her feigned, tear-stained face. She clutched hands with Fleece who seemed in on the bit, wearing their own expression of overdramatic shock as more beantighes hurried over to see what was happening.

Behind the growing crowd, an even louder voice commanded *"Move! Get out of the way!"* and Saffron's frenzied Night Prince shoved himself to the front of the throng, taking one look at Saffron with a pale face and wide eyes. Behind him, Taran sidled up as well, eyes locked on Saffron without a whisper of emotion.

"Ask what it wants!" one student called out. "Maybe we can help it find peace!"

"It's not dead!" Elluin shrieked, stepping toward Saffron furiously—but stopped short when the rowan berries dousing him threatened to penetrate her skin. Her fingers twitched, taking a slight step back, another arrow of water from the lake knocking the headmistress' hand out of the way for good measure.

Saffron let out the breath he was holding, before inhaling another one. He straightened up. He looked at Cylvan, first—before his eyes traveled to Letty and Fleece, as well as the other white ghosts gathered behind them. A reminder of who he was really speaking for.

"I've come with a warning," he said calmly, a wash of excitement spreading over the crowd. "There is a hungry wolf in the Agate Wood viciously killing beantighes on the edge of your campus."

Whispers chittered between the students, like sun singers witnessing morning light over the mountains. Saffron kept his eyes locked on Letty, and she kept her attention on him.

"I am the wolf's most recent victim," Saffron continued, summoning more conspiratorial gasps from the crowd. "I recently fell to my death searching for it. Your headmistress refused to protect her own students, and left me no choice. I wished only to put an end to our suffering, and avoid any suffering of the high fey we serve with so much devotion."

He paused, turning to gaze upon Elluin. More whispers bloomed, hissing her name in tandem.

"Saffron—" Cylvan attempted.

"It's true!" Letty exclaimed. Cylvan's head snapped toward her, but she just kept her eyes on Saffron. Saffron offered her a tiny nod. "We... found him at the bottom of the ridge into Hesper. His... his neck was broken. We buried him beneath the rowan trees in beantighe cemetery last night."

"I told you—a rowan spirit!" someone hissed.

"I've come to warn the rest of you, as the wolf's slaughter creeps closer and closer," Saffron announced. "Your headmistress has still done nothing to stop it, despite swearing on the rule of threes. I make four deaths, and yet she still refuses to heed the threat. Perhaps she does not care if the wolf rips open a student, after all."

More gasps, concerned whispers flooded the ever-growing crowd of onlookers.

"There's nothing to be afraid of, everyone!" Elluin finally turned to address them, but Cylvan's eyes remained locked on Saffron, looking white as a corpse. Saffron wanted to look back at him, wanted to offer a tiny smile, a little nod—but felt the icy kiss of the golden ring against his chest. Like a needle biting into his heart.

"What will you do to protect us, headmistress?" someone asked, Elluin frantically attempting to keep the excitement at bay.

"The wolf has already killed four beantighes? What about Pepper, from my family's house?"

"Is Sunbeam safe?"

"What about Pocket? And Pin? They only just started!"

"Everyone, please," Elluin attempted with a diplomatic smile. "We will ensure someone properly accounts for your servants, and we'll look into this alleged wolf—"

"The first two were foundlings, Arrow and Cloth," Saffron began, Elluin whirling with a fearful look. "The third was Berry of Ferguson. Sunbeam of Finnian has been missing for a week. Who knows if she is the fifth."

"A week!" someone shrieked.

"Who were you patronized by, rowan spirit?"

Saffron inhaled sharply, avoiding Cylvan's gaze. The needle bore deeper into his chest.

"No one," he answered somberly. He let the words sink. The needle drove deeper. "I was... alone when I died."

"These are all lies!" Elluin screeched, making Saffron jump as she pointed furiously at him. "You will not pass the blame, beantighe—what these students do not know is I was already looking into you and your doings—you, who have been dabbling in taboo magic with the help of a stolen library ring. It makes sense that you would weave this lie to hide from responsibility—"

"Taboo magic? A library ring?" Saffron asked with an uncertain smile. "With all due respect, Headmistress... beantighes do not even know how to read."

Elluin's nostrils flared as more whispers spread behind her. Saffron just kept his eyes locked with hers.

"You will not shirk this responsibility any longer." The words escaped him with compelling intention, and silence fell across the onlookers again. "You, who forced us to wait for a third death before you would consider helping us. You, who would rather accuse me of impossible things like reading and magic before showing concern for the students who look to you as their protector."

He couldn't resist the bloodthirsty smile crossing his mouth as fury grew hotter and hotter inside of him.

"Now your own impertinence will spill high fey blood across this campus, until the lake runs as red as I do."

He inhaled deep through his nose.

"My spirit will only rest when I am satisfied with your work. Until then, so long as your students see me walking these grounds... they should consider their lives at the mercy of your competence."

Elluin stared at him. More whispers, more mumblings emerged from the throng of students. And then Saffron witnessed something he never thought he would—even in death.

Elluin bowed her head to him in defeat.

No one else spoke to him after that; no one approached to accuse him of being a liar, or to see if he really was only a spirit. Even other beantighes watched in uncertainty from afar, proof that Letty and Hollow kept the secret amongst only those who needed to know. Fleece, Baba Yaga, the other nightshifts from Fern Room. Saffron wondered if Baba had shared the news with any of the other henmothers, too, and couldn't help but guess how they might feel about his stunt. A part of him wanted to know how they felt about him failing to save Berry, too.

Another part of him didn't want to ever know how anyone felt about his failure to save Berry, on every front. On the Brìghde, beantighe, prince-loving, forest-knowing, map-making, arid magic fronts. Did they think his new attempt at helping was cheap? A mockery? An attempt to clean up the mess he'd left behind, to pursue his own selfish dreams that—weren't even real?

He tried not to think about it. Thinking about it only made him doubt everything, only made the anxiety swell and spin until he had to slip between the trees and catch his breath. Sometimes he considered doing more than just slipping, nearly convincing himself he would be better off disappearing altogether. But he'd already made his exclamation—if he took the cowardly way out, all the students would think the wolf was taken care of, and nothing would ever be done. And Taran would just—keep propositioning more beantighes for more fruits until there wasn't a single human left at all.

He thought about going straight to Taran and offering himself, instead. Saffron knew the woods better than anyone— even without a clue of where to start, he still stood a better chance than anyone else—

But what if Taran refused him? Why would Taran even have any reason to trust or believe him? Especially after causing such a mess, why wouldn't Taran gut him instantly just to make another scene for the scared beantighes in the village? Dragging their lifeless, bleeding rowan spirit back to the gates would only make every single one of them more desperate to help. Taran would soon have wild fairy fruits coming out his ears; and then he would have Cylvan. Every inch, every thought, even decision would belong to Taran through merely whispering Cylvan's true name and making a request.

Damnit.

As the sun set on the first day, Saffron said goodbye to the day-shift beantighes, Letty assuring him Hollow would be on his way to keep an eye out while Saffron decided what to do for the night. But as much as he wanted to keep haunting—he was exhausted. He hadn't had a good night's rest in going on four days. He wasn't sure how much longer he could keep it together and maintain the elegance of a rowan spirit, as well as the elegance of not sprinting into the woods or sprinting straight to Danann House to serve himself up on a platter to either Cylvan or Taran, whoever spotted him first.

But then—Hollow and Professor Adelard passed by where Saffron was pretending to appreciate a rose bush decorated with blooms that matched his crimson color, and Saffron realized their stilted conversation was meant to be overheard.

"Are you sure you really just want me to sit in your *open office* all night, professor?" Hollow said with absolutely no grace whatsoever.

"Yes, Hollow, that's *correct!*" Adelard responded with the forced inflection of a bad actor. "My rare flower needs constant fresh air, and I'm not about to leave the window *wide open and completely accessible* without anyone inside to make sure my things are safe! I would stay myself in the *corner where I keep a sleeping mat*, but I, ah... I actually have a date tonight, you know, the first one in a very long time..."

"Oh, with Professor Dullahan?" Hollow asked with sincerity. "It's about time."

"Wh—what do you mean!" Adelard squeaked. "*About time*—you don't know what you're talking about, Hollow!"

"Everyone knows you've got it bad for him, professor—Letty even did one of these neat fortune-flippers you fold up and put on your fingers, and said you and him were going to get married—Erm... I mean... right, of course. I'll definitely keep an eye on your, um, *flower* tonight, professor. Don't worry about a thing."

"... There actually is a flower, Hollow."

"Ah, yes, of course... *the flower*."

"... The flower is real, Hollow! Please!"

Saffron hunched on the balls of his feet, swallowing his laughter as the two amateur performers bumbled off, Hollow asking more about Adelard's date that night—but before Saffron could follow after them, he spotted two figures walking on the opposite path in his direction. Straightening up, he watched in silence as Cylvan and Taran passed by hand-in-hand, in a way that made Saffron's heart twist up—but not because of the surface-level display of affection. No—it was the way Cylvan's blazer sleeve rode up slightly over the silver cuff shaped like hands, the one that trapped him in the house or by Taran's side. It was the visible bruising on the pale skin underneath, as if... he'd been trying to force it off, without any luck.

Cylvan didn't offer Saffron a glance at all, as if he didn't see him. But Saffron knew he did. He straightened up slightly as they passed by. He complimented the brightness of the roses a little ways further up the walk. And—he was wearing the perfume Saffron liked. Pine and gardenia.

Gazing down at the flowers again, Saffron flexed his hands into agitated fists.

Damnit.

He waited for the campus to clear entirely before hurrying through the dark for the Administration Building, knowing exactly where Adelard's office was, relieved to spot one of the latticed windows indeed hanging open a few inches behind the hedges.

Standing on his toes in order to peek through, he said hello to Hollow on the other side, biting back a laugh when the professor's chair crumpled beneath Hollow's weight in surprise.

"Can I get some help?" he asked, pretending like he didn't notice. "Not all of us are as tall as trees."

Hollow rolled his eyes, but fixed the crunched chair before pushing the window open further, hooking his hands under

Saffron's arms like a toddler and heaving him up inside. Saffron ducked down right when his feet touched the office floor, as Hollow made a big, poorly-performed deal about *the wind* and pulled the window mostly shut again.

"There really is a flower," Saffron commented at the sight of a single bushel of lavender blooms, potted in ceramic with obvious care and attention on the professor's desk. Smiling to himself, he shouldn't have been so surprised. Adelard was, if anything, always prepared to protect his lies and other shady dealings.

In the corner of the room, a cotton sleeping pad, a blanket, and a small pillow, were illuminated in Hollow's single candle-light, and Saffron couldn't hold back the quiet tears of gratitude. Hollow just patted him on the shoulder, helping him to pull off the red veil and nudging him into the corner cleared of books and baubles. He still had to curl up tight in order to fit, pulling his knees into his chest—but he slept as soundly as he would have in his bed in Cottage Wicklow. Especially with Hollow there to keep an eye on him—Saffron couldn't think of a safer place to close his eyes.

The following day, he haunted Morrígan's campus exactly the same, drawing gazes, letting his veil float behind him like lapping red water, demonstrating to the students how the wolf still had not been taken care of and their lives were on the line. He expected more backlash, he expected someone to come forward and demand more proof—but as if he'd already joined the lexicon of other wild things that roamed the ancient campus, people just watched him from afar, sharing whispers as their headmistress was nowhere to be found.

Before climbing into the professor's office window that night, Saffron stopped short at the sight of a book discarded in the grass. His thieving-púca fingers itched, and he scooped it up without much show, tossing it into the room to get Hollow's attention and requesting to be hauled inside again.

Hollow returned to where he was pulling faces at some body parts in jars behind a glass case, Saffron curling up on the makeshift bed and opening the shiny, gold-leafed cover of the book to see what the title was on the inside—and his heart stopped in delight.

An Introduction to Grecian Mythology: Greek Myths as Told By Human Scholars.

"Oh..." Saffron whispered, pausing again when his fingers brushed over something marking a place between the pages, near the middle. Cracking it open, he gasped slightly to find Cylvan's beautiful black quill tucked into the first page of *Hades and Persephone: The Origin of the Seasons*. Ink dribbled across the page, the end of the nib still wet and dripping black pigment as if he'd been interrupted and hid it all away in a hurry.

Saffron bit his lip and flipped to the next page, breath catching again when he found annotations in the margins. Lines under specific passages. Sarcastic comments, thoughtful notes, romantic ramblings amongst the story, the same one Cylvan regaled Saffron with in the library.

THERE IS A MARBLE STATUE BY AN ARTIST NAMED GIAN LORENZO BERNINI THAT DEPICTS THIS SCENE HERE, WHEN HADES FIRST PULLS PERSEPHONE DOWN INTO THE UNDERWORLD; IT'S LOCATED IN A PLACE CALLED ITALY. I'LL TAKE YOU TO SEE IT, ONE DAY.

I SPENT THE YEAR BEFORE MORRÍGAN IN THE WINTER COURT WITH MY MOTHER—I CAN UNDERSTAND WHY HADES WAS SO QUICK TO SNAG SOMEONE WHO BROUGHT HIM WARMTH AND COLOR IN COMPARISON.

DID THE UNDERWORLD HAVE INDOOR PLUMBING? OR DID PERSEPHONE WASH HER HAIR IN THE RIVER STYX?

WHENEVER I SEE YOU WITH YOUR PIXIES, I AM
REMINDED OF PSYCHOPOMPS, WHO GUIDE SOULS INTO
THE UNDERWORLD. YOU AS THEIR MASTER MAKES YOU
MORE OF A HADES THAN I AM; THOUGH I AM NOT
SURE I FIT THE PART OF PERSEPHONE VERY WELL.
POMEGRANATE SEEDS ALWAYS GET STUCK IN MY
TEETH.

SAFFRON LAUGHED, THEN SHUDDERED AS TEARS
dripped onto the pages. He quickly wiped them away, not
wanting to smudge any of Cylvan's words, not wanting to lose
any more of him than he already had. He tried to tell himself it
was just another trick, Cylvan had only done it in a desperate
attempt to try and regain Saffron's trust—but once he finished
the story of Persephone and Hades, he flipped back to the first
myth to read from the very beginning—and found even more
annotations there. The ink was mottled, less crisp, with tendrils
reaching through the texture of the paper. It had to have been
written weeks earlier—long before Saffron ever learned about
Cylvan's trickery.
Damnit...

ON THE THIRD DAY, ELLUIN EMPTIED EVERY RAVEN
paddock to keep students from sending long-distance letters.

On the fourth day, the students themselves were gone once
morning arrived.

According to Adelard—they were sent home while the headmistress investigated. For their own safety.

Saffron never thought she would go that far, knowing it only
hurt her own reputation as someone able to handle issues on her
own campus—but perhaps it was better than parents receiving
letters from their children claiming the headmistress was doing

nothing while they were haunted by a burning crimson ghost claiming a wolf wished to devour them.

That night, Saffron and Hollow argued about what they could possibly do next, and Saffron clung to his new book of myths the entire time. The shape, the size, even the smell of it was comforting in a bone-deep way, a hole in his heart finally refilled by something that perfectly fit.

He was pitching the idea of luring the wolf into a trap, somehow, or maybe just shoving it over a cliff into the river—when a knock came at the door.

With barely enough time to scramble under the professor's desk and properly hide, Hollow answered—and Saffron's blood ran cold at the greeting he gave.

"G-good evening, Lord Taran."

Pulling his knees close to his body, Saffron pressed his hands to his mouth to silence his breaths, knowing they would be practically shrieks in the quiet room. Cylvan's book sat propped between his thighs and his stomach, like a million-pound anchor pinning him to the floor when all he wanted was to leap out the window.

While he couldn't see over the desk, he could peek through the smallest crack of books that shielded the view of him, watching as the fey lord entered the room and closed the door silently behind him.

"H-how did you know this was where I'd be, tonight?" Hollow asked, keeping his voice polite. "If there's something you need, surely someone else—"

"You think I can't read a simple assignment roster?" Taran asked with a handsome smile—before grabbing Hollow by the blouse and slamming him into the nearest bookshelf. While they stood at equal heights, and Hollow was at least twice as broad as Taran was—Taran somehow managed to throw him like he weighed nothing at all, and Saffron lost the ability to breathe.

"Where the fuck are the fruits I asked for, beantighe?" he growled. "It's been a week."

"That's—!" Hollow attempted, grunting when Taran drew and slammed him again. "Since this rowan beantighe thing started —we're not allowed to leave Beantighe Village except for chore assignments! And I've been stuck here watching this stupid plant...!"

Hollow's eyes flickered to the desk, and met Saffron's through the books for a split second. Saffron cursed internally, heart pounding hard and loud as Taran gave the special flower a cursory glance as well, before smiling in exasperation back at Hollow.

"*This* stupid plant?" he asked through his teeth, releasing Hollow's shirt and approaching the desk. Saffron listened as Taran encouraged the flower pot over the edge, where it crashed to the checkered tile floor in a pile of soil and ceramic chunks. Saffron pressed himself back into the wood—before going still as, written around the detached bottom of the pot, he recognized an arid circle. His heart thumped back to life, once. Twice. He carefully extended a hand to pick it up, pulling it under the desk with him.

"Now you have plenty of time to find exactly what I want and bring it to me," Taran smiled on the other side. "In fact—you have all of tonight and all day tomorrow. After that, I think I'll request you at Danann House to make your special delivery... and if you don't come with my wild fruits in hand, I'm going to *gut you*, then give Elluin the go-ahead to *flatten* Beantighe Village in search of your little rowan-fugitive. How does that sound?"

"You can't—!" Hollow gasped, but Taran's hand lashed out, and Saffron watched in horror as hooked claws stretched around Hollow's throat, mid-shift into those of a wolf. Hollow stood petrified, pale, silent, as Taran just smiled at him.

Time slowed as Saffron's thoughts exploded behind his eyes, a thousand possible things racing by. But the biggest, the loudest— was compelled by pure rage.

To expect Hollow to go into the trees and come back out again with fairy fruits in hand, with no map, no guidance, nothing, except a vague notion of an iron gate, some ruins—

The same information given to Arrow, to Cloth—*nothing. Nothing at all.* And Taran knew it, he was setting Hollow up to fail on purpose, maybe because he secretly enjoyed slaughtering beantighes who failed his quest. Or maybe—

Taran wasn't only desperate—he was absolutely deranged.

"Tomorrow night," the fey lord repeated, pulling his hand back again. It returned to five normal fingers, and he patted Hollow gently on the cheek. Finally, he plucked a golden Danann House access ring from his finger, and set it on the edge of the desk over Saffron's head with a *clack.* "Don't be late. You won't be able to explain it to your friends if you are."

If Prince Cylvan could just get away from Taran, get away from Morrígan Academy...

Would he be able to put a stop to everything? If Saffron could get the silver bracelet off of him, would be be able to fly all the way back to Avren? To plead with King Ailir? Surely there had to be *something* he could do, anything at all. Anything.

Would he, if Saffron begged?

Did Saffron have any other options other than to beseech his own patron-prince for his life and the lives of his friends?

If the Crown Prince of Alfidel couldn't help him—then certainly he himself drenched in red didn't stand a chance.

Taran turned to leave. Saffron's mind raced, imagining the gold Danann House ring over him. If he took it first, it would be easy to get into the house and find Cylvan. Ask for his help. Beg on his hands and knees if he had to—

"Oh," Taran said suddenly, and Saffron realized he'd paused next to the door. "I think I hear another racing heart."

Cold sweat dripped down Saffron's back—and he knew he couldn't wait to be found.

Tucking the book of myths in the back of his waistband, Saffron stepped out from under the desk. Hollow whispered for him not to, but Taran grinned wildly at the sight. Saffron could practically see the strings of drool as his mouth watered at the thought of ripping Saffron apart.

Saffron reached for the Danann House ring, silently claiming it for himself and sliding it over his finger.

"You know I'm being accused of dark magic?" he asked. "Apparently a particularly nasty type... that only humans can perform."

Taran laughed under his breath, before Saffron held up the bottom of the broken pot, forbidden magic drawn on its face. Taran's eyes flickered to it, before back to him.

"Want to know what this spell does?" he asked—before slamming his foot against Adelard's desk, sending it skidding into the floor rug. Taran stumbled backward, out of the way, distracted just long enough for Saffron to pitch the ceramic chunk at his face, where it exploded against his nose with a wet crack and a gush of blood.

Taran fell like a sack of meat, Hollow cursing sharply and scrambling away. Saffron wasted no time heaving him through the window into the humid air outside, jumping out right after and landing on him in the grass.

"Hollow, go back to Beantighe Village!" Saffron commanded. "I'm going to take care of it—I'm going to take care of everything!"

"How!" Hollow's hand lashed out, grabbing Saffron's arm and yanking him back before he could take off running. Saffron looked at his terrified friend, at the pallor of his face, the glazed fear in his eyes. Saffron grabbed him, kissing his forehead.

"I'm going to beseech the Night Prince," he said with a weak smile. "Now do as I say, Hollow!"

"Saffron, damnit!" Hollow yelled, but Saffron was already gone, vanishing into the trees like a streak of blood on water.

26

THE FRUITS

Straight into the trees, deeper and deeper until there was almost no light at all. He didn't allow himself to wonder where Taran was, or Kaelar, or Elluin, or anyone else. There was only one high fey he needed to meet, and he knew exactly where they would be. Exactly where Taran had trapped them. He hoped Taran would dwell on that, someday—how locking the prince away made him easier than ever to find and set free.

When the side of Danann House came into view, it was all Saffron could focus on, tunnel vision gripping him like the eye of a storm.

But from that tunnel, he couldn't see the glow of a lantern behind a nearby tree—though he felt when it swung out and crashed against his forehead.

Hot glass and shards of metal exploded outward, his body slamming to the dirt as a gush of blood waterfalled from the center of his forehead. Gasping and convulsing, he grunted and fought to sit up, spitting blood that gathered between his lips. His attacker in the shadows emerged after seeming to appreciate the view long enough, grabbing a handful of Saffron's veil mixed with his hair and kneeling down to meet his eyes.

"Interesting," Kaelar muttered, pushing up Saffron's veil to reveal his strained expression. "And here I thought spirits were incorporeal. Oh—that means *without a body*, in case you didn't know."

Every inch of Saffron trembled from the shock, ears still ringing from the impact, vision blurring in and out no matter how many times he blinked. Combined with the new fiery pain of Kaelar's grip on his hair, he thought he was going to be sick.

"You managed to get Elluin all stirred up like you wanted, you know," Kaelar went on. "Taran really thought you wouldn't come sniffing around over here, either—but *I* knew. I've known this whole time how you feel about the Night Prince, since I was the one who introduced you. Do you remember, Saffron? Why haven't you thanked me?"

Kaelar slammed a knee into Saffron's stomach, making him choke, crumpling back to the forest floor as his eyes watered. Mixing with blood from his forehead, he tasted only salt and rust on his tongue, smeared against the back of his teeth. More gushed in when Kaelar's boot cracked against his jaw, and Saffron spit blood into the grass.

Searching for anything within reach, Saffron finally managed to grasp a rotten stick, swinging it around and smashing it against the side of Kaelar's head. The fey lord stumbled enough that Saffron could force himself to his feet and race for the fence around Danann House's yard—but he didn't make it over before hands grabbed him again. Thrown against it, the pointed tips buried into his stomach, making him curse before he was wrenched around and shoved back. Kaelar grinned wildly, blood dripping from his ear.

"You know—I saw you tied up outside your village," he said with a thrill. "We watched you dangle there on the fence for a long time, debating the pros and cons of tearing you apart. We'd just decided to pop your head like an egg when that old bitch found you and screeched like a beansidhe. I asked Taran to take her out, too, just to shut her up—"

Saffron slammed a knee between Kaelar's legs, reeling back when the fey cursed through his teeth and buckled, slumping over and pinning Saffron back against the fence posts again. Saffron attempted to shove him away, only for Kaelar to grab his hair again—but a thrashing wind suddenly wrenched Kaelar off like clawed fingers, hurling him back into the trees.

"Saffron?"

Saffron turned—and met the eyes of his caged raven on the balcony, staring at him in disbelief.

He wasted no more time, leaping over the metal fence. He ripped through the gardens, kicking ferns and rose bushes and clusters of vines out of the way, leaping for the garden lattice and hiking himself upward. It made his injured shoulder, his stiff wrist ache miserably—but then Cylvan appeared over the high railing, reaching out a hand and calling his name. Saffron heaved himself faster, and was within a few feet of the offered hand, when the lattice shuddered—and he glanced down to find a wild-eyed Kaelar tearing up after him.

Racing up the last few handfuls of the makeshift ladder, Saffron's fingers tangled with Cylvan's, just as a hand wrapped around his ankle and attempted to wrench him back.

"Oh—*fuck off!*" Saffron screamed, slamming a foot into Kaelar's nose and sending him tumbling. In the same moment, claws grabbed him from the other end, yanking him up and over in an instant.

Saffron collapsed into Cylvan's arms, sinking into his body and clutching at him as Cylvan cupped him by the back of the head, repeating apologies over and over again. Stumbling through the balcony doors, they sank to their knees where, inside, the Aonadharcach Suite was as dark as the rest of the house. It smelled of perfumes, alcohol, rotten food; the bedsheets were in shambles, spilled across the floor around the dark mattress; there were clothes scattered in every direction, intermingling with empty bottles of wine, broken glass, jewelry; in the fireplace, dying embers glowed like motes, finding a brief grasp of life when the windows opened and allowed a wave of fresh air to enter. Saffron let his eyes trail over every inch, and the sight of the prince's scattered pieces intermingling with the chaos squeezed his heart.

Clinging closer, unable to resist, Saffron's fingers tangled in Cylvan's long hair while breathing in his perfume, arms shaking from the effort and the adrenaline. There was so much he wanted to say, to scream, to cry, to beg—but he couldn't let himself get distracted, again. Not like the last time.

"Taran—is going to kill Hollow," Saffron finally pulled away. "And Elluin is going to kill everyone in Beantighe Village, Cylvan."

"What?" Cylvan pushed hair from Saffron's eyes, using the sleeve of his tunic to wipe the blood and dirt away. "Who told you that?"

Saffron nearly shouted *"Taran did!"*, but the words caught as he fully regarded Cylvan's face.

Full of cracks.

Pale and hollow, bags under his eyes, cheeks sunken and hair dull.

His eyes were wild and frantic—but bright with concern as they flashed over every inch of Saffron, touching his face, his hair, as if searching for proof that he hadn't actually died falling from the ridge. The prince's expression was a mix of concern and pure, body-melting relief, as if having Saffron within reach again was enough to restart his calcified heart.

"What do you need, Saffron?" Cylvan attempted to smile in reassurance, still pushing hair from Saffron's eyes, again and again as if he couldn't stop touching him. In the dim light through the windows, Saffron saw the silver cuff on his black and blue wrist shine with the movements.

A clutch of regret made his breath stop.

"Cylvan, you..." he managed to speak the words. He had to. What other choice did he have? "You have to do something. Anything."

Cylvan's motions slowed. He looked at Saffron like—like his

stomach still swirled with thorns and blades, with words Saffron had been able to vomit the last time they stood in his room. But Cylvan had kept them, held them, until they grew and festered into a poisonous mire of their own, eating away at him slowly.

He lifted his bruised wrist. He tucked more hair behind Saffron's ear, and Saffron felt how badly he trembled. As if the mire was rising to speak, but he was terrified of what might come.

As if Saffron was both his redemption, and the person he had to convince for it.

"I'm sorry, Saffron, I..."

A piece of ceramic tumbled to the floor with a glasslike sound. Saffron watched Cylvan's perfect facade crack more.

"I can't do anything, anymore..." he whispered, hardly a sound at all. "I can't do anything... No matter what, people just keep getting hurt. If I tried to help Hollow, or Beantighe Village... Taran would only do worse. It would only get worse..."

His eyes lifted weakly to meet Saffron's gaze again. His fingers returned to brush down Saffron's cheek.

"I lost you once, already," he whispered. "Because I was selfish, again. I've always been so selfish. You were the light in my life —and my coming Night nearly snuffed you out."

His pale lips hung open slightly.

"Perhaps... I really do need Taran to tame me," he croaked, expression faltering as he tried to keep his composure. "Perhaps I should just... accept it. If I just propose to him, he'll stop all of this, won't he? And then I won't... hurt you anymore."

What remained of Prince Cylvan broke further. The beauty, the confidence, the power, the affluence, the influence that made up his ceramic armor barely maintained its shape, one wrong breath from crumbling entirely.

Saffron's rare flower was one wrong nudge away from spilling and shattering across the floor. Beneath Saffron's hands, he swore the pieces chipped and gave way where he pressed too hard. The same intangible pieces he'd gathered and returned in the library, promising to protect Cylvan from Taran, promising to be there for him, had broken again.

Had Saffron... turned his back on Cylvan like he once turned his back on Arrow?

No—Cylvan had been intentionally misleading. Cylvan knew the lies he was telling from the very beginning. If anything, Cylvan turned his back on Saffron, first—

But the broken prince on his knees was nothing like the person Saffron met the night of Imbolc. The broken Cylvan in front of him was tired, scared, crumbling beneath the weight of Taran's emotional abuse right in front of Saffron's eyes, and—

Saffron knew how it felt. To be reduced to single-minded survival beneath the pressure of abuse that felt inescapable. It was the same single-mindedness that lead him to turning his back on Arrow. To turning his back on Beantighe Village, potentially leading to Cloth's death, and then Berry's.

And—perhaps the reason Cylvan never mentioned the truth to Saffron in all that time was simply because, like how Saffron put off mentioning the wolf—Cylvan had found such a breath of peace in their nights together that he didn't want to risk ruining them.

Could Saffron ever blame a single person who sought a moment of peace?

His fingers delicately touched Cylvan's face, careful not to catch his nails on any of the edges barely holding together. As if Saffron's final request was finally enough to shatter him beneath the weight. One nudge from collapsing. Breaking. Crumbling into dust.

Saffron—couldn't add anything else on top of him, else he might lose the shape of Cylvan forever. Else Cylvan might actually give Taran what he wanted, including everything Cylvan was, for a simple chance at relieving the pressure. Cylvan was carrying too much, and soon he would break apart into pieces for Taran to puzzle back together into whatever he wanted.

If Saffron wanted to help Hollow, help Beantighe Village, he would first have to ease the burden on his unseelie prince full of cracks—and he already knew how he could. He'd known since the first day of haunting, exactly what a pixie like him could offer. Like the unfurling of apple slices in wax paper. And even though the thought summoned his own poisonous mire to swirl in his stomach—he would do anything to relieve the crushing pressure from the Night Prince who once promised him a chance to live in the Day.

Saffron pressed his forehead into Cylvan's, closing his eyes—and then gently coaxed the prince down onto his lap. Cylvan sank without resistance, and Saffron was relieved to see his pieces stay together once he reclined his head.

"I... found your book," Saffron told him with a calm smile, and Cylvan's eyes cracked open slightly. "Will you really take me to Italy one day? To see the Bernini statue?"

Cylvan's pale lips smiled. He nodded.

"Absolutely," he breathed. "And then we'll visit the Acropolis... and the Colosseum... and then the Pantheon..."

"What are all of those?" Saffron smiled.

"After I made that note, about Bernini... I asked Eias what they recommended."

Saffron stroked the side of Cylvan's cheek as he spoke, trailing fingers under his jaw, down his neck. Holding his breath, he took a moment to appreciate Cylvan's calm face on his lap, eyes closed, like he was finally able to rest again. He swallowed back the nervous mire. He knew what he had to do.

"I... forgive you, Cylvan," Saffron whispered. Cylvan's face contorted like he was finally able to take a breath after drowning, making Saffron's heart throb. "I forgive you for trying to trick me. I understand why you did—and I know you weren't trying to hurt me, specifically... you were just desperate."

Every additional word made Cylvan shudder, as if Saffron cast a weakening spell across him. When he finally cracked open his eyes, they were wet, though no tears dripped over.

"Do you really?" he asked, voice hardly more than a rasp.

"Yes," Saffron promised with a gentle smile. "In fact—I think I'll wipe your entire slate clean. This prince owes this beantighe no debts at all."

"Oh..." Cylvan breathed, a tiny smile lifting the corner of his mouth. "Oh, that's..."

He sank heavier into Saffron's legs. Saffron bit back his own smile, swearing he saw an ounce of the burden lift from Cylvan's back. He continued, hoping to ease more of it—

"And..." he trailed off when, through the open balcony, voices came from the yard. Cylvan must not have heard them, but Saffron did—though he didn't let it show in his hand touching Cylvan's face. Caressing his cheek. He just swallowed back the new lump in his throat. The dryness, knowing what he had to do to take as much of the weight from Cylvan's back as he possibly could.

To take the weight from Arrow. The weight from Cloth. From Berry. From Hollow. All of the weights he should have claimed the first time Arrow mentioned *wild fairy fruits* at all.

Saffron was no longer going to turn his back, claiming he already carried too much. Not now that he'd actually witnessed what it looked like to be buried alive.

"I think I've figured out how to get Elluin off your back," Saffron continued lightly. "About the wolf, at least."

Cylvan opened his eyes again, lifting his head slightly—but Saffron coaxed him back down, gently. The prince didn't say anything, just watched Saffron's face, and Saffron never let his calm smile fade.

A fist pounded on the door. Cylvan jolted, but Saffron didn't move. He just pulled Cylvan back down again gently. He rubbed his hand up and down Cylvan's shoulders, his arm, trailing through his hair.

"You're safe, here," he promised as the door latch rattled. "I promised to keep you safe, Cylvan, remember?"

Cylvan nodded, but didn't close his eyes again. He didn't

relax, just staring at the door as a body on the other side slammed against it. He tightened his grip around Saffron's back like he always did—silently begging him to never leave.

"Do you know what sounds nice?" Saffron went on gently, pushing more hair from Cylvan's eyes as the wood of the door splintered. His next words caught in his throat as Cylvan begged, as his own heart leapt in the first moment of fear he couldn't swallow back. But he knew what he had to do. He knew what he could offer—and he just prayed Cylvan would one day understand and forgive him, too.

"Saffron, please—"

"Close your eyes and sleep, Sybil."

Cylvan's eyelids fluttered closed, and his body went heavy right as the suite's door burst open. Saffron lifted his head to find the wolf standing hunched and rumbling on the other side—but didn't move, didn't stop brushing his fingers gently through Cylvan's hair.

The beast stepped inside, foam and spit dripping from its mouth. It filled the room with the scent of rot and blood, ears pressed flat and the fur on its back wiry and upright. Saffron didn't look away.

"Good evening, Lord Taran."

He breathed in the smell of the wolf deep through his nose, letting it settle in his lungs. Taran stalked closer, heaving with his own furious breath. Saffron never pulled his eyes away, never stopped caressing the sleeping head on his lap.

"Hollow will never be able to find your wild fairy fruits," he said. "But I can."

KAELAR THREW SAFFRON TO THE FLOOR OF THE cramped room, dust kicking up like flurried snow as Saffron immediately scrambled to his feet and slammed his bodyweight against the door as it closed again. *Servants' quarters*, he'd heard

Taran grumble to Kaelar, right before being dragged from the suite as Cylvan was left on the floor for the wolf to loom over. Through a panel in the outer corridor's wainscoting, up the back staircase, and through the first door on his left, Saffron found himself in the calcified remains of a previous servants' bedroom. Stripped bare except for a naked bedframe, a night table, a narrow desk, and a rickety wardrobe, Saffron's eyes lingered on the patch in the dust where his body had landed.

He tried to breathe, but the aged air was bitter and melancholy.

He dug his new book of myths from the back of his waistband and quickly hid it in the wardrobe, whirling around right as the door opened again, and Taran walked in.

His face was still crusted with blood from Saffron's assault with the ceramic disk, and Saffron couldn't resist a tiny smile when Kaelar stepped in and matched. Saffron's main victim of the night was apparently *ugly fey lord nose.*

"Sit down," Taran said. Saffron remained standing. Taran rolled his eyes, but didn't sit, either, just crossing his arms.

"I'm still trying to decide what to do with you," he said simply, and Saffron kept his heart rate under control. "So I suggest you show me a little more compliance."

Saffron still didn't obey, and a vein popped in Taran's forehead. He opened his mouth to snap another command—

"I know what you want," Saffron said before he could. "And you have something I want. We don't have to be formal about it."

Taran's mouth ground into a hard smile.

"And what *do* you want, beantighe? A kick in the ass straight through the veil? A place in Cylvan's court? Do you want Elluin's head on a plate?"

"I want you to stop killing beantighes," Saffron interrupted flatly, and the amusement disappeared from Taran's face. "And I want you to tell Elluin to leave Beantighe Village alone. And I want *you* to leave *Hollow* alone."

"Oh? But I was just starting to like him," Taran countered, and Saffron flushed with anger. "What else, beantighe? Give me your whole list."

"That's all of it."

"Alright. I would say *my turn,* but you seem to already know what I want, don't you?"

Saffron bit his lip, but nodded. Taran nodded his chin in encouragement, and Saffron huffed.

"You... you want wild fairy fruits, right? That's what you asked for from Hollow," he feigned as much ignorance as he could get away with. "I know the Agate Wood best in all of Beantighe Village. I can help you, if you agree to leave everyone else alone."

"How poetic, the rowan beantighe sacrificing himself for the rest of the flock," Taran smiled. "Do you want to know *what else* I want? Let me tell you."

Taran suddenly approached, and Saffron took nervous steps back, bumping into the round window behind him with a small sound.

"I want your tongue on a chain. I want your hands on a platter. I want your entrails decorating the vestibule."

Saffron blinked at him before nodding his head slightly.

"And what of my legs?" he asked, yelping when Taran grabbed and threw him to the naked bedframe, making it creak under his weight. He clutched Taran's arms with wide eyes, trying to smile apologetically, though it kept flickering back to fear.

"M-make a geis with me, my lord!" Saffron attempted, finally getting the smile to stay. "A-a deal. Make a deal with me, then. Would that help you trust me? Here, I'll start—I promise to find and bring back your wild fruits if, in exchange... you never harm another beantighe on Morrígan's campus again, and leave the moment the geis is fulfilled. Oh, *and—!*" he grunted when Taran's exasperated smile split and he shoved Saffron down harder. "And—and let me stay here, in Danann House! Elluin's pride will kill me the second I'm exposed as anything other than a ghost, anyway—I can be your personal housekeeper, or—!"

"And how much time do you think you'll need, exactly?"

Saffron gulped, reeling back his thoughts. "What, to find the fruits? I don't know—more than the day and a half you offered Hollow."

"Give me a date."

"Well—*fuck*, I don't know! The Agate Wood is huge—*urk*—Alright, okay! How about, ah..." he flashed his most charming, innocent smile. "How about Ostara?"

Taran frowned—but Saffron saw a glimmer of interest in his eyes.

"And if you can't find them in time?"

Saffron's mouth twitched. He took his time before answering —and an idea flickered. Two stones, one throw.

"I was, um, using a ring I stole from Prince Cylvan to get into the library—but you know that already, don't you? As well as what Elluin's accusing me of—with the forbidden magic."

Taran didn't nod, but didn't shake his head, either. Saffron's smile twitched wider.

"I heard about this ring, once, that made it so even humans could enchant high fey," he kept smiling. "I thought, if I had a ring like that... well, I wouldn't have to be a beantighe anymore, you know?"

He had to resist the wild, frenetic lightning in his bones from crackling through his teeth.

"If I can't find your fruits in time—I'll make a ring like that for you, instead. Using arid magic."

The pause of consideration might have been only a moment, or an eternity, but Saffron felt every single second like silver needles on his back. He just watched Taran with his nervous smile, as Taran watched him with restrained curiosity.

Finally, the fey lord pulled away, and Saffron let out a gasp and a cough. Taran's eyes flickered to Kaelar.

"Kaelar," he invited. "You still want to patronize this beantighe?"

Saffron's breath caught as Kaelar grinned and nodded.

"Good. He'll need someone to take responsibility for him. Stay here, I'll be right back. We have some formalities to address, after all."

"*No sudden movements,*" the fey lord Magnin whispered, compelling Saffron instantly. "I don't want to pinch you yet, beantighe."

Hanging over where Saffron sat on the edge of the bedframe, Magnin had pale skin and light, yellow-green irises, with long, silvery-blonde hair straighter than hanging silk. Something about his eyes was inherently *kind*, though maybe only because their color reminded Saffron of field grass in the summer. Though the way his hands moved, the way he was careful of Saffron's broken wrist and festering wound around his shoulder, reminded Saffron of Silk.

"Is Cylvan alright?" he asked in the smallest voice. Magnin gave him a smile that matched in size and nodded.

"The prince is downstairs sleeping. He's fine."

Saffron breathed a sigh of relief.

His eyes flickered to where Taran and Kaelar shared a hushed conversation at the dusty desk across from him. Next to it, the fourth high fey of Cylvan's circle, Eias, leaned against the wall with their bright, golden-brown eyes locked on Saffron. With messy black hair, a light-brown complexion, and round glasses nearly as big as their face, they were both boyish and intimidating, making it hard for Saffron to hold their gaze longer than only a moment.

"If Taran lets me, I will look over these other wounds once I'm done here." Magnin motioned to Saffron's infected bite marks and wrist.

"Oh, thank you..." Saffron smiled nervously, uncomfortable with that specific qualifier. *If Taran lets me.*

The sound of ribbon winding through a roller clicked behind Saffron's ears, followed by the sensation of a necklace growing tighter and tighter until it wrapped flush around his throat. Something cold and metallic kissed the skin over his windpipe, making him stiffen.

"This will hurt," Magnin said like a promise, before the kiss crunched into a bite on Saffron's throat. The choker then cinched a few excruciating clicks tighter, making him gasp sharply, a hand flying up to touch whatever tasted him. A cold metal pendant nestled against the center of his throat, a velvet ribbon wrapping around his neck and connecting at a similar piece of silver in the back. Saffron wanted to ask what it was, but felt like he already knew, swallowing nervously when a drop of blood slid from where the silver sunk its teeth.

Magnin then knelt down in front of him, motioning for Saffron to offer his arms. When Saffron didn't right away, Magnin compelled him to do so, and Saffron had no choice. Pushing up Saffron's red sleeves, the fey hooked shining silver cuffs around his wrists, making Saffron's heart pound. They were the same as the one Cylvan wore, though when they hung open, he could see what was on the inside—two shallow spikes emerging from the inner curve. He just clenched his jaw while Magnin adjusted little silver loops on the edges and the spikes nestled into the soft skin under Saffron's wrists.

"Another pinch," the fey muttered, snapping one cuff painfully tight, and then the other, inner spikes digging into his flesh and making his fingers tingle..

"Is one not enough?" he asked bitterly, the choker making his voice hoarse.

"*Silence. Restraint. Disgrace,*" Taran answered, rising to his feet as Magnin stepped out of the way. Saffron didn't meet his eyes, wiping a finger along the dripping blood from his neck, and then the new blood from his silver cuffs. "Three tenets of Queen Proserpina's *means of taming an insubordinate human.*"

Saffron grimaced, holding his breath when Taran suddenly took him by the chin and lifted his face, forcing them to meet eyes. The fey lord touched a finger to the silver pendant on Saffron's choker.

"*Silence.* You will be unable to speak according to boundaries placed in the house."

He grabbed one of Saffron's cuffs, making Saffron wince.

"*Restraint.* You will not be able to *cross* certain boundaries within the house. And by wearing two, on command, they will snap together and bind you. Finally," stepping away, he pulled a long, black sheet of chiffon from a box on the desk. The eyelet lace around the edges told Saffron what it was right away.

"*Disgrace.* From this day forward, you shall drape yourself in black, not unlike that of the veiled queen. To demonstrate your shame for all to see."

Saffron accepted the veil in his hands, rubbing fingers over it.

"What am I ashamed of?" he asked, partially sincere, partially sarcastic.

"Oh, many things," Taran smiled. "For practicing forbidden magic; for using fairy fruits to enchant the prince to do whatever you pleased; and for slaughtering fellow beantighes under the guise of a wolf."

Saffron's eyes flickered up to meet Taran's again, trying to resist the bitter smile. He'd promised to ease that burden from Cylvan, too. How easily these fey did whatever Saffron wanted without being asked, it seemed.

Magnin handed Taran a silver ring, who held it up. It donned a similar motif to the hands on Saffron's ornaments, fingers caressing a narrow dagger between them.

"Whoever wears this ring controls your silver pieces and the boundaries that limit them. For now, because I have given you to Kaelar to patronize..." He handed the ring over, Kaelar grinning and taking it with glee.

"This isn't—" Saffron wanted to say *necessary*, but Taran's eyes were cold. Saffron just closed his mouth again, swallowing back his protests and nodding stiffly.

"I will take care of you, beantighe, until I get what you've promised me—but that does not mean I will be kind. Do you understand?"

Saffron nodded again.

"Now... in order to give Cylvan plenty of time to purge any last of your *enchantment* from his system," Taran smiled as he repeated the falsity, "you will spend the next two weeks here, in the servants' quarters. If you behave yourself, I will allow you downstairs to begin your chores as well as your search in the woods. If you're *really* good... perhaps Kaelar will even continue to patronize you once Ostara comes and our agreement concludes."

"*Restraint*," Kaelar tested his new ring, grinning as Saffron's wrists clacked together. It nearly brought tears to Saffron's eyes, his broken wrist having nothing to brace it.

Still, he just kept his eyes on Taran, doing whatever he could not to let the nausea climb further up his throat.

"Prince Cylvan will be made aware of your circumstances as I see fit to best comfort him. With that said—while I do not know the full extent of your manipulation on him, if I ever have *any* reason to believe you have demonstrated anything other than silent, obedient, *repentant* household servant in the prince's presence, I will command that silver choker to tighten until it lops your head clean off your shoulders. Do you understand?"

Saffron bit his lip, but nodded again.

He wanted to believe that, on top of everyone else being safe —perhaps, if Taran really felt secure in their deal, he might even relax his stringent control over Cylvan. Might allow Cylvan to shirk some of the weight, some of the burden. To heal some of the cracks breaking him. Taran might even show Cylvan an ounce of respect, or affection, or kindness, while Saffron pretended to search for fruits in the Agate Wood day in and day out.

Pretended. As far as Saffron was concerned, Taran would never hold a single wild fruit in his hands. No matter what—there was another geis Saffron was more devoted to fulfilling, and

Ostara would come with a magic ring given to Taran in one way or another.

A satisfied smile crossed Saffron's lips, and he lifted his eyes to all four high fey appraising him. Rising to his feet, he offered a polite bow from the hips.

"I will be sure to exceed all of your expectations, my lord."

EPILOGUE

The room Saffron chose in the attic servants' quarters was the same size as Fern Room in Cottage Wicklow. The bed was also more comfortable once there was a mattress on it, and he wouldn't have to share it with anyone. There was a tiny fireplace in the wall, and a round dormer window he could push open that overlooked the back gardens and Agate Wood in the distance.

It took him all of the following day to sweep decades of dust out, having to walk carefully the entire time as to not make a sound. In the rafters, spiders spun webs, a family of owl finches perched in their nest, and soon, even a few familiar pixies found the hole in the roof tiles and wriggled in to ask where Saffron had been.

Saffron spent the morning trying to find even the smallest things he could to keep him from breaking down entirely. The pixies were a nice addition to the pathetic list. Other small positives included:

The black blouse of shame had the same high collar, wide sleeves, tall cuffs, and fit as his standard white blouse, though it was slightly less ruffly.

The black slacks were a size too small, fitting more like

leggings than formal pants—but they didn't itch at the seams like his dark gray pants always did.

He was able to keep his own derby boots, assuming he could polish out the scuffs from his most recent adventures.

There was a little bath in the corner of the servants' quarters, the fourth floor attic consisting of a dozen other empty rooms not including Saffron's. The water in the bath even ran warmer than the creek.

He'd managed to protect his new book of myths, as well as the prince's ring with the royal crest, which had been tucked under his crimson blouse while Magnin removed every one of Saffron's other campus access rings.

He didn't have his sketchbook with him to be taken, either. It was, hopefully, still tucked safely away with Baba Yaga, along with Cylvan's book and notes on arid magic.

Hollow would be left alone. All of Beantighe Village would be left alone. Things could go back to normal for them, with no more wolf to keep them up at night.

Cylvan was safe in his room, still fast asleep from the enchantment. Saffron hoped it was restful. He hoped the prince was having lovely dreams, and would wake up feeling like himself again.

But no number of small pleasantries within the gloom could protect him from the freezing moment when, through the floorboards, Saffron faintly heard voices speaking—and realized he'd chosen his place to sleep right above Cylvan's suite, and apparently the silencing barrier didn't work through the ceiling.

Lying on his back on the floor, wanting to torture himself by hearing everything, Saffron stared at the rafters as Taran explained to the prince exactly what had happened while he slept.

"Saffron confessed to killing beantighes, as well as to drugging you. I had him sent to Avren immediately—where he may have already been executed. I can send a raven and request clemency if he is still alive, but I can't make any promises. I did it because I care for you, Cylvan—and it showed me how I've fallen short as your

partner. I'm so sorry for letting it go on like this; I never would have allowed that human to manipulate you for so long if I'd known. Let us learn from this and better trust one another in the future, so no one else gets hurt. So that we can grow and be happy next to one another, alright?"

Saffron didn't hear Cylvan's response. He couldn't even picture what Cylvan's face must have looked like. He just listened as Taran left the suite, closing the door behind him.

Saffron closed his eyes. In two weeks, he would be able to step in front of Cylvan again. According to Taran, they would claim his memory threads had been plucked, and he wouldn't recall anything to do with the prince at all—but he would be alive. Cylvan wouldn't have to feel any guilt—

An agonized scream tore through the floorboards, vicious gusts of wind ripping through the suite below and whistling through the cracks beneath where Saffron lay.

He clamped hands over his mouth, stifling his own miserable sobs as Cylvan wept and begged until there was nothing left but shuddering grief to fill the walls of Danann House.

Two weeks. Just two weeks.

"I'll keep you safe," Saffron promised, just as another piece of ceramic hit the floor of the suite below him.

ACKNOWLEDGMENTS

My partner, whose long walks and endless headcanon sessions allow me to build lush worlds with consistent backstories and loveable characters. Also for being there when I cry, when I panic, when I have so much anxiety that I clack tumbled rocks in my hands for hours. Who ALSO painted my incredible, BEAU-TIFUL cover art, without which I don't think I could have gotten the response I did.

Arielle M. DeVito, my developmental editor and copy editor; I appreciate your work and beautiful editorial letters SO MUCH. Thank you for teaching me how to properly use em-dashes as well as always catching my long, meandering sentences. https://ariellemdevito.com/

My beta readers, the first ones I've ever used, who provided not only some incredible developmental and editorial feedback, but also the little confidence boost I needed to keep going.

My past self, for quitting that job that was going to kill me in favor of more time and more stamina to tackle my debut with the respect and attention I wanted to give it.

iWriterly on Youtube for the self-pub advice. Also: Kennie J.D., Dylan is in Trouble, Nick diRamio, Drew Gooden, Friendly Space Ninja, and Jenny Nicholson on Youtube, who played in the background of my burnout-induced days off.

ABOUT THE AUTHOR

Kellen Graves is a queer writer and artist from the Pacific Northwest, where they live with their partner, two cats, and crystal collection.

While this isn't their first novel, it's the first one people get to see.

You can find more info about this release and upcoming releases by following Kellen on social media, or on their website.

HTTPS://SKELLYGRAVES.COM

HTTPS://SKELLYGRAVES.CARRD.CO/

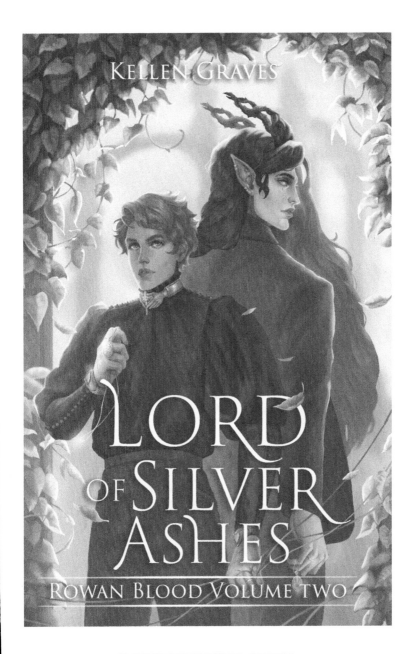

LORD OF SILVER ASHES
ROWAN BLOOD VOLUME TWO
AVAILABLE NOW